TRAITOR'S MOON

TRAITOR'S
MOON

BY ROBERT
NEILL

Doubleday & Company, Inc., Garden City, New York

TO EMMELINE MORRISON
WHO BRINGS DISTINCTION TO
THE SIGN OF SCORPIO

CONTENTS

FLEET STREET   13
MR. BARLOW'S CLOCK   21
INVITATION   26
THE TAVERN IN THE STRAND   35
THE POPISH MIDWIFE   47
VENUS IN SAGITTARY   57
THE LADY OF FASHION   65
THE NEWGATE CAPTAIN   75
LANGLEY OF LANGLEY   82
MISS PENELOPE'S HUMOURS   89
MANSELL OF THORNCLOUGH   97
HOGHTON OF PARK HALL   101
A TALE OF '42   109
THE LETTER-OF-NEWS   117
THE SCENTED GARDEN   123
MR. PAYNE'S INQUIRY   132
SUMMER HEAT   140

MR. GADBURY'S PREDICTION   148

THE MARTIN MERE   156

THE INN AT ORMSKIRK   168

THE WIDOW JUMP   176

MR. BARLOW'S COUNSEL   187

STUDY OF LUNATIONS   198

THE CAPTAIN'S PROGRESS   208

THE YOUTHFUL ANNE   219

MOON IN SCORPIO   228

WARRANT FOR SEARCH   235

THE WHIG JUSTICE   243

THE GREAT POPE-BURNING   251

" 'FORTY-ONE IS COME AGAIN"   261

WIND FROM THE SEA   268

THE GEESE FLY LOW   276

THE SWELLING MOON   286

THE BROKEN NIGHT   295

RED SKY AT MORNING   305

TRAITOR'S MOON

1

FLEET STREET   Mr. Leyburne, the journeyman clock-maker, accounted himself a gentleman.

He was sprung of the old and honourable family of Leyburne of Cunswick, by Kendal in Westmorland, and his pretension had therefore to be admitted. But his friends, though admitting it, thought him rash to insist on it; for it had also to be admitted that the Leyburnes were notorious papists. His uncle George at Cunswick was a papist; his uncle John was a most eminent papist, a priest who had been President of the English College at Douai and was now in Rome with Cardinal Howard; and in this spring of 1679, with all London in a ferment from what Mr. Oates had lately revealed of popish plots, such connections were enough to set any man's neck in danger. So his friends urged, but young Mr. Leyburne was not to be moved. He was himself no papist, he said; his father had been no papist; his uncle Thomas had been the sourest of Puritans; and so much must suffice. There was a streak of obstinacy in him, almost of perversity as his friends said, and the more they counselled prudence the more did he insist on his connections and on his right to regard any gentleman as an equal. To be a journeyman, almost out of his time and within weeks of being free of the Clockmakers' Company, did not, it seemed, suffice for this tall young man with the clear-cut face and the brooding eyes; that he had ambitions of another sort seemed plain, but what they were was known to none, and perhaps not even to himself.

He was in this humour when he first met the Langleys.

It came about in Fleet Street at the end of a grey and misty afternoon in March. Mr. Leyburne, returning from Fetter Lane, had scarcely turned into Fleet Street when he became aware of the elderly gentleman in the russet riding coat who was walking in front of him. A gentleman who wore a riding coat in Fleet Street must surely be from the country, and that in itself would have engaged Mr. Leyburne's interest; but what engaged it a great deal more was the girl who walked at this gentleman's side, holding dutifully to his arm and having every appearance of being his daughter.

It must be supposed that it was something in her walk and bearing, or perhaps some yet more subtle emanation, that stirred Mr. Leyburne's pulse and set his fancy speeding; for the truth is that, being behind her, he could see very little of her. All he could be sure of was a cloak of mulberry velvet and a hat of the same, with some wisps of dark red hair straying between brim of hat and collar of cloak; but that was enough for Mr. Leyburne. Something of life and vitality seemed to peep and beckon from those slim shoulders, and when he was come to within a few feet of them he slowed his walk; and then opportunity was put into his hand.

He had not been alone in guessing that a riding coat in Fleet Street must mean one not versed in the ways of the town. Some fifty paces ahead was the shop of Mr. Gill, the noted clockmaker, who was both employer and uncle to Mr. Leyburne, and by his door two gaudily dressed fellows were lurking. Evidently they had noted this gentleman and his daughter, and they went about their business with practised assurance. One of them came strolling airily towards this country pair and then turned in his walk as if to cross the road; and, as he went, a shining guinea fell from him and went tinkling on the stones. The gentleman could hardly miss seeing it, and he halted while his daughter stooped to take it up. Behind them Mr. Leyburne watched without illusions; he had been bred in the town, and he knew all about this trick.

"Hey, you, sir!" The gentleman called it boisterously, and the fellow in the road turned as he heard it.

"D'ye call at me, sir?"

"To be sure I do. You must be plaguy rich that you spill your guineas on the stones."

"Guineas?" The fellow's surprise was admirably assumed. "Is that mine, d'ye say, sir?"

"I'll suppose it is, since you dropped it."

The fellow came from the road, and he was bowing most politely, his hat aflourish, as he took the guinea.

"I'm grateful to you, sir—vastly grateful. It's an honesty you show that's rare in the town these days. Sir, your servant!"

He was bowing again, and this was the moment for his partner to join the game. He had approached unnoticed, and he spoke indignantly and without introduction.

"God stap and damme!" He was taking the airs of a fine gentleman. "D'ye leave it at that, sir? Ye've no more to say to it than that?" The fellow turned and addressed himself to the gentleman in russet. "Sir, I'm enchanted to meet so honest a gentleman, I vow I am. You'll be pleased to be my guest to a bottle of wine?"

"Why, er . . ." The gentleman in russet cleared his throat noisily. "That's handsomely said. And since you put it so——"

Mr. Leyburne thought it time to intervene.

"You'll permit me, sir . . ." He was speaking quickly to the gentleman. "These fellows are what we call money-droppers. They use this means to scrape acquaintance that they may later fleece you at their leisure. Their proper place is the cart's tail."

"Oh!" The red-haired girl turned impulsively, and her cloak fell open to show that it was clasped only at the shoulder, and by a brooch of smooth red gold. The rogues waited for no more. The first of them leapt at her, and the cloak ripped as he tore at the brooch; at once Mr. Leyburne was on the fellow, and as quickly the second rogue was on him. The three of them went swaying and staggering, while the girl watched excitedly and her father fumbled for his sword. But so much was not needed. Mr. Leyburne was in the apron and cloth breeches proper to a journeyman, and that was enough for Fleet Street; shop doors went clattering left and right of them as journeymen and apprentices came pouring out to the help of their own kind; for a few seconds there was a wild and whirling scuffle, and then the two rogues were in headlong flight with a pack of delighted apprentices whooping after them. Mr. Leyburne scrambled to his feet, and the gold brooch was gleaming in his fingers as he smoothed his ruffled hair and looked quickly round him.

What he saw set him for a moment into quick alarm, for the only person who seemed to have come to any hurt was the one in whom he had the most interest; she had apparently been flung to the ground like himself, and now she was sitting on the stones, blinking ruefully and dabbing with a laced and dainty handkerchief at a trickle of blood that was staining her mouth and chin. He jumped forward in alarm, and then he checked as he saw what it was; the girl's nose was bleeding, and that was all. His sigh of relief was audible, even if his eyes were still anxious as he watched the trickle of blood. But if he was concerned, the girl apparently was not; she picked herself lightly from the stones and grinned in his face.

"It's no matter," she told him cheerfully. "I've hit the street with my nose. That's all."

It was a happy voice, and her eyes were laughing as she spoke. Mr. Leyburne was enchanted. He could see something of her face now, even if it was smeared with blood and obscured by a dabbing handkerchief, and he noted with quick approval the clear firm lines of it, the brown and sunburned skin, and the hint of impudence in mouth and nose.

"You relieve me," he told her earnestly. "Though it's poor welcome, I fear, to this Fleet Street of ours."

She turned to her father in mock dismay.

"That's another," she told him solemnly. "How do they guess we're from the country?"

"To the devil with that!" he growled. Then he fished in the great pockets of his coat and produced from their depths a handkerchief of his own, monstrously big and none too clean. "Here—stanch with this. That flimsy of yours is wetter by now than your face."

The girl took it gingerly, and her eyebrows were lifting eloquently as she let it hang from finger and thumb; the grin flashed across her face again as she looked at it, and then she had buried her face completely under it; they could hear her sniffing vigorously as her father turned to Mr. Leyburne.

"We're in your debt, sir—both of us. As the girl says, we're from the country, and I was in fair way to being finely gulled by that pair. And we're further in your debt for your help thereafter."

"Not so, sir." Mr. Leyburne was quick on that. "We are not all rogues in the town. But I fear that the lady is in need of refurbishment. . . ."

He thought he saw Fortune's hand in this; for the gentleman, after a shrewd glance at his daughter, made a surprising answer.

"Aye," he said. "She'd be the better for her face washed, if so much could be offered. To give you truth, we're all but lost and foundered in this street of yours. But we were making for the shop of Gill, the pendulum maker."

Mr. Leyburne held his breath. Mr. Gill, grave and decorous, pushed through the throng and spoke easily.

"Then you need seek no further," he said. "Myself am George Gill."

"Gill, are you?" The gentleman was plainly surprised. "Why, then, that's well met. I'm told you sell as sound a clock as any. That's my need, and I'll be glad to talk with you soon. But for the moment, as this lad says——"

"Precisely. As my nephew says——" Mr. Gill, standing a shade more erect, corrected him gently. "As my nephew says, the lady is in some need of refurbishing, and if you'll come to my poor house, sir, she shall have it."

His dry tone was not lost on Mr. Leyburne. The gentleman had certainly been a little short, even a little patronizing, as a gentleman was apt to be if he were of the country and did not know what wealth and substance a man might come to in the City. Mr. Gill's offer of hospitality was no doubt sincere; but it would also serve to show this gentleman something which he did not seem to know.

"Why, then . . ." The gentleman seemed at a loss, almost as if he had sensed that all was not quite as he had supposed. "Why, then—I thank you, sir. We'll come most gladly."

That was better said, and Mr. Gill was smiling as he bowed his acknowledgement. Then, with the gentleman at his side, he led the way to his door. Mr. Leyburne, following behind with the girl, passed to her the gold brooch, and her hand touched his as she took it from him.

"My thanks," she whispered. "I'm—I'm most properly grateful."

"No," he answered firmly. "Rather it's I who am grateful to you—who colour so grey an afternoon."

"Colour, do you say? Do you tease me in that?" Her answer came quickly, and suddenly he realized that she was laughing. "Dust and blood and disarray—fine colours I make for you!"

She looked herself up and down comically, and then she was shaking with laughter as they passed into Mr. Gill's shop; but Mr. Leyburne, feeling her fingers quiver, found his thoughts go bounding into chaos.

They passed through the workshop, through Mr. Gill's own room, where the finished clocks were ranged for his inspection, and thence up the stair to a parlour whose height and exactness of proportion must have been new to this gentleman from the country. He checked in his walk as he saw it, and his daughter stood bright-eyed and staring as she saw the tall doors, the moulded wainscot, the ceiling broken into plastered panels that balanced the oaken panels of the walls. Her eyes opened wider as she saw the close-grained walnut of the chairs and table; and then Mrs. Gill, in rustling taffeta and shining lace, rose from her elbowchair to receive her guests. The gentleman bowed.

"You're most gracious, ma'am," he told her. "And since there's none that can present me, pray give me leave. My name, ma'am, is Langley—Richard Langley, of the parish of Bolton in the county of Lancaster. And here's my daughter, Penelope."

Miss Penelope's curtsey was impeccable, and Mrs. Gill was plainly approving as she swept her young guest from the room. Even her sober husband had a smile as he stood by the hearth and spoke to Mr. Langley.

"I don't think she's come to harm. But a glass of wine, sir? And a dish of tea, perhaps, for the ladies."

It was Mr. Leyburne who poured the sweet canary into the tall Venetian glasses, and the three men were chatting amiably when the door swung open again and Miss Penelope came marching sturdily in, her hair set tidy and her face scrubbed clean. She halted in front of her father, and her face was as impudent as her curtsey was correct.

"Do I pass your eye, sir?"

"Indifferently."

It came as a low growl, but his face had softened and there was a warmth in his tone. And then Mrs. Gill was in again with the serving-girl who bore the dish of tea. She poured for her guest from the tall silver pot, and Mr. Leyburne hid a sly amusement. Tea, he thought, was new to Miss Penelope. She would have heard of it, of course, as she would have heard of the other fads of the town, but she would hardly have tasted it; country ladies were seldom as close to the fashion as that; and, even when they were, it was not every gentleman who could and would pay thirty-five shillings a pound for dried leaves to please his womenfolk. But Miss Penelope had some qualities, and if she was ignorant of this rite she was certainly not going to say so; she went at it courageously, keeping a wary eye on her hostess and matching every movement, and she succeeded brilliantly. Mr. Leyburne nodded his approval; it was what he had expected of her.

Then Mr. Gill claimed their attention. He addressed himself to Mr. Langley, who was now much at his ease with a second glass of canary.

"You were saying, sir, that you had some business with me?"

His tone was brisk, and Mr. Langley shook himself and became brisk in his turn.

"Aye," he said, "I have it in mind to get me a new clock—of the pendulum sort. It's true, is it not, that they go more exact than others?"

"There's no other sort that goes exact at all." Mr. Gill was almost didactic about it. "Pendulums were brought out of Holland twenty years back by Mr. Frohmanteel, and now there's no clockmaker free of our Company who will make without them. But was it a table clock you had in mind, or a long one?"

"I suppose it would be the long one. I want it to stand at the foot of my stair."

"Exactly. Then you'll need a long one—and if you have also Mr. Hooke's new escapement, you shall have a clock, sir, of a most excellent exactitude. It shall not vary through the month by more than a minute, or two at most."

"In a month?" Mr. Langley seemed to have been duly impressed. "That's so, is it? And I'd thought the rogue was bragging——"

"Rogue, sir?"

"Your pardon, Master Clockmaker." Mr. Langley caught his daughter's eye and seemed to find there something that set him laughing. "The truth is, I've a neighbour who's fairly earned that name. And lately he's bought him a new clock, and he's mighty full and proud of it. He had it here, in Fleet Street, of a Mr. Tompion——"

"Then he may rightly be proud of it. If it's of Mr. Tompion it will most surely run as true as I have said."

"Aye, but . . ." Mr. Langley hesitated and then plunged at it. "But I'll not be worsted by the rogue, in clocks or aught else. Now tell me, sir, do your clocks run as true as Mr. Tompion's?"

But Mr. Gill declined that one.

"Permit me to own embarrassment, sir." He had his grave smile as he spoke. "But my clocks run as I have said. And now, sir, if you will come below . . ."

"Aye, to be sure." Mr. Langley heaved himself to his feet. Mr. Leyburne, amused at this tale of neighbours' envy, made ready to follow; and then, to his open surprise, Miss Penelope had a word to say.

"By your leave . . ." She had come quickly to her feet, and her face was eager under her vivid hair. "By your leave, Mr. Gill, I myself desire to buy a clock——"

"You also? Another clock, is it?"

"Aye." The sudden smile that lit her brown face set Mr. Leyburne catching at his breath. "I would have a small repeating clock for my own bedchamber. I—I have a small gift of money, and I would expend it so."

"By all means." Mr. Gill's smile was broadening. "Then if you will come below also, you shall see the repeating clocks."

"Yes, but . . ." Miss Penelope paused as though she had a doubt; and then she added what set Mr. Gill's eyebrows lifting in surprise. "But—it must be of Mr. Barlow's sort."

2 MR. BARLOW'S CLOCK

Mr. Gill was not without cause for his surprise, for this Mr. Barlow was a man of mystery, a puzzle to all the clockmakers of London.

Mr. Tompion, whom all allowed to be the first of clockmakers, had lately roused the interest of the Company by making what he called repeating clocks—clocks which would repeat, at demand, the chime of the hour and quarter last struck. Nobody had thought of such a thing before, but there could be no dispute about its convenience; every clockmaker had therefore been anxious to make these clocks, and many had asked Mr. Tompion for leave to use his design. But Mr. Tompion, usually the most obliging of men, had for once refused; the design, he had said, was not his; it had been brought to him by a Mr. Barlow, and whoever wished to use it must ask leave of Mr. Barlow. And when he had been asked where Mr. Barlow should be sought, he had answered that he did not know.

In itself it was no great matter; for repeating clocks, once the idea of them had been put about, had not been found hard to design, and soon every clockmaker had been offering repeaters of his own sort. Trade was therefore satisfied, but curiosity was not. Who was this Mr. Barlow who was so ingenious with clocks and yet not known to the Clockmakers' Company? Why should he so mysteriously disappear after carrying his design to Mr. Tompion? And why should Mr. Tompion so steadfastly refuse all information about him? Mr. Gill had asked these questions as often as anybody, and as vainly; and now this red-haired girl from Lancashire was speaking as if she knew at least as much about Mr. Barlow as the clockmakers did. It was not matter for wonder, therefore, that Mr. Gill should be surprised.

His answer, when it came, was an evasion.

"Of Mr. Barlow's sort? That may be more difficult. However, if you will come below . . ."

He took them to the room behind the workshop, the room private to himself whither the finished clocks were brought for his inspection, and at once Miss Penelope was nosing round the room with a delighted interest, before coming to a halt at a sleek and shining clock. It was finely done in a clear and smooth-grained walnut, and its long door had an oval of floral inlay; above it, the hood had the classical design that was usual, and the shining dial was flanked by pilasters and surmounted by a moulded cornice and a delicate pediment. Mr. Gill swung the door and disclosed the swinging pendulum within.

"The Royal," he explained. "Thirty-nine and one tenth inches, and beating seconds exactly."

"Aye, no doubt." Mr. Langley seemed more concerned with the outside of the clock than with these details. "But what's this?"

He was pointing to the floral inlay on the face of the door, and Mr. Gill answered him placidly.

"It's new," he said, "very new, and we call it marquetry. The case, as you'll know, is of walnut, veneered on English oak. But in that oval the veneer is not of walnut. It's of a dozen woods, each of a different hue, and the pieces so placed that you have the shapes of flowers."

"Aye, aye." Mr. Langley nodded with satisfaction. "Mansell's not got that. But what's above here? It'll show the moon?"

"Of course. There are few clocks sold today without calendar-work. Here it is . . ." Mr. Gill showed the slot in the dial and the painted moon that swung behind it. "You may know at a glance which nights will serve for the visiting of neighbours. And here are the days of the week and the dates of the month———"

"And how of the price?" Mr. Langley sounded decided.

"If exact as this one, four-and-twenty guineas. But it need not be exact as this one. The case, now—it need not be of walnut. You could have olivewood, or ebony . . ."

Mr. Leyburne let this flow past him. It was not talk that could hold his interest at this moment, and plainly the natural end to it would be that Mr. Langley would agree for his clock and then depart, taking his daughter with him; and that he, John Leyburne, would never see either of them again. Already she seemed to have forgotten his existence, and his thoughts were desperate as he asked himself what could be contrived.

He came from that abruptly as he saw that the talk had changed. Apparently the clock had been agreed for, and now it was Miss Penelope who held the centre. She was asking to be shown a repeating clock, and Mr. Gill was genial and benevolent as he set one on the table before her. It was a pretty thing, ticking gaily as it stood square and sturdy on the table; a neat and compact thing, done in ebony with gilt mounts, and driven by springs instead of weights that it might be light enough to be carried by the hinged and gilded handle that surmounted it. From its side trailed a silken cord, and Mr. Gill quickly showed what this was for. He set the hands to a minute before six o'clock; then he waited; and as the hands came to the hour two silvery bells chimed the four quarters and a third bell gave the hour. Mr. Gill advanced the hands by a quarter hour, and again the two bells chimed the quarter. Again Mr. Gill waited; then he pulled sharply at the silken cord, and at once the bells chimed out again, first the six beats of the hour that was gone and then the short tinkle of the quarter. Miss Penelope glowed with pleasure, and her father stared, fascinated.

"Thus you have it," said Mr. Gill. "Pull at this cord and straightway you know which quarter hour was last—which is as much as you need to know in the nighttime. And it spares you a temptation to rashness."

"Rashness?" Miss Penelope spoke darkly, and with the air of one accustomed to being so accused. "What rashness, if you please?"

"Firing a candle within your bed curtains."

His answer came promptly, and Miss Penelope's lifted eyebrows showed that it had gone home. Then, in an instant, she had changed, and she had the clock excitedly in her hands, lifting it and peering at it and listening to its tick; she pulled the cord again and listened delightedly to the chiming bells, and then she was rubbing her fingers along the smooth grain of the wood. For a moment it seemed certain that the clock would be hers, and then a shadow of doubt swept over her face; she put the clock down and looked Mr. Gill in the eye.

"It's beautiful," she said, "and I'd ask no better. But tell me, sir—is it of Mr. Barlow's sort?"

"I think so much might be said." Mr. Gill spoke with a nice precision. "Mr. Barlow, as I understand, did first devise repeating clocks. That was a clock of a new sort. And this clock is of that sort."

"Aye, sir. I see that. But is this of the sort that Mr. Barlow did devise? Are its workings those that he devised and drew?"

Mr. Gill was cornered. He had to admit that they were not. This clock, he said, did all that Mr. Barlow's clock had done, but its design and workings were his own; and, if he might ask it, were they the worse for that?

Miss Penelope stood silent; and then suddenly her smile was alive again.

"No, sir," she told him. "I'm very sure they are no whit the worse for that. This, indeed, is just such a clock as I would have. In spite of which . . ." She paused, and obstinacy was plain in her shapely face. "In spite of which, sir, I must needs have Mr. Barlow's, even though it should be a worse clock. You see . . ."

She paused again, and Mr. Gill was quick to assure her that she was wholly free to choose. But she would not be silenced, and she went courageously at what was almost an apology.

"There's a sentiment in it," she explained slowly. "I had a gift of money in December that last was. I—I came to twenty years the first day of that month . . ."

Once again Mr. Leyburne had quick thoughts. This gave her the age he had guessed, and it was just three years less than his; he thought that very proper.

"And I chose to use it for the buying of a clock, because it—it was given——"

"Mr. Barlow's clock. Precisely." Mr. Gill was smiling. "I'll suppose, then, that you're acquainted with Mr. Barlow?"

She nodded.

"He's—he's been most kind to me."

"And generous, no doubt." Mr. Gill showed how his thoughts were running, and then, nobly, he forbore to ask questions. "But I must regret that I cannot serve your need in this. Only Mr. Tompion makes in Mr. Barlow's sort."

"Where I've said we won't go," growled Mr. Langley suddenly. "We don't follow after Mansell."

Mr. Leyburne's wits went as smoothly as his clocks, and he wasted no time.

"By your leave," he said quickly, "there's nothing of moment that need hinder you in this. I'll myself procure from Mr. Tompion such a clock as you speak of, and you may make the purchase from Mr. Gill. So much can be arranged within the Company."

He turned to his uncle as though to get confirmation of this, and for a moment Mr. Gill was pleased to show amusement.

"My dear John," he answered, "if you care to put yourself to the trouble I'd be the last to gainsay you. No doubt you'll do a kindness and, as you say, it can be arranged within the Company."

His dry smile, which his nephew was beginning to find disconcerting, turned suddenly to Miss Penelope, who was in no way disconcerted. She smiled happily back, and then turned a beaming face to Mr. Leyburne.

"Is this earnest?" she asked him. "You don't jest with me?"

"Not I!" He was fervent in that, and her smile broadened as she caught the note of it.

"How then?" she asked. "Do I come here to get it?"

"No." He was decisive about that. "It's I that shall bring it to you. You'll permit so much?"

"Permit?" Miss Penelope was charming. "I'm honoured, sir—and grateful."

"There's one thing," Mr. Langley cut in suddenly in his low growl. "Here's Tuesday, and we set ourselves for the North on Thursday. What of that?"

"We'll take account of it and contrive accordingly." Mr. Leyburne concealed his dismay and spoke firmly. "I'll bring the clock tomorrow night. Now if I may know where you are lodged in London?"

"Not in London. We're lodged in Westminster—the King's Arms in Tothill Street."

"I'll wait upon you there, sir."

They parted on that. Mr. Langley was cordial as they took their leave, and his daughter, holding dutifully to his arm as they walked away, suddenly spoiled the decorum of it by twisting impulsively for a smile and a wave at Mr. Leyburne, who was standing by the door to see them go. It sent him into the house in a dream, and it was as much as he could do to give a proper interest to the talk at supper. He made some wandering answers, and after the third of them Mr. Gill sat with his dry smile and then slyly changed the topic; he looked at the panelled ceiling and wondered what might lie between Miss Langley and the mysterious Mr. Barlow. Mr. Leyburne rejoined with sudden interest, and for a moment his talk was brisk. Then he broke off in the middle of a sentence and sat staring in something near consternation; the alarming thought had occurred to him that this Mr. Barlow might perhaps be a young and personable fellow.

3 INVITATION The workaday world was no more than opening its shutters and finding its tools when Mr. Leyburne made his way along Fleet Street to where the Three Crowns hung above Mr. Tompion's shop at the corner of Water Lane. Mr. Tompion, astir with the earliest as his custom was, received him genially and asked how he might serve a fellow clockmaker. He was promptly told, and then he pursed his lips and looked regretful; he doubted whether he had such a clock, but Mr. Leyburne might come to his room and see.

They went and they saw, and Mr. Tompion's forebodings were justified. There was a table clock in gilt and ebony, but it was not the repeater that Miss Penelope desired; there was a repeater in silver and walnut, but it had not the appearance that Miss Penelope desired; there was no clock that wholly met her desires. Mr. Tompion shook his head, and Mr. Leyburne looked at the two clocks; then he suggested that they were much of a size and shape, and that the movement of the one might with no great difficulty be put in the case of the other. As a suggestion it was reasonable, but it set Mr. Tompion blinking; he was accustomed to suppose that his clocks, once made and passed, were as perfect as clocks could be, and he was not used to journeymen who suggested they should be altered; he said so, and Mr. Leyburne, perceiving that he was on delicate ground, decided to stick to the truth.

"Truly, sir, it's out of the common course, I know. But it's a matter of a lady. She—she knows her mind on this most exactly, sir. And for my part, I—I have an interest, and . . ."

He broke off in some confusion, and Mr. Tompion scanned him keenly and then burst out laughing.

"You've an interest, have you? And I thought you said this was to serve Mr. Gill." Mr. Tompion chuckled happily; he was himself a bachelor, but he was not the less genial for that. "I've heard it whispered, young man, that it's time you had a wife to cool your humours. Let me see now . . ."

He gave his shrewd glance to the clocks and seemed satisfied. Then he led to the workshop, and one Hopkins, a journeyman, got his orders. Mr. Tompion wandered off, still chuckling, and Mr. Leyburne breathed more easily; he and this Hopkins had been apprentices of the same year, and they knew each other. He perched himself comfortably on the bench as Hopkins peered at the clocks and began to ease the securing screws.

"What the devil!" said Hopkins. "What is it, John? Can't you make a repeater in your own shop?"

"Better than you, my boy. But it was one of the Barlow breed that was called for."

Mr. Hopkins grunted, and suddenly Mr. Leyburne was alert. There had been more in that, he thought, than mere displeasure at an unwanted job; and at once he was asking himself if there was something to be learned here.

"Who is this Barlow?" he asked casually.

"Ask the Pope," was the surprising answer.

"The Pope?" Mr. Leyburne still sounded casual. "Do you take me for a papist?"

"I take Barlow for one."

Mr. Leyburne was startled. He found this thought disturbing, and he had some ado to keep his casual air.

"You think so?" he asked lightly. "Why? I'd not supposed you knew the man."

"I don't. But I've seen him. He seems to come to town each half year, and when he does, he looks in here—to collect his moneys, I suppose."

"He'd be a fool if he didn't. You've sold enough of his clocks. But what manner of man is he? Of what age and sort?"

"Age? Forty or more. A slender fellow with greying hair and his eyes dreaming. Blue-jowled, with a sallow face and the look of a shave yesterday—never today."

Mr. Leyburne nodded, glad that the advantage in looks and age lay with himself.

"It's a pretty picture," he said slowly. "But why a papist?"

"There's not a doubt of it. Tompion all but said so."

The man shut his mouth suddenly, and Mr. Leyburne stayed carefully casual. This Hopkins, as he well knew, was devoted to his master, and would certainly say no more unless he were assured that nothing would be turned to the hurt of Mr. Tompion; and dealings with a papist could be turned to the hurt of any man. Mr. Leyburne nodded affably.

"Did he so?" He had the easy air of an old friend. "Then we'll suppose Barlow's the better sort of papist, if Tompion knows him. Tompion's got more sense than Oates. But what did he say? I've an interest in this—and I don't gossip."

"No?" Hopkins eyed him again and then seemed reassured. "You know what the times are like."

"I do. But this isn't a matter of the times. It's a matter of a lady."

"Is it?" Suddenly Hopkins was grinning as if he had heard tales of Mr. Leyburne and the ladies. "Then if that's how it is——"

"That's just how it is. And now if you please, what did our Tompion say?"

"Say?" Hopkins seemed quite at his ease now, and suddenly he put down clock and tools and spoke lucidly. "I've told you that Barlow comes each half year, I know not whence. He was here in October—in that same week when Godfrey was murdered. And he came here—to the shop. He stayed his half hour, and then Tompion let him out by the side door yonder. And as Barlow went I heard Tompion warn him to be careful. 'Look you to it,' he said. 'The town's none so safe this week for men of your thinking.' Those were his words—and what should they mean except that the man's a papist?"

Mr. Leyburne nodded, and his casual air had slipped from him. This was convincing; for it had been for the papists, and for no others, that the town had been none so safe in those October days when Sir Edmund Godfrey had lain murdered and Mr. Oates and the others had been telling of a Popish Plot. Decidedly it had been for men of papist thinking that the town had been unsafe—and was unsafe yet. Again Mr. Leyburne nodded.

"I agree," he said quietly. "And my thanks for being told."

"You sounded urgent. And we're not strangers. But why——"

"It's a matter of a lady. That's all." Mr. Leyburne was speaking quickly. "But believe that I'm grateful."

"It's no matter—if you keep it close. But for how it should help you to a lady——"

"It doesn't—so far. Which is why I'll ask you for a service more."

"But what?"

"This way." Mr. Leyburne marshalled his thoughts and then spoke carefully. "What I really want is a word with Barlow. He—has the lady's ear."

"The devil he has! Then——"

"Listen! It's no jest with me. You say Barlow was here last October?"

"What of it?"

"If he comes each half year he should be back again next month— in April. Now if he does, will you point him out to me?"

"Point him out? Why, yes—if I can, and if there's no more to it than that."

"It's a matter of a lady, and no more. Now will you point him out to me?"

"Surely." Hopkins was grinning openly. "But what's this of a lady? And is she to have this clock—when I've had the guts out of it for you?"

It sufficed, and a half hour later Mr. Leyburne was back with the clock in Mr. Gill's workshop; and at once he went at a self-imposed task. He began with a bead of gold which he beat flat and trimmed to a shapely oval. Then, clearly and delicately, he engraved it in fine-cut letters: *P.L.: Dec., 1678.* He inspected them minutely before he gave the plate a final polish and screwed it carefully to the base of the clock, where it shone and twinkled against the ebony and gilt. And suddenly he was smiling as the fancy came to him that these letters need not necessarily become outmoded when Miss Penelope should have been prevailed upon to change her name. Mr. Leyburne did not want for self-confidence.

The blue haze of dusk was upon the streets when he went abroad again. The clock, delicately wrapped, was carefully under his arm, but this time he was not the clockmaker—nor did he look it. This was Mr. Leyburne, the cadet of a gentle house, and his dress and bearing showed it. Nor had this been difficult, for he was independent of his modest pay as a journeyman. His father, youngest son of a John Leyburne of Cunswick, had prospered in the town before his untimely death, and had been able to leave to his only son enough to permit him to indulge his fancies in clothes and in some other things. All that had been needed tonight was to choose from a well-stocked wardrobe, and what he had chosen supported admirably the dignity that belonged to his name. He had coat and breeches of golden brown, and the coat, wide and full, hung open to show the cream brocade of his long waistcoat and the wide sash of golden satin that girt it about the middle; he had a modest periwig, and there was a touch of richness in the lace of his cravat and the paste buckles of his shoes. He carried, too, a slim steel-hilted sword, and this was not wholly for display; the streets of London were none too safe when darkness was upon them, and in these days, when the Mohawks and the Brisk Boys added perils beyond those of footpads, it behoved any man who stirred at night to wear a sword and to know how to use it.

He went delicately. He picked a careful way along Fleet Street, and at the first opportunity he hailed a hackney coach and had himself driven. It was too late in the day to go by water, and the only other way to Westminster was the long miry lane called King Street, and he was set tonight on a visit for which he preferred to arrive clean. He achieved it, and with greater speed than he had expected, for he was in Westminster in less than an hour. He walked into the King's Arms with a fine air of consequence, and inquired imperiously for Miss Langley; the landlord bowed, and Mr. Leyburne was invited abovestair and shown into the low oak-panelled room that was private to the Langleys, a room snug now with curtains and candles and a sea-coal fire. He clicked his heels in the doorway and at once it was plain that his name had meant nothing here. Mr. Langley, courteous and puzzled, was standing stiffly to welcome this unknown gentleman, and Miss Penelope was correct and formal at his side. Mr. Langley bowed, and Miss Penelope began her curtsey. Then, even as she sank into it with a billowing of skirts and a swish of taffeta, her face twitched and changed, and suddenly a smile was on it; but it was a friendly smile, and she kept it while she halted and looked him up and down; and then she coolly resumed a curtsey that now seemed to be deliberately deep.

"Sir—your servant!" She was still sunk in it, and her eyes were dancing with mischief. Mr. Leyburne bowed again, and this time it was to her.

"What the devil!" said Mr. Langley suddenly. Plainly he did not understand this byplay; just as plainly he did understand this look on his daughter's face, and he was eyeing it with dark suspicion. Mr. Leyburne thought it time to enlighten him.

"We met yesterday, sir—at Mr. Gill's. And I fulfil a promise. I bring Miss Langley's clock."

"The devil you do!" Mr. Langley stared; and slowly recognition came upon his face.

"What the devil!" he said again, and had another look at the cravat, the gleaming buckles, the periwig and sword. "Who—— What d'ye say your name is?"

"Leyburne, sir. John Leyburne."

"Leyburne?" Mr. Langley's eyes opened a little wider. "It's a name we know in the North Parts."

"Aye, sir. We're of Westmorland."

"Cunswick, do you mean?"

"Exactly, sir." Mr. Leyburne saw no need to add that he had been born in London and had never in his life seen Cunswick, nor even Westmorland.

"Oh!" Mr. Langley looked baffled, and while he still stared his daughter slipped in front of him and held out her hands for the clock. She unwrapped it excitedly and set it on the table, and his cheek brushed against her hair as he bent over it to hook the pendulum into position and set it ticking sturdily. He stepped back, his breath coming quickly, and he had a sparkling glance from her excited eyes. Then she had turned to the clock again, and her face was alive with pleasure as she saw the deep glow of the gilt against the ebony; and at once she must jerk at the trailing cord and hear the tinkle of the bells that tolled the hour and quarters. She threw him another delighted glance, and then she saw the plate of gold that gleamed beneath the dial; she peered keenly, and then, with no pretence of dignity, she dropped on her knees by the table to read what he had engraved on it.

"I did not ask for this."

She had turned to him, still kneeling, and if her words might have meant displeasure her eyes corrected that; and he had to steady his breath before he dared to answer her.

"Therein should lie the pleasure of a gift."

"You think well." She spoke slowly, and then she jumped lightly to her feet with her forehead puckering and her head tilting.

"You look well, too," she told him cheerfully, and by that she seemed to rouse her father. He addressed himself to Mr. Leyburne.

"Well or not well," he said bluntly, "you give me to wonder. I'd supposed you to be the journeyman."

"I am, sir—by day."

"Aye, but——"

"He's Mr. Gill's nephew," said Miss Penelope quickly. "So much we were told yesterday."

"That's one thing. Leyburne of Cunswick is another. However—a glass of wine, if you please?"

That sounded like recognition, and Mr. Leyburne was quick to accept. His host waved him to a chair by the fire, and it was Miss Penelope who poured the wine and carried the glasses. He lifted his in salute to her, and at once she lifted hers; and deliberately he let the glasses touch before he drank.

"I don't know what you find to chatter of, both of you," said Mr. Langley gruffly. "I've said I'm lost in this. You make clocks, you call yourself Leyburne, and you talk of Cunswick. Am I to be enlightened?"

"Surely, sir," came the sober answer. "But truly, it's not matter for wonder. My father was a younger son. He came to the town, prospered here, and was wed here—to Mr. Gill's sister. It's no uncommon tale, sir. You'll have heard the like before?"

"Oh aye—if it runs that course. Then you're set to be a Master Clockmaker?"

"It would seem so. Yet at times I doubt it." Mr. Leyburne contrived a laugh. "I'm not sure, sir, that I have the taste for town life. But I come out of my journeyman's time next month, and I'm minded then to see something of the country before I settle."

"Aye, aye. You'll learn best by visiting—just as we learn when we visit the town. It's always of interest."

That was disappointing; an invitation to do his visiting in Lancashire would have been more to the point; but Mr. Leyburne was not easily discouraged, and his answer came smoothly.

"Aye, sir. There's always something in the town. Pray, sir, were you at the Rolls on Sunday?"

His question was neither so innocent nor so simple as it seemed. The preacher at the Chapel of the Rolls last Sunday had been the Dean of Canterbury, who was fast rising to be the favourite preacher of such men as Mr. Langley seemed to be. The Dean had a talent for persuading his hearers that they could be excellent Christians without wrestling with anything very difficult, and Mr. Langley seemed to be precisely the sort of man who would heartily agree with that—unless, of course, he were a papist. So Mr. Leyburne flung his question and then waited. The answer satisfied him at once.

"Aye, to be sure we were. I'd not have missed it. But are you saying that you were there?"

Mr. Leyburne had not said so, but he had in fact been there, and for precisely the same reason. He said so now, and at once Mr. Langley surprised him by looking pleased.

"That's good," he said heartily. "It's uncommon good. Do you know, Mr. Leyburne, I'd been supposing you to be a papist——"

"What!" Mr. Leyburne sat suddenly erect. "A papist, sir? Truly, sir, I——"

"Aye, aye. But take it not amiss. What else should I suppose—of *your* family? But where's the wine?"

Mr. Leyburne gasped, and called himself a fool for not having foreseen this; it was obvious, but somehow he had never thought of it, and now he had to pull his wits together quickly while Miss Penelope saw to the wine again; and soon he was explaining about his Puritan father and his Puritan uncle Thomas, who had owned Cunswick until at his death it had passed to George Leyburne, the next brother.

"He being a papist," said Mr. Langley quietly.

"Aye, sir. And so's my other uncle—John, like me. He's a priest among them."

"So we've all heard. But what are you? A dissenter?"

"Far from it, sir." He was quick on that, guessing that Mr. Langley probably regarded all dissenters as a seditious rabble. "I'm neither the one nor the other, sir. Like you I—I hear Dr. Tillotson."

"You could not do better." There was a heartiness in Mr. Langley now. "Why the devil should the dissenters have all the preachers? But the wine again, if you please. . . ."

Mr. Leyburne sipped it thoughtfully. There was another matter that he wanted to probe, and he went at it as slyly as before. He looked steadily at Miss Penelope.

"Mr. Barlow is a papist, is he not?"

For once she was almost disconcerted; she stared at him as though she could find no good answer, and when she did it was an evasion.

"I did not suppose that you knew Mr. Barlow."

"I don't—though I've heard talk of him. But you, I take it, know him well?"

"Very well. But——"

Suddenly her father came to her help.

"That's no matter," he said firmly. "It's the way of things in Lancashire. There's many an honest man in that county who has papist neighbours and finds them civil folk—for all that's said of plots in London. And as with others, so with us. And that's the short of it."

His tone dismissed the topic, and Mr. Leyburne suffered it to pass. If it did not tell him more of Mr. Barlow, at least it sorted with all that he had heard of men's ways in the North Parts, and he was satisfied. He was still satisfied when he rose to take polite leave and wish them pleasant journey on the morrow. He called for a hackney coach, and while he waited for it he stood at leisure.

"I've said," he remarked casually, "that I'm minded to see something of the North Parts when my journeyman's time is out. That will be this summer. To be more exact, it's been in my thoughts to ride north for Kendal and make my respects at Cunswick."

He waited breathlessly by the hearth; and Mr. Langley made the perfect answer.

"Kendal? Then you'll need to ride through Lancashire. It's a road none so distant from my gates."

"You turn off at the Boar's Head," said Miss Penelope brightly. "It's three miles north from Wigan town."

4

THE TAVERN IN THE STRAND   It was a full three
weeks before the Fates gave Mr. Leyburne what else he had asked
for; and he might not have asked for it if he had foreseen how they
would give it.

He chose, on an April afternoon, to spend an hour of leisure at
the theatre. He thought the theatre a very proper place for a gentleman, and when he heard that the Duke's Company had revived Mr.
Payne's *The Fatal Jealousy* at Dorset Garden he at once determined
to see it. He went alone and he went at his ease, dressed again as he
had been that night in Westminster; and with the clothes came memories and the image of Penelope Langley. She was still with him when
he came from the theatre in the early dusk, and it was perhaps to
savour the dream that he halted in Salisbury Court and turned into
the Red Lion for a chop and a glass of claret. He was in no hurry,
and when he came from the tavern the April night was soft and clear
under a shining moon; it blended with his mood as he strolled up
Fleet Street, and he had come almost to Water Lane before he was
abruptly roused to the present.

The moon was above the river, and at the corner of the lane the
shadows were deep; but there were lights in Mr. Tompion's shop, and
the journeyman Hopkins was holding a lantern while apprentices put
the shutters up. Mr. Leyburne, on the other side of the street, was
clear in the moonlight, and the friendly Hopkins turned to wave a
greeting; and at that exact moment a man came quickly from the
shadows of Water Lane and was for a moment in the lantern light
before he plunged again into the shadows as he turned westward
along Fleet Street; and then, as Mr. Leyburne was making slowly
across the street, Hopkins came towards him.

"Did you see him?" He spoke urgently, and Mr. Leyburne was
almost alarmed.

"Who? The man yonder——"

"I mean Barlow. He's just left—from our side door."

"The hell he has!" Mr. Leyburne was wide awake now. "That fellow who made off?"

"Who else? You asked me to point him out."

"I did. And I'll be after him. My thanks."

"Aye. But John——"

"Yes?"

"He spoke of a friend he was to meet, and he said he was late. So if you want him you'd best hurry."

Mr. Leyburne did want him. He very much wanted this Barlow who could tell him of Penelope Langley, and already, after another word of thanks, he was hurrying in pursuit; and it was not a very hopeful pursuit. His glimpse of Barlow in the lantern light had shown him no more than a cloak of black and a hat of black, wide and low-crowned; and beyond that he had nothing but Hopkins' description of a sallow-faced man of forty who might seem in need of a shave. It was little enough; and if the man were hurrying to meet a friend he might turn quickly into any coffeehouse or tavern; and there were enough of both in Fleet Street and the Strand beyond.

He moved into the middle of the street, where the line of moonlight lay, and here he was able to move at a decent speed, careless of who saw him. He went quickly, watchful of the shadows on his left and of the track of moonlight ahead, which Barlow might at any moment cross. He was heedless of all else, and as he drew near to Chancery Lane he was taken wholly by surprise. From the arch of the Inner Temple there came a sudden rush of men, whooping and shouting, and before he had found his wits they were upon him; his sword was jerked from its sheath and flung on the cobbles, and as his hat followed his sword he was gripped by the arms and swung to face the moon. The men were all round him, jostling and pushing, and in the moonlight he could see them clearly; a half dozen of gay and gaudy sparks, reeking of scent and wine, all of them young, tipsy, and dangerous. At once he understood, as any man in the town would have understood; these, beyond doubt, were the Mohawks.

He stood tense and silent, knowing only too well what his danger was; all the town knew the Mohawks as swaggering sprigs of fashion who ruffled it through the streets at night, breaking windows, wrecking taverns, offering violence to men and insult to women. They had an ugly name; and Mr. Leyburne, his sword gone and the press of them round him, knew that he would be lucky if he escaped with no more than insult.

"Who the hell's this rat?"

The words were bawled in his face, and, insult though they were, he pressed his lips tight and made no answer; it was not wise to make answers to the Mohawks, and the man who made one was likely to be held down while his nose was slit to the bone. It had been done to some others, and Mr. Leyburne knew it could be done to him; so he kept silence, and, with eyes that were twitching with anger, he noted keenly the looks of the man who had spoken. He was a man who might be remembered, a tall and burly fellow, perhaps in his middle twenties, and elegant in bottle green laced with gold; a man with a round and florid face, hard unwavering eyes, and some wisps of hair pushing untidily past the fringes of his wig; a man whom Mr. Leyburne might at any time have disliked and to whom at this moment he felt murderous.

"Who the hell is he?" The man shouted it, and then suddenly he bellowed a laugh. "God sink and blast me! What's this fleabag round his ears, hey? Look at it!"

They hooted with drunken laughter, and Mr. Leyburne's short periwig was suddenly snatched from his head and flung to the cobbles with his hat and sword while the burly man pushed his face close and stared insolently.

"God's life!" The voice came bawling again. "There's no sport here. We'd best seek elsewhere. The night's still young."

It was almost a command, and it was promptly obeyed. Mr. Leyburne was spun round and a vicious kick sent him sprawling on the filth and mud of the cobbles; and before he had picked himself up the Mohawks were away, roistering it down Fleet Street in search of some other prey; and from the shadows of the Temple arch a half dozen others, who had the look of servants, moved watchfully after them.

There was nothing to be done, no retribution that Mr. Leyburne could exact if he wished to live till morning. There was nothing for it but to quell his fury as best he might while he wiped the worst of the filth from his breeches and did what he could to his wig before setting it on his head again. A glint of steel in the moonlight showed where his sword lay useless on the cobbles, and he slammed it viciously into its sheath before he made his way along the street with what poor dignity he could; and he was so filled with fury that he wandered blindly on, all thoughts of Barlow forgotten in the intensity of his anger.

He was far past Temple Bar when he became aware of his surroundings, and then he halted and began to look warily about him. He was in the middle of the Strand, and opposite to him was a tavern; it was dimly lit, and it had an air of gloom, but it could no doubt supply a glass of wine; the thought was compelling, and he moved across the road, only to halt once more as he saw the painted sign that swung above the door. It was a leaping horse, vividly done in white, the paint of it flaring in the moonlight, and Mr. Leyburne stood stiffly as he considered it; for this was no ordinary tavern, as well he knew. Six months ago there had been the Reverend Titus Oates, a clergyman of the Church of England, to tell of the great plot the Jesuits had hatched to kill the King and all the Protestants; and Mr. Oates, who was most oddly well informed of all their secrets, had revealed that in the spring of last year the Jesuits had held a great consult to perfect their plot, and had held it at this very tavern, the White Horse, in the Strand. It therefore followed that this White Horse tavern was a noted sink of villainy, a place frequented only by papists, and of those only by the worst and most villainous; it would compromise any man to be seen in this place, and ordinary prudence commanded a man of sense to go elsewhere.

But Mr. Leyburne was not at this moment a man of sense. He had had his fill of prudence this night; and then, while his jaw was stiffening and obstinacy was coming into his face, he remembered the papist, Mr. Barlow. This, surely, was the tavern of taverns where a papist might make a meeting with another, and Mr. Barlow might well be inside it at this moment. That thought decided him, and at once he squared his shoulders, clapped his hand to his sword hilt, and went swaggering in.

The little room was dark and low, with only a candle on the bar and another on the chimney breast; three fellows were at ale by the dying fire, and a drowsy woman was lolling at the bar. Mr. Leyburne looked about him with distaste, and then he saw in the shadows another door which surely led to the inner room the hostess would keep for folk of the better sort; he called shortly for wine, marched to this second door, and flung it open.

The inner room was as dark and small as the other, and the fire in its tiny hearth was almost burnt out; a single candle burned at a small table where two men sat deep in talk. They turned as he burst in, and it was plain that they were not pleased; one pushed his chair back noisily, and his stare was enough to snap Mr. Leyburne's frayed temper.

"What the devil?" he demanded truculently. "Do I offend you, sir, by entering a public tavern?"

"No." The man came lazily to his feet and stood tall and loose-limbed. "But you offend me infinitely when you take that tone."

"Do I so? And what would satisfy you, pray?"

His hand was on his sword hilt, and his angry eyes made his meaning plain. For a moment the other man was silent, his face an impassive mask. He was a big man, tall and powerful, with a lean bronzed face, a big jutting nose, and a mouth which at another time might have suggested humour.

"So much?" he said quietly. "I'm to suppose, then, that you're a gentleman?"

"Sir!"

"Be at ease. If you assert that you're a gentleman I'll believe you. It's merely that it was not apparent from your manners."

Mr. Leyburne almost choked; but then, while he was on the brink of what would have made it worse, the hostess was in with the wine he had called for, and that gave him a chance to recover.

"You'll do well to believe it," he said firmly. "My name, sir, is Leyburne—John Leyburne."

"Leyburne?" The man echoed it quickly, and his tone had changed. "That's a name——"

He broke off, and his brown eyes were keen and steady as he seemed to ponder it.

"Of the Cunswick Leyburnes?" he asked quietly. "Of Cunswick by Kendal?"

"Of Cunswick, Skelsmergh, and Witherslack, all by Kendal," came the prompt answer; and the tall man nodded, as though he, too, could have recited the names of the Leyburnes' estates.

"I am Nevil Payne," he said gently. "And I should be sorry to offend any of your house."

Mr. Leyburne began to be appeased, and he had the unhappy thought that his manners had certainly not been of the best; he had, too, the thought that he ought to know this man, that he had heard of Nevil Payne before; and while he groped in his memory the other man, the man still sitting at the table, spoke for the first time. He was a smaller man than Mr. Payne, and he had been so still and impassive that he had all but escaped notice; but now he leaned forward so that the candle gave him full light, and at once Mr. Leyburne's thoughts went leaping. He saw the slender figure, the pale ascetic face with the lines of middle age, the faraway look in the dark dreaming eyes; he saw the high forehead, the greying hair, the chin left blue by an insufficient shave; he saw the cloak of black and the broad-brimmed hat that lay on the table by the candle; and at once his thoughts went leaping to the name he could give this man. It was not indeed a certainty; but surely, at a guess, this might be Mr. Barlow.

But whoever the man was, he was speaking; he was addressing himself to Mr. Payne, and there was something compelling, something almost of authority, in his soft voice.

"Certainly you must not quarrel," he said firmly. "Mr. Leyburne perhaps spoke a little ill, but it would seem from his looks that he has lately been treated ill. That perhaps excuses——"

Mr. Payne followed the lead at once, with one quick look at Mr. Leyburne's mud and disarray.

"Aye," he agreed. "What has come to you, Mr. Leyburne, and from whom?"

"Mohawks—as I came from the theatre."

The answer was short, for his thoughts were elsewhere; but Mr. Payne seemed satisfied.

"That suffices," he said briefly. "We all know the Mohawks. They're pests beyond all bearing. Sit you down, sir, and we'll brim these glasses."

Mr. Leyburne obeyed; it was plainly a moment for tact.

"My thanks," he said briefly. "And I fear I must regret some hasty words."

He let his glass clink against the other, and then he looked searchingly at the lean and vital face before him.

"I don't recall you, sir," he said. "Yet it's in my mind that I should. At the least I've heard your name."

"Most men have," said Mr. Payne easily. "What piece did they perform, pray, at the theatre?"

"It was called *The Fatal Jealousy,* and it was a most——"

He stopped abruptly as understanding came to him; for all men knew that *The Fatal Jealousy* had been written by a Mr. Payne. He looked across the table and saw the slow smile and the twinkling eye, and suddenly he was smiling back.

"Your pardon, Mr. Payne. I've been slow of understanding."

"Pardon granted," said Mr. Payne briskly. "But permit me to present Mr. Webster. . . ."

"Mr. Webster, is it?" He stared again at that pale ascetic face, and suddenly he decided to risk it. "Now at a guess I'd have said it was Mr. Barlow."

The pale face froze to ice. By the side of the table Mr. Payne turned sharply, his eyebrows drawn down and his lips pressed tight; at this moment he looked oddly like a hawk.

"What's this?" he said softly. "What is it that you say?"

Mr. Leyburne saw that he had blundered, and he was in haste to set it right.

"It's no matter," he said quickly. "It's merely that I'm a clockmaker, and that I've lately been dealing with repeating clocks—of Mr. Barlow's sort."

"Ah!" It was almost a sigh of relief, and for a moment the two men glanced at each other. Then the smaller man spoke quietly.

"So?" he murmured, almost in inquiry. "But I had not supposed that I was known by face to the clockmakers here."

"You are not. But we are all curious about the man who carried a design to Mr. Tompion. I had heard that he was a man of such-and-such sort and that he came to town each half year. And it chanced that I saw you come from Mr. Tompion's this night. And so——"

"And so by another chance—or would it be a design?—you came

upon me here. It's very well, Mr. Leyburne, and I'll own to being Edward Barlow. But that's for your private ear. To all others I'm Mr. Webster. Is that understood?"

"Perfectly." Mr. Leyburne raised his glass. "Your good fortune, sir! To speak as a clockmaker, I'm honoured to meet with one so adept in our mysteries."

"Hardly an adept. Call me a mathematician rather than a clock-maker. But what of yourself, Mr. Leyburne? Cunswick and clock-making scarcely run together."

That had to be answered, and Mr. Leyburne left nothing to chance; he was in speech with the one man who could tell him about Penelope Langley and he would leave nothing unsaid that might help him to establish himself. Mr. Barlow listened placidly and when the tale was at an end he poured the wine again.

"George Gill, do you say? And your uncle? I'd call you fortu-nate, Mr. Leyburne. But tell me, is it true that Mr. Gill makes repeat-ers with a coiled spring instead of a straight one for the striking train?"

"To be sure he does. And he sees good reason for it. A coil spring gives some advantages . . ." Mr. Leyburne became professional and launched himself upon an explanation of this. He was countered by some shrewd questions, and soon he was involved in an argument that grew too technical for Mr. Payne. He uncoiled his long legs and got lazily to his feet.

"The devil take your springs," he told them both. "Myself, I like to hear your little bells go jingle, but for how it's done . . ." His big shoulders shrugged. "I'll leave you to it and get me to the Rainbow. There'll be some gossip there."

His good-humoured smile disposed of their protests, and with an easy nod he wandered out by a discreet side door that seemed to lead into a yard.

"I think he has affairs," said Mr. Barlow, as if in explanation, and Mr. Leyburne nodded. He was by no means sorry to be alone with Mr. Barlow, and he made no delay about coming to what was in his mind.

"I heard of you lately, sir, from another—who is far from being a clockmaker."

"Indeed? But you set me to wonder. From whom, may I ask?"

"Miss Langley."

Mr. Barlow's eyebrows went up, and plainly he was in high surprise; then his cool ascetic face softened as a smile woke in it, and stayed and broadened.

"What? My little Penelope?"

He asked it softly, and Mr. Leyburne, who would have given much to be able to say those words himself, had a quick moment of jealousy. It was gone as quickly as it had come, for a single look at Mr. Barlow was enough to prove it groundless; then he had recovered himself and was probing for information.

"Aye," he answered. "We spoke of you in talk of clocks, and she admitted to knowing you."

"So she should," came the dry answer. "I am permitted—by courtesy, you understand—to stand to her *in loco avunculi*. It's a fiction that pleases us both."

The smile was still with him, and there was something in it of memory and much of happiness. Then, quite sharply, he seemed to come to earth again.

"But I do not understand," he said quickly. "When was this? And where?"

"Here in London. She was here with her father, and it chanced that I was able——"

He got no further. Instead, he came leaping to his feet, Mr. Barlow with him. From the outer room there came the sudden crash of a door burst open, and then a rush of feet, a splintering of glass, and a high flurry of voices, wild and blasphemous; and if anything more was needed to announce that here were the Mohawks again, it was quickly supplied. There was the crack of a blow and a sharp cry of pain, and then the door came quivering as a booted foot caught it; the gust of it set the candle flickering as a man came storming in, big and burly, and one look at him was enough for Mr. Leyburne. Here once more was the green-coated fellow who led the Mohawks, and for a moment he stood at gaze, his red face hot and sweating; then, as he saw the men by the table, his eyes dilated, and suddenly his great voice came bellowing.

"God's life! It's Barlow!"

It was a howl of triumph, and at once he was leaping forward, his sword flashing murderously. Then Mr. Leyburne recovered his wits, and anger flared in him again to spur him on. His long arm swooped, and the wine bottle went hurtling into Greencoat's face, sending him reeling and spluttering with sudden pain. In the same instant Mr. Barlow sent stand and candle clattering to the floor, and in the darkness his hand was on Mr. Leyburne's arm; he was quick and decisive, with the coolness of a man not unused to sudden dangers, and Mr. Leyburne was spun round and pushed quickly to the wall. Mr. Barlow fumbled for the latch, and then the small side door swung softly open, and moonlight was flooding over them.

Mr. Barlow seemed to know the way, and Mr. Leyburne, who certainly did not, was glad enough to follow. They sprinted across a cobbled yard, and then through inky shadows down an arm-wide alley; in another moment they were in the Strand and were running quickly by the wall. They were on the south side and therefore in the shadow, hard to see, and with a good hope of escaping unseen, and then disaster came. If they could not be seen, they could also not see, and Mr. Barlow, who had the lead, ran headlong into a pail that some slut had left by her door; he gasped with the pain of it, and went staggering and lurching, swaying out of the shadow into the full light; and from behind them, from the mouth of the alley, there was a shouting and a running of feet.

Mr. Barlow did his best. He went on pluckily, for all the pain of his lacerated shins; but he was plainly lamed, and from behind came an exultant yell from the man in green. He was full in the moonlight, his sword flashing and his long legs carrying him quickly; behind him were two more men, and Mr. Leyburne, glancing anxiously over his shoulder, had no illusions. They came to Arundel Street, and Mr. Barlow was leading down it towards the river when Mr. Leyburne stopped and turned. The moon was above the river and there was no shadow here that could hide a limping man; and Mr. Leyburne had had enough of flight. He was not born of that breed, and he had remembered what he had been made to swallow from this Greencoat earlier this night. That was enough, and it was a Leyburne of Cunswick who turned in the moonlight, hard-eyed and truculent. There was a dry ring of steel as his sword came out, and then he waited, his nostrils dilated and his sword point quivering. There was a clatter of feet as Greencoat turned the corner with two fellows with him who looked like servants; and then their clatter died abruptly as they saw what awaited them.

For a moment there was silence. The two servants held back, and Greencoat came on alone. He came boldly, and then he halted, blown and panting, a bare sword-length away.

"By the pox!" he shouted. "What's this? A rat that fights?"

Mr. Leyburne made no answer. His heat had faded now, and his thoughts were cool and clear. In theory his knowledge of the sword was sound, for he had been taking lessons earnestly since it had first occurred to him that a gentleman ought to do so; but this would be different from the polite exercises of the fencing room, and he was too intent on that to be distracted by words. He stood poised and ready, his back to the moon and his eyes alert and watchful. He saw the angry face before him, and its quick intake of breath; he saw the sword come up, and the sudden glint of moonlight on the hilt of it. Then it flickered and dipped, and he felt the hard thrust of it against his own as he parried the lunge that came so quickly.

What followed was so swift that he was astounded. With breath and temper under control, and the light behind him, he had more advantage than he knew; and the first exchange told him that Greencoat's swordsmanship was a rough thing at best. After that he dealt coolly. The second exchange showed him the way of it, and the third exchange ended it. He held back until Greencoat came forward in a great stamping lunge. He had expected that, and he was ready for it; he deflected it, stepped swiftly inside it, and then ran his man through the shoulder. It was cleanly, almost precisely, done, and the ease of it surprised him.

Greencoat lurched. His sword went clattering on the cobbles, and his cry of pain was shrill and sudden. He sagged to his knees, his left hand snatching at his shoulder and the blood spilling blackly down his arm and over the laced cuffs that were so white under the moon. The two servants pressed themselves against the wall, and Mr. Leyburne, suddenly seeing them there, wasted no time; he lifted his wet point, and without a word he was at them. It was more than they had stomach for; they were, when all was said, no more than lackeys —with a taste for rough sport, no doubt, but not for sport so rough as this. They turned, the pair of them together, and ran for their lives, bawling wildly for help and rescue.

Mr. Leyburne laughed and refrained from pursuit. He was excited now, and exhilarated; his first encounter with the naked steel had been a triumph, and the thought was surging in him that he had, after all, borne himself as became his name. Then he remembered Mr. Barlow, and what he saw surprised him. Mr. Barlow, clear in the moonlight, was down on his knees by the wounded man in the road; he had pulled the soft sash from the fellow's waistcoat and already he had it tight about the wounded shoulder, stanching the blood and supporting the torn flesh. Mr. Leyburne fidgeted with impatience. This, no doubt, was the way to lay treasure in heaven, but at this moment on earth, with the frightened lackeys still howling for their fellows, he thought it out of season; and even as he groped for words to say so, there was a babble of angry voices and then a clatter of running feet to give warning. There was no time to waste, and Mr. Barlow was plainly far from being a fool; he spared one quick glance for Greencoat, who seemed to have fainted, and then suddenly he took the lead, running quickly down the street towards the river.

Mr. Leyburne followed, sickeningly aware that the whole street was silver in the moon and that there was not one shadow in which to lose pursuit. His sword was still in his hand, and his grip was tightening on it as he glanced round without hope. And then, before the pursuit had gained the corner, Mr. Barlow stopped abruptly at the tight-shut door of a darkened house; there was a key ready in his hand, and, with the smooth click of a well-oiled lock, the door swung open. Mr. Leyburne stepped hastily after him, no questions asked, and a heave of his shoulder sent the door swinging shut again. In the utter darkness Mr. Barlow fumbled, and a bolt slid smoothly as the pursuit went roaring past.

On a landing above them a door clicked open, and a shaft of yellow light fell quavering across the stair. At the stairhead a woman appeared, white-faced and anxious, holding a single candle aloft so that its light came spilling down the stair to find Mr. Barlow's white face and pick a glint from the steel of Mr. Leyburne's sword. She recoiled at the sight of it, and the candle shook in her hand.

"Mother of God!" she quavered. "Are you preserved, Father?"

5   THE POPISH MIDWIFE   For a moment Mr. Leyburne's
wits failed him; he did not perceive why Mr. Barlow should be so
addressed, and he scanned this woman closely in hope of enlightenment. Certainly she was of attractive looks. She was small and trim,
with corn-coloured hair and eyes of vivid blue, and her small round
face, with its smooth skin and pouting lips, was taking colour again
now that she had been reassured. He saw the glint of a wedding ring
on her neat hand, and from that his eyes strayed to Mr. Barlow, who
could surely give her no more than a dozen years in age. Then, while
he still pondered the oddity, she had dropped on her knees before Mr.
Barlow; and plainly she was seeking a blessing and as plainly he was
giving it.

Mr. Leyburne pressed back against the bolted door as surprise
gripped him; and at once he had the memory of this man down on his
knees by the wounded Greencoat—which was proper enough, no
doubt, in a priest, out of season though it had seemed at the time. But
here, certainly, was something to be reckoned with. In these days a
popish priest stood in much danger of hanging, and the penal laws
could cut not only at a priest but at any who gave him aid and comfort. Mr. Leyburne stood stiffly while the uneasy feeling grew in him
that he had got himself involved in something deeper and more dangerous than clocks and Mohawks. But the thing was done; there was a
man run through and a priest brought safe away, and nothing of it
could be undone. He steadied himself and looked again at Mr. Barlow's pale and friendly face, and at once he remembered that this man
had some cordial link with Penelope Langley; that was enough for Mr.
Leyburne, and his decision was immediate.

He put up his sword and stepped forward into the candlelight. Mr.
Barlow saw him and turned to do what was needed; he addressed himself formally to the lady.

"For preservation," he said, "I am wholly indebted to this good
gentleman. Permit me therefore—Mr. John Leyburne."

Mr. Leyburne bowed, and the lady stared at him with her blue eyes wide and startled.

"Oh!" she gasped. "Father, you mean——"

"No." Mr. Barlow resolved her confusion promptly. "I think he is hardly old enough to have been President of Douai."

Mr. Leyburne found himself smiling; he had not before been confused with his priestly uncle, and he hastened to a disclaimer that should slyly assert his credentials.

"It's my uncle," he explained, "who has held that dignity. And others of my family have held priestly status. But for my part, ma'am, I'm of the laity."

She accepted that with a smile that was almost merry, and she went belatedly into her curtsey. That seemed to remind Mr. Barlow, and he took his formal tone again.

"Mrs. Cellier," he said pleasantly, "is my present hostess, and at all times the friend of all of us."

Mr. Leyburne bowed again, and he did it partly to conceal the thoughts that had gone racing in him as he heard her name. For he had heard of Mrs. Cellier. Everybody had heard of Mrs. Cellier. She was commonly known as the Popish Midwife, and she did indeed ply a midwife's trade; but she was known also as a hot and zealous papist, and the gossip ran that she harboured priests, fomented plots, and had had a hand in the managing of witnesses who were to give the lie to Mr. Oates in the forthcoming trial of some Jesuits. Mr. Leyburne had heard it roundly asserted in the coffeehouses that the lady was in much need of a hanging and was as like as not to get it before the year was out. She was dangerous company, and he knew it.

Then, with his resolution unaltered, he was telling her politely that he was greatly honoured.

"I've heard much of you, ma'am, and you may guess what it is that I've heard. Ma'am: your most humble servant——"

"The honour's mine, sir, I assure you. It's not every day that I may have in my poor house one of so fine a name. But be pleased to step abovestair—and you, Father. Anne! Anne! Bless the girl! Where are you?"

She was lighting them up the stair as she called, and before they had gained the head of it a serving-girl came running, young, soft, and

pretty. She got her orders quickly; supper was to be served, and at
once; there was a guest of quality, and she was to lay the Spanish silver
and bring the sweetest wine. It came as a rush of words, rippling and
musical, as Mrs. Cellier waved her guests into her trim and elegant
parlour. And elegant it certainly was. It was a square and spacious
room, richly done in oak, and it had a fine green carpet on the shining
boards, and green curtains flowing by the shuttered windows; there
was green cloth in the seats of the high-backed chairs, and a rug of
green lay before the hearth where the sea-coals hissed and flamed.
Above the hearth, on the carved stone shelf, the candles were bright
in their silver stands, and the gleaming oak of the table had another
pair. Mr. Leyburne's keen glance took it all in; the lady, it seemed,
had an excellent good taste and the means to indulge it.

She had also a fine hospitality. Her supper was of the best, and it
had service worthy of it. There were capons, sizzling and golden-
brown, supported by potatoes and sparrowgrass, and all of it eaten off
painted porcelain plates with two-pronged forks in the place of common skewers; there were apples, and cream, and wheaten bread, and
the pale canary wine; there were nuts, and sugar, and ginger, and a
fine French brandy to lace the fragrant coffee. And with it all there
was Mrs. Cellier, colourful and vivacious, her blue eyes sparkling and
her hair golden under the candles as the wine gave speed to the talk
and lured them all from silence.

Nor were they an odd number. For before they were ever at table
there came a knocking at the door below—a knocking whose rhythm
set Mrs. Cellier hurrying down the stair; and then she was back, and
with her was the long-legged Mr. Payne, his brown face set and grave.
His eyes, keen and hard now, were suddenly on Mr. Leyburne in an
oddly piercing glance; yet when he spoke it was with relief, and to Mr.
Barlow.

"Love of God!" he said. "I've been sweating for you like a lathered
horse. I'd thought your business done. What was it?"

"Meaning what?"

"What *should* I mean? I was scarce away when I heard it—like the
rabble setting about some rogue in the pillory. And again I ask, what
was it? That tavern looks like a Quakers' house when the constable's
been in."

"Then we must do something for the hostess." Mr. Barlow was speaking gravely. "But for what it was, it was all but the taking of me. It was Mr. Leyburne here who brought me off——"

"The devil he did!" Mr. Payne's glance was suddenly keen again, and then he seemed to relax. "He did well. But how was it done?"

"By a bloodshed, I grieve to say."

"Bloodshed? And you grieve for it? But I'm not sure that I do." The lean humorous face was matching the sardonic tone. "Phlebotomy has its uses, and I can think of some I'd prescribe it for. But of your charity, let me have the tale."

They told it to him at leisure, the one prompting the other as they ate; and Mrs. Cellier, at her best with three men round her, held them back with her eager questions. It was a tale much to her liking, and it was plain that Mr. Leyburne stood high in her esteem on account of it; she had some pleasing words for him, and Mr. Barlow had some quiet ones which pleased him more, seeing that it was Mr. Barlow who had touch with Penelope Langley.

"Mohawks, do you say?"

The words cut quietly into his speeding thoughts, and with a start he realized that the question was for him. It was Mr. Payne who had spoken, and Mr. Payne had changed; he was thoughtful now, and there was authority in his eyes. Mr. Leyburne met their glance, and suddenly he knew with certainty that here was a man of no common quality; he made haste to answer.

"I took them to be Mohawks. What else, pray?"

"It's what I ask. A man in green, you say?"

"Aye, bottle green. But——"

"An odd taste that—for Mohawks. Commonly, such sprigs run out in gayer hues."

"Aye, that's true." Mr. Leyburne was puzzled. "But you speak, sir, as if you have some thought in mind. . . ."

"I have." The answer came grimly. "Who wears green ribbon?"

Mr. Leyburne sat up startled. He had not thought of that, but the answer was plain. It was milord Shaftesbury's men—the Country Party, as they styled themselves—who affected green ribbon, and Mr. Leyburne did not like the Country Party. They were the militant Protestants, with fierce hatred for the Duke of York and no friendly

eye for his kingly brother; they were hot against the prerogative and
a deal hotter against popery. They had a brisk and noisy following in
the City, where they flaunted it with tags of green ribbon; and of late
they had made for their leaders a Green Ribbon Club with chambers
in a Fleet Street tavern. Mr. Leyburne had cause enough to know of
it, for this King's Head tavern was at the corner of Chancery Lane,
and whenever it pleased milord Shaftesbury to lean from an upper
window and address his men, Fleet Street would be blocked by a
stamping cheering rabble, and every shoulder with its knot of green
ribbon. Mr. Payne's question, therefore, did not lack meaning, and
Mr. Leyburne made no pretence about it.

"You mean the Brisk Boys?" he asked.

Mr. Payne nodded. Milord Shaftesbury had been boasting that he
had ten thousand Brisk Boys at call, and he had been sending bands
of them to roam the streets by night to show his power and to put fear
into any who might oppose him. Apparently Mr. Payne knew all about
this, as his answer showed.

"It has that look," he said. "I know the Boys brag of wearing the
ribbon when they roam at large. But I've heard of some special bands
that have *not* worn it—and without it they might pass as Mohawks.
That might suit them if they sought some special prey and did not wish
to be known as themselves." He turned to Mr. Barlow. "I wonder
now, did they come upon you by no more than chance?"

"I do not know."

His tone was dry; it brought a hard stare from Mr. Payne, and it
set Mr. Leyburne remembering a detail he had forgotten.

"I mind now," he said slowly, "that this Greencoat fellow did
address you by name."

"Yes." Mr. Barlow was as quiet as ever; and then he shrugged his
shoulders as though accepting a necessity. "I'd hoped not to speak
names," he said. "Commonly they bring trouble. But if you will have
it, this man in green was Roderick Mansell."

"Was he now?" Mr. Payne whistled softly. "He being now run
through?"

"Yes."

"Then there's an end to doubts. Brisk Boys they were. Mansell's of
the Green Ribbon Club, and as pretty a rogue as breeds. But that's no

matter. What signifies . . ." Mr. Payne hesitated and seemed to be choosing his words. "What signifies is whether Mansell and his crew came upon you by chance, or whether they were hunting you—and concealing that by aping Mohawks. Now which was it?"

Mr. Barlow seemed to be engrossed in the peeling of an apple. He kept his eyes to his plate as he answered.

"I have said that I do not know."

"Which in that tone suggests that you do. Or, to give you strict truth, that you do not know but could make a sharp guess."

"As a mathematician I deplore guesswork." The decanter was steady in Mr. Barlow's hand as he added brandy to his coffee. "And will you tell me of any sufficient reason why Colonel Mansell should think me worth the hunting? Am I of such consequence?"

"Not above some scores of others. That's what teases me. And it seems that you do not intend to help."

"Guesses seldom help. And here's a matter in which a guess might touch another."

Mr. Barlow looked up at last, and there was authority as well as decision in his face. Mr. Payne looked at him steadily.

"You'll perceive that I seek your safety?"

"Of course. And believe that I'm grateful." The pale face had relaxed, and a smile was on it again. "For your part, you'll perceive that mine's a work in which safety may not always come first."

"Love of God! Do we not know it? Is there a doubt of it in these butchers' days? And you take no heed to safety."

"*In solo Deo salus.* Can I say more?"

For a moment the two men were eye to eye, and the room was tense. Then Mr. Barlow recovered himself; his face relaxed and he was almost easy when he spoke.

"What is it that you would have me do?"

Mr. Payne held silence and considered him gravely; then he spoke with crisp precision.

"Your safety shall at least come as near to the front as it may. And as things now are your safety is not in London. You may get you gone —and quickly. I'll breathe better when you're back with your pigs and ducks."

"In Lancashire?" Mr. Barlow seemed almost amused. "And why, if you please?"

"Because it's needful. It will be prudent to suppose that Mansell was in search of you. That was bad enough, but now it's a deal worse."

"Why?"

Mr. Payne pushed his chair back and looked as though the question was almost too much for his patience; then he steadied his breath and began to speak deliberately, in the manner of one explaining to a child.

"Because there's a man run through. That's why. A man who's of the Green Ribbon Club, and of some note there. What may have been Mansell's own affair is now the affair of the whole crew, from Shaftesbury down. There's vengeance in it now. They'll be about it in earnest, and they'll raise such a hunt as you'll not withstand. Am I plain?"

The authority was in Mr. Payne's voice now, and the other seemed to accept it. He nodded thoughtfully.

"In matters secular I allow you to be the master. Nor do I wish to bring trouble on any." He had a quick glance at Mrs. Cellier. "It shall be as you say."

"It had best be." Mr. Payne spoke grimly; then his chair scraped sharply as he pulled it round, and suddenly his eyes had found Mr. Leyburne and had pulled him erect in his chair; there was a force in Mr. Payne.

"You also, Mr. Leyburne. You'll note that it touches you as keenly —if not more keenly. You pinked your man this night, for which I'm grateful. It was well done, and timely. But it will bring you also within the scope of their hate."

Mr. Leyburne sat staring, speechless under the spell this man was casting. Then Mr. Payne relaxed; the lazy smile woke again on his brown face, and he permitted his eyes to move. Mr. Leyburne sighed and found his voice again.

"Aye," he said. "I'd not thought of that, but I'll not doubt the truth of it."

"Don't." It came grimly. "I've no wish to cast shadows upon you, but there's a need to be plain. And the plain of it is that your neck's none too safe."

"Neck!" It was Mrs. Cellier who spoke, and the single word was shrill. "What's this? You can't mean——"

"I can and do," he cut in firmly, and his tone silenced her. "I'm not here to jest; and I speak the truth of things."

Mr. Leyburne sat stiffly, trying to show a coolness that he did not feel. He had realized that he would hardly survive another brush with the Brisk Boys if he were so foolish as to let them catch him again in the streets at night; but what Mr. Payne had come to now was a different matter, and bleakly devoid of comfort. He felt his throat twitch, and to cover his discomfort he spoke with an assumed ease.

"Hardly so much, surely? It was but through the shoulder, and that won't kill the fellow."

"Shoulder's enough to be criminal assault. And that's capital."

"Assault!" Mr. Leyburne was suddenly indignant. "It was not assault. It was an affair——"

"It will be what they care to say it was—if it comes to trial. They have the witnesses, and you have not. You could hardly call Father Barlow, unless you've an itch to hang in his company. Good company, I grant you, but . . ."

Mr. Leyburne sat silent. He had wit enough to see the logic in this, and he had no itch to hang in anybody's company; and then, to his unspeakable relief, he saw that lazy smile again.

"You may be of better cheer than you look," said Mr. Payne pleasantly. "It's none so desperate. You say you had not seen these men before?"

"Not to my knowing."

"Then we may suppose that they do not know you, nor where you may be sought. And if you show a proper care, it will tax their wits to find out. I think that all that's required of you is a change of clothes and a decent prudence."

Mr. Leyburne began to breathe more easily; if no more than that was required of him he thought he could supply it. He said as much, and Mr. Payne had another hint to offer.

"You've said you live in Fleet Street. Keep your eyes alert as you go past the King's Head tavern. That these men of the Green Ribbon do not know you is no reason why you should not know them. It's a prudence in these days to know a Whig when you see one."

"A Whig? What's that, if you please?"

"If it's new to you, no matter." Mr. Payne dismissed the point abruptly, and at once he was speaking to Mr. Barlow again. "Day-break, if you please. And now it grows late, so I'll not delay you further. I'll be away, and Mr. Leyburne with me."

He was imperious about it, and he swept their protests aside. There were farewells, and exchanges of thanks and good wishes. Mrs. Cellier was insistent with the spiced wine of departure, and Mr. Leyburne found her a distraction; at this moment he was seeking a word with Mr. Barlow.

He had it on the stair as they went softly down, and because his time was short he came to the point at once.

"In the tavern, sir, you spoke of Miss Langley. You'll be seeing her soon—in Lancashire?"

"Deo volente, I shall."

"Put me in her remembrance if you please. Assure her that I'm her servant always."

"To be sure." There was faint surprise in Mr. Barlow's voice. "I did not know that you were well acquainted."

"We are not. That's what's to be mended. And I hope soon to ride to the North Parts myself."

"If so, I shall hope to see you there. I'm in your debt, remember. Meantime, I'll serve you as best I may. Most certainly I'll be your Mercury."

There was no time for more. Mr. Payne was already sliding the well-oiled bolt. There were last hurried words, and then the door was open; they stepped quickly through, and behind them the latch clicked and the bolt slid softly.

Arundel Street was deserted, cold and empty in the moonlight, and for a moment Mr. Leyburne shivered and gazed regretfully at the tight-shut door that hid a man who was to ride at dawn for the North —and Penelope Langley. But he was given no chance to linger there in sentiment. The moon had swung in the sky since it had lighted him for swordplay; the light lay aslant across the street, and on Mrs. Cellier's door it was vivid; opposite there was inky shadow, and sud-denly Mr. Payne had him by the arm and was thrusting him into the dark pool of it.

"That," said Mr. Payne softly, "is the first step towards prudence.

Do not stand in the moon to point which door you've come from."

"My thanks! I had not thought of that."

"No. But it matters little this time, and I think you are gifted to learn. Certainly you did well tonight."

Mr. Leyburne was still seeking an answer as they walked briskly into the Strand and turned towards Fleet Street. Mr. Payne kept warily in the shadows, and his question came abruptly.

"Mr. Leyburne: do you care to tell me what creed you hold to?"

"Creed?"

"You know well what I mean. Rome, or Lambeth, or Geneva— which?"

"Why, I—I suppose it would be Lambeth."

"That at least is honest. I might even say that it is *at last* honest."

"How, if you please?"

"Pray do not grow heated. There's not cause for it. Also, though you did not lie to Father Barlow, you did at least mislead. You know well what he supposes you to be. And you intended him to suppose it. Now why, I wonder?"

There was silence, broken only by the steady tramp of their feet on the stones. Mr. Leyburne's thoughts went twisting, and he knew that this big and forceful man was not to be imposed on by evasions. There seemed nothing for it but the truth.

"Why," he said at last, "you'll have heard me, on the stair yonder, speak of Miss Langley. . . ."

Mr. Payne laughed softly.

"So that's the set of it? Then I'll wish you joy, even though I do not know the lady. She has some link with him?"

"Yes. She told me as much."

"Did she indeed?" Mr. Payne seemed thoughtful. "And she lives in Lancashire? Where, do you know?"

"In the parish of Bolton, as her father said. You turn from the road at a certain Boar's Head, three miles north of a place called Wigan— wherever that may be."

Mr. Payne nodded.

"I leave you here. I'm for Lincoln's Inn Fields. You'll be for Fleet Street?"

"Yes. I'm lodged with my uncle there."

"We part here then. Have a prudence, as I've said. And watch for Whigs and their faces. If you've aught to tell me or to ask of me, I'm not hard to discover. You may find me in the coffeehouses, and often at Mrs. Cellier's. God keep you!"

He was away on that, flinging an affable nod as he crossed the street with his long-legged stride. He plunged again into the shadows and was gone; only his quick footfalls broke the silence, and suddenly Mr. Leyburne was tired and lonely.

He turned and moved slowly into Fleet Street, hugging the shadows and treading softly. The evening was alive again as he walked, and the scenes of it passed before his eyes in a dreamlike medley—the men in the tavern, the flight, the gleam of the moon on swords, and Greencoat lying prone; and Mrs. Cellier in the candles, and Mr. Barlow's smile, and his telling who this Greencoat was. And suddenly, as he came to the door, the thought of something else came stabbing through his mind and brought him to a startled halt.

He had had the memory of Mr. Langley peering at the marquetry panel of a long-case clock and saying with satisfaction that Mansell had not got that.

6

VENUS IN SAGITTARY   Almost to his own surprise, Mr. Leyburne slept that night soundly and well. But when he had at last roused and had pulled his bed curtains to the glowing sun of an April morning he was at once aware that he had been thinking in his sleep; what had been dark and vague had now come sharp and clear, and he pondered it thoughtfully as he dressed.

It seemed plain enough. Mr. Barlow, who seemed to be papist, priest, deviser of clocks and self-styled mathematician all in one, had recognized this Greencoat and had named him Roderick Mansell; and since Mr. Barlow knew little of the town it seemed to follow that he must know this Mansell out of the town. And where should that be but in Lancashire? And where in Lancashire but in that part—whichever it might be—where Mr. Barlow was neighbour to the Langleys?

Mr. Leyburne grew alarmed. Undoubtedly Mr. Langley had spoken of a neighbour Mansell—which, if it did not mean this Greencoat, must surely mean some other of his family. And undoubtedly this Greencoat had enmity against Mr. Barlow, who had refused to say more because the matter touched another. And who should that other be but Penelope?

To a cool head this might have seemed rushing to conclusions, but Mr. Leyburne's was not a cool head where Penelope Langley was concerned, and he went to his breakfast in a truculent humour, urgently asking himself how he might best learn more of this Greencoat Mansell and his doings in Lancashire.

Thought of Mr. Payne occurred immediately. Mr. Payne seemed to know a great deal, and he had a way of seeing to the roots of things, of making comments that were uncommonly shrewd. Mr. Leyburne nodded thoughtfully; decidedly he must ask Mr. Payne.

He slipped away in the dusk, as soon as work was done, and he went discreetly in russets, bare of adornment except for the gleam of his sword hilt. He came to Arundel Street as the first shafts of moonlight began to glimmer on the windows and the painted signs, and the trim young serving-girl whom Mrs. Cellier had addressed as Anne made no difficulty about admitting him and conducting him at once to the parlour abovestair. But here was disappointment. Mrs. Cellier was there, to be sure; but with her, instead of Mr. Payne, was a stranger, a man whom Mr. Leyburne did not know.

But Mrs. Cellier was welcoming. She acknowledged his bow most graciously, and at once she was coming to him, vivid under the candles with her golden hair and her deep blue eyes.

"All's well," she told him quickly. "All's well. He was safe away by daybreak, and well horsed. So all's most happy—though that's thanks to you, sir."

Her voice came rippling, a musical stream of sound, and when she had spoken she did not wait for an answer. She waved to the man at the table, and at once she made the presentation.

"Gentlemen, permit me: Mr. John Gadbury—Mr. John Leyburne. . . ."

Mr. Leyburne, as he made his bow, had a vague feeling that he had heard this name before.

"Your servant, Mr. Gadbury."

"Yours, sir." Mr. Gadbury got hurriedly to his feet, and he, also, seemed to be searching his memory. "Leyburne, d'ye say, sir? Why, surely . . ."

He was a big man, too big for his clothes, for his suit of sober brown was tight upon him; he had thick legs, a portly middle, and a round red face that looked like a harvest moon. He had a mop of sandy hair, long and curling, and there was a wide smile slashing across his red face and contrasting oddly with an air of consequence that he seemed to take to himself. He turned to Mrs. Cellier, as though asking for enlightenment, and she hastened to supply it.

"Mr. Leyburne," she explained, "is the nephew of Father Leyburne."

"Ah! Of course. . . ." Mr. Gadbury lost his puzzled look, and his face beamed with approval. "Certainly your servant, sir. A most religious family——"

"Not all of us, sir. Truly, we've had among us a Puritan or two."

"No matter for that." Mr. Gadbury dismissed it airily. "That may easily chance. If Jupiter hold the ninth and be afflicted by Saturn, some heresy might properly result. It's a cold heresy, sir, that afflicts the Cropheads—cold and sour, and that's the true humour of Saturn."

Mr. Leyburne stared blankly and wondered if he had heard aright. Then Mrs. Cellier interposed quickly.

"There's nothing of the Crophead in Mr. Leyburne, if you please." She sounded almost indignant. "You have it wrong, sir. . . ."

"I do not have it wrong," said Mr. Gadbury loudly. "It is not my wont to have it wrong. The stars do not have it wrong, ma'am, and nor do I."

He nodded vigorously, and Mr. Leyburne called himself stupid. No wonder he had heard of Mr. Gadbury! Everybody had heard of Mr. Gadbury the astrologer, whose books were so widely read, and whose reported embracing of popery had lately been a source of gossip in the town.

"Of course, of course. . . ." Mrs. Cellier's voice came fluttering. "I only intended, sir, that it is wrong to suppose that *this* Mr. Leyburne has the sourness. It was by his sword, sir, that Father Barlow was brought safe away when they were attacked last——"

"Attacked, is it?" Mr. Gadbury waved her into silence and then pursed his lips judicially as he gave attention to Mr. Leyburne. "Your sword, was it, when attacked? That will be the Scorpion in you, sir. It's ever a sign to give good measure when attacked."

"Indeed, sir?" Mr. Leyburne was feeling a little lost. "And do you say that I have this . . . er . . . this sign upon me?"

"By your looks, Mr. Leyburne, I'd say you reek of it. You'll not take it amiss if I ask when you were born?"

"Why—why, sir, it was in '55, on the Gunpowder day—the fifth of November, sir."

"Exactly so!" Mr. Gadbury nodded sagaciously. "Sol in Scorpio. But the time of it, if you please?"

"It was late in the day—an hour before midnight, as I've been told."

"That's vague, sir. However . . ." With a resounding thump, Mr. Gadbury sat himself in the chair by the table. "You're in Fortune's smile, Mr. Leyburne. I came here this night to cast a figure for our hostess—of a rogue Dangerfield who imposes on her."

"He's not a rogue, sir."

"Madam, he is. But since the fellow was born in your year, Mr. Leyburne, it follows that I have the ephemeris under my hand. . . ."

He was flicking rapidly at the pages of a thin book, and Mr. Leyburne watched with interest. Then Mrs. Cellier motioned him to an elbowchair and poured wine for him, moving warily on tiptoe lest she disturb the sage at the table. Mr. Leyburne lifted his glass and then gave amused attention to the table. Mr. Gadbury had finished flicking his pages, and now he was muttering to himself while he made inky scratchings on a circle of the heavens he had drawn on a sheet of paper. His pen spluttered noisily as he put the signs of the zodiac round his circle with frequent references to his ephemeris, apparently that he might put them in their proper places. Then he scrawled figures on paper, as though he were computing sums, and next he was at his circle again, writing planetary symbols in a loose and scrawling script. His mutterings continued, and Mr. Leyburne's amusement grew.

"So!" Mr. Gadbury's labours came to an end. He flung down his pen, and his forehead puckered as he held up the paper and scanned his figure attentively. "I said you reeked of Scorpio, Mr. Leyburne, and here's the Moon combust——"

"I—I beg your pardon?" Mr. Leyburne was hard put to it to keep a proper gravity as he met Mr. Gadbury's prescient stare. "You mean the moon's afire, sir?"

"I've said there's Sol in the Scorpion." Mr. Gadbury spoke with a laboured patience. "And here's Luna within the same degree—combust, as we say, from the Sun's near beams. And so, Mr. Leyburne, with the luminaries both so tinctured, it's not matter for wonder that you should show us something of the Scorpion."

"I—I see." Mr. Leyburne was by no means sure whether this was a compliment or not.

"Pay no heed to William Lilly, sir."

Mr. Gadbury spoke loudly with a sternly outstretched finger, and Mr. Leyburne was startled. He had never heard of Mr. Lilly.

"It's a disgrace, sir, a scandal, that such a canting rogue should set himself to ply the royal art. A poor thing, sir—a poor creaking thing with his wits corroded by disuse. William Lilly, indeed!" Mr. Gadbury did not seem to think much of his fellow astrologer. "He knows no better, sir, than to spatter mud upon the celestial sign. Read my *Reasonable Service,* sir."

"I beg your pardon. . . ."

Mr. Leyburne said it helplessly, and Mr. Gadbury snorted at his ignorance.

"My *Reasonable Service for the Celestial Sign Scorpio,* wherein you will find the true and just defence thereof against such calumny." Mr. Gadbury snorted again and pointed his pen impressively. "And if that content you not, read also my *Just and Pious Scorpionist,* wherein you may learn what talents and virtues that sign did bestow upon that great and upright judge, Sir Matthew Hale, lately gathered unto God."

"I'll—I'll endeavour it, sir." Mr. Leyburne was shaking with laughter behind his wooden face, but Mr. Gadbury was already on another slant. He had picked up his paper again and was poring over it with twitching eyebrows.

"How now?" he demanded suddenly. "Taking it to want an hour of midnight, you're a fortunate fellow, Mr. Leyburne. For Leo holds the ascendant, and therein is Jupiter. The greater fortune, sir. Fire in fire, and rising." Mr. Gadbury made some clucking noises. "In square to the luminaries, both of them—you'll be something imprudent, Mr. Leyburne, and perhaps with an itch for men's esteem. Yet always with a touch of Fortune's smile. But what's this?" Mr. Gadbury tapped noisily with his quill. "No planet in the seventh, yet the Moon applying to milady Venus. She'll show your attachments of the heart, Mr. Leyburne."

"I beg your pardon. . . ."

Mr. Leyburne could think of nothing else to say, and once again Mr. Gadbury grew impatient.

"I am saying, sir, that the planet Venus, as figured herein, will tell us of the lady to whom you'll be attached. Venus in Sagittary—hmm! That might sort with such an ascendant."

"Might it, sir? And pray, what might it be?"

"What I've said, sir. Venus in Sagittary. Denoting a lady born within the Archer—early December, perhaps."

Mr. Leyburne's amusement left him abruptly. Suddenly he sat erect.

"What's that you say?"

His voice came with a snap, but Mr. Gadbury was too absorbed in his figure to give heed to anything else. He was still prodding it with his pen, and his eyebrows were twitching again as he spoke.

"She has the hot glance of Mars—red in his own Ram, and all but exact in trine. Hmm! There'll be some strife before you have her, Mr. Leyburne. And it will colour the lady, too. She'll have a wild and wayward mood—and perhaps some redness of the hair."

Mr. Leyburne was on his feet, stiff and tense, and with his breath coming quickly.

"What the devil!"

"The devil nothing!" Mr. Gadbury was suddenly indignant. "I tell you, sir, what's written in the heavens, and you may believe or disbelieve as your humour runs. *Magna est veritas.*"

"*Et prevalebit.*"

The response came from Mrs. Cellier. She had been sitting quietly by the hearth opposite Mr. Leyburne, and now she intervened quickly, as though she feared some quarrel between her guests. She spoke soothingly, and to Mr. Leyburne.

"You'll surely not dispute it with Mr. Gadbury, sir? He has very great learning in these subtle things."

"Aye, ma'am. So I've heard. I did but——"

"Of course, Mr. Leyburne, of course. We've all heard of Mr. Gadbury's skill. But pray, Mr. Gadbury, what of this other figure which you cast at my poor asking?"

"Of this Dangerfield, ma'am?" Mr. Gadbury burrowed among his papers and produced another sheet. "Here it is, and the fellow, as I've told you, is a rogue."

"Oh! But—but indeed, Mr. Gadbury. I———"

"I thought you said, ma'am, that you allowed me to have some skill in this?"

"Indeed I do. Most certainly I do." Mrs. Cellier was growing agitated. "But in this case, sir, Mr. Dangerfield has perhaps———"

"Mr. Dangerfield has perhaps a pretty face. I've known women imposed on by as little."

Mrs. Cellier sat in silence, her mouth turned sullen, as if the shaft had gone home. Mr. Gadbury spoke petulantly.

"Where is this Dangerfield at present, ma'am?"

"In—in Newgate, alas!"

"He would be!" Mr. Gadbury sent his pen clattering across the table. "Is more needed, ma'am, to point a rogue?"

"The debtors' side, sir—that only." Mrs. Cellier was almost fluttering. "He's no criminal, sir. It's for a poor five pounds that he's cooped in hold. And I thought———"

"You thought to pay him free. Don't deny it, ma'am. It's plain in your face. And what then?"

"I—I'd thought to use him to collect some debts due to me. I———"

"God give me calm!" Mr. Gadbury's chair went creaking back. "Debts, d'ye say? By such a rogue?"

"Aye. But—that is . . ."

She was almost incoherent, and Mr. Gadbury glared at her. Then he drew his chair forward again, picked his pen out of the litter, and began tapping viciously at the paper in his hand.

"Here's Saturn holding the mid-heaven—the cold one who is the doom of men. Here he hangs—in fiery Leo—hangs and broods, and waits. And here is Mars within orbs of square. In Taurus, ma'am, where he's weak and earthy. Here's treachery, ma'am—treachery of a perjured rogue."

"Oh, but——"

"It's not all." He swept her into silence again. "Here's Luna. She lies by the nadir—and that same Saturn does oppose her. Now mark . . ."

The petulance had gone from his voice. He was speaking slowly now, and plainly he was in earnest.

"Saturn on high, and the temporal light opposed—which is how it's figured here—and death shall have a horrid shape. And let that light be in a human sign—as here it is—and it shall be death by the hand of man. Thus, ma'am, shall end this Dangerfield."

The paper, fluttering from his hand, went rustling to the table, but he took no heed of it. He sat stiffly in his chair, tense and silent, his sombre eyes intent on the woman who faced him. Mr. Leyburne did his best to break an unhappy silence.

"It would seem," he said slowly, "that this Dangerfield is more entitled to sympathy than trust."

"Oh, aye. Let him have sympathy—a hogshead of it, if you will." Mr. Gadbury was almost sardonic. "But as Mr. Leyburne says, ma'am, do not give him trust."

But Mrs. Cellier's lips had set tightly; her delicate forehead was wrinkling, and obstinacy was plain in her face as she spoke.

"I'll not doubt your talents, sir. Yet all knowledge is not yours, and some things are known to me, known deeply, sir, as you cannot know . . ." She had her hand on her heart to point her meaning. "And I do know most truly, that Thomas Dangerfield, come what may, will most surely be true to me."

"God pity you!" Mr. Gadbury snorted his contempt. "You've Mercury combust in the Fishes, ma'am, and your wits are addled. How of it, Mr. Leyburne? How to keep a fool from her folly?"

But Mr. Leyburne could see no reason for getting involved in this. He was not interested in Mr. Dangerfield, and he had affairs to attend to. He came briskly to his feet as he remembered what they were.

"You'll give me leave?" he asked politely. "The truth is, ma'am, I've need to consult with Mr. Payne. Can you tell me, pray, where I should seek him?"

At once she was a ripple of words, commending his wisdom in seeking Mr. Payne, regretting his departure, pressing him to come again. He listened impassively, and when he had a chance to speak he asked her again where Mr. Payne should be sought.

"At this hour, sir, in the coffeehouse, no doubt."

"Aye, ma'am—no doubt. But which coffeehouse, if you please? Which does he mostly use?"

"Why, he—he uses many. There's the Grecian, round the corner there, and the Rainbow, and the Union in Cornhill, and Will's, and Man's, and Child's in the churchyard, and Procter's by the Charing Cross."

Mr. Leyburne blinked with surprise, and Mrs. Cellier nodded vigorously.

"It's true," she assured him. "Mr. Payne uses all of them, and more besides."

"Indeed, ma'am?" Mr. Leyburne decided not to argue the point. "I'm much obliged to you. Your servant always! Mr. Gadbury, yours!"

7 THE LADY OF FASHION   The April night had taken a chill when the soft-faced Anne shut the door behind the departing guest. Moonlight was flooding down the Strand as he came out of Arundel Street, and at once his thoughts were with this enigmatic Mr. Payne who was so crisp and competent, who wrote plays, managed papists, and haunted such an odd assortment of coffeehouses. For odd it certainly was. A man used a coffeehouse to meet men of his own trade or men of his own leanings, and not unreasonably, therefore, a man might use two coffeehouses. But why should anybody use Man's, which was a centre of fashion, Child's, which was a haunt of the clergy, the Grecian, where they argued politics, Will's, where Mr. Dryden pronounced on poetry, and the Rainbow, where they exchanged gossip at large? Certainly it was odd, and Mr. Leyburne was no nearer to understanding it when he came to Devereux Court and plunged into the Grecian.

But here he was unlucky. The place was thronged as usual, but there was no sign of Mr. Payne. Mr. Leyburne retraced his steps and went on into Fleet Street, and there, between the Middle Temple and the Inner Temple, he turned into the celebrated Rainbow; and this time luck was with him. His first glance into the blue haze of the smoke-filled room showed him the man he sought. In the press of men who stood in groups, smoking and chattering as they sipped their coffee, one group was conspicuous by having a woman in it; and on the fringe of this group, leaning indolently against the wainscot and apparently intent on the lady's talk, was the long-legged Mr. Payne.

Mr. Leyburne stood staring by the coffee bar while he fumbled for his penny. This was not precisely what he had expected; it was not precisely what any man would have expected, for a woman in a coffeehouse was a rarity. In general they left such places to men; and any man, going to his coffeehouse, took it for granted that he would meet and talk with men. It was not precisely forbidden for a woman to enter a coffeehouse, and it was not perhaps even improper; but it was certainly an indication that the lady's tastes were not domestic, and Mr. Leyburne, viewing this lady critically, had no difficulty in believing that of her. This lady took the eye. She stood erect, taller and slimmer than the usual, and her slender sharp-featured face, with its straight nose and thin lips, had a fashionable pallor that surely owed something to art. She was in the fashion in some other ways, too. Her gown, of a stiff golden silk, had wide sleeves slashed open at the front to give excuse for jewelled clasps, and at the neck it had an immodesty of cut that suggested Whitehall. Over it, trailing loosely from one shoulder as she stood under the candles, was a cloak of soft black velvet, vividly lined with crimson satin and held to the shoulder by another jewelled clasp. Her deep gold hair, falling in curling ringlets against the velvet, lost nothing by contrast with the black; and to complete the contrast she had cloak-ties of cloth-of-gold, deep and rich, that exactly matched her hair. Even Mr. Leyburne, inexperienced in such matters as he was, knew at once that this elegant lady, so poised and assured amid the group of men, had ways other than the wifely and maternal.

A tap on the coffee bar took his attention, and he saw that the server was impatiently proffering his cup. Hastily he found his penny and flung it down; and when he turned with the cup in his hand, the lady had turned also. She was looking directly at him, and for a moment her eyes met his. Then, almost in the same moment, she had turned away again, and he heard her ripple of laughter as she gave ear to a blue-coated gentleman who was jesting at her side.

Mr. Leyburne was startled, and without knowing why. On the face of it there was nothing odd in this; that a lady, chatting idly with some gentlemen, should glance at a newcomer, and should at once resume her talk when she saw him to be a stranger, was surely in the common course of things. Yet undoubtedly Mr. Leyburne was startled; the lady's eyes had had some quality to which he could not have given a name, and the thought lingered in him that her glance had not been idle, and that she had some purposes that did not go with her air of leisured ease. Then he recovered himself; he moved purposefully forward, and at once he was halted. Mr. Payne, still indolent against the wainscot, turned lazily, and for an instant his face darkened; it was no more than a twitch of his eyebrows and a quick pucker of his forehead, but it was enough. Mr. Leyburne halted abruptly, knowing that he had been warned.

He retreated to the bar and watched. Mr. Payne was in no hurry. Very much at his ease he withdrew from the chattering group and moved to the hooks by the bar to take up hat and cloak. Without haste he adjusted his cloak; then he clapped hat on head, and without so much as a side glance at anyone he strolled lazily to the door and was gone. Mr. Leyburne had wit enough to look the other way. Then, with what he hoped was the same casual air, he followed; he put down his untasted coffee and took a soft departure.

The moon was moving to the river, and by the door of the Rainbow the shadows were deep. In the gloom Mr. Payne confronted him suddenly.

"Are you mad?"

"Mad?" Mr. Leyburne echoed the word blankly.

"Mad, I said." Mr. Payne spoke with laboured patience. "I counselled a decent prudence, did I not?"

"Aye, to be sure. But wherein have I——"

"We'll walk, if you please." Mr. Payne suited action to word and stepped out briskly. "What's that street across the way?"

"Why—Chancery Lane, of course. But——"

"And the tavern at the corner?"

Suddenly Mr. Leyburne began to understand.

"It—it's the King's Head."

"Just so. With the Green Ribbon Club quartered abovestair. You live in Fleet Street, do you not?"

"I do."

"So you'll be known here to many."

They were passing by Mr. Tompion's shop, and the moonlight came out of Water Lane as a dazzling shaft. Mr. Payne turned full-face and spoke incisively.

"It's the coffeehouse most used by the Green Ribbons. It's also the house where you're surely known to half the company. And now it's the house of all houses where you must needs stand peering at the bar to draw all eyes upon yourself. Do you perceive nothing in that?"

Mr. Leyburne did, but he tried to sound at ease.

"I saw none tonight whom I saw the last night—nor any who saw me last night."

"I'll pray you're right. But the room was crowded and you can't be sure. But be that as it may, you'll please note the imprudence and bring more wit to your doings in future. What took you there tonight?"

His tone was peremptory, and for a moment Mr. Leyburne thought he ought to resent it. Then, even as he thought of that, he found himself answering; it was not easy to resent Mr. Payne.

"I was in search of you," he admitted slowly.

"Why?" The answer came with sudden sharpness. "Is aught amiss?"

"Why, no. At least, not in that way."

"Good." Mr. Payne's glance was keen, and then suddenly an easy humour had him. "Then it may keep till we're behind doors again. Child's, I think, will suit our need."

"In the churchyard? The house the clergy use?"

"Precisely. We may talk at ease there, knowing that none will listen."

"Why not, if you please?"

"It's not the way of the clergy. It's what they expect of the laity."

His light tone had its effect, and Mr. Leyburne began to feel better as they went briskly up Ludgate Hill.

"I did have the thought that you'd some odd tastes in coffeehouses," he said.

"How so? Who told you?"

"Mrs. Cellier. I was inquiring for you. . . ." He explained it briefly, and Mr. Payne laughed.

"She might have spared you perplexity. She knows what trade I drive."

"But I do not." Mr. Leyburne permitted his tone to express his curiosity.

"No? I do not brag of it. But my letters-of-news are held in some esteem."

Once again Mr. Leyburne felt surprise. He had not associated Mr. Payne with letters-of-news, though he knew as well as any man that the writing of them had become a trade in the town. Every country gentleman, and many a divine, too, was urgent for news of what was passing in the town and Parliament, of how men's thoughts were drifting and what course the affairs of state were running; and since the law was inflexible against the printing of such news it followed that the writing by hand of letters-of-news had become a profitable trade.

Mr. Payne was pleased to explain himself further. Deep in the shires of England there was many a papist gentleman who wanted papist news; and Mr. Payne, at once a zealous papist and a mature and seasoned writer, had found in this an opportunity that exactly matched his talents. He knew what his customers wanted, and he brought a fine skill to the gleaning of it. Day after day, he would be about his quest, changing gossip in what was left of St. Paul's, pushing in at the Old Bailey or at Westminster Hall, slipping into the Great Gallery at Whitehall, hearing what was said and guessing what was whispered, observant of faces and demeanours and the come-and-go of coaches; above all, roaming from coffeehouse to coffeehouse, mixing with all men, heeding, noting, listening, ever sifting the endless gossip. Mr. Payne had a deal of work to do before he could compress his gleanings into the terse and simple text which he dictated each Saturday afternoon to the score of writers who attended him in a discreet room by Covent Garden. The country gentleman paid a guinea a quarter for their weekly letters, and they had value for their money.

Mr. Leyburne listened with interest, knowing now why Mr. Payne was so well informed on so many topics. He said as much as they came to the top of Ludgate Hill, and Mr. Payne laughed.

"It's prudent as well as profitable to be informed. But here, I think, is Child's."

He turned aside in the shadow of the cathedral and led through an arched and lighted doorway; and at once it was plain that this was not the Rainbow. Here, to be sure, was the same clatter of cups and scurry of servers, the same thick air redolent of coffee and tobacco, the same groups of standing, chattering men. But here also was a difference; there was not a man here who was not in decent black, and hardly one who had not the white bands of a divine. Nor was there any woman here; and if there had been, she would assuredly not have glittered in satin and cloth-of-gold.

They laid their pennies on the bar, and Mr. Payne, cup in hand, led sinuously across the crowded floor. Mr. Leyburne, following at his heels, had further proof from scraps of talk that this was not the Rainbow; one group was asking whether the papists would accommodate themselves to the oaths prescribed by the Test Act; another was disputing whether a comprehension should now be offered to the dissenters; a third was agreed that resistance to the King was a damnable sin; and a fourth was amazed at the choice lately made to fill a vacant deanery. Decidedly, this was not the Rainbow.

"So!" Mr. Payne settled himself comfortably in a nook by the wall. "We may now return to present affairs. What sent you in search of me?"

"That?" Mr. Leyburne had to pause and think before he could remember what it was. "It's—it's touching this Mansell of yesternight."

"He's in bed, we'll hope."

"No doubt. But please to tell me—who is he, and what is he?"

"He's of Shaftesbury's following, of the Green Ribbon Club, and said to be climbing there. Probably he's a dissenter too."

"I see." Mr. Leyburne steadied his breath and then came to the heart of it. "Does he know Miss Langley?"

"So that's what teases you!" If Mr. Payne's smile was born in amusement it continued in understanding. "But remember, if you please, that I do not know the lady."

"Mr. Barlow knows her. He said as much."

"So I noted. You said she's of Lancashire—of the parish of Bolton."

"Wherever that may be—I did. She said you turn away at the Boar's Head——"

"Three miles north of Wigan. Precisely. Do you know these places?"

"Not I." Mr. Leyburne hesitated. "I've not yet been through the North Parts."

"No?" Mr. Payne's smile was quizzical for a moment. "I don't know them well myself, though I've ridden that way. But Bolton's a sink of Cropheads. It's where they butchered the Earl of Derby in the time of the Rebellion. They had his head off in the market place."

"So I've heard."

"So have all men heard. But Wigan's different. It's a loyal little town. They know the decencies in Wigan. See . . ."

Mr. Payne dipped a finger in his coffee and drew wet lines on the table to show his meaning.

"For Lancashire you do not go to Chester."

"No?"

"Not unless you want a swim. For in those parts there's a river they call the Mersey, and there's but one bridge by which you may cross it. That's at a place called Warrington. And once across that bridge you're in Lancashire."

"Yes?"

"From Warrington the road runs north, and it's perhaps a dozen miles to Wigan—a pleasant little town, and loyal, though it's now of perhaps more charm than note. But once you're out of Wigan, on the Preston road, you're in the parish of Standish, where dwells Mr. Hoghton of the Park Hall. And in this house you'll commonly find Father Barlow."

"Oh!" Mr. Leyburne was all attention. "And this Bolton?"

"Lies to the east here." Again Mr. Payne drew wet lines on the table. "As you ride north through Standish there's high ground to your right, and that's the parish of Bolton. It's a vast place, and Bolton town, where the Cropheads breed, is in this corner. But here to the northwest, where it marches with Standish, it's moorland. And that's where your Langleys must be if you've to turn at the Boar's Head."

"So?" Mr. Leyburne was staring at the wet lines on the table. "So they're neighbours to Mr. Barlow?"

"Father Barlow, if you please. But also, if you please, to Sir Henry Mansell of Thornclough."

"Who?" The question came with a snap.

"He's a justice in those parts, and father to that Roderick whom you laid abed last night."

"I hope so. But what more of these Mansells?"

"Of the father, not much. I'm told he's Shaftesbury's man, like his son. He's of substance. He's a justice, and probably he's a dissenter. And like as not, in the Usurper's day he was a damned rebel. That's all of him."

"It's perhaps enough. What of the son?"

"Ye-es. He's of some interest." Mr. Payne's voice came softly. "The fellow came to town three years back—to seek his fortune, no doubt. As I've said, he now wears the Ribbon, and in those circles he's rising. But of late, I think, he's given some hostages to fortune."

"Meaning what, if you please?"

"Mrs. Waring." Mr. Payne was speaking slowly, and his eyes were steady. "Mansell's had a deal of her company of late, and no doubt of her favours, too."

"And who, by your leave, might Mrs. Waring be?"

"Did you not note her this night—in the Rainbow?"

"That?" For a moment Mr. Leyburne's voice rose in surprise. "The woman in the golden silk, you mean? With the cloak of black?"

"Lined with crimson. That same. Black and crimson might almost be called her colours these days. Have you seen her chariot?"

"Not I."

"I thought you might have done, since you dwell in Fleet Street. It often waits by the King's Head there. It's a pretty toy—done in black with crimson panels, and a lively pair of greys to draw it."

Mr. Leyburne nodded. He had indeed seen this chariot, and he had noted that it was slung on Colonel Blount's new and risky device of steel springs in the place of leathers. It was modern as well as elegant.

"I'd wondered whose it was," he said slowly.

"It's hers. Or at least she'd say it was."

"A nice distinction."

"An obvious one. I've never heard that she's any money. Or if she has, she doesn't spend it. And since Mansell's had her company and favours, we may suppose he's been at charges for her. And not light ones either. The lady isn't cheap."

"I see. Which is to say that her status is also obvious?"

Mr. Payne shrugged.

"It's a guess, no doubt. But I don't know what other use a man should have for Mrs. Waring. Unless indeed . . ."

Mr. Payne seemed lost in contemplation of his coffee, his fine eyes clouding as his thoughts grew deep.

"Unless?" The reminder came softly.

"There's just this—though it's drawing a bow at a venture." Mr. Payne looked up sharply, his eyes alert again. "The lady's in the fashion—very much in it, as you'll have noted. She's had attachments before Mansell, and some of them in high places. Perhaps she parted on friendly terms. . . ."

"Perhaps she did. But what of it?"

"I've said it's a bow at a venture. But such a woman, moving where she is free to move, might do a deal to lift Mansell in this world. It's that sort of world. A whispered word as the wine runs low—Mansell would not be the first who's risen that way."

Mr. Payne's short laugh was contemptuous. "That might suit Mansell. He's an ambitious rogue, and if head and heart could march together, as it were, that might account for his willingness to spend more on the lady than his purse can spare."

"It's that way, is it?"

"There are no certainties in this. But that's the gossip. And you've seen the chariot."

Mr. Payne beckoned to a passing server and called for a pipe and more coffee, and thereafter he retreated into silence and a haze of tobacco smoke. Mr. Leyburne, thoughtfully stirring his fresh coffee, sat in the same brooding silence.

"Would you suppose," he asked suddenly, "that this fellow Mansell is attractive to a woman?"

"What?" Mr. Payne seemed startled, and then his smile flickered suddenly. "I've not yet discovered what it is that makes a man attractive to a woman. That's a secret the sex does not impart to us. But why speak of attraction at all? Need you suppose that the lady's heart is engaged?"

"No." Mr. Leyburne spoke obstinately. "But if it is not, and if the lady is as well placed as you say, and Mansell as short of money——"

"The devil!" Mr. Payne sat up suddenly, alert and attentive. "I had not thought of that. But it's as you say. She might surely have flown higher, and it's odd that she should not. That might bear looking into."

Mr. Payne relapsed into silence again as he rekindled his pipe. Then his tone changed, and he spoke briskly.

"But at present there's no more than I can tell you. And now I think we have perhaps been seen together for long enough. It would be prudent to depart separately. . . ."

Mr. Leyburne took leave politely and without regrets. Much as he had come to like Mr. Payne, he was not at this moment sorry to part from him. He wanted to consider this, and his thoughts were busy as he went alone down Ludgate Hill, patiently sorting the confused impressions of the night. And for once, Penelope Langley did not hold the centre of his mind. Into it there had now come another image—a bright clear image of the fashionable Mrs. Waring, glittering under the candles in her gold and her black and crimson, and turning suddenly to him with her inscrutable and disturbing glance. It was an image that stayed with him in spite of his attempts to cast it out, and it brought him no thoughts that were comforting.

He moved quickly along Fleet Street and came to the lane by the Whitefriars; and there, drawn up in the gloom of his own shadowed side of the street, was a hackney coach, the candles flaring smokily in its lanterns. He stared at it idly, wondering who visited in Fleet Street at this dark hour; and then, as he went past it, three men were suddenly upon him, and before he had guessed what they were about they had him expertly by wrist and elbow.

Without a word they hustled him past the coach, and then he saw that beyond it, and hidden by its bulk, a smaller vehicle was standing —a slim neat chariot, whose outlines he knew at once, though its colours were lost in the gloom.

"What the devil!" he snapped.

They took no heed of that. They thrust him forward into the light of the chariot's lanterns, and a man who was standing by its door seemed to incline his head as though for a whispered word with someone within. Then, as if satisfied, he came slowly forward.

"You'll be John Leyburne?" he said curtly.

"I am. And what the——"

"Keep your breath for Tyburn. You'll need it there." He flicked a paper between his fingers. "Here's the justice's warrant. You're for Newgate. Felonious assault on Colonel Roderick Mansell. . . ."

8 THE NEWGATE CAPTAIN   It seemed to Mr. Leyburne that his chance of hanging was considerable. The oddity of the treatment he was getting had left him without illusions.

There was no doubt of the oddity, and it had begun at the moment of his arrest; for he had been taken at once to Newgate, and it was there, within the walls, that he had been taken before the justice for first hearing and formal committal to the prison that in fact already held him. He had, moreover, recognized the justice at sight as Sir William Waller, as bitter and bigoted a member of the Green Ribbon Club as might be found, and what had followed had well matched his expectations. There had been as witnesses the two fellows who had attended Colonel Mansell and had run for their lives so ingloriously in the moonlight. The justice had as good as told them what to swear to, and they had as promptly sworn to it. Sir William's pen had scratched viciously as he signed the mittimus, and now Mr. Leyburne lay despondently in Newgate, awaiting trial at the Old Bailey and the all but certain prospect of a hanging at Tyburn; he knew only too well what sort of juries the present sheriffs were apt to name.

He lay alone, and that was another oddity; for on a charge of felony the common course would have been to fling him into the common hold and then allow him to buy his way into whatever food and comforts he chose to pay for. But he had been given no such chance; he had been kept alone in a damp grey cell and he had been permitted no visitors; even Mr. Gill had been refused admittance, and there had been neither word nor letter from anybody. Mr. Leyburne, as hope faded, realized grimly what this meant; his enemies were giving him no chance to concert anything, nor even to prepare a defence.

It was when a full three weeks had gone by, when April had run its course and the half of May had followed it, that the interruption came. It came on a wet and windy night, a night more proper to March than May, a night which even the walls of Newgate could not conceal, when the darkness came before its time, and even the rain came somehow in to set the grey walls shining with beads and rivulets. Mr. Leyburne, stretched on the straw that served as his bed, was lying back in what comfort he could find, and staring dismally at the small high window which the last glimmer of dusk had turned to a square of ghostly grey; the roaring of the distant wind came faintly as a sigh that seemed to match the mood of Newgate, and Mr. Leyburne turned wearily, hoping against reason that he might be blessed with sleep this night. Then abruptly he stiffened and rose tensely on his elbow as a turnkey's boots scraped on the stair, and the grating in the door took sudden outline against a yellow shaft of light.

Mr. Leyburne sat up in alarm, tense and watchful, as feet crunched to the door. The shadows changed as a lantern was lifted high; there was a pause and a clink of keys, and then the clatter of the great lock and a surly creak of hinges; the door swung open, and in silence a man stepped in, his hat pulled low and his cloak drawn tight about him. His gloved hand held a lantern, and he set it carefully on the table as the door was pulled and locked behind him. The turnkey's feet scraped noisily as he took himself away.

"Mr. Leyburne, is it not?"

The man spoke smoothly, and if his voice had not the quality that speaks of breeding, it had at least a tolerable imitation of it; and certainly his manner was courteous. Mr. Leyburne, stiffly on his feet, bowed his acknowledgement.

"I am, sir."

He matched his tone to the other's, and then stood, stiff and alert, acutely conscious of his grime and dirt and his three weeks' growth of beard. But the stranger seemed to notice nothing of that. His left hand came from under his cloak clutching a bottle of wine and a pair of glasses; he set them carefully on the table by the lantern, and then he spoke again.

"Here's earnest of friendship, Mr. Leyburne."

"How, if you please?"

Mr. Leyburne was wary and suspicious, and the stranger permitted himself a bland smile.

"It's to drink to our better acquaintance. And also to one who is friend to us both."

"Indeed?" Mr. Leyburne was as stiff as before. "And may I know who that may be?"

"This letter will inform you."

Again his hand came from beneath his cloak, and in the lantern light he placed a folded blue-sealed sheet. Mr. Leyburne stared, and then decided that some courtesies would be proper. He hooked the low stool from the wall, set it by the table, and waved the stranger to it.

"Poor seating, I fear, but the best I have."

The stranger bowed and seated himself. Mr. Leyburne sat on his bed, and in the same silence he took the letter and saw his name on it in an unknown hand; that sufficed, and he broke the seal and read:

I never change. The captain, who serves both me and you in this, will assure you of that. I professed myself at your service and I am at your service still. So are those good others whom you know of. Wherefore is order taken for your enlargement, and the captain, who is skilled in sly affairs, has the management of it. He will not fail, nor I change, and, if it please God, you may soon—if you will—be once again the guest of

Elizabeth Cellier

Her image flickered before Mr. Leyburne's eyes as he looked up stupidly. He looked down again and read a second time; and as the sense of it began to seep into his mind there was a clink and gurgle from the table. The stranger had poured the wine, and he was smiling as he set the glasses.

"If you please . . ." He was holding his glass aloft. "To our good friend, Mrs. Cellier!"

"Mrs. Cellier!"

In courtesy, Mr. Leyburne could do no less, and his glass rose to match the other's. Both men drained their wine, and at once the stranger poured again. He lifted his glass alone.

"Your speedy enlargement, Mr. Leyburne!"

Mr. Leyburne bowed. The strong sweet wine, drunk quickly after weeks of the poorest food, had been a potent stimulant, and he had sense enough to leave the second glass untouched. But the one glass did its work; it warmed him and heartened him, and suddenly he found his thoughts flowing easily. His mind was alert and his eyes were eager as he looked again across the table, and now he saw that the man had loosened his cloak and was settled at his ease. His dark aquiline face was sharp in the lantern light, and Mr. Leyburne looked at it with full attention. It was a handsome face, clear-cut and regular, with smooth dark cheeks and flashing white teeth that looked the whiter for the dark eyes and the thin black eyebrows. There was energy in this face, and force enough to hold attention. A woman, if she were none too wise, might have found fascination here, and certainly the fellow had an air; his manners were decent, and he aped the gentleman with a smooth and practised skill. But Mr. Leyburne saw more than that; he saw the greedy downturned mouth, the thick voluptuous lips, the slyness in the restless eyes. He looked again and was satisfied. Here beyond doubt was the captain, skilled in sly affairs, whom Mrs. Cellier had written of; though whether he was indeed a captain, and of what, were questions which it would no doubt be wiser to leave unasked.

Mr. Leyburne raised his glass and made pretence to sip at it.

"Your good health, Captain! I take it that I may address you so?"

"By all means, sir. And my name is Dangerfield. Captain Dangerfield—at your service."

Mr. Leyburne stiffened and clung tightly to his wineglass while the memory came to him of Mr. Gadbury, the astrologer, pronouncing on this man's ways and nature. And what had Mrs. Cellier said? She had surely said that this Dangerfield was himself confined in Newgate; he had been cooped in hold for debt, and to Mr. Gadbury's fury she had purposed to buy him out. Mr. Leyburne looked once more and saw the captain's well-cut coat of blue, the snowy lace at his neck and wrists, the ring that flashed on his finger; beyond doubt the captain had lately come to prosperity as well as enlargement, and it might be guessed that Mrs. Cellier had paid for both. That, as Mr. Leyburne quickly reminded himself, was not his affair; but certainly he need not doubt further what sort of a captain this was.

"Now, touching this letter, Captain . . ." He made his voice sound affable. "There's a deal here I do not understand. I do not even understand how you were able to come to me tonight. I've been forbidden all visitors."

"Just so." The captain had poured himself a third glass of wine, and there was satisfaction in his smile as he lifted it to the light. "But the clink of a guinea is music in a turnkey's ear—especially if you know how to choose your turnkey."

"I see." And indeed Mr. Leyburne did see. He had no difficulty in believing that this man would know exactly how to choose a turnkey; the captain's knowledge of turnkeys was probably extensive.

"I see," he said again. "But what's this of enlargement? You know the charge I'm held on, and you know what men are pressing it. You'll hardly bribe a way through that?"

"No?" The captain drawled it as he fondled his glass in the lantern light. "No? Though it might be contrived at need. But here there's not the need. Why spend so much when there's a cheaper way?"

Mr. Leyburne, remembering that his own neck was at stake, began to get impatient.

"What way?" he said curtly. "I'll be obliged to you if you'll be plain with me."

"By all means." The captain filled his glass for the fourth time and then leaned across the table with a suave air of confidence. "Then bethink you, Mr. Leyburne, that there are three witnesses to testify against you, and three only. There's Colonel Mansell, and a pair of lackeys who say they were with him in the street that night. And that's the sum of it—three, and no more."

"It's enough. Even two would suffice."

"True . . ." The captain cut him short with an airy wave of the hand. "But what if there's only one against you? Colonel Mansell against Mr. Leyburne? That's one to one, and no court can convict on that."

"One?" Mr. Leyburne was staring at him. "But what of the two lackeys? What of them?"

"I'll take them off."

"You'll what?"

"A venal pair of rogues." Captain Dangerfield coughed virtuously. "And if they won't melt to the clink of guineas, they'll certainly melt to a slit throat—or even to the thought of one. You may leave them to me, if you please."

"Oh!" It seemed to Mr. Leyburne that the less he said to this the better. "By all means I'll leave them to you. But you're sure of this?"

"Perfectly. You'll not be so sweet as to suppose that it's a new thing? And now, if you please, to details . . ." Captain Dangerfield upended the bottle and stared gloomily at the clouded dregs that trickled into his glass. "This is Saturday, and they tell me your trial's set for Wednesday—before which, however, you'll have been told that they've put it off. I doubt if they'll mention that they've lost their witnesses."

"So do I. They've told me nothing in this place yet, and I've no reason for thinking they'll tell me of this."

"No? It—it might be so." Gloom seemed to be settling on the captain as he eyed the empty bottle. "Yes, it might be. They'll perhaps think fitter to say no word, and leave you here to rot."

"What's that?" Mr. Leyburne set the table quivering as he leapt to his feet. "Hell and——"

"No! No!" The captain was on his feet also, and it was plain that he was startled. Then he collected himself. He pressed his face into the old suavity as he resumed his seat, and the sly gleam was back in his eyes as he spoke again.

"Not so," he said smoothly. "They may indeed be so minded, and it's well that you've raised it. We'll ensure that they don't achieve it. That will be done by milord Shaftesbury's contriving."

The captain seemed amused, and Mr. Leyburne, whose sense of humour did not extend to this affair, saw nothing here that was funny.

"Shaftesbury!" he snapped. "Are you drunk?"

But Captain Dangerfield was staring absently at the table; his hand closed casually over Mr. Leyburne's untouched glass, and he drained it at a gulp; then his eye was brightening as he spoke.

"Ah!" he said, with the air of one admiring his own cleverness. "That's to be explained. Milord, d'ye see, is hot for what he calls liberty, and that's his cry just now while he presses through the Parliament what he calls a Habeas Corpus Act. . . ."

"A what?"

The captain blinked, and then he explained it further. With this act passed, any man in hold might at once, and of right, have himself brought before a judge, who must order his instant enlargement unless good cause to the contrary could be shown. It was an act, said the captain, designed to clip the claws of the King if he should be minded to practise so against milord and his wearers of the Ribbon.

"That's the short of it," said the captain, after a fruitless test of both the empty glasses. "But it will serve your need, Mr. Leyburne, as well as theirs. All you'll have to do is—— Blast the fool!"

Boots were crunching on the stair again, and the captain glanced angrily over his shoulder as a fist hammered on the door. He struggled to his feet as a key grated in the lock.

"I'll have to leave you," he grumbled as the door was pushed open. "I could agree for no more than a half hour, and it's gone. This will be gaoler's rounds, and this rat's got the wind in his guts. Fare you well— and be of good heart. You can trust me. You can always trust Tom Dangerfield."

Without another word he had lurched to the door and was gone, the empty bottle clutched tightly in his hand, while a scowling turnkey snatched up the glasses and the lantern and followed him out with an angry slam of the door. The lock rattled, the lantern light swayed and faded beyond the grating, and then Mr. Leyburne was alone in the dark, torn between hope where there had been no hope, and a clear perception that he could certainly *not* trust Tom Dangerfield.

He had some endless hours to endure in the days and nights that followed. Wednesday passed without word or hint of trial, and almost a full week more had gone before he at last knew that the captain, whatever his common courses might be, had told the truth in this. On a Tuesday night, when dusk had softened the shadows and turned the grey walls black, a lantern flickered again behind the grating, and when the door creaked and opened there were three turnkeys and the gaoler there. They were not communicative, and they offered nothing of explanation or apology. They merely conducted Mr. Leyburne down the stair, across the exercise yard, and to the great gate of the prison. In a surly silence they unlocked the wicket, thrust him through, and bade him go to the devil; and the door thudded behind him as he lurched into the darkening street.

He stood gaping, bewildered by the unexpected and not knowing what would follow. Then, as he collected his wits and looked about him, he saw, dim in the dusk, the vague dark outline of a hackney coach that waited there unlit; he saw the leather door curtain pulled aside and a half-seen man step quickly out, tall and towering in the gloom.

"You're very welcome," said Mr. Payne. "Now, into the coach with you. . . ."

9

LANGLEY OF LANGLEY   June was in its own, and the roads were white with dust and loud with the hum of bees when Mr. Leyburne at last took horse and departed for the North. He rode in the gilded sunrise of a limpid pale blue morning, and he rode lazily, seeing no cause for haste and much for thankfulness. The summer sun and the fanning wind soothed him as he trotted along the white rutted ribbon of the road, content to savour to the full the blues and greens that are England on a summer's day; and a week and a day had passed before he came out of undulating Cheshire lanes and went trotting down through marsh and meadow to a gleaming river, across a long stone bridge, and into the streets of Warrington; and that roused excitement in him, for here was the county of Lancaster.

He rode differently on the morrow. He was in Wigan before noon, and there in the market place, in the shadow of a gracious church, he halted at the sign of the Dog for strange new cheese and ale of surprising strength. Then he was pressing on, alert for the Boar's Head, which lay at a fork of the road; and here again he halted, to bestow some crowns, speak his name, and ensure that letters from the post bags should be kept in safety for him. He made very sure of it, and then he was away again by the right-hand fork, climbing over hill and dale to the rolling moorland that must be Bolton Parish. The heat of the sun was fading, and the light was turning gold when he came at last to the crest of a hill and saw below him the dry-stone wall of a gentleman's park and the belt of trees that must conceal a house. He halted and looked searchingly. Then he went clattering down the slope and along the run of the wall until he came to tall sycamores, a trimly painted lodge, and gates of fine-wrought iron; and at that he drew rein again and stared in something like dismay. This dignity and air of opulence were not quite what he had expected.

His face was hardening as he walked his horse through the open gates, past the lodge, and up the smooth-rolled gravel of the drive; and when he rounded a bend and saw the house he halted yet again as dismay came back to him. Assuredly this was not what he had expected. This great house, set in green lawns and squares of hedge, was in the modern style; it had a symmetry and a considered balance; it had a door precisely in the centre, with a window neatly above it and matching windows left and right; it had a portico and a moulded pediment; and if it had such necessaries as servants and a kitchen it permitted nothing of them to show in its dignified façade. It was dignity in stone, but it did not blend with his memories of the wayward Penelope.

The crunch of feet on gravel cut into his thoughts, and he turned to see a fellow in livery hurrying nervously from the lodge; he swept a servant's bow and asked how he might serve the gentleman.

"Is Mr. Langley within doors?"

"Mr. Langley, sir?" There was surprise in the voice. "No, sir. He seldom visits here, sir."

"Visits?" It was Mr. Leyburne's turn to be surprised. "What's that you say? This is Langley House?"

"No, sir." The man stayed civil, but his tone had slyly changed. "This is Thornclough, sir—Sir Henry Mansell."

"The devil it is!" Mr. Leyburne wheeled his horse abruptly. "My regrets, then, that I've entered."

The gravel spurted under the hooves as he made hurriedly for the gates and the open road, asking himself urgently what blunder he had made. But there was not much further to go. In a mile there was parkland in sight again, and gates again by a dusty road; but this time the keeper was alert by his gates, and if he had less dignity than the other he had in its place a welcoming grin.

"Is this Langley House?" He was taking no chances here.

"Aye—that it is!" It came heartily, full-toned and rich, and suddenly Mr. Leyburne was smiling.

"Good!" he said as heartily. "And Mr. Langley?"

"They'll know yonder."

The man jerked a thumb at the trees that must screen the house, and Mr. Leyburne went trotting cheerfully up the gravelled drive; and when the house came in sight he had a sigh of relief as he stopped to gaze. This was not Thornclough.

Decidedly it was not Thornclough. Here was nothing trim and neat, nothing of symmetry and considered balance. This rambling house had grown through the years under many hands; it had some black-and-white timbers, simple and straight, which had seen two centuries pass; it had some later timbers, with the black beams rioting into lozenges and circles; and it had a wing, where some departed Langley had built in stone, so that here was a gracious doorway and mullioned windows with slender transoms. There was ivy, old and safe as the house, rooting in the stonework, blurring the lines of door and window, and throwing back the blaze of colour from the flowers by the fringing turf. And as he sat his horse and looked, the house called softly to him across the lawns; and at once he understood. This old house was sentient, and it could do what Thornclough could not do. Thornclough stood aloof and beautiful for the stranger to admire; but this house called the stranger in.

There was St. Christopher wrought in iron as the knocker on the door—a gracious thought, surely, in whoever had put it there. He knocked and waited, while his heart pounded with excitement and his straying eyes saw the grey stone blackened by the arch of the door, as though by some fire of long ago. Then there were footfalls and the rattle of a latch, and the door swung to disclose a white-haired man in russets; and he asked no questions; he merely swung the door more widely, and made a bow which was plainly a request that the stranger should come in.

Mr. Leyburne went in. He went into a panelled hall, cool and dim in the style of an older day, with panels no wider than a plank of oak may be. He saw the doors left and right, the low straw-plastered ceiling, the oaken stair with the balusters and the moulded rail; he saw the long-case clock from Mr. Gill that ticked at the foot of the stair; and he turned pleasantly to the man who waited.

"Mr. Langley?"

"I fear he's out riding, sir."

"Oh! And Miss Langley?"

"Certainly, sir. I'll tell her, sir. But who——"

"Mr. Leyburne—John Leyburne."

"I'll tell her at once, sir. Pray be seated, Mr. Leyburne."

The man pulled an old leather-back from the wall, set it some six inches from where it had been, and waved the guest to it. He gave his courteous bow and then departed softly. Mr. Leyburne ignored the chair and stood stiffly. He glanced out through the open door, and saw the green grass and the blackened stone; he turned again to the mellowed oak and the measured ticking of the clock; he looked at his dusty boots and felt for the set of his cravat. Then there were footsteps, brisk and light, and the sharp click of a latch. He swung round, almost on his toes; and through the door, with a tap of heels and a rustle of taffeta, swept a bright-eyed lady who was clearly of an age to be Penelope's grandmother.

Mr. Leyburne gaped; and the lady, head erect and shoulders squared, halted in mid-floor to consider him. She took her time at it, viewing him from head to foot with shrewd and steady eyes, and when she spoke her voice was crisp and clear.

"Mr. Leyburne?"

"Ma'am . . ."

Belatedly he was bowing as he asked himself who she was and what he should say to her. He had known that this moment would be difficult, for he had sent no warning of his coming. He had preferred to arrive unheralded, representing his intrusion as a visit of courtesy made on his way to Cunswick and relying on good will and his native wit for more; he had his tale prepared for that, but he could hardly tell it to this formidable and unknown lady.

"You seem at a loss, Mr. Leyburne."

Her voice cut crisply into his thoughts; and as he braced his shoulders and met her eye, he saw, to his unspeakable relief, the hint of a smile on her lined face.

"Would it perhaps have been Miss Penelope Langley whom you wished to see?"

"Ma'am . . ." He was bowing again. "I'll not deny it, ma'am, I did indeed hope——"

"You'd be a fool if you didn't." Her smile broadened while he

gaped at her. "But she's riding with her father—who is my brother.
I am Arabella Langley."

"Your—your servant, ma'am."

"You have already served me, Mr. Leyburne. And you are very
welcome here."

It was an odd answer, but he made the best he could of it; it might
serve as an opening.

"I'm grateful, ma'am. I had feared I might be intruding. I'm on
my way to Cuns———"

"You were on your way to Langley House, Mr. Leyburne. We had
some warning of your coming. And you are very welcome here."

That cut him short and left him staring; and then the smile left
her face and she was speaking gravely.

"When you served Edward Barlow you served me. You are as welcome here as you would have been at Cunswick."

He could do no more than bow again while quick thought told him
that warning of his coming must have been sent by Mr. Payne, who
no doubt kept touch with Mr. Barlow.

"There's one thing more, Mr. Leyburne, and then I'll see to your
comforts." She was looking him steadily in the eye as she spoke.
"What service it was that you did to Edward Barlow we do not know,
and we do not seek to know. This is a county in which it's sometimes
wiser not to know. Secrets have dangers, and no doubt you share one
with him. But be assured it is a secret safe. It is not shared with any
here."

Her voice died away, and he stood in silence, grateful for an assurance whose meaning he well understood. Mr. Payne had done some
plain speaking about this. The charge of felonious assault which had
put Mr. Leyburne into Newgate had been neither tried nor dismissed;
it had merely been allowed to lapse for want of evidence, and it could
be both revived and pressed if he should be heard to admit that it had
indeed been his sword that had wounded Colonel Mansell. In short,
as Mr. Payne had grimly put it, he could very easily talk his way to
Tyburn; and he would sleep the better if the truth were known to
nobody.

He met Miss Langley's eye and read understanding there. This was
the secret she was assuring him they did not know.

He was bowing in silent acknowledgement when she spoke again, and in a different tone.

"I think I hear . . ."

She moved quickly to the door that still lay open to the lawns and the sunlit evening, and as he followed he heard the clop of lazy hooves and a soft jingle of harness. He was at her side, looking over her shoulder as a pair of horses rounded the bend by the shading trees; and into the sunlight of the lawns came Miss Penelope, elegant and at ease at her father's side.

She saw him on the instant, and she was waving gaily as he ran to take her stirrup.

"Now don't start bowing," she told him cheerfully. "It's too hot. But I'm glad to see you. We all are."

"Aye, aye. We are indeed." Mr. Langley spoke gruffly as he swung to the ground. "We're glad to see you, Mr. Leyburne."

"Sir—to command!"

"It may be for you to command us. Since you've come into this county, Mr. Leyburne, it's fitting you should know how things stand here—for this is not London. For one thing, we've a plenty of papists here. They grow like currants in these parts. And for another thing, they're not newcomers. The oldest families in this county are like as not to be papists. And that, Mr. Leyburne, makes a difference."

"Aye, sir. I understand that. My—my own family——"

"To be sure. Of Cunswick. I'd remembered that, or I might have said less on this. But we do, some of us, have papist friends."

"Surely, sir."

Mr. Leyburne was puzzled. He did not see the need of this explanation. But Mr. Langley had not yet done.

"I spoke of some of us," he said slowly. "But not of all of us. We've men among us of your true London breed—men who lean fondly to Geneva, and mutter and grumble at our Church. There's no liking for papists among such men—nor any mercy either. For these are not the loyal gentlemen of Lancashire. They're not loyal, and often enough they're not gentlemen either—by any proper count. These are the men, or the sons of the men, who took arms against their King— fought against him, laid hands on him and butchered him."

"I—I know, sir."

Mr. Leyburne spoke softly and had no answer. The man before him had changed, his face had hardened, and now he was in a brooding silence. Then, quite suddenly, he returned, and his eyes were on his guest again.

"Your pardon, Mr. Leyburne." The smile was on his face again. "For a moment I let memory take me. But you'll perceive how it is," he said. "These men grew fat in the Usurper's day. They ruled England then. They smashed the churches, swam the witches, and burned the Maypoles. And fat they grew, on the lands of men who had gone with their King to Holland—or paradise. And how now, Mr. Leyburne? How is it now?"

Mr. Leyburne shook himself, almost startled by the sudden question. But at least he knew the answer; he had seen enough and to spare of such men—and he remembered Newgate.

"Now, sir——" He spoke with sudden warmth. "Now, sir, they call themselves the Country Party. They hate the King and they're fanatic against the Duke. They'd commit any treason to exclude him, aye, even if it were selling all England to any usurper who'd have her."

"You say it well." Mr. Langley spoke grimly. "Any treason, as you say—in their hearts. Though truly, here in Lancashire there's little they can do but harry papists—and they do that with an eagerness. For our papists are loyal. They're loyal and they've shown it. That was in the time of the Rebellion. I do not think there was one disloyal papist in this kingdom then. They rode to their King, all of them, with their sons, their tenants, their plate, their swords and horses. And they did for him in their hundreds. And they'd do the same for his son if the need should be. That's the core of this, Mr. Leyburne. Men disloyal to the King will attack his friends. And the papists are among his friends."

"I see," Mr. Langley said slowly. "So you have your troubles— even here in Lancashire."

"We have," retorted Mr. Langley forcefully. "Ned told us you were coming, and dropped us a hint or two." He seemed to hurry over this. "You'll be newly come, I suppose?"

"Of course he is," said Miss Penelope briefly. "He's still in his boots."

"Aye, aye. But at least he's safe come. And I'm glad of that."

"So am I," said Miss Penelope, and she sounded almost truculent. "I've been wanting you this last month—and badly."

"Truly now . . ." He faced her in delighted embarrassment. "Truly, you do me too much honour."

"No, I don't. I'm telling you the truth. I did want you. My clock won't go."

She sounded as truculent as before, and he stared at her, crestfallen and aghast. For a moment she returned his stare, her brown face solemn and her eyes as steady as his. Then, to his infinite relief, the smile was in her face, lighting it and quickening it, and sweeping every care from his glowing thoughts.

10 MISS PENELOPE'S HUMOURS   Miss Penelope had a way of making her wishes plain.

Mr. Leyburne, coming lazily to breakfast the next morning, found her as fresh and sunny as the morning itself. She was in a riding habit, and certainly it was of the mode. Her coat was of leaf-green serge, laced with silver, and it was cut like a man's, long in the skirt and tight in the waist, with the great cuffs turned broadly back to show the shining silk of the reverse. Under it, she had a shirt of white silk, foaming with lace at neck and wrist, and secured by a silver clasp that gleamed and sparkled in the sun; her pleated riding skirt, of the same leaf-green serge, was impudently short so that another gleam of silver came from the spurs that were already buckled to her yellow boots. She sat with her back to the window, with the morning sunlight flooding on her; behind her, the latticed casement was open to the southwest wind, and Mr. Leyburne saw the blaze of her sunlit hair and the sparkle of her green and silver against white clouds and the blue of a summer sky. It was an attractive and alluring picture, and it was not spoiled by the sly thought that it had perhaps not come about wholly by chance and the grace of God.

Miss Penelope was apparently at her best this morning, and her best was very good. She said all the right things, and she said them charmingly. She inquired of his health and of his night's rest; she hoped he would enjoy his visit; she was interested in his horse and solicitous for his comfort; and she wondered if he would care to see something of the countryside this pleasant morning.

He found polite words for the obvious answer; and a half hour later they rode out together into a soft warm wind under sailing clouds in a sea of blue. She led him behind the house and up a steep and grassy track that brought them to a bare hillside beyond; and then on and on, and up and up, till they came at last to a vast and sunlit moor where the grass grew tufted and the wind sang and the curlews called. Here she halted, and together they sat their horses in silence, looking down at the valley below and the rolling prospect beyond.

"Where are we?" he asked briefly.

"Anglezarke Moor," she answered as briefly. "I hope you like it."

"I do."

"Good! You're supposed to. That's why I brought you."

"Very proper of you."

"Of course it's proper." She almost snorted. "Aunt Arabella says it's proper, so it must be. She has a devotion to what's proper."

Miss Penelope's own devotion to it, he thought, was perhaps less apparent now than it had been at breakast. She was sitting brisk and erect, her chin uptilted and the plumes in her beaver all aquiver in the wind. He looked keenly and thought that her nostrils were aquiver too.

"I see." He edged his horse round so that he might face her more directly. "It almost sounds as though you'd no wish to come here. Where did you wish to go?"

"The Park Hall."

He took warning at once, and picked his words slowly.

"That's a Mr. Hoghton's house, is it not?"

"It is. It's also Uncle Ned."

"Meaning—Mr. Barlow?"

"Of course. What was it you did for him?"

It came bluntly, in her own direct manner, and it was the question he knew he must not answer, to her or any other; no doubt she had some qualities, but discretion might not be among them.

"It was no great matter," he told her. "But I do not think I should say more. It's Mr. Barlow's tale, when all is said, and since he did not choose to speak of it I should surely not tell it when he is not here."

"That's just it." There was a glitter coming into her eyes. "Why is he not here?"

"I don't know. But should he be?"

"Of course he should."

"Why?"

"Because I want him. I've wanted him for a month."

"I see. But——"

"If we stay here much longer we'll have the horses chilled—after that climb."

He would have been better pleased if he had thought of that himself; but it was plainly true, and he followed her lead as she turned her horse. Together they ambled along the rim of the moor, jogging knee to knee in a silence which now seemed amiable. He broke it cautiously.

"I still don't know why you wanted him."

"To mend my clock, of course."

"But—but Miss Penelope——"

"Miss Penelope be damned!"

"I beg your pardon?"

"Granted, Mr. Leyburne." She had become sardonic, but she had a friendly smile that eased it. "But I'm not going to be called Miss Penelope by a man I see at breakfast. So if you're to stay in the house you'd best stop it. You can call me Penny, as everybody else does. What do they call you?"

"John."

"Good! Then that suffices."

"Suffice it shall." Between amusement and pleasure, he was laughing openly. "No more of Miss Penelope then. But I still don't understand about Mr. Barlow. I don't properly know who he is. He's not truly your uncle, is he?"

"No. He . . ." Her brown face was puckering as she considered it. "He's a Booth out of Warrington by birth. That's his true name. And one of the Booths, it seems, once did a deal of visiting—here."

"Oh?" He was meeting her level gaze and finding it eloquent. "You mean he had some encouragement?"

"I don't suppose he'd have kept coming if he hadn't." The sardonic note was back in her voice. "But you might remember I wasn't there. I was still in heaven."

"I beg your pardon?"

"Or wherever it is that girls come from. I'm talking of '38 now, and I'm not as old as *that*. But Aunt Arabella is."

"Oh!" Again her level eyes explained her meaning. "I see. And what followed?"

"I don't know. But we do know he didn't marry her."

"You think he wanted to?"

"I think she wanted him to. Or would have done if . . ."

"If what?"

"It's plain enough, isn't it?" She had turned her eyes away now and was stroking her horse's neck. "The man was a papist. All the Booths are. And Aunt Arabella isn't—and won't be."

"I see. And then?"

"He married another." Her shoulders shrugged lightly. "And soon a son was born——"

"Your uncle Ned?"

"Of course. And then the Rebellion came. And Uncle Ned hadn't got a father."

"You mean . . ."

"I mean Marston Moor. But his mother was a Barlow—of the Barlows of Barlow, by Manchester there. And when she died he went to live with them, and he took their name. So off he went to Lisbon, to a college there, and then back home on the Mission, as they call it. And of course they would have to send him just here."

"But you don't mind, surely?"

"Of course I don't. But it makes for scandal. Aunt Arabella says he's just like his father, and she fusses after him as though she were his mother. And some people, of course, must needs have it that she *is*. Some people are like that."

She was looking away, seeming to scan the blue haze that was rising in the heat, and he tried to speak lightly.

"But of present affairs—you need not, surely, be concerned to see him now. Your clock's mended."

"Thanks to you." She turned back to him quickly. "And I haven't thanked you properly for that."

"Nor need you. It was a simple task enough. You had done no more than unseat the pendulum. I'm almost glad you dropped the clock."

"Why?"

"Because it allowed me to serve you."

"Oh, ho!" The sardonic note was back at once. "Good out of evil, is it? Last Sunday's sermon. Text from II Samuel, 16:12. And a damned prosy sermon it was!"

"What?"

"That's what Aunt Arabella said. It's the only time we've thought alike this past month."

"Is it? But why?"

"I've been trying to tell you. It—it's a month and more since he was last here. That was when he brought me messages from you——"

"Oh . . ." For a moment the blue sky faded from his view, and there was a single candle flickering on Mrs. Cellier's stair while Mr. Payne watched impatiently and a smiling Mr. Barlow made promise to act as Mercury.

"And it was the next day I dropped my clock." Her voice roused him quickly from the memory. "So I wanted him to come to mend it. After all, it was his clock. But he didn't come. The devil knows why he didn't, but he didn't. There's something kept from me in this. And when I wanted to go to the Park Hall for him, they wouldn't let me."

"You mean your father wouldn't?"

"No, I don't. I could have wheedled him. I can always wheedle a man. It was Aunt Arabella."

"I see." The disgust in her tone had set him smiling. "And why will they not let you visit the Park Hall?"

"On a lack-wit tale that it's a papist house."

"But isn't it?"

"Of course it is. But what's that to it—in this county? I've been there a hundred times. Will Hoghton and I used to romp together as children. I once pushed him into the lake there."

"I'll well believe it. You should have been whipped for it."

"I was. But why can I not go there now?"

"Perhaps . . ." He hesitated and then plunged at it. "I don't know how it is in this county, but I do know it in London. I've some cause to. And with half the town carrying flails, and Oates and his crew bellowing a new plot every twenty minutes, it could certainly be thought unwise to visit papists. It wasn't so once, but it is so now. The times have changed—since Oates."

"They haven't changed as much as all that—here. And my father knows it. But he won't ride with me to the Park Hall. And there's none other I can ask—to such a house. People are shy of it. And Uncle Ned doesn't come, though he used to come each week. I tell you, there's something kept from me here."

"Yes . . ." Her eyes found his, and suddenly he knew what was expected of him. "But, Penny, could you not ride to the Park Hall with me? Could I not serve you as escort?"

"Oh!" She drew rein and halted. "It is a papist house, you know. And if times have——"

"I've dealt with papists before. And I've a papist name, so none will count it odd. And certainly I'd be glad to see Mr. Barlow again. So what do you say?"

She faced him gravely and then she nodded.

"Believe that I'm grateful," she said quietly.

"It's agreed then. How of your father? Will he give consent?"

"My father?" Her chin was tilting, and the smile was spreading on her face. "I've told you about that. You may leave him to me."

"I will. And your aunt?"

"I leave her to you. She's been vowing thanks to you for a month, so——"

"I'll attempt her then. Where is the Park Hall, by the way? Is it far?"

"Ten miles, perhaps. It's in Standish, just across the post road."

"Good! Then we'll go tomorrow."

"Tomorrow's Sunday."

"Monday then. Now . . ." He faced a smiling Penny. "What more?"

"What you will. That's Thornclough down there."

She was pointing down to the valley below; and there, on its further slope, were trees and smooth walks and a trim house set in lawns; and for all the distance and the shimmering haze of heat he knew at once that this was Thornclough. He could not mistake the lovely form, the cold elegance, the hard unwelcoming beauty of the place.

"Yes," he said slowly. "I got there yesterday, by mistake. A family called Mansell, is it not?"

"Yes." She had become suddenly alert. "But how did you know? Which did you meet?"

"None." He was picking his way carefully. "I met none but a lodge-keeper—who spoke of Sir Henry Mansell."

"Oh, I see." Something like a grin was appearing on Penny. "I was hoping you'd meet Roddy."

"Who? Who the devil's Roddy?"

Her chin was tilting again as she eyed him mischievously.

"Roddy," she announced calmly, "is Colonel Roderick Mansell, only beloved son of Sir Henry and Lady Mansell of Thornclough."

"Is he?" He spoke with an impassive face. "And who calls him Roddy?"

"I do."

"Why?"

"Because he doesn't like it. Do you know him?"

The sharp question took him by surprise, and he all but plunged into a rash denial; then he checked himself and looked at her steadily.

"I've heard of him," he said carefully.

"Have you? You haven't heard of him from me. Who was it? My father?"

"No." He was sticking delicately to the truth. "It was from Mr. Barlow."

"Oh? I haven't heard of this. When?"

"It—it was in a tavern. In London." The words seemed to come of their own accord. "I was in talk there with Mr. Barlow, and some men came in. And later Mr. Barlow named one of them to me as Roderick Mansell."

"Oh, I see." She sounded almost disappointed. "So you didn't talk with Roddy?"

"No. But is he a friend of yours?"

"Now is he?" She cocked her head to one side and affected to consider that. "I sometimes wonder. And so does he."

"That sounds tangled." His breath was coming more easily now. "May I be enlightened? And shall we ride back? It gets hot here."

"It gets hot anywhere today. But as you please."

They wheeled their horses, and he had a sigh of relief as they turned their backs on Thornclough. But Penny had not done with the subject, and she went on with it while the horses ambled quietly along the track.

"I never saw much of Roddy till this year," she explained. "Of course we did meet sometimes as children. We were neighbours, so we couldn't help doing that—even if we did have fathers who could only just be brought to wave hats at each other on Sundays."

"Why that?"

"They were rebels." A backward jerk of her head towards Thornclough completed her meaning. "Still, you do meet your neighbours sometimes, even if you don't want to. And when Roddy and I met we generally didn't want to." She seemed to brood on it. "He was older than I, and you couldn't have called him sweet. He used to pinch me, and pull my hair, and tease me about it. So it can't be supposed he liked me. Once, when I bit him, he didn't. I know that. So with one thing and another it could *not* be said that I was queen of his young heart—or wanted to be."

"And now?" he asked quietly. "Is the peace made between you?"

"I suppose so." She was stroking her horse's neck again. "Certainly Roddy's changed. He's learned some manners since he went to London. And I will say he's been attentive—lately. Has all London gone savage?"

"*What?*" He was taken aback by the suddenness of her question and her change of tone. "What do you mean?"

"I don't know what I mean." She had swung to face him again, and she was speaking forcefully. "I'm not told enough to know what I mean. There's too much kept from me. But there's Uncle Ned, who's a papist, set into a danger that's not named. And you get him free of it. Then there's Roddy, who's of the Geneva sort——"

"In heaven's name, why bring Mansell into this?"

"Because he's hurt. Didn't you know that?"

"Hurt?" His eyes had narrowed suddenly. "But how, if you please?"

"In the shoulder. His arm's been slung till this last week."

"But *how*, if you please? How was he hurt?"

"That's what's odd. He was going to his house one night, it seems,

walking and alone. And as he was going down the Strand he was set
on by a crew of papists."

"What!" He gazed at her in stupefaction.

"Yes. By six of them, in the moonlight. They rushed from Arundel
Street, and they were on him before he could draw. He never saw
them till too late."

"The devil he didn't! Was he blind, do you think, or drunk?"

"He was neither. He—he was dreaming."

"Was he? What of, I wonder?"

"Me. He told me so."

11 MANSELL OF THORNCLOUGH   John Leyburne's
feelings towards the sly cunning of Roderick Mansell had turned by
morning into something near amusement. His first response, indeed,
had been so far from amusement that it had almost deprived him of
speech; he almost choked at the thought of such unchecked effrontery.
But later, when he was quiet in his bed that night, when he had drawn
his curtains and was brooding in the dark, another thought crept upon
him. True, he dare not speak the truth about the affray in Arundel
Street; but neither dare Mansell. Mansell had told his tale of an attack
by papists; he had spun it as a lure for Penny; and, having spun it,
he would now have to wear it, or proclaim himself a boasting liar.
The truth was that neither of them dare accuse the other; and John
laughed softly in the dark as he gave himself to considering the possibilities.

It was well that he did; for the inevitable meeting with Mansell
came sooner than he had expected. It came the next morning, which
was Sunday. That inescapably meant church—Standish Parish
Church, with all the gentlemen within miles assembled with their
wives and families; and it was very soon apparent that here, as elsewhere, the rites of Sunday were as much social as religious. No sooner
was service done than the churchyard was a throng of people, pacing
the gravelled walks and sauntering in the sunshine as they took their

weekly chance to meet, change gossip, hear the news, and appraise each other's clothes. John was assiduous in attending Penny, and Penny was plainly enjoying herself; she had a pretty talent for banter, and she was very willing to display it. It thus came about that he was too deeply occupied to observe the approach of the dignified gentleman in fine black velvet, and it was not until the buzz of talk died about him that he took warning. He spun then on his heel, and there was the gentleman in black; and there, too, gay in blue and silver and a waistcoat of lemon taffeta, was Colonel Roderick Mansell.

But Colonel Mansell had to wait for attention; it was the elderly gentleman who claimed it first, and already he and Mr. Langley were bowing ceremoniously, their hats aflourish and their long beribboned canes at arm's length. The ladies made their curtseys; and then Mr. Langley spoke frostily.

"Sir, permit me to present Mr. John Leyburne, my present guest. Mr. Leyburne, Sir Henry Mansell."

Mr. Leyburne was ready. The buckles of his shoes went flashing as his high heels clicked, and his bow was perfect as his hat swept elegantly.

"Yours, sir," he was murmuring. "Always to command. . . ."

He stayed courteously uncovered, but his eyes were busy as he stood in a proper silence. Certainly Sir Henry was of a presence proper to a justice. He was a man of full six feet, erect and vigorous, disdaining a periwig and wearing his own short-cropped hair, grey and flecked with white; his pointed beard, retained from an earlier day, was silver against the black of his velvet; only some white Dutch lace relieved the black; not a ring sparkled on his finger, not a brilliant on his shoes. They were signs not to be mistaken; this man was of the Puritan sort, the picture of many who had prospered in the days of the Lord Protector. He had the gravity and unadorned sobriety those times had valued, and the vigour and strength of countenance they had demanded. It was a face that could impress, even if the eyes were a shade too close and the lips a shade too thin; but now he was smiling gravely, a nice blend of dignity and courtesy.

"At your service, Mr. Leyburne. A friend of Mr. Langley must be welcome here. He will find us all his friends. But permit me now to present my son—Colonel Roderick Mansell."

It was admirably done, and there was nothing to do but bow in acknowledgement; and for the first time John looked directly at Roderick Mansell. Beyond doubt it was the same man. Here were the ice-blue eyes, the round red face, the burly shoulders, exactly as they had been in the tumult of an April night—except that the red face was vastly redder now than it had been then. Colonel Mansell, in fact, seemed to be on the point of choking, and that gave John an advantage he was quick to take. He had full command of himself, and already his hat was aflourish and his left arm sweeping his cane aside; his bow was impeccable as his heels clicked delicately.

"Sir, your most obedient! At your service always. . . ."

He had chosen the phrase with care as he lay abed, and he saw at once that it had been understood. It was a phrase proper to the occasion; but it was also the phrase in which a man might accept the challenge of swords. Colonel Mansell might take it as he pleased; and before he could speak, John was following it up.

"Miss Penelope was telling me of you, sir—of your hurt, and the way you were beset by rogues. I had to say I did most readily believe it."

The cold blue eyes grew wider. To be told that his tale had been believed was perhaps not quite what the Colonel had expected; and John nodded affably.

"Aye," he went on. "I've myself some knowledge of the rogues who infest the town at nights. That's to say, I've knowledge of their ways and of the work they do. But as to who they are"—his shoulders shrugged lightly—"I'm as ignorant as you."

Colonel Mansell stood a shade more erect, and his breath came noisily; but plainly he had seen the bargain that was offered, that silence should be matched with silence; and slowly, in his turn, he nodded.

"You've a pretty trick of words, Mr. Leyburne, and I'll not dispute what you say. We may be at one on that."

It was acceptance; and for a moment, as the blue eyes met the hazel, there was understanding; and behind the understanding was hostility, cold and implacable.

"Roddy! Have you no word for me today?"

Penny's voice came suddenly and sharply, as though she were not used to being left aside while gentlemen talked. Mansell turned to her at once.

"Damme!" He had an air of keen surprise. "But what's this? It's new, Penny—and you're outmoding all Whitehall. It's perfect."

It was shrewdly said, and by a man who had fully recovered his wits. Penny glowed with pleasure as she turned a little to one side and the other to display her riding habit the better; plainly Mansell had not seen it before.

"You like it?" She was preening herself again.

"Like it? There's witchcraft in it. I'll vow you saw it in some crystal."

Penny's eyes widened, and John watched unhappily. There was an adroitness in Mansell that he had not suspected; and he had himself seen this habit yesterday and had not wit enough to comment on it. There was something to be mended here.

"You'll come riding with me—in that." Mansell's voice came sharply, forceful and assured. "I'll not forgive you else. Now when's it to be, Penny? What of tomorrow?"

Perhaps he was too assured, for Penny's chin began to tilt.

"That's difficult," she retorted calmly. "I've a guest to look to, and he takes my time."

"The devil he does!" Mansell snorted angrily, and suddenly John intervened; he thought it high time to be in this talk again.

"True," he said cheerfully. "And it's my intention to take more of it. My regrets, Colonel."

He had an easy smile as he saw the red face getting redder. Mansell's lips pressed tighter; he turned his shoulder to John and spoke purposefully to Penny.

"He does not take the whole of it, I'll suppose and hope. So what of tomorrow? Will you ride with me then?"

"Tomorrow, now?" For a moment Penny stood considering. "Tomorrow," she said calmly, "Mr. Leyburne does indeed take the whole of my time. He's escorting me to the Park Hall."

"What!"

Mansell's voice snapped, and Penny looked innocently from the one man to the other.

"I've some affairs with Will Hoghton there," she explained, "and it's proper that I should have some escort over such a distance. And Mr. Leyburne has very kindly——"

"Precisely so," said John, and Penny nodded cheerfully.

"So that's tomorrow," she said. "You'll understand how it is, Roddy . . ."

"What?"

"Our fathers differ on much. But there's one thing they seemed agreed on."

"That it's time we ceased to keep them waiting."

The men turned quickly as she looked at the gate, and it was at once plain that she was right. Sir Henry Mansell was impatiently at the gate, and, beyond it, Mr. Langley and his sister were sitting their horses stiffly. John took his chance quickly.

"Then we'd best be departing. But remember me, Colonel. Always at your service. . . ."

12 HOGHTON OF PARK HALL The post road through Standish to the North was glittering in the morning light. The hedgerows were a chequer of blue and pink and green, and the white dust went swirling as the horses crunched along, slow and lazy in the July heat. Penny, riding with her coat unbuttoned and her hat pulled low, waved a gloveless hand and pointed.

"There, John!" she said eagerly. "In those trees."

"The Park Hall? I don't see it."

"Of course you don't. That's what trees are for."

The white dust was dazzling on the road, and his eyes were puckering as he saw the belt of woodland; and already Penny was urging her horse to a trot as she entered a narrow lane. There was less than a half mile of it, and then there were gates and a lodge and a curving gravelled drive, and then what was not so usual—what indeed he had never seen before. For here, strong and sturdy, was the Park Hall, a genial mellowed house set to face the sun, and with its back to a great circle of trees; and here, in front of the house, the lawns ran smoothly down to a great shining lake, a glittering sheet of silver, dotted with the green of lilies and the images of the trees and the flower-set lawns. His eyes were so held by the sheen and colour of it that he was all but startled when a sudden call of greeting came from the house, and Penny was waving happily to a man who stood smiling in the arch of the door.

"Penny!" he was calling. "You're welcome indeed!"

"You're sure?" She was smiling down at him as he came out to her. "I never know what guests you have here, Will—not if you can truly welcome others."

"We can always welcome you, Penny. And just now we've no guests at all. So it's easy."

He held her stirrup for her as she slid deftly to the ground; and from the corner of the house a groom came running to take the horses.

"Thanks!" she said briefly. "This is John Leyburne. He's a guest of ours. John, permit me—Will Hoghton."

"You're welcome also, Mr. Leyburne." Will Hoghton had an easy smile as he spoke. "Any guest of Penny's will be welcome." He hesitated, and then spoke firmly. "I've said you're welcome, and that's plain truth. We've not met before, Mr. Leyburne, but your name's not strange to me—nor your doings either."

"My doings?" John spoke doubtfully, and then he looked again at his host, keenly and appraisingly, and liked him. Will Hoghton was perhaps of his own age, a sturdy broad-shouldered fellow with crisp brown hair, steady grey eyes, and a cheerfully turned-up nose. There was honesty in his brown face, and a fine air of confidence; and with it he had an infectious smile that would win him friends in any place. Again John Leyburne found himself smiling; and he knew already that he liked Will Hoghton.

"I see," he said diffidently. "But my doings have perhaps been set too high."

"They're more likely to have been set too low, if I know our man. It's not often he tells all he knows."

"You mean Uncle Ned?" Penny cut in crisply. "Now it's of that, and of some more, that I've come to learn. There's too much kept from me of late. So where *is* Uncle Ned? I want him."

"So that's it? But I'm sorry, Penny." Will Hoghton was looking at her steadily. "He's not here."

"Not here?" Her eyes were glittering suddenly, and there was a flush coming into her cheeks. "Where is he?"

"Not here. That's all I know."

"You mean he's out of the house this day?"

"I mean he's away on his journeyings. I told you a moment since, we've no guest at all just now. I'm sorry, Penny."

"Blast your sorrow!" She muttered it viciously and then glared angrily at him. But that was wasted on Will Hoghton. He stayed in a placid ease, looking good-humouredly into her angry eyes; and suddenly her mood changed and she was twitching with amusement.

"I'm sorry, Will," she said cheerfully. "That was poor courtesy to show you."

"It's no matter, Penny. But come to my father. . . ."

He led them through the arch of the door and into a wide, stone-flagged hall, cool and shady, where a clock ticked sleepily and bowls of roses were white and red on the benches beneath the windows. Penny stood on no ceremony. She pulled off her hat and flung it with her whip to add to the litter of fowling pieces and fishing rods that lay jumbled between the roses.

"How is your father?" she asked.

"None so well. The gout has him again."

"In this heat?"

"It's the lake, he thinks. He says there's a rheum rises from it."

"It's very like. You've my sympathy, Will."

"Not I. My father, surely?"

"No—you. My own father has the gout too, in the winter. It's not good for the temper."

"Then heaven send, Penny, that you never get it."

Will Hoghton gave her no chance to reply. Instead, he led them to a square and panelled parlour, where the windows were set wide and the sun was dazzling on the polished floor. Full in the warmth and light of it an elderly gentleman sat in an elbowchair, one bandaged foot propped on a stool and one hand toying with a mug of ale. Temper or no temper, he gave them courteous welcome; he put aside the closely written sheet he had been reading, and he expressed himself pithily as soon as John Leyburne had been presented.

"You'll be very welcome, Mr. Leyburne," he said, "now and henceforth. You've done good service to Father Barlow. And beyond that, as I'm told, you move in good company." He flicked the written sheet between his fingers as though in explanation. "The newsletter—fresh this morning. And I'm told you know Mr. Payne?"

"I have that honour, sir, though I'd not known that his letters came to you."

"Aye, they come. I subscribe for them gladly, and I'd not be without them."

His eyes strayed suddenly to the close-packed writing as if his thoughts were still with it, and Penny spoke with understanding.

"We'll not disturb you, sir," she said quietly. "If you'll give us leave to talk with Will . . ."

"With all my heart!" Mr. Hoghton seemed relieved, and he was sunk in his newsletter again before his visitors had even got to the door.

"Prettily spoken, Penny," said Will Hoghton as he pulled the door to. "He fidgets the week through till the letter comes, and then he's sunk in it till dark. And this week . . ." He laughed softly. "But let's to the garden. It's cooler by the trees."

He led them down a stone-paved path through the coloured garden and along the rim of the lake, and there, in the leafy shade of the chestnuts, chairs had been set, and a low squat table. A servant followed them, apparently unbidden, with thick cool mugs of ale.

"There!" Will Hoghton saw that his guests were at ease. "Are you contented, Penny?"

"In this—yes." She settled herself back and looked him in the eye. "You were saying that your father's more than usually sunk in his letter this week. Why this week?"

"Because it has more to relate this week. There's been a battle, it seems, in Scotland——"

"What's that?" John cut in sharply. "Of the rebels, do you mean?"

"Aye. And they're dispersed, and by the Duke of Monmouth."

"The devil!" Penny was sitting bolt upright. "What's this, Will? Rebels—and battles in Scotland?"

"It's news to you? But Mr. Leyburne speaks as though he's heard."

"Of rebels, yes." John made his answer as he saw the question in Will Hoghton's eye. "That's to say, I heard before I left London that there was trouble again in Scotland. The tale ran of an archbishop murdered—Sharpe, I think his name was—and of men in arms, and the Covenant proclaimed again. The last I heard was of some affray at a place called Drumclog."

"You have it pat." Will Hoghton nodded calmly. "And in today's letter there's a last note, written in a margin, of His Grace dispersing these Covenanters at a certain Bothwell Bridge—just that, and no more."

"No more than that?" said Penny. "Then what's it to do with me?"

"Nothing, I should say. But you were urgent to know why my father is so deep in that letter."

Penny snorted.

"I thought it had news that could touch Uncle Ned—and tell me where he's gone, and why. Where is he, Will? You must know."

"But I don't." Will was as calm as ever. "He left us some two weeks since. He did not say where he was going nor why. He never does, and we never ask. He packed his saddlebags and was gone. That's all I know."

"Or care, by the sound of you." Her angry eyes passed from the one man to the other. "Where is he, John? Can you guess?"

"London, if you want a guess. He goes each half year, I'm told, and he may go betweentimes, too, for aught I know."

"What does he go for?"

"We may suppose that he has affairs."

"And Will knows what they are—and doesn't mean to tell me." She wheeled on him angrily. "Isn't that so?"

"No." Will was watching her steadily. "I've told you already I don't know where he is—and I don't know what he does, either."

"Don't you?" She was viewing him doubtfully. "And I suppose you'll next say that if only you did know you'd tell me?"

"No, I shouldn't."

It was as firm as it was unexpected, and for a moment Penny sat gaping at him; and in that silence he spoke again.

"Penny, why do you probe so hotly into his affairs? All being said, they are not your affairs. Why do you do it?"

His quiet tone robbed the words of offence, and Penny did not flare into anger. Instead, her words came as quietly and steadily as his.

"Because there's something kept from me here. I've said that to John, and now I'm saying it to you."

"What's kept from you?"

"If I knew that, I shouldn't be asking. But something there is. He's stayed from me for a month and more, though he knew I wanted him. And I've been forbidden straitly to seek him here—on a lack-wit tale that your house is suddenly grown dangerous. Then there's John here. He was with Uncle Ned in London and he did him some great service —but I'm not to be told what it was. He'll not trust me with so much. And now there's you—saying that if you did know his doings you'd not tell me. So it seems you don't trust me either?"

Will Hoghton looked at her steadily.

"None of us mistrusts your goodwill, Penny," he told her quietly. "But mischief may be done otherwise than by intent. A word let slip, or a hot answer—and you're something given that way——"

"More than most?" Her chin was tilting again.

"A deal more. But also—and what's much more——"

"What?"

It came as a challenge, and there was a crackle of fire in her voice. John, forgotten by both of them, glanced uneasily from the one to the other, from Penny, sitting tensely in her chair, as hot as the sunlight that was flooding over her, to Will Hoghton standing a yard from her, cool and collected, his strong brown face alive in the rippling light that came through the swaying leaves. Will's eyes were as steady as ever when he made his answer.

"What's more is that you see a deal more than sense or decency would permit of Roderick Mansell."

Penny thrust herself back in her chair, her face quivering.

"Did—did you say decency, Will?"

"I did." Plainly he was not intimidated. "I know what Mansell is, and what a breed he comes of—and so do you. And I know also—as do you—that there's a gallows and a quartering block for Ned Barlow, if the Mansells can but take him."

"Are you saying that I would——"

"No, I'm not." She had jumped to her feet in fury, but the snap of his answer cut her short. For a moment he had the faintest of smiles as he watched her quivering face. "No, Penny. I'm not saying you'd betray Ned Barlow to Mansell or to anybody else. It's as sure as God lives that you'd not—wittingly. It's what you might do unwittingly that frightens me—what you might let slip. That's why I said you see more of the fellow than sense permits."

"You said decency, if I heard you right. That's another word, and you said it to my face, and in John's hearing."

Her quick side glance was a plain hint that John should support her in this, and it was hard for him to disregard it if he wished to keep her goodwill. Yet he spoke reluctantly; he was much in agreement with Will, and certainly he liked the man too well to wish to quarrel with him. Yet something was plainly expected.

"Perhaps," he said quietly, "the word decency could be accounted too strong here."

"No, it couldn't," came the blunt answer. "Forgive me, Mr. Leyburne—I've no wish to be offensive. But here's a matter in which you speak of what you don't know. But I know, and Penny knows. And if she needs to be reminded she's but to glance at her father's door."

"Door? I don't see——"

"Precisely. But Penny does. And again I say it's not decent for a Langley to show such sweetness to a Mansell. I'm sorry, Penny." He was looking her straight in the eye. "But since you press to know why things are hid from you, there's no honest answer but that."

"I see." She said it grimly, with her cheeks flushed and her mouth pressed tight. "I'm schooled indeed. And so, I suppose, is John, who's been well told that I lack the decencies." She turned on him suddenly. "John, can you yet bear with me enough to escort me home?"

"Penny! You know well that I——"

"Can you? And will you?"

"Penny!" Will Hoghton spoke softly. "That's needless, as you've been well told. None mistrusts your goodwill. I did say that. There's nothing held against you but—a mistake."

"And a lack of decency. John, will you call for our horses, please?"

He stood stiffly as he perceived what she was thrusting upon him. In embarrassment he looked to his host; and, to his infinite relief, Will Hoghton nodded. There was even the hint of a smile on his face.

"I'll spare you the task, Mr. Leyburne," he said quietly, "I'll call for them myself."

He turned on his heel and walked firmly to the house. John looked at Penny, and neither of them spoke. In an awkward silence, they moved after Will.

It was an embarrassed departure and it began a silent journey. They spoke little as they rode, and that little was about nothing. Penny seemed disposed to brood; and John, all his sympathies with Will Hoghton, had sense enough to know that this was not at present a safe topic for him to comment on. It was not until they were back at Langley House, had dismounted and were come to the door, that either of them spoke of it. Then Penny stopped suddenly in her walk and was staring at the door.

"What did Will say?" she asked abruptly. "That if I needed to be reminded——"

"You need but glance at your father's door—whatever that might mean."

"It means . . ." She was still staring at the lintel. "It means Will's right, blast him!"

"How is he right?"

"He'll tell you." She wheeled suddenly to face him. "He likes you. Did you know that?"

"No." He hesitated. "How should I?"

"By believing me. I know his looks and his ways. He likes you."

"I think I like him."

"So I noted. And you were with him against me."

"Penny, I——"

"Oh yes, you were. And you were right, too, though you didn't know it. And I'm glad you like him. He's worth it. So you may ask him about that door."

Penny turned on her heel and walked into the house; but at the foot of the stair she turned for a last thrust.

"And if you think I'm to be spoken to like that by Will Hoghton, you're wrong. If Roddy Mansell wants me to ride with him, I shall. And I shall *not* talk of Uncle Ned."

13

A TALE OF '42   That came true, and earlier than might have been expected. For the very next morning, breakfast being scarcely done and Penny in a scratching humour, there was a scamper of hooves on the gravel, and a gay jingle of harness. Penny jumped to her feet and went running to the window as a gentleman in mustard taffeta swung nimbly from his saddle and came marching to the door. Mr. Langley sat stiffly in his chair, no pleasure showing in his face, and, behind him, John stood as stiffly; for this gentleman in taffeta was Roderick Mansell.

Even John had to admit that the fellow did it with an air. He came in boldly, and he brought something of the manners of the town with him. His bow was in the mode, deep and swift, with his heels clicking and his white-plumed beaver sweeping. He did it as though he meant it, and then he stood erect, very straight and strong, and waited for his answers. From Miss Arabella he got a nod as she sailed from the room; from a hastily departing Mr. Langley he got little more than a grunt; and from John he got his thrust returned.

"Sir!" The bow was as fine as his own had been. "Ever at your service, sir."

Colonel Mansell had an affable nod for that, and for a moment he waited in silence—and in vain. John had no intention of leaving the fellow alone with Penny, and he stood his ground firmly. Another nod seemed to show that that was understood, and thereafter Mansell ignored him. He had an easy smile as he turned to Penny, and from a pocket deep in the long skirt of his coat he produced a slim packet softly wrapped in silk.

"If you'll honour me, Penny? I told you on Sunday you'd seen your habit in some witch's glass. One trifle you perhaps did not see—and I exist to serve you."

It was finely said, and it had Penny between surprise and pleasure. She took the packet in her hands, fingered it excitedly, ripped off its seal, and flung the wrappings open.

"Roddy!"

Her smile was of delight as she spoke; and then she dropped the wrappings and held before her eyes a pair of fine laced riding gloves in soft green leather, with silver lace done into stars on the backs and running in dazzling lines along the cuffs. She held them happily under John's disgusted nose.

"Aren't they beautiful?" she cried.

"Admirable, no doubt," came the stiff answer, and Roderick Mansell smiled confidently.

"I spent the day scouring Bolton for them," he explained. "And I had to stand over the glover while he moved the lace as I directed. But here they are. And if you'll honour them by putting them to your riding habit——"

"Honour them!"

She had already thrust her hands into them, and now she was preening her wrists while she looked at the gloves from every angle. Mansell's smile broadened.

"The habit was divine, Penny. I told you so at once. But no! Please, Penny—not brown gloves!"

"They were all I had."

"Then now you've better." His smile grew even broader. "Don't you agree, Mr. Leyburne?"

Mr. Leyburne nearly choked. He did agree. He was, in fact, quite sure of it; and he was just as sure that he ought to have thought of this himself. But already Mansell had turned from him, and his forceful eyes were meeting Penny's.

"There's just one thing I would ask," he was saying. "Let me see the gloves married to the habit—on you, Penny."

His quick side glance through the open window did the rest. Penny's eyes turned with his; and there were the trees, green against summer blue, and the lawns and the smooth-rolled gravel; and on the gravel a grey horse waiting, nuzzling against a patient groom. It was not a lure that Penny would resist, least of all in her present thwarted humour.

"Roddy!" she said excitedly; and then suddenly there was something of dismay in her face.

"But, John!" she said, and almost with contrition. "What of you? Won't you—won't you ride with us?"

"My thanks!" He bowed frigidly. "I'll beg to be excused."

"But why? Oh, John, you're not——"

"Why should I be? But I've letters that claim my time this day."

It was almost true, as he sourly told himself. If he had not letters to write, he had perhaps letters to collect, and he would be better employed collecting them than in moping while Penny rode with this unspeakable Mansell.

It was a thought that persisted, and a half hour later, when Penny and her smiling cavalier had trotted out of sight, John rode for the Boar's Head, meditating sourly on the gloves and on this Will Hoghton, whose bluntness had done so much to put Penny in this wayward mood.

But it was a steep and hilly road, down and up, and down again, and always there were sun and moor and sky, the soft padding of the horse, the sigh of the wind in the rippling grass. Little by little his humours eased, and when he came at last to the inn by the fork of the road he was hot and thirsty and dreamily content. He dismounted and consigned his horse to an ostler, who came running with memory of a crown once flung; and from the cool dimness of the inn the landlord came, in the same good memory of a guinea.

It had been money well spent, and he was well remembered here. Certainly there was a letter for Mr. Leyburne; and if he should be minded for a quart of ale, there was shade in the garden. . . .

Mr. Leyburne was exactly so minded. He followed through the rush-strewn ale room, through the stone-floored kitchen, and out into a green and leafy garden. And there, pleasantly at his ease in a garden chair, an ale mug in his hand, and his feet propped on a low stool, was Will Hoghton.

"Well come!" he called cheerfully. "I was hoping you'd seek your letters this day."

"Why, so I do. But——"

"No need to stare. My father was urgent for letters again, and from one cause and another . . ."

A drawer came with ale and the landlord with a letter, a single folio, directed to Mr. John Leyburne at the Boar's Head. John put it unopened in his pocket and then gave his attention to Will Hoghton. Their mugs lifted as the landlord moved away.

"How's Penny?" asked Will. "She's not with you?"

"No. She's—she's riding."

Will's eyebrows rose in a plain question, and John nodded.

"Mansell," he said tersely, and for a moment Will stared thoughtfully at his ale.

"From yesterday?" he asked slowly. "From what I said?"

"Yes. And Mansell's impudence. He brought her some gloves . . ."
He explained it briefly as he sank into a chair, and Will nodded his understanding.

"I'll be called tactless, no doubt. But I'm not a penitent. I was at least honest. And as for Penny—if you must speak of impudence, why confine it to Mansell?"

It was John's turn to nod, and the feeling was upon him that he and Will were likely to agree on most things; the sense of harmony between them was unmistakable.

"Yes," he said slowly. "She's perhaps not an angel straight from heaven."

"Heaven!" Will grunted with disgust. "She should be slapped. But you see now why Father Barlow has been avoiding her of late? She'll not see *him* if she rides with Mansell."

"Yes, but . . ." John remembered that there was more to ask. "But what's this of the door, please? You told Penny to view her father's door . . ."

He told how she had done so and what she had said, and again Will nodded.

"If she won't explain it, I suppose I may," he said. "But you'll have noticed that door—with the blackened stone in the arch and lintel?"

"Why, yes. But you're not saying it was Penny——"

"Not so much." Will laughed openly. "No, Penny did not fire that door. You may acquit her of that. And it was done before her time—or ours. It was powder that bit into that stone—a petard in the rebellion-time, when they blew the door and mastered Langley House."

"The rebels, you mean?"

"Rebels, as damned as any, and out of Bolton town. A half troop of horse, and pikemen supporting—the whole in command of Major Henry Mansell."

"What! Of Thornclough?"

"He was not then of Thornclough. But certainly the same man—now a knight, and a justice of the peace and quorum. The Usurper made him that."

Will Hoghton pushed himself further back in his chair and took another pull at his ale. Then he told a quiet tale. In '42, he said, when John Langley of Langley had betaken himself to his King with his horse and his sword and his servants, young Henry Mansell, a gentleman then of only the lesser sort, had marched his troop to the house and had demanded its surrender to the Parliament; and with the force he had brought he should hardly have found dispute. But Arabella Langley, just turned three-and-twenty, had stocked her larders and barred her doors; and for five long days, with no more than nine true servants as her force, she had given him shot for shot in the King's name and her own. There had been dead men in the house and out of it before the end came—when the great flash of the petard sent the door into blazing ruin, and the hard-faced pikemen came pressing in to uphold the writ of Parliament.

"Aunt Arabella, was it?" John spoke softly. "I had not heard of this. And then?"

"Then she was prisoner among them, until they tired of her and let her go. And by that time her father was dead."

"Dead? You mean——"

"I do. He died in battle, his son being at his side."

"Richard?"

"Aye—he that's your host today."

"I had not heard this, either. And then?"

"It's a common tale enough. A garret in Amsterdam."

Will Hoghton told the tale almost bitterly. When all was done, the King dead and loyal gentlemen in ruin, young Richard Langley had found nothing for it but exile—a garret in Amsterdam, as Will had said. There, as the years had dragged by, Arabella had contrived to join her brother; and there, putting all to the hazard of faith, Richard Langley had found himself a wife. And in '58 the Langleys had come quietly home—not indeed to their own, but at least to England and the kindness of faithful friends. Penny had been born that year—and her mother had died in that.

"God's mercy!" John almost whispered it. "But what a tale it is! And is there more to tell?"

"Something." Will Hoghton was sitting erect. "Their lands were sequestered. They were seized to the commissioners and sold, and most of the land, a fair two thirds, went to Henry Mansell at a fool's price. That's how he came by what built Thornclough. He'd known what he was about when he embroiled the Langleys in siege and war."

"And yet he——"

"Aye, aye." Will waved him into silence. "But note, if you please, that the Langleys had never sold their land. It was sequestered—taken from them. And that meant, do you see, that when the King was back, and some colour of justice done, the land came back to them—and not a penny saved to the Mansells of what they'd paid for it."

"And what of that? It was rightly so."

"No doubt. But do you see what follows?"

"I do not think I do—from your tone."

"No? But you'll see at least that the Langleys have no love for the Mansells, nor any cause to have. That was what I reminded Penny of when I told her to view the blackened stone."

"Aye, that I see. It's plain enough."

"Yes." Will had a soft smile for a moment. "That stone could be cleaned, you know, if old Richard wished it. It would be no great task. But he'll have none of it. It shall stand so, he says, to his sister's honour——"

"Well said! I grow warm to these Langleys."

"Aye, aye. But we lose this tale. The Mansells, then, were left with Thornclough—all fine and new, and not wealth enough to keep it. That's the devil that bites the Mansells now. How to pay the charges that Thornclough brings."

"Is it now?" John was leaning forward with his brow furrowed. "Then there's something odd here. I—I've seen something of Mansell —Roderick, I mean—in London, and he flaunts it lavishly. Though——"

He broke off. The memory had come to him of a chariot, fine in black and crimson, and of Mr. Payne, speaking thoughtfully of a Mrs. Waring, who could not be accounted cheap.

"Though what?" asked Will quietly.

"Though I've heard it asked where he finds the money."

"You may hear that asked here too. But . . ." Will hesitated. "Does no thought come to you on this?"

"Thought?" John snapped the word in sudden anger. "My thought is that Richard Langley must be out of his wits that he permits Penny to know this rogue—let alone go riding with him."

"It's matter perhaps of Father Barlow."

"Of Father—— You set riddles, surely?"

"This county's full of riddles. But when all is said, the Mansells are the Langleys' neighbours, and to forbid Penny to know them would be discourtesy, the grossest. It might well provoke Sir Henry to strike back where he can. And that's the rub—he can. He's a justice, remember. And the Langleys, with a priest flitting in and out, are in no position to provoke him. Do you see?"

"Yes—damnably."

"Good!" Will spoke almost grimly. "Have you got the answer yet?"

"Answer to what?"

"I was telling you that guineas are now none too plentiful at Thornclough. And I'd asked if any thought had come to you. Has it?"

"No—not specially. What's in your mind?"

"Only that Penny's an heiress."

"Good God!" He was almost out of his chair. "Are you saying——"

"No, I'm not. I'm merely asking—guessing, if you like. And your guess will be as good as mine. But it could be so."

Will's quiet voice died away, and John sat rigid, his thoughts whirling. It certainly could; it was not even out of the usual, and there would be as many to account it good sense as to condemn it. John stirred uneasily, and the thought came that it must surely have been an urgent need that had called Mansell from the distractions of the town and the charms of Mrs. Waring—the so expensive Mrs. Waring. He was hardly the man to feed his soul on rustic pleasures.

"Tell me"—he looked steadily at Will—"is it a new thing that Mansell should visit here from the town?"

"No." The answer came promptly. "He's been here some three times this last winter."

"After Penny?"

"No. At least, I've not heard of that. I'd have said he was after the geese, not love."

"Geese?" It was the townsman speaking. "What geese, if you please?"

"On the mere there." Will jerked his head to the west. "There's good rough shooting round the Martin Mere, if you don't mind getting your feet wet. Apparently Mansell doesn't."

"The devil he doesn't! That's rustic sport surely?"

"What of that? He was bred here, when all is said."

"No doubt. Yet . . ." John was trying to tell himself that this could be believed. Fine gentlemen of the town did at times have a taste for rough sports, as well he knew; but somehow it was not quite his conception of Roderick Mansell.

"No doubt," he said again. "But where is this Martin Mere? And what is it?"

"It's over to the west there, between Ormskirk and the coast. And it's what you might suppose—shallow and reedy, and marshy by the rim. And it's of a size, too—a vast desolate place. You may ride a score of miles to circle it, and never see a soul."

"And you may shoot geese there?"

"If you've skill enough. It's not a 'prentice sport."

"And Mansell? You say he spends his days at that?"

"Not now."

"Why not?"

"Because you don't shoot geese in summer. There are no geese to shoot. It's a winter sport—and you don't spend your days at it. You go at dusk. But does it signify?"

"No, I suppose it doesn't. But I'm obliged to you for telling me so much. Believe that I'm grateful."

"There's no cause for that. It's we who are in your debt, and you know why. And that brings me to one thing more you should know."

"Yes?"

"Father Barlow—be not surprised if you see him. He's back. He was in at dawn, and his first word was of you. He wants to see you. There's something on his mind."

14

THE LETTER-OF-NEWS The letter that had been directed to Mr. Leyburne at the Boar's Head stayed unopened in his pocket as he rode thoughtfully back to Langley House, and it stayed forgotten until he was back in the house and in talk with his host. Penny, it seemed, was not yet back from riding, and Mr. Langley was disposed to be apologetic. John cut him short politely.

"Not so, sir. I'd occasion to seek my letters at the Boar's Head, and here's one. It may be a letter-of-news."

It was; and since Mr. Langley was plainly curious, they at once broke the seal and pored over the closely written text together. Nor did their interest flag, for it told a tale of Covenanters astir in Scotland, of the murder on the Magus Moor of the Archbishop of St. Andrews, of a Captain Graham of Claverhouse who had come with his dragoons upon an armed conventicle near Glasgow, and of the rising that had swiftly followed his repulse in that affray. True, the affair seemed over; the Duke of Monmouth had soon dispersed the rising, and all seemed very well. But Mr. Payne's last paragraph was disquieting:

Yet all is perhaps not so happily concluded as might from these appear. Those in the town who are of the Green Ribbon Club and the like places (being now called by many Whigs, or Whiggamores, after some shaggy and unwashed cattle thieves from whom Covenanters are bred in Scotland) are not minded that it shall easily conclude. The Dutch, too, are of the covenanting sort, loving neither kings nor bishops, and they may be expected to meddle if they can. And in Scotland the Earl of Argyle is surely of the same mind as milord Shaftesbury here in London. All are fit allies to stir what more they may, and it only wants that someone shall concert the whole; of which it is further to be noted that one Robert Ferguson, whom some call the Plotter, has of late been flitting between Amsterdam and London, and has never in his life had any business but to concert plots. Wherefore it is concluded that further mischief is brewing, and it is thought by some that Oates will find yet further filth to vomit up; or that if he does not, milord Shaftesbury will find it for him and put it in his mouth.

"God's life!" Mr. Langley threw the letter from him, and it fell fluttering and forgotten to the table. "Here's a pretty tale! Rebellion in the land again!"

"Not in this land, sir. Surely in Scotland only?"

"So far. But what shall come—times being as they are? Damn all rebels!" He picked the letter from the table again and stared at it with smouldering eyes. "Who is this Oates? And why?"

"You—you don't know of him, sir?"

"How should I?" Mr. Langley let the paper flutter to the table again as he flung himself back in his chair. "You're to remember we're in the country here, and all we learn of the town is what's in letters. And all the letters are like this one. There's always a word of Oates, and never a plain tale of who the fellow is. And now I'm asking you. Who is he?"

"Aye, sir. I see. But as for a plain tale—there's nothing plain about it."

"Very like. But who is he?"

"He's a rogue, sir, if ever one was bred. I saw him at the Old Bailey, the day he swore against Coleman, and I'd not thought Creation held the like. A short thick brute of a man without a neck, and a head that seems to stick from his shoulders. And his mouth is in the middle of his face. He has a brow low as an ape, and a chin long as a beard. And from mouth to chin is as long as from mouth to brow, so it's as I said—in the middle of his pasty face. And when he speaks he whines and slobbers."

"He would." Mr. Langley grunted in contempt. "We knew that sort in the rebellion-time. But who is he?"

"The devil knows. But they say his father was a Dipper out of Essex."

"A what?"

"It's the word that goes, sir. It seems they once bred a sect there who baptised by dipping folk in rivers, in the nighttime. And this fellow—the father, I mean—was a minister among them."

"And did the dipping, hey?"

"He did. But they threw him out of that for having too much sport of it when it was women to be dipped. But the fellow got him a son, and dipped him, I suppose, as Titus."

"Being the rogue we speak of?"

"Just so. And the King coming home and the Church of England looking big again, this Titus Oates got himself into holy orders." John laughed. "There was a man in a coffeehouse who told me the fellow spent half his nights thieving his neighbours' hens."

"A very pretty parson!" Mr. Langley sounded sardonic. "Pray continue."

"I don't know it all, sir. But it seems there were complaints to the bishop, and with that and some more this Titus may have thought he was not like to prosper much in the Church of England. So he turned papist—after a fashion."

"What fashion?"

"His own. That's to say they took him, and then he asked to be a Jesuit."

"The devil!" Mr. Langley stirred himself and began to pour ale with the air of a man who needed it. "And did he make a Jesuit?"

"He did not." John accepted an ale mug thankfully. "I've heard much said against the Jesuits, but never that they're fools. They soon had the measure of Oates. But it does seem true that while they were sniffing at him they let him live in their seminaries—at St. Omer in France, and at another in Spain. And that's where his mischief brewed."

"But how?"

"Because when they'd got the reek of him, they threw him out. And at once he was back in London, bawling of treasons he said he'd nosed among them. That was last summer—about a year ago."

"Oh? But what treasons?"

"All you could think of, sir, and more. But the core of it was of a consult of Jesuits held in London that April."

"In London?" Mr. Langley sounded scandalized.

"Aye, sir, in London. At the White Horse——"

John broke off as memory cut him short; memory surging of an inn sign, white under the moon, of Mr. Payne and Mr. Barlow in a darkened room, of Roderick Mansell and the Brisk Boys storming in. The whole sweep of it went past his eyes before he found his voice again and looked his host in the eye.

"At the White Horse in the Strand," he said quietly. "Or so Oates said. And he said that they talked of killing the King."

"God's life!" Mr. Langley sat up, startled. "Of killing the King?"

"Aye, sir. He was to be shot and stabbed and poisoned, and I know not what more. And then the papists were to swarm into the streets and fire the town——"

"Good God in——"

"Oh, aye, sir. But remember, if you please, that this is what Oates said. It need not be true."

"Ah! To be sure!" Mr. Langley sat back again and breathed hard. "To be sure, then. It's what Oates said. But what more did he say?"

"Not much. For the truth is there were few of consequence who believed him. Nor would there have been, but for justice Godfrey."

"Godfrey? The man who was murdered, is it?"

"That same, sir. Sir Edmund Berry Godfrey—a justice of the peace for Middlesex, and as good a one as most."

"No doubt. But how is he in this?"

"Why, sir, there was a fellow Coleman, a very hot and busy papist —and perhaps not a very honest one. But he was secretary to the Duchess of York, and that gave him colour for sending letters to the French Court—letters of treason, as it does truly seem. And that gave Oates his chance."

"How?"

"He'd nosed something of these letters when he was among the Jesuits. And by Michaelmas he'd made noise enough to get called before the Privy Council, and this time it was Coleman he meant to swear to. But it seems he didn't trust the Council."

"What's that? It was *he* that didn't trust *them?*"

"I meant he didn't trust the Council to believe his plot and publish it. You'll know, sir, that nothing may be published of what passes before the Council unless the Council so resolves. That was Oates's risk—that he might be disbelieved and suppressed. And he didn't mean to be suppressed."

"No? But how——"

"Very prettily, sir. Very prettily indeed." John was at ease now, and the talk of a score of coffeehouses was clear in his memory. "There was just one way, sir, and that was to go first before a justice of the peace and swear an information. Depositions before a justice can't be suppressed, as you'll well know. They must go to the High Court."

"I see." Mr. Langley spoke softly. "I see indeed. And Godfrey was the justice?"

"Exactly. So the deposition was sworn, and then the thing had to go on. But it might not have gone far if Godfrey had not been murdered."

"It was murder, was it?"

"What else could it be?" John shrugged his shoulders. "He was missing for five days—and well I remember them. The whole town was at it, searching for him. And then he was found by Primrose Hill."

"Where's that?"

"A mile out of town—near St. Pancras Church. He'd been strangled, and his neck broken, and his own sword thrust through his middle. And some other hurts, too. He couldn't have done them *all* to himself. And it wasn't thieves either, because his pockets were untouched. So the whole town swore it was the papists."

"To stop that deposition?"

"The deposition had gone forward. It had been sworn a fortnight before he disappeared, and he'd done his duty. He'd sent it forward in the proper way. So what the truth of it is, God knows. But that's what the town thought—papists. And after that it was Oates as the saviour of the nation. That's what they called him, and to hint you disbelieved him was to call yourself a papist—and you were halfway to Tyburn then. There was no man safe in the town at all—nor is yet, if you're at odds with Shaftesbury and his crew."

Again cold memory came surging, and John's voice faltered and failed in the chill of it. Newgate was very near and cold and grey, and Mr. Payne's quiet voice was warning him of what might come if he let out the truth of the affray with Roderick Mansell—Mansell who was at this moment riding with the laughing brown-faced Penny. John thrust his feet against the oaken floor, and suddenly his head went back as his mind cleared. There was not space enough on one earth for himself and Mansell, and more must be done than sit and wait. He must take some active course. . . .

"Shaftesbury, do you say?" Mr. Langley's question cut sharply into his thoughts. "How does Shaftesbury come into this?"

"Shaftesbury?" John had to wrench his thoughts to that before he could answer. "Because he leads the Country Party. And the Country Party, however they may style themselves, are men who love the King no better than they loved his father. They were warmer to the Lord Protector——"

"We'll say the Usurper, if you please." Mr. Langley's voice had become an angry growl. "But I know what men you speak of. My neighbour Mansell, hey? That breed?"

He had no quick answer, for John sat silent while again his thoughts went ranging; ranging to the church at Standish, with Sir Henry Mansell prim in his plain black velvet; to the sunlit garden of the Boar's Head, and Will Hoghton's soft-voiced tale; to the wind that was quivering on the moor, where Penny was riding now with Roderick Mansell. The silence lengthened; and, as his thoughts came back, he looked across the table and saw his host, silent and rigid, his eyes turned to the panelled wall as though they would see through it to the blackened stone by the door of Langley House. And again he heard Will Hoghton telling gently of siege and war, and of Arabella Langley, who had given shot for shot.

"Aye, sir," he said quietly. "Of just that breed—from all I've heard."

His host turned sharply, as though startled by a voice. Then he shook his wits together and came briskly to his feet, as though there were something here to be forgotten and passed quickly by.

"The ale be damned!" he said firmly. "Where's the wine?"

He found it in the press behind him and sent it splashing into the tall-stemmed glasses. John stood silent, thankful that the talk could be changed.

"Mr. Leyburne—your prosperous ways!"

"Yours, sir!"

The glasses clinked and parted, and Mr. Langley sank back into his chair with a sigh of relief. But then, as though the matter still gnawed at his thoughts, he looked across the table again.

"So that's Shaftesbury, is it?" he said slowly. "But tell me then, how comes the King to let it pass?"

"Why, sir, I—I think he has to. This faction of Shaftesbury's, they taunt the King with plotting popery and hatching a tyranny. And they're strong in London, and elsewhere, as I'm told. So strong that not even the King may seem to flaunt it that the papists are his friends . . ."

Once again John faltered into silence as memory came surging back once more—of Will Hoghton saying that only for the sake of Edward Barlow did Richard Langley keep a freezing peace with the family of Mansell.

"*Are* they not his friends?"

The question came abruptly, but this time John could meet it firmly. He looked his host in the eye.

"Yes, sir, I think they are his friends—as they are friends to some others. Yet he, like some others, may find it prudent not to say so— the law being what it is."

"Aye . . ."

It was hardly to be heard, but there was understanding in it. And then, before another word was found, the crunch of hooves and the tinkle of harness came clearly through the open window. Both men turned on the instant, and they were at the window as Roderick Mansell swung lithely from his saddle and ran to Penny's side as she dismounted. She stood for a moment, close to him and looking up to him, while the sunlight gave a blaze to her hair and gleamed and twinkled on the silver lace of her habit and her fine new gloves; and in silence the two men watched through the open window.

"God's life!" growled Richard Langley.

The pale canary went spilling on the table as the tall glass twisted in his hand; and John, looking hard-eyed into the sunlight, was thinking of a night when he had run this fellow through the shoulder— instead of through the heart.

15

THE SCENTED GARDEN   For a moment longer Penny stood close to Roderick Mansell, her face upturned to his greater height, and seeming to be in earnest talk. But it was not for long, and she did not bring him into the house; instead she stood by the blackened door, slim and straight in the sunlight, while he rode off at a gay canter, his hat aflourish and his head turned back as he waved.

Penny waved acknowledgement, and in the sunlit window the two men looked at each other in silent understanding; in the same silence they moved apart as Penny came boisterously in.

"Now what's this? Do I catch you at secrets?"

She had halted in the doorway, and she spoke gaily as though she were teasing them; but her glance had been keen, and now her eyes were wary as though she had sensed their disapproval. She was plainly suspicious when she spoke again.

"You're very silent, both of you."

"We give you our attention. That's all." Her father spoke stiffly. "We'd supposed you'd have something to say to us."

It was not encouraging; it almost asserted that she had something to explain, and Penny's eyes grew steady as she faced him.

"I came to say, sir, that I'm safe returned, and no harm done. And I've been returning a courtesy—which I hope is proper."

She came slowly forward as she spoke, almost to the table, and now she tossed her gloves lightly on its shining top; they were the green-and-silver pair that Mansell had brought her, and they showed plainly what the courtesy was that she had been returning.

"Aye—proper enough." Her father spoke slowly. "But I could wish you had not had need to do it."

The regret in him was plain, and Penny met his eye unhappily.

"Then I'm sorry," she said simply. "But he did bring me the gloves. And it was kind of him, and thoughtful. And when he pressed me——"

"There was more to it than that, Penny, as you well know. However . . ."

He would perhaps have left it at that, but Penny would not evade it. She slumped into a chair by the table, and for a moment sat brooding, while an outstretched hand toyed with the green-and-silver gloves.

"Aye," she said suddenly. "You may have it so. Call it ill temper if you wish. I've been so checked and schooled these last days——"

"By me?"

"No—not in this. It was—it was Will Hoghton."

"Then I'll not probe into that." Her father spoke more briskly. "And if the fellow was owed some courtesy, it's perhaps as well he's had it. It can be called at an end, no doubt—now?"

There was almost a question in his last word, and Penny looked away, her fingers tapping nervously on the table.

"It's not . . ." She was in plain embarrassment. "He pressed me that I should go——"

"Go where?" There was a rumble in her father's voice, and Penny turned to meet his eyes.

"They've built some new stables at Thornclough lately. And he pressed me that I should ride to view them. I said I would—on Saturday."

"God pity you!" It sounded like exasperation. "You heeded that tale?"

"But it's true. They *have* built the stables. I've seen them building. And——"

"Did it occur to you that you've a guest in the house?"

"It did." The answer came defiantly. "And I did my best. John"—she turned to him in sudden agitation—"I did ask you to come with us this morning."

"You did." John spoke quietly. "But I asked to be excused. That was natural, surely?"

"Was it? Why was it?"

"Because I did not know—and I could not well ask—what terms you and Colonel Mansell might be on. It was prudent to suppose that I might have been intruding."

"A courtesy, and I should no doubt thank you for it. But I did want you to come. And I've told Roddy I want you to come on Saturday to see those stables. I mean it. Now will you?"

Her smile was suddenly on her face, and it changed the whole look of her. She was eager, inviting, and friendly, and her spell was too strong for him. He yielded at once.

"To be sure I will—since you wish it."

There was a wave of exultation in him at her ardent tone; and with a flicker in her eye Penny made him think again. Very coolly she turned to her father. "All being said, sir, it will look better if I do not ride alone with Roddy twice in one week."

"It would look better still if you rode with him never in one week. But settle it with Mr. Leyburne. . . ."

That, as the afternoon wore on, might have been thought precisely what Penny had set herself to do. She departed to rid herself of her dusty riding clothes, and when she reappeared, cool and sleek in a deep cream taffeta that gave her hair its chance, her mood seemed to have changed with her clothes. She was lazily at her ease, friendly and charming, and she eyed John as though she had never had an interest in any other; and she showed a fine coolness in seizing what chances offered. For Mr. Langley, as might have been expected, had a word to say of Mr. Payne's letter-of-news; and Penny, hearing mention of rebels, seized on that at once. She must needs have the whole story, and her aunt was in agreement. Miss Langley also wanted the story told; and Penny, with one cool eye on her father and the other on her aunt, put in a stream of comment so impeccably cavalier that aunt and father alike were soon in high approval, while John sat back in silence. It was beginning to dawn upon him that Penny, for all her wild ways, could not properly be called simple.

Nor could she be called forgetful; for, supper being done, she turned herself to John again and asked politely how he had fared with Will Hoghton. But he, too, had wits that could turn smoothly, and his quick glance towards her aunt was hint enough for Penny; the air of the garden, she announced, would be cool at this late hour.

It was, for the sun was down and the heat of the day had passed; the western sky was still a reddening gold, but above it the blue of night was taking form, and in the east the first warm stars were aglow; the lawns were velvet, and the scent of phlox and roses was heavy in the windless air as they strolled at ease along the paths between the flowers.

"And what," said Penny, "did Will Hoghton say?"

"A deal of things," he answered lightly. "But mostly of your family."

"Of my family? Or of me? Which?"

"I said of your family. You told me to ask him of that stone blackened by the door."

"Oh! And——"

"And he told me."

"Did he truly?" Her voice came quietly. "And of Aunt Arabella?"

"Aye. And of how yours were loyal when there was rebellion in the land."

"Aye . . ." She seemed almost disconcerted. "And now I—I should not be riding with Roddy Mansell. Is that it?"

He turned to face her in the fading light.

"To put it clearly—should you?"

Her face was white as she looked up at him; and then quickly her head was down and she was taking a bloom from the tall phlox plants in the border by the stone-flagged path.

"No," she said at last. She was crumbling the bloom between her fingers, and the white petals went fluttering as she spoke. "I should not. Will said it yesterday, and I told you he was right. But when you live here—in the country—and with so few . . ."

The last of the petals went fluttering, and she seemed intent on the white blur of a moth that hovered in the border. The silence had lengthened to a strain before John spoke.

"So few?"

He prompted her gently, and suddenly she had turned towards him, her white face lifting as if in defiance.

"You don't know the country, do you, John? In the winter when my father has the gout, and there's snow on the moor, and every road a mud bog?"

"No." He was staring at her in the gloom. "I don't know it then."

"Or ever. You're a townsman, and you don't know." Again she turned away, and again she picked the white phlox petals to set them crumbling through her fingers. "And even if you were not a townsman, you still wouldn't know."

"You're tearing those plants to pieces."

He sensed that she was between two moods, and could be dealt with firmly. His fingers closed over hers and pressed them sharply, so that the petals she was holding went showering to the grass; with a touch on her arm he turned her, and together they moved slowly down the scented path.

"What is it," he asked quietly, "that I would not know?"

"The country." She had made no protest, and the soft pull of his arm brought her close against him as they walked. "If you were not of the town you'd still be a man. And you could ride, and make your friends, and go a-visiting. . . ."

"I see." The memory was quick in him of her eagerness to be

escorted to the Park Hall, where she must not go alone. "I—I had not thought of that."

"Men don't. Why should they? But it's still true—in the country."

"I suppose it is." The light had all but gone, and he was peering again to guess her mood. "But I'm to learn of the country now, I hope."

"Do you? But why? What brought you to the country?"

She had stopped in her walk, and suddenly her voice had changed; the dull tone had gone, and now there was a ring in her voice as though she were alert again. He eyed her warily as he summoned his forces for the direct answer.

"You know well enough what brought me to the country."

"Do I?"

"You do. You're not a fool, Penny."

"No?" There was airy innocence in her tone, and in the gloom he saw her head go back as she poised herself. "Of course I remember you did have a need to visit Cunswick. A duty, I think you called it—and very proper, too. Aunt Arabella said——"

"We're not speaking of Aunt Arabella—or of Cunswick either. I didn't go to Cunswick. I turned from my road and came here."

"And you've had nothing but trouble since." Suddenly her tone had changed again. "At the Park Hall, and at the church with Roddy, and today when I went——"

"It's no matter. It's no matter, any of it. But you know why I came here."

"I don't. How should I?"

"You knew it that night in Westminster when I brought you your clock. Even then you knew that we should meet again—that I should seek you out. I all but said so. And all else was in your eyes."

"Oh?"

She seemed on the brink of an answer, but it never came. From between the flowers the moth came wheeling, to go lurching and dipping along the border. Penny seemed to watch it as it faded into the gloom that was deepening beneath the hedges, and suddenly John felt her fingers on his arm.

"Listen . . . !"

It was an urgent whisper, and he was almost startled by it. But he threw back his head, and at once he heard what she had heard—the soft clear beat of hooves on grass, the unhurried tread of a horse that seemed to go discreetly, through the night rather than through the day. And suddenly Penny had left his side and was running quickly to the hedge and the deepening shadows.

He followed her in alarm, and together they passed through the low gate and were in the paddock beyond the hedge. The last gold of the sun was shut from them now, and all was gloom and the clear blue of a starlit sky; and in the gloom there was the faint blur of a horse, and a man dismounting.

"What's here?"

It was a quick mutter as alarm came surging, and he felt blindly for the sword he had not got. But Penny felt none of that. She went running to the rider, and at once she was standing close against him while his hands were lightly on her shoulders. Then the man turned, and his quiet words came clearly.

"So we meet again!" said the soft-voiced Mr. Barlow. "And I'm glad indeed it's granted."

Penny had deftly taken his horse and now he moved quietly forward, cloaked and hatted so that there was no more to be seen of him than a blur in the night. But out of the darkness his hand came, cordial and ungloved, and John took it willingly.

"I'm glad also," he said. "And I know Penny is. She's been asking for you."

"The need's past," said Penny coolly. "My clock's mended now."

"Good!" Mr. Barlow's soft laugh was understanding. "Be thankful that Mr. Leyburne came safe to mend it for you. But is your father within? And your aunt?"

"To be sure."

"Then you'll keep my horse—as always?"

"As always."

Without another word she turned and was walking the horse across the paddock, along the hedge, and to the stables that lay beyond. She merged into the shadows, and Mr. Barlow laughed softly.

"A difficult child! But she has a way with horses."

They moved together over the grass towards the gate in the hedge; and here Mr. Barlow paused.

"My visit is in part to you, Mr. Leyburne. Let me discharge some duties while I may." He was feeling beneath his cloak as he spoke. "I've been in the town these last days, and I've been in talk with Nevil Payne——"

"He's well, I trust?"

"Excellent well. But first, I'm to say he has sent letters-of-news to you, and bids you pay heed to the affair in Scotland. He grows sure we have not heard the end of it."

"Yes?"

"And second, he sends you also a private letter, which is here. Again I'm your Mercury, you see."

The friendly tone and the memory roused by that phrase had their effect. John spoke warmly as he took the proffered sheet.

"My thanks for both—this time and last. You show me kindness indeed."

"Have you not earned it?"

They walked slowly up the scented garden, and Mr. Barlow had yet a word to say.

"I'm to bid you also, have a care of the Mansells, even if you be provoked. And especially of Roderick."

"Roderick? Yes . . ." John spoke grimly. "A pretty tale he's told to Penny. But tell me, sir, what does the fellow do in these parts?"

"I wish I knew—except make court to Penny. But his ways are his own. I saw him not a half hour back——"

"Tonight?"

"Tonight indeed—as I came here. Riding to the west, not far from Standish, and a servant or two with him. I had to press into a thicket to stay unseen."

"That's odd, no doubt. But I did not mean his ridings-out and comings-in. I meant, rather, what is it that brings him to Lancashire at all?"

"Yes?" Mr. Barlow halted in the shadow of the house. "But you'll have something in mind, by your tone."

"Yes . . ." John hesitated. "Truly then, I've heard it hinted that these Mansells are short of money, and——"

"And that he would therefore wed with Penny. Yes—I've heard that hinted also."

"And you believe it?"

"That's difficult." Mr. Barlow spoke with a dry precision. "It might involve us in disputation about the nature of belief. Let us say merely that it is not new in the world that a needy man should wed where money is."

"Exactly. Which is to say that you do believe it?"

"I've called it possible, no more. Yet if I might offer counsel——"

"Gladly."

"Yes . . ." Mr. Barlow seemed to be weighing his words. "In my one capacity I might commend you to the Epistle to the Romans—the last verses of the twelfth chapter."

"Oh?"

"And in more worldly vein, I would have you reflect on the death of Sir Edmund Godfrey—and the vengeances that followed." Mr. Barlow's voice was almost a whisper. "They are still hanging men in London."

"Do I not know it? But——"

"As much might follow on the death of Roderick Mansell, even if it were in a duel—if it could seem to have been forced upon him."

"Now truly, I have never said——"

"No man ever does." There was calm authority in Mr. Barlow's voice. "But your thoughts have been straying on that road. And, expediency apart, at the end of that road there is a pit."

Behind them was the click of a latch and the creak of hinges, though not a candle burned; from the discreet darkness Penny's voice came softly.

"Come you in now. All's prepared."

"Aye, we come." But Mr. Barlow as he went had a whispered word. "Not in that way—ever—at peril of your soul."

It was the voice of authority. There was finality in it, and utter certainty, and John stopped unhappily in the loom of the blackened door.

"Aye," he muttered. "It's no doubt so. But some way there must be. This fellow Mansell——"

"To be sure." Mr. Barlow's hand was softly on his arm. "He plans a knavery, and is therefore to be checked. And when you set yourself to what is lawful, you may expect that God will point the way."

"I hope you're right."

"You may be sure I am." The authority was back in the soft voice. "Perhaps He has already done it."

"Oh? And how?"

"Perhaps He has worked through Nevil Payne. Did I not bring you a letter?"

16 MR. PAYNE'S INQUIRY

It was midnight past and gone when Mr. Barlow at length took leave and passed through a darkened door to the horse that Penny held for him in the shadows of the garden. But John knew nothing of that, for he had been in bed a full hour by then; it was surely proper that he should withdraw and leave them to talk alone, and he had hoped that the merit of it would not be marred by its having run with his own wishes; for the truth was that he had been eager to read this letter from Mr. Payne. He had read it twice in bed, with his candle dangerously within the curtains; and now, with the curtains set wide, he was reading it again in the cool fresh light of morning.

My letter-of-news, which I'll suppose you've now had from the Boar's Head, will have apprised you of what's public. The Scottish affair may be of greater weight than is supposed, for it will suit Shaftesbury's interest too well for him to let alone. There is great coming and going between here and the Low Countries, and if you pass by the door of the Green Ribbon Club you may hear as many Dutch voices as English; nor is there any want of Scotchmen here, from which I'll guess that Argyle has a hand in what is stirring. All the Green Ribbons buzz to and fro like wasps when the honey's out; and it's odd that Roderick Mansell should be out of town just now.

This, I think, is your just concern. There will be a reason for his betaking himself to the rustic glades, and it imports to know what that reason is. Father Barlow, though discreet, yet plainly thinks that Mansell seeks a fortunate marriage there; and perhaps he does; all tales have it that he's pressed for money. But his true fortune lies with Shaftesbury, who has more to give than any rustic heiress. So I'll suppose there is some further cause, and if you could lay it open, you might both dispose of

Mansell and furnish a tale most hurtful to Shaftesbury and all his crew.

Now here's an oddity, if your wits can fit it into place. You'll remember I promised to inquire into Mrs. Waring, and why she should give her golden charms to one as ill supplied with gold as Mansell is. I found nothing to give a hint on it, and lately I turned to the women's gossip; and plainly the one who could best sieve that was Mrs. Cellier. You know she plies a midwife's trade, and among ladies of some quality, and is thus well placed to hear what's said in their parlours and lying-in rooms. She comes now to say the whisper runs in such places that if you would have lace of the finest Dutch, and at a price below what's honest, you should apply to Mrs. Waring. The lady, it seems, is well furnished with such stuff —for a purchaser recommended to her as discreet. Mrs. Cellier herself bought a parcel and has shown it to me. I am not expert in the prices and qualities of lace; but Mrs. Cellier, who is, has assured me that this could not have been sold at such a price if it had paid lawful dues to the Excise.

You'll see what's hinted? That Mrs. Waring mends her purse by selling smuggled lace is like enough; it sorts with all that's known of her. But from whom does she have the lace? If we could answer that it's from Mansell, he'd be in flight to Holland the next day. And it has perhaps its probabilities. If he can furnish such lace and she can sell it, they serve each other's need; which might perhaps account for the giving of her favours there. Certainly he's spent more money than he's supposed to have; and certainly, also, he's in touch with Holland—as are all these Whigs. Is he perhaps a slyer dog than we'd supposed? Is it for touch with Holland that he serves milord and flaunts the Green Ribbon?

As I say, it's tempting; but I do not see that it explains his visitings in Lancashire. Had it been Essex, I'd have believed it better. That fronts on Holland, and it's made for such a work, with marshes by the sea where what you will might hide. But Lancashire?

Yet I tell you hopefully, for the question what he does there is still to be answered. You may perhaps come across some hint that might be a pointer. Wherefore do I acquaint you of this.

Mrs. Cellier desires to be brought most kindly to your thoughts. Gadbury, who is as mad as ever, desires also to be commended to you. He says that Mars in your natal figure is now progressed into the Bull, whence it opposes some conjunction in the Scorpion, Venus, however, holding a trine. What this may mean I know not, but Gadbury seemed to speak as though it were in some sort auspicious. That it may indeed be auspicious shall be the prayer of

Nevil Payne

Beyond a doubt it was interesting. The first reading by the flickering candle had roused interest enough; and now, in the cool light of morning, John found that his thoughts of it were clear. That Mansell was smuggling lace for Mrs. Waring certainly fitted the probabilities, as Mr. Payne had said; and Mr. Payne had not heard Will Hoghton telling quietly of Mansell's going night after night for the geese on the Martin Mere—going at dusk, with the winter dark to follow; and this mere was vast and desolate, set about by marsh—surely a place, as Mr. Payne had put it, where what you will might hide. John was out of bed and half into his clothes before the other thought came leaping, of Mr. Barlow pressed into a thicket while Mansell went riding west; and to the west, surely, lay this mere by the sea—and there were no geese in summer.

John came to breakfast with his thoughts aglow. Certainly it was tempting; certainly it was to be looked into. Just as certainly it was not to be blurted out at the breakfast table; but, with a decent discretion, something might surely be learned about this Martin Mere.

It was Penny who showed him the way of it. She suddenly declared that she had been ill-mannered to Will Hoghton the other day and must therefore seek him to render due apology. She came out with it defiantly, and her father's leave to visit the Park Hall was given with so little surprise that John came to suspect that Mr. Barlow had been talking to him.

They rode without delay, and it was no more than noon when they came to the lake by the dreaming trees, with Will Hoghton out on the gravel to give them friendly welcome. He was wholly unchanged, as calm and placid as before, and he greeted them as though no heated word had ever passed. His father, he said, was worse than before with the gout; and as for Father Barlow, he was safe returned and safe abed.

"Abed?" John was not yet used to the nocturnal ways of priests.

"But what else?" Will seemed a little surprised. "He'll have been to a half dozen houses in the night, and an office to say at each. No wonder he sleeps."

The easy hospitality was as unchanged as Will himself. There were the cakes and ale, the chairs under the trees, and Will's quiet friendliness to lead them into talk. Nor had Penny forgotten why she had come. She flung her hat aside to let the sun come dappling on her; then she produced the most charming of smiles and made her apologies in a voice of honey. Will received them placidly, and all was harmony. John stared thoughtfully at his ale mug and decided that his moment had come; he addressed himself lightly to Will.

"Did Father Barlow tell you he had some escape last night—near Standish?"

"No?" There was concern in Will's voice, and Penny was showing a plain interest.

"It's nothing, no doubt. He said he had to press into a thicket as some men went past—riding west."

"Oh, I see." Will's smile was almost of relief. "They'd be from an alehouse, at that hour."

"Would they? But the first of them was Roderick Mansell."

"What!" His hearers spoke together, and John was at pains to stay placid.

"Or so Father Barlow said. And I'll suppose he'd know."

"But . . ." Penny's curiosity, which never slept too deeply, was certainly awake now. "What was Roddy doing there?"

"Riding west."

"I know. But why?"

"That's what I'm asking. What lies west from Standish?"

"Ormskirk."

"And what's at Ormskirk?"

"Nothing—these days."

"Then where did he go?"

"That's what I'll ask him—on Saturday."

"No you won't, Penny." He had expected this, and he had the answer ready. "It might set him to ask who saw him. And if he should guess aright there might be a snare set soon for Father Barlow."

"Oh! I——"

"Exactly." Will cut in suddenly and firmly. "You'll hold your tongue on that, Penny."

Slowly Penny nodded. Evidently she had seen the point, and John was satisfied. He turned to Will again.

"This Martin Mere you were speaking of—it's west from Ormskirk, isn't it?"

"The mere? It's west and north. But——"

"You said he had some taste for shooting there?"

"Why, yes—in winter. But I told you you don't get geese in summer."

"Then where did he go? And why?"

John sipped his ale placidly and with the air of leaving this to the experts. They were looking at each other blankly.

"There's duck," said Penny doubtfully. "There are always mallard on the mere."

Will shook his head.

"You don't shoot mallard in August. Why should you? They're too young."

Penny sat silenced, and John decided she must be teased a little further.

"Then it must have been Ormskirk," he said easily.

"Why Ormskirk?" She sounded almost testy. "It's dead and empty these days. Why should any man ride there at night?"

"He might have an assignation, I suppose."

"Oh?" Penny received that coldly. "And with whom might he have an assignation?"

"With any you please. There's Mrs. Waring——"

"Who?" Penny had jerked upright. "Now who the devil is Mrs. Waring?"

"A friend of his—though I've not heard that she's in Ormskirk."

John sat back as though he had lost interest in this chatter. Will Hoghton looked at him steadily, and his eyes had an understanding gleam.

"Does the lady shoot duck?" he asked slowly.

"I think it most unlikely."

"Then why suppose——"

"I don't. I suppose only that if a man has an assignation with one lady in London, he may have an assignation with another in Ormskirk. I've heard such tales."

"Ah!" Will nodded sagely and then seemed to wait for Penny; and Penny snorted at him.

"Will! I want the truth of this—and you'll please to find it for me."

"But how?"

"How you please." She glared at him fiercely. "If you can't, I'll ask Uncle Ned. Between you, you've ears stretched for every whisper in this county—and you need not deny that."

"Why should I? We need to know what stirs, if *he's* to be kept safe." He turned calmly to John. "That's another secret out."

"What is?"

"That it's a duty among our folk—of our faith, I mean—to keep eye and ear alert, and to pass a word at need. So something might be learned here."

"Yes?" John was speaking gravely now. "And it's perhaps of importance. You could discover where he was?"

"Hardly so much, perhaps. But . . ." Will paused to consider. "If he was in Ormskirk—how many horses, did you say?"

"Two or three."

"Then they may have been heard. It's a quiet town o' nights. And there's Tom Greenhalgh who keeps the Rose there——"

"Good! And of the mere?"

"I think we may at least learn if he was shooting there. It was a night of no wind, and the mere must have been quiet as a grave. Any shooting would ring for miles."

"I'll hope you're right. You'll remember that I have not yet seen this mere. I'd like to."

"You would?" Will glanced quickly at the sundial over the great door. "If you want no more than to *see* it—what of that, Penny?"

"Aye." She nodded absently. "He must have been shooting there."

"To be sure. But I was speaking of our seeing it today."

"Oh!" She shook herself into attention. "You mean from Parbold?"

"Of course." He turned to John in explanation. "It's a hill with a prospect, and from it you may see the mere. Now what do you say?"

"Say?" John rose quickly to his feet. "I say horses, and at once."

They were away within minutes, Penny riding happily between the two men. Will led them to the south, but soon he was edging away, more and more, until they were heading almost to the west; and now the ground was rising and the horses' fine canter became a trot, and the trot a patient walk, and it was Penny who insisted on stopping to water them where a tiny stream went rippling across the track. Almost an hour had gone before they found the top of the rise, and when they came to it John sat, staring in surprise.

It was no gentle slope like the one they had climbed, for in front the ground fell steeply and to an almost level plain; north and south it stretched, flat and level, till it merged into the distant haze; and to the west the haze was lit by a shimmer of distant silver that might have been the sea. Beneath them, seeming almost at their feet, a river curled by the hill and went winding and twisting to the north; and to the northwest, lying between this river and the sea, was a vast sheet of water, sleek and shining in the sun. It filled a half of the plain, and John knew at once what it must be.

"This is Parbold Hill," said Penny suddenly. "And that's the mere."

She waved her hand at the great water, and John's interest grew. He studied it intently, and at once he was aware that it was no smooth unbroken water; black patches in it were surely islands, and a vague darkness round the rim suggested a marshy shore; here and there, faint dots might have been trees growing in the water.

"I'd not supposed it was so big," he said slowly.

"Big it is, and shallow." Will Hoghton was taking up the tale. "And it's not at its biggest now."

"Why?"

"Because the summer's been dry. You see the river?"

"Below here?"

"Yes. It's the Douglas. It joins the Ribble up to the north there, beyond Rufford. And it's near Rufford that the mere drains into the Douglas."

"I see."

John was reminding himself that his true concern was a smuggling of lace, and he did not see what this mere had to do with that. He lifted his gaze to the silver streak that shimmered in the distant haze.

"That will be the sea, I suppose. How far might it be from here?"

"Oh . . ." Will paused to consider. "A dozen miles in all."

If lace were coming in at all it must surely be from the sea, and John nodded absently as he considered it; he must find a reason soon for looking more closely at this sea and the shore that bounded it. But meantime . . .

He tore his thoughts from that and gave attention to the view again.

The great plain was not desolate. Wisps of smoke and a glint of sun on whitened walls told of habitations here and there; mostly they were hamlets, but in the centre there was a place of decent size.

"That's Ormskirk," said Will suddenly. "And down there in the trees, halfway to Ormskirk, is Lathom House."

"Lathom?"

"Where the earls of Derby lived, until it was battered in the rebellion-time. When the siege was done the house was not for men to live in, and that's why the Earl lives elsewhere now."

John nodded, and then Penny thrust herself suddenly into the talk.

"And that's why there's nothing now in Ormskirk. It used to live on those who had affairs at Lathom, but there's nothing of that now, nor of Ormskirk either. It's no place for any—assignation, as you call it. It's a forgotten place."

"Very suitable, perhaps—for an assignation."

"I don't like your talk, John." She tossed her head back petulantly. "You've an odd and pressing interest in this Mrs.—what do you call her?"

"Mrs. Waring."

"I'd forgotten. She's nothing to me. I'm only telling you that Roddy wasn't in Ormskirk last night. He couldn't have been. He was shooting duck on the mere."

John nodded and turned gravely to Will.

"You'll remember to ask who heard that shooting?"

"I will. But now . . ." Will looked thoughtfully at the sun. "I'm an hour from home, and you're a deal further. Penny, what do you say?"

"I say we'd best be off. There's nothing of interest here."

She was almost haughty as she wheeled her horse and went trotting down the eastward slope, leaving the men to follow or not as they chose; and thereafter she led them a pretty chase. She took one look over her shoulder and then shook her horse to a canter that soon became a hand-gallop. She and her horse knew each other, and they were of matching spirit; and when the men at last came up with her by the gates of the Park Hall it was with the rueful belief that they might not have done so if she had not intended them to. She was grinning broadly when they at last ranged alongside, and her grin persisted as she said friendly farewell to Will.

But later, as she and John trotted demurely home, a brooding silence seemed to grip her. It lasted until they were well across the post road and were making into the hills. Then, suddenly and almost defiantly, a question came from her.

"This Mrs. Waring," she said indignantly. "What's the woman like?"

17 SUMMER HEAT

That Penny's curiosity should be stirred about Mansell's doings was precisely what John had intended when he mentioned Mrs. Waring's name. But he had not supposed that more than that would follow; and what actually did follow so startled him that he came to wonder whether there might not be just such a Fate in things as Father Barlow had seemed to foretell.

For on the following afternoon Roderick Mansell came to Langley House again, riding gaily and cheerfully to keep his tryst with Penny, who was pledged to ride with him to Thornclough to see the new-built stables; and this time John did not stand aside. He said blithely that he would certainly ride with them. Penny looked pleased; Mansell caught Penny's eye and did his best to look pleased; and the three of them were away together, with a gay clatter of hooves and a swirling trail of dust.

Certainly Mansell was at his best. He had learned something of polish in the town, and now he gave a fine performance; he kept a cheerful small talk going as they rode, and he was not so crude as to keep John from a share in it. He was gay and witty; he had some scraps of French to give a flavour of the Court; he turned some sly compliments for Penny; and when she asked him darkly how he spent his evenings in the town, he laughed and answered that he spent them as the mode was, at talk in the coffeehouses or at wine with other gentlemen. Nor was he disconcerted when she asked him bluntly whether it was only gentlemen he sat at wine with; he even turned it to advantage by retorting fervently that there was not a flower in dusty London to compare with an unplucked rose in Lancashire. His bold eyes made his meaning plain, and Penny did not look displeased.

They were at Thornclough before more could be said, and there was the dry-stone wall, the tall sycamores, the iron gates and the brightly painted lodge. But that, it seemed, was not their way; for Mansell led them up the dusty road till it turned sharply round the end of the park; and here was another gate, simple and of wood. It was not a thing to take the eye, but Mansell drew rein with a fine air of hospitality.

"In here," he said briefly as he dismounted and swung the gate for Penny. She walked her horse into the park; John followed her sedately, and then Mansell came trotting quickly past him to Penny's side. He led them up a grassy slope, and there below them, nestling by a fringe of trees, were the new-built stables, squat and sturdy in stone.

"There!" Mansell waved broadly. "Complete at last—and much needed. We may put a score of horses there."

"You may indeed," said Penny expertly. "But why so many? You've not the need of them. And you've stables by the house too— for a dozen horses and more."

"Yes. But they spoil the prospect there." Mansell was quite calm about it. "You'll note that these are by the trees, and, by them, screened from the house."

They were; they were very fully screened, for the belt of trees was thick, and nothing showed of the house beyond. John looked attentively; these stables were screened from more than the house, for they were so far down the slope that the ridge hid them from the road. It was very discreet; and the thought came surging that here was something odd. It was not only the expense incurred in building stables surely bigger than even Thornclough needed. The placing of these stables was an oddity in itself; for was it usual to build stables a half mile from the house and not a hundred yards from the road? But if these stables were for a purpose not disclosed, then did that purpose sort with Mr. Payne's suspicion? Seemingly it did not, for lace would not burden many horses, nor call for any spacious loft for storage.

John came out of his thoughts. He took a glance at the others and saw them deep in talk by the gate; and deliberately he walked his horse down the slope. He was almost disappointed; for stables they plainly were, complete, but not yet in use. Mansell had even spoken the truth about numbers, for there were ten stalls to a side; yet John's suspicions stayed alert; there was an air of purpose about these stables, and that purpose was not obvious; and it did not fit with tales of a straitened purse.

He made the circuit of the deserted building, and then it occurred to him that he might do well to see where Penny had got to. But she was not hard to find, and as soon as John was on the ridge again he saw her and Mansell by the gate, sitting their horses in the road; they were still engrossed in each other, and Mansell, hat in hand, was leaning forward and seemed to be speaking earnestly. John's head went back sharply and his forehead puckered; it seemed high time to intrude on this, and his face was purposeful as he walked his horse quietly down the slope. He came to the gate and then a hearty laugh set his head jerking up again. Apparently Mansell had made some jest, and now he was bowing from his saddle with a gay wave of his hat; and Penny, vivid in the sunlight, was tossing her head archly, her face alive with laughter.

It was at this moment that interruption came, and John had excuse for being startled. Like the others, he had been too intent to pay heed to anything else, or he must have heard the clop of horses' hooves and the sharp clatter of wheels on the sun-baked road. The sounds burst upon him suddenly; and then, before he or the others had moved, the horses were round the bend—a pair of fast-trotting greys, yoked to a chariot he had seen before.

For an instant there was confusion and alarm. The chariot was almost on top of Penny and Mansell, and there was a wild slither of hooves, with the coachman almost on his back as he hauled at the reins. Penny swung her horse deftly, and at once Mansell was at her side, one arm round her as though he would protect her from any harm. The chariot lurched to a halt, shuddering on its fine steel springs, its crimson panels grey with dust. Mansell took one startled look at it, and then in an instant he was off his horse, had run to the chariot, and had wrenched open the door. He was bowing as he held it open; and out of the chariot, cool and elegant, came the fashionable Mrs. Waring.

She was elegant indeed, but she did not fit the scene. She was in deep cream taffeta, with the lightest of travelling cloaks in her favoured crimson, with the deep glint of gold in its cords and clasp; and in her own setting it might have been admirable. But here was the grey stone wall, the spreading trees, and the white snake of road; and it was not the setting for Mrs. Waring. But that did not disturb her poise. She came lazily from the chariot, as assured as when she had stood in a coffeehouse one April night, and there was cool displeasure in her face as she looked from Mansell to Penny and then back to Mansell.

"Unlooked-for pleasure!" said Mansell gallantly. "Felicity newborn!"

"Who is Felicity?" asked Mrs. Waring calmly.

"Madam!" Mansell was plainly out of countenance. "My meaning, surely——"

"Oh, that?" She cut him short, and had a contemptuous glance at Penny. "I had supposed that perhaps—— It's a name with a rustic ring."

The slight shrug of her shoulders said the rest, and Mansell whipped round with an anxious glance at Penny; and he had some cause for anxiety. She was sitting her horse stiffly, poised and erect, with her head lifted and her lips pressed tight. But she made no answer; and into the silence came Mrs. Waring's trilling laugh.

"Who is your rustic Venus, Roderick?"

Mansell gasped. Then, red-faced and unhappy, he did his best to mend it. He bowed formally to Penny, and then to Mrs. Waring.

"Permit me, ma'am, to present Miss Penelope Langley, of Langley—the Queen of Hearts hereby."

"Is she?" Mrs. Waring took one cool look at Penny and then turned to Mansell again. "The worst of these country girls, Roderick, is that, once turned twenty, they fatten at the hips. She has traces of it now."

Mansell stood speechless, and, under the trees by the gate, John stirred slightly in his saddle. He had made no move so far. Mansell was finely embroiled, and John could see no reason to raise a diversion for him; it was better to stay forgotten under the shading trees. But that last from Mrs. Waring set him stirring to look at Penny. She had shown already more forbearance than he thought she had, and something might now be expected. That, and in that tone, meant open war.

He had not long to wait. Penny's head moved slightly. She spoke to Mansell and wholly ignored Mrs. Waring.

"You did say 'of Langley,' did you not?"

"Of course. But——"

"And it's *I* that am to be presented to *her*?"

The flush faded from his face, and for a moment he was almost pale as he saw his dilemma. For, as Mrs. Waring was at least ten years the elder and a married woman, it was proper that she should receive, and that Penny should be presented—it being supposed that they were of equal status. And Penny was quite plainly asserting that they were not.

"Penny!" There was desperation in his voice. "Penny, I——"

"You have the wrong notion of it." Penny cut him short, and coolly looked Mrs. Waring up and down from head to foot. "It will be easier, Roddy, to have no talk of presentation. Just name the woman. That will suffice."

A faint hiss of indrawn breath came from Mrs. Waring. It checked almost as it began, and then she was a shade more erect than before. Slowly, almost lazily, she turned her shapely head as though to see what this interruption was. Her long eyelashes dropped contemptuously, and her nose seemed to lift in scorn. Languidly she turned to Mansell, and her voice had become a drawl.

"Ah! Native here, no doubt?"

It was admirably done, and in the sleek elegance of her London salon it might have succeeded. But here she had not that fine setting; she was in the hot sun of a country road, and, which was worse, she was on foot. Penny, still mounted, was looking down on her, and was not to be dominated. She waited for Mansell to answer, and then, when no answer came, she spoke crisply.

"I still don't know her name, Roddy. By the looks of her, I'd guess it to be Abigail."

It was John's turn to gasp. For since Abigail was generic for ladies' maids, and especially for those of the less reputable sort, this could properly be called the bludgeon rather than the rapier. And it had plainly hurt; Mrs. Waring's lip was quivering, and there was a flush of red in her carefully pallored cheeks. Mansell pushed himself hurriedly in front of her.

"Penny! If you please! You have no right——"

His voice quavered and died as Penny looked him fairly in the eye. Plainly she was unrepentant, and for the first time she turned her eyes directly on Mrs. Waring.

"I could think of another word," she said calmly; and her tone left no doubt of what that other word was.

"God in heaven!"

It came viciously as Mrs. Waring's temper snapped. She came forward in a leap, thrusting Mansell aside with her shoulder, and for a moment it seemed as though there would be combat. Mansell was after her on the instant, and in the shade by the gate John swung hurriedly from his saddle. Yet it was neither of them that saved it; for interruption came, quick and startling, as an unknown voice broke in.

"Och, no! Ye'll please not to do so, ma'am."

It came from the door of the chariot, a strong vibrant voice redolent of Scotland, and it had immediate effect. It gave pause to them all, and set them to turn and stare at the chariot and at the odd face that had appeared at its open door. For odd this face certainly was, and one not to be forgotten easily. Here was a sharp and thin-jawed man, quick and alert, with piercing deep-set eyes and a great sharp Roman nose. He had a big brown periwig pulled low above his eyes, its ringlets clustering thickly over cheeks and forehead—and surely with intent. For one glance showed that the skin of his face had some contagion; it was of an angry blotchy red, almost as though a fire were glowing in it, and the clear white of his teeth showed vividly against the red.

He thrust head and shoulders through the door of the chariot, and his head shook in disapproval.

"Och, no!" he said again. "Colonel, ye'll not permit it? Ye'll forbid it straitly?"

But Colonel Mansell was past forbidding anything. He stood gaping, his mouth open and his voice gone. The man in the chariot thrust his head and shoulders still further forward, and the rest of his lean body seemed to tumble after them as he stepped into the road, his keen eyes blinking in the light. He came forward a pace or two in a stooping shuffling walk, and then he halted; and John, standing quietly by Penny's stirrup, noted for the first time that the man had the bands and black of a divine.

Mrs. Waring was the first to recover. She had, after all, been travelling with this man, and might be supposed to understand the matter better than the others. She slipped forward now, with her temper controlled and her face impassive.

"Colonel Mansell." Her tone was smooth and easy. "Permit me— the Reverend Mr. Roberts."

It was formal, perhaps too formal; and John, alert and watchful at Penny's side, seized on that at once; for this man had just addressed Mansell with a deal less formality, and not at all as though he were a stranger. But Mansell seemed to find no oddity in it. He was bowing at once, the short easy salute that a gentleman might give to a divine, and he was murmuring politely that the honour was entirely his.

"Mr. Roberts is my cousin," said Mrs. Waring calmly. "I regret it if we surprise you, Roderick, but I'd some affairs to ask your advice of, and Mr. Roberts most kindly made my escort."

"I'm in his debt," said Mansell gallantly. "Count me your friend, Mr. Roberts. Whoever serves your cousin, serves me."

It was promptly said, and properly, but it had a ring of unreality. It put John in mind of some scene from a play; and at his side Penny snorted.

"Cousin be damned!" she said suddenly, and leaned down to John. "She wants to marry Roddy, and she's brought the Levite with her."

"Lassie! Lassie!" Mr. Roberts was shaking a reproving head at her. "You've no call to be making that assertion. For the one thing, it's false. For the other, it's malicious. It's the imputing of scandalous conduct to this good lady."

"Which good lady?"

Penny's voice was challenging, but the Scot was not disconcerted. He looked her in the eye and spoke simply.

"I mean my good friend Mrs. Waring."

"*Who?*"

Penny's question crackled, and her quick glance at John was a hint that she had heard the name before. Then, after one frosty stare at the lady, she turned again to Mansell.

"Perhaps," she said steadily, "I may now be enlightened, Roddy?"

"I've been trying this last half hour to enlighten you." He sounded exasperated. "The simple truth is that here is Elizabeth Waring, who is not only my good friend in the town, but also my partner in certain ventures of profit. That's not odd, is it? It will be of those ventures that she's here to speak with me. And Mr. Roberts, as you've heard, has given her his escort. That's not odd either. And is there any reason against her receiving some courtesy, now she's in this county?"

"Is there any reason against her showing some?"

Mansell gave it up. Red-faced and tight-lipped, he stood in silence, his eyes steadily on Penny. Slowly, and in the same silence, he turned to Mrs. Waring, as though in hope of help. Her response was immediate.

"We waste our time here, Roderick," she said firmly. "It's hot and it's dusty, and it's altogether rustic. Also I've matters of importance for your ear. I did not drive the length of England without some cause. So perhaps you'd best escort us."

She turned as though it were agreed, and Mr. Roberts had manners enough to hold the door of the chariot as she entered. He climbed in after her with a lithe agility that set the delicate vehicle swaying and bouncing on its springs. The coachman gathered up his reins, and a little bell tinkled sharply. The lively greys jumped forward, and the dust shot up behind the slender wheels as Mansell found his stirrup.

"Roddy!" Penny was sitting stiffly again, and her voice came icily as he swung into his saddle. "I'm here to see those stables, and you've not yet shown them to me."

"No . . ." He checked as he turned his horse. "You'll perceive a difficulty. I did not contrive it, and on Monday I'll be wholly at your service. But just now—forgive me!"

The dust spurted as he gave his horse the spur. John's abandoned horse reared in quick alarm, and he had to catch and soothe it. When next he looked he saw the chariot a furlong down the road and already turning through the elegant gates that led to Thornclough. Mansell was alongside it, close by Mrs. Waring's door.

Penny had never moved. She was sitting rigid, her face set and hard, but as John mounted she slowly walked her horse close to his.

"So!" she said steadily. "He knows which voice to answer. A fly-blown ladies' maid!"

It was perhaps unjust, and it was certainly untrue. There was a deal more to Mrs. Waring than that, as John well knew; but he had wit enough to make no answer, and suddenly Penny spoke again, and sharply.

"You spoke of her the other day, John. Do you, also, know her in the town?"

"No." His answer came promptly, and then he chose his words with care. "I've seen her in the town, and I know *of* her in the town. But I do not know her. I've not in my life exchanged one word with her— nor desired to."

"Good!" Her voice was grim, and again she was looking down the thin ribbon of the road to where the dust still smoked and swirled by the gates of Thornclough. Slowly she turned her head and looked John in the eye.

"You were hinting at an assignation the other day. And I didn't believe you—then."

18 MR. GADBURY'S PREDICTION

The morrow being Sunday, and attendance at church being a duty that few could evade and not many wished to evade, it seemed to John that here were some possibilities of trouble. For if Sir Henry Mansell should choose to exchange some words with Mr. Langley after service, as he had commonly done of late, and if Mrs. Waring should be in his party, as might well be expected, then, with Penny in her present humour, it seemed plain that anything might happen. It was not a prospect that commended itself to John. He had no objection to Penny's quarrelling with Mrs. Waring in private, but a public uproar in the churchyard was another matter; it verged on scandal, and perhaps on irreverence, and it ought to be avoided if possible. It gave him an anxious evening, and, as the event showed, without cause. The Reverend Mr. Roberts attended service next morning, as was proper in a divine, but there was no sign of Mrs. Waring, nor of Roderick Mansell; and Mr. Roberts, when presented by Sir Henry, had no more to offer than some decorous comments on the sermon. So all was peace, and John rode home at Penny's side with a growing belief that this was working out most happily.

When they were home that seemed even more probable. For there was a letter waiting, brought that morning by a groom from Thornclough. Penny pounced on it, broke the seal with an angry rip, and pored over it angrily; apparently it gave her no pleasure, for suddenly she crumpled the sheets and flung them to the floor.

"From Roddy," she said briefly.

"Yes? What?"

"What you'd guess." Her foot ground the crumpled sheets against the floor. "Presents his apologies and says he can't show me his stables tomorrow after all. Did he think I wanted him to?"

"I don't know. But why can't he?"

"Says he's for London tomorrow. Urgent affairs. Fortune at stake—and God knows what!"

"Ye-es . . ." He spoke warily. "And how do you see it, Penny?"

"See it?" Her angry eyes showed how she saw it. "She's away back tomorrow and he's riding with her—or riding in her love cart with her. That's how I see it."

"Ye-es." He was still wary. "Perhaps you're right."

"Of course I'm right. Who pays for the blasted thing? They'll put the Levite in the boot, I suppose."

"It hasn't got a boot. And why the Levite?"

"Judges, 17:10. I've asked who pays for it."

"That?" He eyed her thoughtfully, considering whether some hint might not be dropped here. The tale of the smuggled lace was still high in his thoughts—and Penny would not be a less active ally if her curiosity were stirred a little.

"That?" he repeated slowly. "It's a nice point. I've heard it said that he pays for it himself."

"Meaning that she's what she looks?"

"I haven't asserted it." He was picking his way carefully. "Myself, I see a difficulty in believing it."

"I don't. What difficulty?"

"Has he money enough? Do the Mansells clink their guineas freely?"

Her face sobered suddenly as the sense of that went home.

"No." She spoke slowly. "They don't. They're at shifts for half a guinea."

"Then she's not what you've supposed."

"Yes, she is. She doesn't gull me, if she does you. I'm not a man."

Penny's snort seemed to dispose of the wits of men, and John watched her coolly.

"Then how does he pay?" he asked blandly. "You'd hardly call her cheap."

"Cheap! She's——"

"Exactly. But how does he pay?"

She stared at him blankly; and at that he left it, thinking that he had perhaps said enough for the moment. Penny might ponder it by herself, and the exercise would do nothing to damp her curiosity. John went off to write an overdue letter to Mr. Payne.

He took it next morning to the Boar's Head, and Penny rode with him in a humour that well pleased him. She was cool and amiable, as though to show him the reverse of her feelings to Mansell, and she was full of curiosity about whatever might touch the matter she had most in mind. He told her he had a letter to despatch to Mr. Payne, and at once she was asking who Mr. Payne might be; and she pressed it so warmly that she had to be diverted with some talk of Mr. Payne's being the trusted counsellor of Father Barlow. It lasted till they were at the Boar's Head, and at once John was busy with the landlord, arranging that his letter should be put in the postboy's bag this week. And what of last week's bag? Had it held anything for Mr. Leyburne?

It had. The landlord produced a letter, and John stared at it in surprise. For this was not in Mr. Payne's incisive hand; this was a round and scrawling script, generous in its curves, untidy in its details, and certainly a script that John had not seen before. Quickly he broke the seals, peered at the foot of the sheet, and saw it to be signed "John Gadbury." His eyebrows must have lifted in surprise, and Penny's interest promptly overflowed.

"What's that?" she demanded bluntly. "It seems to set you in a flutter."

"Hardly so much. But it's unexpected."

"It seems to be. You looked like a tickled trout."

She was sitting cheerfully on the low bench that ran by the open windows, and suddenly her grin was evident as she buried her face in a pewter mug of ale. He drained his own as he watched her, and then he decided that more might be done this day.

"It may keep," he said lightly, and slipped the letter into his pocket. "Will it please you to ride to the Park Hall?"

"It will. But why?"

"I'm curious about this Mrs. Waring."

"Oh?" Penny's chin had tilted suddenly. "But what's that to the Park Hall?"

"You were something urgent the other day that Will Hoghton should catch some whispers."

"Of Roddy on the mere, you mean——shooting?"

"Or perhaps at Ormskirk. Will may have learned something now."

"Perhaps. But what's it to do with the trollop?"

"Penny!"

"Yes she is. But she wasn't on the mere. She wasn't even here then."

"No. But there's an oddity in this."

"I don't see it."

"I know you don't. But you haven't seen Nevil Payne's letter."

"His letter-of-news?"

"No. A private one. Father Barlow brought it."

"The devil he did!" She was on her feet at that. "You never told me."

"Because it was a private letter. But as things now are——"

"Yes?"

"I think you should know of it—and Will also."

"So do I. And what was it?"

"I said Will also. That's why we go to the Park Hall." He looked her coolly in the eye. "You'll wait till then."

Penny said nothing. She banged her empty mug down on the bench and went briskly out, and she was calling for the horses as John followed her.

Will Hoghton, quiet and friendly as before, gave them the same greeting and led them again to the turf under the trees. His father, he said, was abed now with the gout, and was inclined to blame the lake.

"He's perhaps right," he added. "Though myself I'd regret it if we lost the lake. But how may I serve you?"

They told him and he answered them at once.

"Something I've learned," he said, "though perhaps not all you'd wish. First, there was no shooting heard from the mere that night. And you'll remember it was a still night. If there had been shooting it *would* have been heard."

"Yes." John nodded thoughtfully. "And what of Ormskirk?"

"I do not think he was in Ormskirk that night. It chanced that there was a child sick there and a woman astir, and if there had been horses she'd have heard them."

"Then where was Mansell?"

"The devil knows. But I've done my best."

"I'm sure you have." Penny cut suddenly into the talk. "And it's a good best too, Will. But John's got a letter—from Mr. Payne, and he's to tell us of it."

"A letter-of-news?"

"No." John spoke firmly. "It was a private letter. But some of it may touch this affair."

As quickly as Penny's interventions would let him, he told Will of the coming of Mrs. Waring and of the encounter by the roadside; and then he brought out Mr. Payne's letter and read it to them. They listened intently, Will Hoghton in a grave and attentive silence, and Penny with a brightening eye and some gasps of excitement. She waited for nothing as he ended.

"That's it!" she burst out. "That's why she's come."

"What is?"

"That is. She's sold all the lace and spent all the money, and now she's come for more."

"More lace? Or more money?"

"Both. I thought she was in a hurry."

"Ye-es." John eyed her almost with amusement. "Why did she bring Mr. Roberts?"

"Because she's a woman. She could not well journey without an escort. She'd set every inn and every postboy talking if she did. And that's why she dressed him as a parson. A most seemly escort!"

"And why must Roderick Mansell return to London with her?"

"Because she's fondled him and pawed him and dripped on his neck. That's why."

John had sense enough not to argue. He gave a nod that might have been assent and then he turned to Will Hoghton.

"You're silent on this, Will. May we know your thoughts?"

"On this tale of smuggling?" Will roused himself and then spoke steadily. "I agree with Mr. Payne. It's tempting, but it's not probable. Here's not the place for it. Essex, yes. Lancashire, no."

"Ye-es. Though he does speak of the Essex marshes. And you, I think, spoke of marshes by this Martin Mere."

"And elsewhere, if it comes to that. But you were speaking, surely, of lace coming in from the sea. You don't sail ships into a marsh."

"No. But a marsh could give a reason for riding to the coast on a winter night."

"The devil!" Will sat up suddenly. "You mean—to shoot geese?"

"What else? And I don't doubt he does shoot geese."

"I know he does," said Penny quietly. "I've seen the geese he's shot."

"Have you now?" Will turned to her quickly. "At Thornclough, you mean? And how were they brought back?"

"On a pack-horse."

"Oh!" Will's soft whistle was eloquent. "Dead geese loaded, and under the geese—lace? Is that it, John?"

"Or something like it. But Will—what manner of coast is it beyond the mere?"

"Flat and sandy."

"Sandy, is it?" John paused to consider. "Not good then for a ship standing in with cargo?" .

"Not good at all. As unpromising a coast as might be, I'd say. A ship would need to lie off a quarter of a mile at least. Even the fishing ketches do that, and the jolly boat lands the fish."

"You ease my mind." John spoke crisply, and Will looked at him in surprise.

"How?"

"I'm not a sailor. But I'd guess that where you can land fish you may also land lace. It's no heavier than fish, and it's less bulk."

"I think you could," said Will slowly. "And I've heard those ketches called weatherly craft."

They looked at one another in silence, and then Will spoke decisively.

"It's possible. And, that being so, it's probable. Now what next?"

"Make it more than probable. We must show that it's indeed being done. And all we know so far is that it won't be done this week."

"Why not?"

"We may suppose Mansell commands it. And he's for London this day. His letter to Penny told us that."

"*And* who he's with," said Penny darkly. "They'll be in the love cart together and———"

"Is that sure?" Will's voice came sharply. "Have they truly gone to London? Or do they merely wish it to be supposed so? But I think you may leave that to me."

"How?"

"As before. We've our ears stretched for whispers, as I think Penny put it. Give me a day and a night, and I'll tell you whether Mansell's left or not."

"Good! Now is there more?"

"Hardly—till then. I think we're in debt to Mr. Payne for his letter. You'll write to him of these doings here?"

"I've done so. Penny and I are just from despatching it at the Boar's Head."

"Well said! You did not find there a letter-of-news? One could be due."

"No. But . . ." John's hand was suddenly in his pocket. "But there *was* a letter, and I'd forgot it till this moment. It's from Gadbury."

"Who?" Penny spoke quickly, and plainly curiosity had her by the ear again. "Who's Gadbury?"

"He's an astrologer."

"Oh, John!" She was gurgling with amusement. "But what does he write of?"

John looked inquiringly at Will. Will promptly nodded, and John unfolded the letter and read aloud the big and sprawling script. Mr. Gadbury was not the tidiest of writers.

I lately desired of Nevil Payne that he should add to a letter he was then writing to you certain warnings deriving from that figure of your nativity cast by me at Mrs. Cellier's. I expounded the matter to Mr. Payne and had his assurance that it should be in his letter. But this forenoon, chancing to espy him in the Grecian, I was put much out of humour by learning that what he had written was not what I had desired him to write and that he had allowed you to suppose that the late progression of Mars into Taurus in your figure is to be accounted auspicious.

Mercury in yours being held by the Goat, I do not doubt that you will readily perceive that Mars, being come to the house of the Bull, is there placed to oppose that conjunction in the Scorpion whereof I told you, Luna being there combust. Some strife and turbulence is therefore to be expected, and in these days some peril may run with that. To which it is to be added that Mars, being this instant month and year in temporal transit of that degree, the matter is present and urgent.

I add for your consolation that Mars, being natally within the Ram, holds the trine of milady Venus, within the Archer; which most fortunate circumstance must most powerfully soothe and mellow him. I do not doubt, therefore, that what is now presaged will not be beyond your power to surmount.

The Scorpion shall signify yourself in this; and being ever the sign of secret things, I make no doubt that what is presaged shall present itself as a secret, dark and deep, to be plumbed and laid bare. The Bull, you will note, is of Earth, and it is therefore to be supposed that your mystery will have to do with some rustic place; also, perhaps with water—the black smooth water wherein the Scorpion broods.

All being plain, I take my leave. Mrs. Cellier stays hale and ardent, though much given to entertaining that fellow Dangerfield—the Captain, as he must needs be styled. It's a foolishness she'll have cause to regret, as I weary myself by saying, but she'll not be warned. Nevil Payne is in health and heartiness, and speaks most kindly of you. That all may commend itself to you is the prayer and purpose of

John Gadbury

They came to the end of it, and Penny rolled over, shaking with laughter. Will Hoghton flopped back into his chair and stared blankly at John.

"Will you tell me," he said slowly, "what it means?"

"But why the livestock?" said Penny. "Bulls, goats, rams———"

"And scorpions. Just so!" John spoke soberly. "I know. It's odd. He's an odd fellow. But he told me once———"

"What?" It was Penny, curious as ever, and John was looking her in the eye as he answered.

"He said I'd find in affairs a girl of December birth, who should have some redness of the hair———"

"Oh?" She was sitting upright suddenly. "Did he indeed? And what more?"

"More? Will—*you* shall judge of this. He said she'd have some wild and wayward humours."

"That's true—true indeed!" Will was smiling as Penny tried to look indignant and succeeded in looking pleased. "But, John, I do not think you should laugh too much at Mr. Gadbury."

"I don't—since then."

"No." Will picked up the forgotten sheets and fingered them thoughtfully. "It's an odd letter, I'll grant, but what little I can grasp has a prick of truth. A secret matter in a rustic place? And water? Black smooth water. That's the picture of the mere in winter. There are grey skies then, and the reeds hang still, and the geese come low."

He was speaking softly, his face impassive and his grey eyes clear and steady. Penny sat erect, the laughter gone from her, and in silence she nodded. John spoke quietly.

"I can believe that. But I must see more of this mere—and of the coast that lies beyond it."

19

THE MARTIN MERE   He rode out with Penny the next morning, and her zeal matched her competence. She led briskly to the post road and across it, and then steadily up the long rise to Parbold Hill; and there below them were the wide flat plain, the winding river, and the shining, tree-dotted mere.

"How did you name that river?"

"The Douglas. And you're going to see it closer. Now down here—and with a care."

She slipped in front of him and led to the narrow track that curved dangerously down the face of the hill; and he was thoughtful as he let her have the lead. This was not quite the Penny he had known, and there was nothing wild or wayward in her now. She was easing her horse very safely and steadily down the loose grit and stones, her fingers sensitive to every lurch of the horse and her eyes watchful for every fault of the track. Her vivid hair was beginning to stray in the wind, and wisps of it were fluttering against the soft russets she was riding in this day. He thought it a charming untidiness, and he was smiling as he watched it; and at once his own horse slid and stumbled, with lurch and quick recovery and a shower of loose stones spilling down the track. Penny halted instantly, and she made sure that her horse was at ease before she turned in her saddle. Then she looked at him steadily.

"Were you watching the track, John? Or the mere?"

He looked at her ruefully.

"To speak the truth, I was watching you."

"Oh!" Her voice stayed cool. "That doesn't make safe riding here."

"Or elsewhere—as I've known these many weeks."

"Have you?"

It was still cool, but her eyes had narrowed. He met them steadily, and suddenly she had looked away and was intent on the spreading plain and the distant glint of the sea. Quietly he walked his horse down the track till he was almost at her side, and then she turned to look him in the eye again.

"You're not frightened of a fall?"

"Yes." He answered her after a pause. "I am. But it's a risk I must take. That's all."

"All?" She spoke slowly and as though she were weighing it. "Can it be all?"

"Why not?"

Her horse pawed at the track, and a stone went tinkling in the silence. Penny turned on the instant, wary and alert, and she leaned forward to pat the horse's neck; she seemed intent on that as she spoke again.

"When a man rides dangerously there may be others fall with him."

She stayed for no answer, and he sensed that at this moment she wanted none. He followed her in a thoughtful silence, and thereafter neither of them spoke until they were down to the plain, had crossed the low bridge, and were trotting easily by the bank of the little river. Ahead a patch of woodland took the sky, with some houses nestling close, and Penny explained that it was Rufford.

"That's where we join the mere," she said. "From there we can turn west and skirt the mere."

He could already see the sheen of it, little more than a mile away, and the scattered trees that rose from it were plainly in his view. Penny kept steadily along the river track, and little by little it converged on the mere; he followed where she led, and soon they were away from the river and riding warily on thin and sedgy turf. There was no track now; the spongy turf was soft under the hooves, and the black soil oozed from it as the horses trod. A fringe of trees hid the mere for a mile and more, and then, as the trees ended, Penny led towards the water; and as they came to it John knew that he was indeed at the mere at last.

The spongy ground was flat, so flat that it was hard to tell where the water's edge was. It had, indeed, no edge; it was rather that as they approached it the ground became blacker and softer and wetter; there were pools here and there, and the pools became larger and closer; and then there was water, black and cool, rippling in the northwest wind. Yet there was no view of distance; the water was rippling in a forest of reeds, with tall bulrushes bending and swaying above them. Between the stems the black water was green with duckweed and eelgrass, and speckled with the yellow flowers of bladderwort; and between the pools were mare's-tails, green and sturdy, and little flowers in pink and white, which Penny said were bog beans. And above were white clouds and blue sky and a dazzling radiant light.

"It grows thickly," was John's comment at last.

"It does. One day there'll be a man with wit enough to drain this mere. There'll be good ploughland when that's done. There's a heart in this black mud. But, John——"

"Yes?"

"Listen."

He flung back his head and put all his mind to hearing. For a moment he thought she had heard something, and then he knew she had not; it was silence, not sound, she was calling his attention to. There were the sigh of the wind in the reeds and the soft lap and ripple of the water; and that was all. There was nothing of sight or sound to tell of time or man. The quiet seemed eternal, and suddenly the loneliness of the place was upon him. Nothing stirred on the mere; it was desolate, timeless, and forgotten.

He turned slowly to Penny.

"Mr. Payne said it well. It's a place for silent things. I've not known such quiet. Is there not a bird on the mere?"

She nodded.

"There's coot and merehen—if you startle them. And, of course, the duck." She pointed to a place beyond the reeds. "They'll be in open water now, idling through the day."

She turned her horse and walked from the water till the ground was firmer, and neither of them spoke as she led him steadily on; the mere, he discovered, did not encourage talk.

Under the hooves the ground was rising, gently and steadily. Soon his eyes were clear of the reeds and rushes and he could see beyond them; and there in his sight was the whole vast sheen of the mere, dazzling in the sun, stretching away till he could see no certain end to it; low reedy islands dotted it, and here and there were trees, some on the islands and some stark from the water.

"This is the Mere Brow," said Penny suddenly. She drew rein in the shade of wind-bent willows and sat shielding her eyes as she looked at the shining water. "It's the only brow there is, and there's no other view across the mere. Do you see the duck? Don't look under the sun. Look to the side there—those dots."

He shielded his eyes as she had done, and then he saw them, floating and lazing on the shining water.

"Mallard," said Penny briefly. "Or mostly."

He nodded.

"And what next?"

"North Meols."

"North what?"

"North Meols. It's the parish we're in, and there's a church by the sea and some houses."

They were on a slope again now, dropping from the low rise of the brow, and soon they had turned the corner of the mere and were riding down its seaward flank; but always they were edging to the coast, and suddenly they were in a sodden marsh, with pools and rivulets and mud that squelched and stuck.

"It's a river here, in winter," said Penny. "It's where the mere drains to the sea."

They splashed across the narrow channel and came to what was almost a bridle track.

"Water Lane," said Penny briefly. "And we're finished with the mere."

In another minute he saw her meaning, for as they took the faintest of rises the ground began to change beneath them. It began to slide rather than stick, and there were streaks of gold in the black.

"Sand," said Penny. "And here's the sea."

They were on thin turf now, a narrow belt of it, and beyond it was sand, dry and undulating; and beyond that was more sand, smooth and gold and wet, and then the seething white of the breaking surf. It stretched far out, dazzling in the sunlight, to give proof that this was a shallow shore; and beyond it was the heave and shimmer of open water.

They let the horses pick their way through the shifting sand, where needle-pointed marram grass shivered in the boisterous wind; then the long dead seaweed crackled under the horses' hooves, and they came to the clean sand of the beach, damp and ribbed and firm. At the water's edge they halted, and John looked about him curiously. The sunlight on the creaming surf had a power that made him shield his eyes as he peered; and under the shore, a bare quarter mile from the surf, a half dozen ketches rode at moorings. At once his eyes found Penny's.

"It's a fishing village," she told him quietly.

"You mean North—North Meols, was it?"

"Yes. And Birkdale too."

"What's that?"

"A hamlet—in the hawes yonder."

"Please." He saw her laughing at his puzzled face. "Please to remember I'm not of this county. What might hawes be?"

"Those are—those hills of sand."

She was pointing to the south, down the long flat acres of sea-washed sand; and now he saw that at its landward edge it rose into great wind-piled hills, steep and curving, thickly beset with the straggling marram grass.

"That's the hawes," she said again. "And Birkdale lies behind it—a half score cottages—and they *all* fish there."

"I see." He gave attention to the anchorage again. "And those are fishing boats?"

"What else?"

"It's what I ask." He turned to face her. "Are they fishing boats? Or could one, perhaps, be from further parts?"

"Meaning from Holland?" Her eyes turned to the sea again as she studied the dark hulls of the ketches. "I don't know. They're the sort I've seen before. But . . ."

A shrug of her slim shoulders completed that, and then she waited in silence for him.

"It could perhaps be discovered," he said thoughtfully. "And this—this Birkdale is yonder in the hawes, you say? What's beyond it? More hamlets?"

"There's Ainsdale—but that's set back from the sea. It's on the ploughland by the moss." She smiled at him as she forestalled his question. "A moss, in this county, being what you'd call a marsh—or any soft ground."

"Thanks!" He looked thoughtfully around the deserted beach. "Sand and sea. And hawes and wind. That's all. As Will said, not a promising spot. Nevertheless——"

"What?"

"What I said before. If you can land fish you can land lace. We'll see more of this beach if you please."

"Shall we?" Penny was looking doubtful. "You see where the sun's travelled to? And we *did* promise to call on Will. . . ."

"Yes." He let his eyes leave the summer sparkle of sea and sand, and then he was smiling as he saw Penny, grave and composed, waiting silently for him to speak; and quickly the thought came that Penny had been most oddly grave and composed throughout this day.

"Yes," he repeated. "It must be close on four. But you're grave this day, Penny?"

"This is your day," was her swift answer. "And it's mine to help, not to take the day."

"No?" He was speaking as gravely as she had done. "But perhaps it's yours to make the day—for me."

He saw the quick catch of her breath, but she made no spoken answer. She was to seaward of him, and she had edged almost into the surf, so that the first white foam of it was sizzling by her horse's feet. He made no move to follow, but sat very still, content to see her poised against the blue sky and the green and white of the tumbling water. For a moment she stayed, still and erect, intent on the horizon, while the sea-wind found her hair and set her white plumes trembling; then slowly she turned her horse so that her back was to the sea, and deliberately she looked him in the eye.

"It's a day shared, John. It could not be made for you alone."

"Penny!"

Her horse was walking now, coming towards him from the surf, and quickly he swung to meet her; his ungloved hand found hers, and for a moment her fingers were warm in his. Then, as she moved slowly past him, he leaned across and lightly kissed her cheek.

A quick pressure of her fingers answered him, but she spoke no word and she did not look round; instead she slipped her fingers out of his, and then her horse's walk became a gentle trot as she made steadily towards the tumble of grass and sand she had called the hawes.

"As I was saying . . ." she said cheerfully as he came up with her.

"Oh?" His voice expressed his sudden doubt. "And what were you saying?"

"That it was time, perhaps, for us to leave this shore."

"Yes." He caught her steady glance and decided to be satisfied. "I think perhaps it is. And indeed . . ."

He was looking at their shadows, leaping and jogging before them as the hot sun found their shoulders, and Penny nodded her approval.

"It really *is* late," she said. "And I wanted time for the Park Hall. Will might have a word for us tonight, and I want to hear it."

"Of Mansell, you mean? And his departing for London?"

"What else?" She sounded almost grim. "And Will said he'd stretch an ear——"

"Then let's hope he's done so."

He had. They came to the Park Hall when the shadows were long and a flame of gold was spreading in the western sky, and Will was decisive about it. He carried them indoors at once.

"It's no hour for the lake," he told them. "I like your face as it is, Penny."

"Oh?" Penny's head had reared, and the old familiar tone was back in her voice. "Meaning what of my face, if you please?"

"That it will not be bettered by being lumpy. The midges are out by the lake. Besides, you can eat better by a table."

They needed no persuading after such a day; and, as they quickly found, there was more to Will's hospitality than that. For he took them to a discreet and private parlour that was overlooked from nowhere, and here, plain and most unclerical in russet breeches and a leather jerkin, was the soft-voiced Mr. Barlow; his cloak and riding boots lay ready, and the cold meats and pastries on the table suggested that he had newly supped and was ready now, after his day of sleep, for the darkening countryside where the duties of his office lay. But of these he made no mention, and he seemed to be in no hurry; his eyes lighted at the sight of Penny, and for John he had a handshake of obvious warmth.

"I've yet an hour," he said cheerfully. "It's scarcely dark enough yet—for me."

He waved them to the table, and while Will propped himself against the hearth it was Mr. Barlow who plied the guests with beef and ham and ale.

"It's to be observed of these three," he said smilingly as he was carving for them, "that each brings a savour from the other two. Which I take to be proof that the Creator knew His business excellently. Is it to your liking, my Penelope?"

But there was no more than a grunt in answer to that. Penny had her mouth full, and Mr. Barlow was smiling as he went to the end of the table and seated himself comfortably.

"I hear you've been to the sea," he said genially. "And what's to tell?"

"Little."

John answered briefly and then looked inquiringly at Will; and from the hearth Will nodded.

"Father Barlow knows of our talk the other day," he said quietly. "Of the lace, I mean. And he knows what you went to look for on that shore."

"Good! But I can't say that we found it. You could land lace on that shore just as you could land fish, but I do not see what that mere has to do with it. It's desolation, and nothing more."

"Just that." Will nodded his agreement. "Though its geese give excuse for a man to ride that way. But . . ."

Will's voice died away, as though he would pass this talk; and, at the head of the table, Mr. Barlow seemed to accept it. For a moment his smile seemed to flicker, and then he was looking gravely at John. Across the table, Penny put down her knife and sat, expectant.

"I took it upon me the other night," he said, "to foretell that a way might be opened for you. And it seems that the letter I brought did indeed open a little of it. But now there is more, and to some it would seem a chance. But *I* shall say that here is design—a working out of things. You'll know where Ormskirk is?"

"I think so. You see it from Parbold Hill—between the hill and the sea?"

"Just so. Now mark . . ." Mr. Barlow leaned forward in his chair. "There's an inn at Ormskirk, the Rose—which is to say the Red Rose. It was a good house once, when the earls of Derby were at Lathom, and always it had guests of quality. But that's gone now, since the Derbys went. And also there's another, the Rising Sun, built opposite —a new and shining place, all glass and varnish. So the Rose is withered these days, and almost it's become an alehouse only. But Tom Greenhalgh, who keeps it, is of the true sort——"

"One of your faith, you mean?"

"I do. Now here's the seeming chance which I shall call design. There was a kitchen woman taken sick at the Rose, and it seemed proper that I should go to her. Which, last night, I did." Mr. Barlow smiled shyly. "But she was somewhat mended, and I had not the work to do that I had feared, and I had therefore a moment for a word with Tom Greenhalgh. And—with no question put by me—Tom Greenhalgh had a tale to tell."

Mr. Barlow had a darting glance at Penny, who had suddenly come erect; and then his grave eyes were on John again.

"What he had to say was this. On Sunday night last—or, more truly, Monday morning, it being then past midnight—he was waked by sound of horses opposite and a soft knocking at doors."

"Opposite?"

"At the Rising Sun, I mean. One George Rimmer has the Sun, and Greenhalgh loves him not. Also, he had heard such sounds before. So this night he rolled from his bed and went peering through his window. There were three men there with horses, and, while he looked, the door of the Sun was opened and they were let in."

"Yes?" John spoke softly, and Penny sat in tense silence; she had even forgotten to eat.

"They were not there for long. He thought, indeed, that they did no more than call for a traveller's cup——"

"Something urgent, surely, if they woke the inn at that hour?"

"He thinks they did not wake it. The knocking was very soft, and the door was opened very quickly."

"They were expected, you mean? And the traveller's cup prepared?"

"It could be. And perhaps they needed it."

"Why?"

"Perhaps they had been on the shore."

"Ah!" It was a quiet sigh from Penny, and for a moment her eyes found John's. "You'll see cause to think that, Uncle Ned?"

"It's a guess, no doubt." Mr. Barlow was as steady and unhurried as before. "But Greenhalgh had an interest. He admits it. For he'd seen such doings at the Sun before—in the winter nights, he says."

"Oh?" It was John's turn to interrupt. "As if men were for shooting geese, would it be?"

"It might be. But Greenhalgh says that when these men came forth from the Rising Sun there were three of them—one who seemed to lead and two who had the look of servants. And as they rode away there were four horses for the three riders."

"What's that? A pack-horse, do you mean?"

"No. A saddle horse—saddled, but with no rider."

There was a sigh and an ease of breath in the silent room. Penny, bright-eyed and attentive, spoke first.

"And what shall it mean?" she asked.

"Mean?" Mr. Barlow seemed to be musing. "But the moon was

falling, and it was time for me to be away. So I could not hear more of it from Tom Greenhalgh. And indeed, my Penny, I think that can be your work, yours and Mr. Leyburne's. But for what it means, our Will has made a guess."

"Has he?" Penny twisted quickly in her chair. "And what guess, Will?"

"Guess is the just word." Will's voice came slowly and deliberately. "But these three riders came from—where?"

"The shore, it's hinted."

"Yes. And you'll note that the man Roberts, who came with Mrs. Waring——"

"The Levite?"

"If you call him so. He was at the church on Sunday, you say—and he's not been seen since."

In a thoughtful silence they exchanged glances. Then Penny spoke decisively.

"He's taken ship," she said firmly. "That's what's hinted, I suppose?"

"Hinted is nicely said. But it could be so."

"It certainly could." Penny almost snorted over it. "Now how do we learn more?"

"That?" Mr. Barlow took the talk again, and now he sounded almost whimsical. "I think, my Penny, that you should fall into talk with the Widow Jump."

"What! She couldn't be called *that*."

"Oh yes, she could. And Jump she is—Margaret Jump, relict of Robert Jump of Birkdale."

"Birkdale?" John spoke sharply. "That hamlet by the sea—where they fish?"

"Just so. The last cottage in the hamlet."

"Oh, ho!" He looked meaningly at Penny. "When do we ride?"

"Tomorrow." Her answer was prompt and vigorous. "But Uncle Ned, will this Jump know of these affairs?"

"She might. She's a widow, and widows are commonly well informed. But . . ." Mr. Barlow suddenly ceased to be whimsical. "But please to note that folk of our faith have a duty to see and listen—but not to talk. Not to talk, that is, to strangers."

"As we are. Yes?" Penny's voice was grave again. "Then how——"

"By a signal given. When you are come into talk with the Jump, or with Tom Greenhalgh, be pleased to loosen the top two buttons of your waistcoats—both of you. That is all."

"Thus?"

Penny came to her feet in her mannish riding habit and suited action to word. Mr. Barlow nodded gravely.

"Precisely. And thus you loosen tongues as well as buttons."

"And that's a secret, Penny."

Will had spoken sharply from the hearth, and Penny gave assent at once.

"It's quite safe, Will."

"I know—or you'd not have been told. But I hope you learn something. You might. This widow is well placed to note that shore. And also she has a son, one Jimmy, who goes shrimping."

"I'll buy his shrimps. Aunt Arabella can pot the brutes. Do you know what shrimps are, John?"

"I don't. And——"

"Peace, both of you!" Will waved a protesting hand. "There's more to talk of than shrimps. Listen. . . ."

His tone called for attention, and at once he had it. Penny's grin withered and was gone. John sat alert and waiting.

"It was Sunday night, you'll remember—or Monday morning— when these riders were in Ormskirk. Later on Monday, about an hour short of noon, that chariot—the black-and-crimson one—drove out from Thornclough. Mrs. What's-her-name——"

"Waring?"

"Yes. She was in it, with bags loaded as though for a journey. Roderick Mansell, with valise and servant, rode by it, seemingly as escort."

"Yes?" John had seen Penny's grimace and was answering for her. "So they *have* gone to London?"

"No, they haven't."

"What?"

"They've gone, certainly, but not to London." Will's voice came slowly. "The chariot made away from Thornclough, and then it turned —north."

"North?"

"North, I said—as though for Scotland. Now can your wits cut that?"

20

THE INN AT ORMSKIRK   From the top of Parbold Hill John stared thoughtfully down at the shining mere, the straggling plain, and the low huddle of houses that was Ormskirk.

"Do we ride through Ormskirk?" he asked.

"We do." Penny, sitting soberly at his side, was answering with a clear precision. "We keep south of the mere today. It's the quickest way to the shore. But why?"

He followed her warily down the stony track, and in silence they came safely to the bottom. He let her pass in front of him over the narrow low-walled pack-horse bridge, and they were trotting again before he answered her.

"Because," he said slowly, "I'm minded to drink a cup of ale at this loyal inn."

"The Rose?"

"I did not mean the Rising Sun." He looked at her steadily, and saw her brown face rising and falling to the trot of her horse. "Do you know who the Rising Sun is, by the way?"

"Who? Did you say *who?*"

"I did." He saw her eyes grow keen as they met his. "I've heard men of a certain sort say it in the town—and they've been speaking of the Prince of Orange."

"The devil!" said Penny, and relapsed into silence. Evidently she had seen the point.

The horses went clattering on the cobbles as they entered the little town. And there in the market place was the Rising Sun, fine and new and shining, as Will had said; and there, facing it from the southern side, was the lesser inn, old and worn, twisted and leaning in timbered black-and-white. It was quiet and faded, its door deserted, its black beams dulled, its plaster none so white. But its quiet was gracious; it had a dignity that had stayed from its better days; and above its door, glinting redly in the sun, was the formal circlet that was the Rose of Lancaster. They dismounted and evidently they had roused interest, for a lad came running to take their horses, and hard behind him came a man who must surely be Tom Greenhalgh. He came quietly and without haste, a man turned sixty, white-haired and none too firm of foot; but he carried himself with dignity, and his laced cravat and buckled shoes gave consequence to his well-cut russets. He bowed politely and asked how he might serve the gentleman.

"A cup of ale, if you please—two cups."

John was at pains to speak lightly, and his smiling glance over his shoulder showed whom the second cup was for. The landlord looked, and at once there was something more than professional suavity in his face as he glanced through the open door and saw what its lintel framed; the sun was vivid in the market place, and Penny's hair was aglow and her silver lace agleam as she stood between the horses and spoke earnestly to the lad who was waiting. Evidently he was being told exactly what the horses were to have, and the landlord beamed approval.

"It's few ladies that ride to my door in these days, sir," he said. "And it's fewer still take thought for their horses—or even know how to."

"She knows," said John briefly.

The horses clopped on the cobbles as they were led away, and Penny came marching sturdily to the door, a smile breaking on her face as she came. That, also, was not lost on the landlord, and he bowed his welcome. Penny acknowledged it graciously.

"We've been hearing of you, and of your house," she told him coolly. "Mr. William Hoghton spoke of you—as did another, also."

If more had been needed to assure them a welcome, that supplied it; and at once they were led to a discreet and cosy room that looked to the lawns and flowers of the garden. The latticed window was wide to the summer wind, and the room was a sparkle of smooth-waxed oak and gleaming brass as the landlord came with the crystal cups of ale. John took his thankfully, lifted it, and turned to seek Penny's eye. But Penny was not heeding. Her alecup was forgotten in her hand, and her thoughts were far away. She was standing stiffly in mid-floor, and, with her head thrown back, she was staring at the wall above the fine stone hearth. A portrait, done in oils, was hanging there, lighting the blackened oak with the deep gold of its frame; and below it, left and right on the smooth-dressed stone, were flowers, fresh and fragrant in their vases. The landlord had turned too, and behind Penny he was standing rigid. But John paid no heed to that; his eyes were on the portrait that hung there in such dignity and honour.

It was of a man in the best years of life, fine-faced and strong, plainly a nobleman and a soldier. His beaver was gallantly aslant, and his cloak was open to show a breastplate of gleaming steel. The blue sash of the Garter lay across the steel, and from his collar his George was pendent. One hand lay lightly on his sword, and the other held a commission with dangling seals. But it was the head, thus set in splendour, that caught and held the eye. It was a head worthy of the splendour, a fine and massive head, poised and alert, with wide level brow, a strong jutting nose, and a hint of humour in the firm-lipped mouth; the eyebrows were thick and long, and even in the canvas there was a gleam of authority in the brooding deep-set eyes.

A boot creaked in the silent room as John stirred suddenly.

"A head of quality," he said slowly.

"Aye, sir." The landlord turned. "Of quality indeed! And they took it off."

"Off?" John stiffened again as a memory came rushing. Quietly he stepped forward to peer at a strip of gold that shone beneath the portrait. It had lettering short and simple. *The Most Honourable James, Seventh Earl of Derby. Nat. 1607 Ob. 1651.*

"Aye—off," came the whispered words behind him. "In the market place at Bolton."

"Ah!" John spun round, memory clear and questions surging. He knew, as all England knew, of this Earl of Derby who had died by the axe at Bolton; he had served his King till his King was dead; he had served the young King until a day at Worcester, and then he had plucked that King from the rout and had led him in safety to Boscabel; and thence he had ridden north alone—to capture, and the death a king had died. But how had his portrait come to this dying inn, and why should it have such splendour?

Penny had turned in silence, and now she met John's eye; and at once she had caught his thought and was answering it.

"We're hard by Lathom—here," she said quietly.

"Aye—Lathom," said the landlord, and almost to himself. "Lathom that was."

Penny nodded.

"You knew him—of course?"

"I knew him."

"And you rode to the wars with him?"

"To the Rebellion." He corrected her gently. "I did. I was his body servant then."

"I would that all good gentlemen had been so truly served."

Penny moved from below the portrait and settled herself by the window on the sunlit bench that ran beneath it. It was as though she were now leaving this to John, and he put his shoulders comfortably against the oaken walls as he sipped his ale.

"This house opposite," he said easily, "this Rising Sun—who has it?"

"George Rimmer," came the prompt answer, and Tom Greenhalgh's voice had hardened perceptibly.

"Aye, Rimmer it is." John sipped his ale again. "Did this Rimmer ride also to the Rebellion?"

"To the Rebellion is justly said, sir. So indeed he rode."

"Ah!" John nodded. "You perhaps met with him as you rode?"

"I did." Again the answer was prompt. "He was there that day in the Wigan Lane when they beat us from the town."

"When?" Penny spoke suddenly from her window seat. "That day Sir Thomas Tyldesley was slain?"

"Aye, ma'am. That day." Tom Greenhalgh's voice was firm and steady now. "They lined the lane with their musketeers, hidden in the hedges, and they shot us down as we came. Sir Thomas was wounded and unhorsed, and they shot him by the hedge." Again the man's eyes turned to face the canvas. "And *he* was most valiant that day. He'd seven shots in his breastplate, and cuts in his beaver, too. But we got him to the Dog in the market place, and thence by night away."

"That was well done." John spoke soothingly. "But of this Rimmer?"

"Aye, he was there." The old voice was in open anger now. "He was of those who shot from behind the hedges. A sergeant, sir—in Lilburne's musketeers."

"A sergeant, was he? And now has the Rising Sun—a well-named house, I'd say."

"Well indeed, sir! You know its meaning?"

"I do. But he's guests in the night, I'm told—riders who come from nowhere, and have no very honest look."

"Has he so?" Tom Greenhalgh stiffened, and then looked warily from one to the other as though he would know more of them. "Has he so?" he repeated doubtfully.

Penny came quickly to her feet, with the sunlight flooding on her riding clothes. In silence she put a hand to her waistcoat, and deliberately she loosed two buttons. In the same cool silence John did the same, and then he looked squarely at Tom Greenhalgh.

"We've cause to know of this," he said quietly.

"Aye, sir?" The man spoke firmly, his voice steady and his face clear. Evidently he had no doubt now. "What is it that you would know of?"

"These riders who came in the night—the morning of Monday, was it not?"

"Aye, sir, in the dark hour—before the dawn." The man hesitated. "I was waked by sound of horses, and, making a guess what it might be, I went to my window. But by that time they roused the Sun. There was an ostler leading in the horses—the men being all dismounted. And while I looked they were let in also."

"Yes." John nodded thoughtfully. "And four horses when they left?"

"Four it was, sir. First a man who rode alone, as if he were the gentleman—a big man, sir, thick in his cloak and his hat pulled low. Then two who followed, and their hats were smaller and their cloaks shorter, as would befit servants. And one of these led a horse, saddled."

"And they rode which way?"

"Eastward, up the market place there."

"Just so." John paused to consider. "And whence did they come in this dark hour? Oblige me by guessing."

Tom Greenhalgh was not unwilling; but he took his time at it before he spoke slowly.

"I've seen such men before, sir—and led, as I think, by the man who led this time. There was something in the loom of him and the way he has with a horse."

"Yes?"

"It's been in the winter nights, sir, and always at the first of the moon. And always it's been the same—two men from Standish way, two by the Scarisbrick road, and three who would come alone, by this road or that. And always they'd meet at the Sun, and always they'd be expected."

"How's that known?"

"No knocking, sir, and no waiting. The first fall of a foot, and there'd be a door open and an ostler with a lantern."

"And then?"

"Why, sir, they'd stay perhaps a quarter hour, and then away all together, to the west—the Scarisbrick road."

"Being also the road for the Martin Mere?"

"It is, sir."

"Thank you. And then?"

"Why, sir, nothing—for the space of hours. And then horses again from the west, and again the door unbolted, and the ostler's lantern lit."

"And they'd stay how long?"

"A half hour perhaps. Time enough for spiced ale and to bait horses. And then away again, to the east."

"All of them?"

"No, sir. Four men only, as though the three who rode alone were now gone elsewhere. And there would be pack-horses now, with loads slung—long and narrow."

"Long?" John echoed it sharply. Then, with his mind still on that lonely shore, a ship standing in, and a jolly boat rocking in the surf, he put another question.

"But, Master Greenhalgh, we were speaking of Monday last gone and of the riders you then saw. They were the same men, you think?"

"Aye, sir, or at least he who seemed to lead them was."

"To be sure. Being of the two that in the winter have ridden in from Standish way?"

"No, sir, from the west—from Scarisbrick way."

"What's that?"

John's question was sharp with surprise. For if this leader, the big man thick in his cloak, were Mansell, then he should surely have come from Thornclough by the Standish road.

"He was of the two from the west, sir," said Tom Greenhalgh firmly. "It was the other two that came from the east."

"Thank you. That's to be remembered."

He stood in silence, asking himself if there was more he could inquire into, and a glance at Penny brought a faint nod. She came briskly to her feet, and her smile was charming as she spoke crisp thanks to Tom Greenhalgh.

"And I also," said John. "We're indebted, and you'll see us another day. Would you be pleased to call for our horses?"

Tom Greenhalgh was at Penny's stirrup when she mounted in the sunlight, and she waved smiling thanks; but she was thoughtful as they trotted out of the cobbled square, and as they walked their horses up the low rise to the church she spoke slowly.

"Two from Standish, and two from the west. Do you see who those were—from the west?"

"I don't. I've been puzzling it. But do you?"

"Yes. It was Roddy, and a servant with him."

"But why from the west? He'd be from the east—through Standish."

"No, he wouldn't. You're a townsman, John, and you've not shot geese."

"No. But——"

"Now listen——"

They had turned into a narrow curving lane by the churchyard wall, and Penny drew rein and for a moment sat in thought. Then she spoke her mind clearly.

"It's a matter of smuggling, is it not? That's work for darkness, so the helpers ride by night—two from Thornclough and three from hereabouts. And they meet at that inn, the Sun, yonder."

"Yes, but——"

"Listen. There's geese to be shot, to cover it all. But you can't shoot geese by night. You must do it at dusk, and then only."

"Why?"

"It's the way of geese. That's why. They spend the day by the mere, working the fringes of it, picking grass and seeds and grain, if there is any. They hide well and they're hard to come at. But at dusk they come together and then they all take flight."

"Whither?"

"Out to the sea—to the sandbanks. They spend the night there. So if you'd shoot them you must do it at dusk. Now do you see it?"

She peered at his puzzled face, and then spoke slowly as though she were explaining it to a child.

"Roddy must be at the mere by dusk. So he leaves home early, a servant with him and a pack-horse. And he does not show himself in Ormskirk. He takes the lonely tracks to the mere. He shoots his geese and he leaves them—and his pack-horse—somewhere by the mere. Then he rides back to this inn and meets his helpers, who've ridden in the dark."

"The devil!" He was beginning to see it now, and Penny nodded as she drove it home.

"They meet here. Then they ride west—to the shore. They get the lace, carry it to the mere, and put it in the pack-horse baskets. The dead geese go on top, and then all's done. It's three men to their homes and four for Ormskirk here. There's a halt at the inn to bait the horses and get hot ale, and then they're for home—by Standish. Is it so?"

"Yes." He was meeting her eyes steadily. "It's so. And on Sunday night——"

"They put the Levite to a ship, and then led his horse home."

"In the dark hour. Yes . . ." He considered it carefully. "Why put the Levite to a ship?"

"Why not?" Penny was grinning suddenly. "He's no beauty."

He was laughing at her as they walked their horses to the crest of the lane; but then, as they went down the curving hill below the church, Penny sobered suddenly. She looked across at John and spoke thoughtfully.

"What roused Tom Greenhalgh, do you think? At just that hour and moment?"

"A knocking at doors, he said."

"Which was very soft and did not rouse the Sun. But he did rouse and he got from his bed and he saw just what was needed. And then he must think to tell Uncle Ned, the one man who——"

"Who might know what it could mean. Just so. You're calling it a working out of things?"

"It's what *he* would call it." Penny fell silent, and then pursued her thought tenaciously. "And Tom Greenhalgh, of all men! Who was body servant to the Earl—and does not love such rebels as this Rimmer, who keeps the Rising Sun."

21 THE WIDOW JUMP   They came out of Ormskirk on a track of stones and sun-baked mud, and the dust went swirling from the steady trot of the horses as the way wound north and west to the coast. Penny had fallen silent, and John was glad enough to be silent too. He had some thoughts to disentangle, and the more he considered them the more did he think that some working out of things was needed here. For Mansell, it now seemed, was served in this affair by George Rimmer, who had the Rising Sun—George Rimmer, who had been a sergeant of musketeers and was perhaps of the same mind still, a man whom Mr. Payne would no doubt have called a Whig. And was it only by chance that he and Mansell, Whig and Whig, were joined in this? Smuggling, after all, was a capital offence; and did they risk their necks for no more than some guineas gained from lace? Or was some deeper purpose served by these forays in the dark?

"There's the mere——"

Penny's voice brought him abruptly from his thoughts; and now to their right the great mere was in view, smooth and glittering beyond its fringe of reeds and marsh. John roused himself and viewed it with interest.

"This being its southern end?" he asked.

"What else? That's Scarisbrick we've ridden by, and you may call it the end of places. It's marsh and sand now, and then the sea."

He nodded as he noticed the telltale softness of the ground.

"We keep close to the mere," he commented.

"We must. Look yonder . . ."

She was pointing broadly to the left, and at once he saw that there again was marsh. It was land, flat as any table, with straggling willow trees, and clumps of reed and rush to show where water lay; and beyond, in the middle distance, was the shine and gleam of water and the sturdy shape of a windmill.

"Halsall Moss," said Penny briefly. "And that's the Otter Pool by the mill there."

"Another mere?"

"Hardly so much—though it's a mile and more across. That place yonder is North Meols, which you saw before."

It was ahead of them and to the right, perhaps three miles away, and again he nodded as he recognized the outline of its church. And then he was looking ahead along the track, where also the low white lines of buildings were coming into view. Penny saw his glance.

"Birkdale," she explained. "And yonder by the pool, seaward of the mill—that's called Ainsdale."

It was under the sun, and he had to shade his eyes before he could make out the thin straggle of cottages that huddled beyond the mill. And suddenly the eerie desolation of this place was pressing upon him as it had done before. These poor hamlets, set far and lonely in this sodden plain, did nothing to break the spell; and it was the mere that cast the spell. It imposed itself, and all this land was no more than the fringe of it, dominated by it, a place not of men but of wind and reeds and geese; always and over all was the brooding silence of the mere.

The horses went steadily on, and once again the track was changing as the stickiness went out of it and the streaks of sand appeared; then there was thin sod on the sand; and at last there were hills of sand, steep and wind-blown, crowned and faced with the trembling marram grass. The thin turf ran between the hills, and the soft green of it was a riot of purslane and saltwort, of sea rocket and goosefoot.

"This is the hawes," said Penny. "There's a half mile at least of it."

He thought it more than a half mile, for the horses found it hard going; they lurched and slithered in the shifting sand, and no sort of track could be discerned at all.

"Tell me," he said, as they slithered down another slope, "how does one know what track to ride in this?"

"You don't," said Penny promptly. "You keep the sun on your left ear and hope for the best."

Apparently it sufficed, for they came to another crest, and suddenly there was the ribbed and level sand and the broad white line of the breaking surf. Penny drew rein and flung her head back, sniffing noisily at the clean cool scent of it.

"What now?" she demanded happily.

"The Widow Jump," he answered. "I think we'll seek her."

She nodded, and in an amiable silence they trotted a half mile southward, along the beach, and then plunged into the hawes again, along a trodden track which the folk of the hamlet no doubt used for their journeys to the shore. It brought them to a huddle of cottages, low and simple, with thatched roofs and limewashed walls that were flaring white in the noonday sun; nets were drying on a timber frame, and on the thin turf a man squatted on a stretched-out sail, busy with needle and canvas. Penny hailed him, and he answered in a broad accent that John scarcely understood; but Penny nodded and walked her horse down the trodden track past the cottages.

"It's the last one," she explained. "He says it's beyond the others."

It was a hundred yards beyond the others, and one look at it showed that someone took a pride in it. The thatch was trim, the lime-wash fresh; the windows twinkled, the door was bright and scrubbed; there was a patch of garden at the front, fenced with willow, and the path to the door was strewn with shells and set about with limewashed stones. Beyond the garden a two-wheeled cart was standing, its shafts cocked into the air and its timbers white with salt; a stable behind the cottage suggested a horse to draw the cart.

They dismounted, and Penny led briskly up the path, her boots crunching on the sliding shells. A latch rattled, and then the door swung open to disclose a woman who must surely be the Widow Jump. She was small and slim and thin of face, and she set John in mind of a thin and perky sparrow. But she had the sparrow's vigour too, and it showed in the sharp lines of her face and the keen brightness of her eyes. She stood staunchly on her threshold, poised and alert, and ready, as it seemed, to defend her home against all comers. John eyed her warily; the widow, he thought, was showing more suspicion than welcome; and while he was considering what to do, Penny slipped past him and did it.

She went about it briskly, and her way of it surprised him. She walked up the path with a grin on her face that took the widow's eye; then she halted and looked round at John; then she turned to the widow again, and her grin was broadening as she spoke.

"He's from London, and he doesn't know what shrimps are. So I want to give him some."

"He doesn't know?" The widow's voice was as sharp as her face. "Then I'll give him one, if that's all he wants."

It came defiantly, as though to assert that John and his needs were nothing to the Widow Jump. It could hardly be said that she was ingratiating, but Penny nodded cheerfully and then spoke as bluntly as the widow.

"He wants more than one. He wants a lot—and I want some too. So may we come in?"

"Aye—if you want to."

It was a matter of indifference to the widow; her tone proclaimed that clearly, but Penny was not disconcerted.

"We do," she said. "It's what we've come for."

She had a quick backward glance at John, and then she marched briskly in. He followed, and then he was in a gloom that at first seemed darkness after the white walls and the sunlit sand. The low room had a smooth hard floor of sand and lime, and the walls had the same smooth dressing; a shining table, with stools against it, took the centre, and at the side, under the one small window, a waxed and polished dresser held mugs and dishes of gleaming pewter. Behind the table, in the shaft of sun from the open door, was the hearth, and its fire was crackling in splashes of blue and yellow as the salt-caked driftwood flared and spluttered; over the fire was a copper pan, with steam blowing from it in curling wisps, and the salty tang of it brought all the fragrance of the seas into the little room. Penny was sniffing happily as she seated herself by the table and pulled her hat off; and as John followed her example he became aware that the Widow Jump had thawed.

She was busy at the dresser, pouring ale and cutting bread, but the glances she spared for Penny were almost friendly, and she looked almost pleased when Penny did not wait for the filled ale mugs to be brought to the table, but went instead to the dresser and took them from it. John watched attentively as Penny wandered again to the dresser, mug in hand, and carried the plate of sliced and buttered bread back to the table. The widow's glance was plainly approving, and coolly and deliberately Penny winked at her; and to John's intense surprise that seemed to conquer the widow completely. She was positively mellow as she came to the table and set before Penny a flat pewter dish that seemed to be filled with a yellow crust of butter, and then she hovered attentively, as though to be sure that her guests lacked nothing.

Penny flourished a spoon and dug it fiercely through the butter; and then she was spooning out what looked to John like pink and curling slugs, oddly bent into curves. She watched him quizzically as he took a cautious nibble, and then she had caught the widow's eye and they were both shaking with amusement as he tried another. Apparently they had come to an understanding, and suddenly Penny was praising the shrimps. The Widow Jump smiled happily.

"There's nowt about 'em except being fresh," she answered. "They're from this morning's ebb."

"Then there's someone to be thanked for that. Do you know what it means, John?"

But John had his mouth full. The brown barley bread and the strong cool ale seemed to blend perfectly with the odd salty tang of the curling things, and he was hungry enough to savour them all. And Penny banged a spoon on the table to get his attention.

"It means," she said firmly, "that you get shrimps at low water— when the tide is at ebb. You push a net through pools, and you bring them back in a horse and cart."

"A horse and cart? On the shore?"

"Yes." For a moment her eyes met his. "It's firm enough on that sand for horses—isn't it?"

She flung her head up to ask the widow's agreement, and John began to be interested.

"Aye, that's it—though I'm not saying there's not a bit more to it. But that's the way of it." The widow was hovering with the ale jug as she spoke. "It's my lad that gets 'em. He's away at Ormskirk at the market now."

"Is he? And out with the ebb to get them first? It's early rising."

"Aye—early enough. But there's nowt in that, when it's your trade."

"No? But if he has to follow the ebbs he must be on the banks at all hours?"

"Oh, aye. Any time o' day—and night too, if there's moon enough."

"Just so—day and night."

There was a faint hardening in Penny's tone, and across the table her eyes met John's; and suddenly understanding came to him. Penny had not been chattering idly, and she had done more than win the woman's good will; she had led this talk of shrimps to the exact opening that was needed.

"Ormskirk, do you say?" Penny was talking to the widow again. "Then he'll be back soon, no doubt?"

"Aye, soon enough now."

"Yes." Penny paused and seemed to be weighing her words. "You'll forgive so many questions, Mistress Jump?"

"Surely. But——"

"Because we've more to ask yet—and of another sort."

Penny's tone had changed; and deliberately, and for the second time that day, she loosed the top two buttons of her waistcoat. John turned, and with the same slow care he loosed the buttons of his own.

The widow stood staring, her face gone impassive while her eyes moved from one to the other. Then she seemed to relax.

"I was just at asking you how you'd come by my name," she said slowly.

Penny looked quickly at John, and then she seemed intent on smoothing her skirt; plainly it meant that she was now leaving this to him.

"Your name was told to me," he said quietly, "because I had need of it. My own name you may know. I am John Leyburne."

"Aye?" She had recovered from surprise and seemed to have accepted him. "But what is it you want of me?"

"There have been men in the winter nights, and perhaps again this week, who have come to this shore in a way I need to learn of. That's the core of it."

"Those?" Certainly she was showing no surprise. "Aye, we know 'em. But it's Jimmy you should rightly ask——"

"Your son?"

"That he is. And as the lady said, he's on the banks at all hours. That's his trade."

"I'm glad it is. He'll know more of this than any other?"

"Aye." She nodded; and then her face darkened. "Unless, maybe, it were Richard Rimmer."

Her shrewd eyes were very keen and steady, and he knew at once that this was not idle; she was telling him something, and he nodded easily.

"And who, if you please, may Richard Rimmer be?"

"He's of Ainsdale—down the beach yonder. He has the mill there."

"Ah!" He turned quickly to Penny. "Is that the mill——"

"Yes." She was bright-eyed and prompt. "We saw it as we rode. By the Otter Pool."

"I see. But of this Richard Rimmer—what's to be said of him, Mistress Jump?"

"He likely knows what you're asking."

Her tone said the rest, and John looked at her steadily.

"What manner of man is Richard Rimmer?"

"He's a damned rebel."

That was blunt enough, and her set face and steady eyes showed that she meant it. But John thought there might be more to probe.

"Meaning that he's a rebel at heart? Or was once a rebel in arms? Which?"

"He's the one and the other—both."

"So?" John's thoughts were of another Rimmer he had heard of this day, who had once been a sergeant of musketeers. "So this Rimmer rode to the Rebellion, did he?"

"And back—more's the pity."

"What was he?"

"A sergeant—in Ireton's regiment. And he's not forgot it."

The widow did not seem to like Richard Rimmer, and John eyed her critically. But the steadiness of her face reassured him; there was honesty here, and this tale would be rooted in more than malice. He nodded.

"And what does he do now?"

"He has the mill by the pool."

"Aye—by day. But it's of his nights that I'm here to learn. And there may be something hang on it."

"I'd be better pleased if there'd be some folk to hang on it."

The retort was prompt; and John, almost to his surprise, found himself approving. He was beginning to like the Widow Jump; there was a staunchness in the woman.

"That might follow," he said carefully. "But tell me——"

Then interruption came. There was sound of a horse from the track beyond the garden, and boots crunched in the loose shells.

"The lad's back," said the widow briefly. She moved nimbly round the table and darted through the open door. Penny followed with a quick interest, and when John came up with her she was standing in the doorway, looking to the garden where the widow was in rushing talk with a man; he had been leading a horse to the stable, and plainly he was Jimmy Jump. He was short like his mother, but there the likeness ended; he was a sturdy thickset fellow, perhaps in his early twenties, with a boyish grin, a mop of sandy hair, and wide shoulders that hinted at strength beyond the common. He gave proof of it while they watched, for suddenly he stretched his arms over the horse and had the saddle and two wide panniers off together in one unbroken movement. Then he led the horse to the stable, and Penny nodded with approval.

"I'll get ours baited too," she whispered, and John left her to it as she went quickly into the sunlight; in matter of horses Penny did not need help.

He moved quietly back to the table, and it was a full ten minutes before the others joined him; when they did, it was at once apparent that Penny had not been wasting her time.

"This," she said briefly, "is Jimmy Jump. Jimmy, this is Mr. Leyburne."

Jimmy had a pleased and happy grin, and it was plain that he approved of Penny. His greeting to John was a nice blend of politeness and independence, and when he had dealt sturdily with a great mug of ale he showed no reluctance to talk. He had evidently been told what the matter was, and he came to it in blunt and homely words.

"Aye," he said heartily, "there's been goings on on this beach the winter through—aye, and I mind summat of it the winter 'fore that."

He needed little prompting, and what he said did not lack meaning. He explained again that his shrimping must be done at the ebbs of the tides; and on days when the ebbs were at dusk and dawn he would make use of a moon, if there should be one, to light him home after dusk, or to the banks before the dawn. And sometimes, by the light of a swelling moon, he had seen horsemen on the sand and a lugger standing in.

"Swelling?" John queried the word sharply.

"When the moon's new," he was answered. "Not the full, and not the wane either. A glimmer o' light, d'ye see? But not too much."

"Yes." John nodded thoughtfully. This sounded likely enough. "But what's this of a lugger?"

"Aye, that . . ." Again Jimmy had a lucid tale to tell. From time to time he had sighted a lugger cruising offshore, or hove to if there had been a punch in the wind; and certainly it had been a lugger, a two-masted lugger with a running bowsprit, a pair of jibs, and broad lugsails to the fore and main. Jimmy described it in detail, and John heard with interest; he gave full attention as Jimmy went on with his tale.

Jimmy's sharp wits had soon connected this lugger with the horse-men who came by night, and always at the same season. It had been an easy guess that something was to be landed or perhaps taken off; but once, on a clear cold night in March, he had seen how the thing was done. And John was sitting tensely forward as Jimmy said his say.

It had been a day of cold northerly airs and pale winter sun, and the night had been clear and still, with coruscating stars in a cold and naked sky. Jimmy had been working the distant banks, which were difficult to come at and difficult to leave, and for that reason he had not had his horse and cart; he had preferred a stout creel slung from his broad shoulders, and even so he had waited till the silver crescent of the moon was above the hawes before he began his journey home. He had gone carefully, moving always to the moon, always up its silver trail, and he had kept his eyes alert, as a man needed to do on the banks at night. He had been still a half mile from the hawes when he saw the horsemen, clear and black against the moon; and at once he had remembered the lugger that had been in the offing, hard against the western sky, when he had come to the banks at dusk. He had turned at that, and at once he had seen the dimmed red light that glowed beyond the surf to tell of the lugger's creeping in. That had not surprised Jimmy; but when he turned to the shore again there had been another light to be seen—a light that seemed to hang in the hawes and was very clear and steady.

"Where," said John softly, "was this light?"

"Ainsdale way—three miles or so to the south'ard. Or that's what I thought."

"Thought?"

"Aye—and a fair take-in it was." The memory seemed to be teasing Jimmy. "Listen . . ."

There was no doubt of their listening as he went on with his tale. He had been walking steadily up the silver trail of the moon, seeing this light to the left of it, and suddenly the light disappeared; and, as he pondered that, he had seen that the horsemen were likely to pass closer to him than seemed to sort with his safety on that lonely beach. Jimmy had been prompt. He had made away to the left; and he had gone no more than twenty paces when the light in the hawes had reappeared. That had been puzzling, but Jimmy had wits that matched the need. He had waited, squatting low on the sand, until the horsemen were safely past, and then he had moved quietly back to the line he had been walking; and the light had disappeared. He retraced his steps, and it appeared again; and when he had continued so across the moon trail he had again lost the light and had again found it when he came back. In short, said Jimmy, this light was a leading light, shining along a line only, and the lugger had only to keep it steadily in sight in order to make the beach at a predetermined point.

"Nice!"

There was a stir in the silent room as if John's short comment had given them relief. Penny eased in her chair and turned to catch his eye. The widow moved quickly with the ale jug, and John stretched his legs and sat back.

"There's one thing," he said thoughtfully.

"Aye?" Jimmy was alert at once.

"It seems this lugger was landing her cargo at the ebb of the tide.

I'm not expert in this, but would it not be better done on the flood—at high water?"

"Not on this coast it wouldn't." Jimmy's answer was prompt. "It's a shallow beach here, and flat, and they'd have to put a boat down to land anything. At ebb they could lie close off a bank, and it 'ud be easy. At flood they'd get no closer in, or not much, and the lads in t'boat would get a half-mile pull—and surf, too."

John accepted that without argument; Jimmy no doubt knew. And then Penny intervened suddenly, leaning forward in her chair as though she were impatient with this talk of tides and coasts.

"It's no doubt important," she said. "But Mistress Jump was telling us of Richard Rimmer—and now we seem to have lost him. Has he some part in this?"

"He has an' all." Jimmy's retort came heartily, and he had a homely grin for Penny before he plunged into the tale of it.

That leading light, it seemed, had been a sore puzzle to Jimmy. He saw readily enough why it had been needed, but he did not see how it had been done. How could a light be made to shine along a line, with darkness left and right? The problem had occurred to him at once, and he had at once tried to solve it. He had left the horsemen to their own affairs and he had plodded sturdily over the sand towards the light, determined to learn where and how it hung in the hawes—and the same thing had happened; the light had disappeared. It had disappeared as he walked to it, and when he went back along his tracks it appeared again. And Jimmy's native shrewdness was plain in his face as he explained what this must mean. The light was not in the hawes at all; it was behind the hawes and throwing above them, so that the loom of them cut it from him as he drew too close; and at that he had begun to guess the answer.

He had confirmed it by daylight and at leisure. The hamlet of Ainsdale, he explained, lay down by the Otter Pool, a mile and more inland, and on the lowest of the ground. A low and sandy ridge screened it from the sea, and this ridge was itself screened by the hawes beyond, so that from the shore there was nothing to be seen of either ridge or hamlet—except on one line, where the hollows between the sandhills chanced to lie in a sequence that made a gap. Jimmy, standing on the shore next day, had looked along that line and had seen, through the gap, the low and sandy ridge; and beyond the ridge he had seen the one tall building the hidden hamlet held—the mill by the Otter Pool, the mill of Richard Rimmer, sometime sergeant in Ireton's Horse.

22   MR. BARLOW'S COUNSEL   Long miles lay from the

sea to Langley House, and John, waving his beaver cordially as the horses sent the dry sand spurting, knew well enough that they were late. He said as much to Penny; and Penny promptly looked mutinous and said that, late or not late, she meant to see this mill of Richard Rimmer; she had never passed close to it, and now was the time.

She had her way, for John was tempted too; and soon they were through the hawes and out on the open shore, where the wind tugged at their cloaks and the rising tide was creaming along the sand in sizzles of green and white. They went briskly, exhilarated by the wind and the light and the scream of the soaring gulls, and they all but rode too far. It was Penny's keen young eyes that saw it first, the thin straggling gap in the long wall of the hawes. She drew rein abruptly as she pointed; and John, ranging alongside, looked through the channel with her and saw, against the distant sky, the thin dark arms that moved against the blue. In silence, his eyes met hers, and she nodded her agreement; these were the turning sails of Richard Rimmer's mill.

After that it was easy. They turned into the gap and went through the sliding sand until they came to the thin soft turf of the ridge beyond; there was a trifling descent, and then the land stretched flat to the score of cottages that huddled by the turning mill. It was scarcely a half mile distant, and its slatted sails dominated fields and hamlet alike as they cut their arcs against the sky. For fields there were, poor and salty though the soil might be, and the track to the hamlet passed through kale and cabbage and potato. There were pigs grunting on the baked mud between the houses, and hens ran squarking as the horses trotted through; dogs barked, and children came running in excitement, and startled faces peered through doors as John looked right and left and Penny swung her horse nimbly to avoid a crawling child. And then they were past the houses, and the mill was a hundred paces distant, its sails turning steadily and the creak and rumble of it coming plainly up the wind.

"We'll gawk at the pool," said Penny brightly. "We're expected to do that, and they'll not account it odd."

It was well said, for it gave excuse to inspect the mill. The pool lay behind the mill, shining and sparkling in the afternoon sun, a sheet of water, perhaps a mile across; the dark soil by its rim was flat and soft, and would plainly be underwater if the pool should rise in winter—as its fringe of reeds and rushes suggested that it did. Only by the mill was the margin clear, and here they halted and looked about them. Apparently Ainsdale had uses for the Otter Pool. A causeway of loose flat stones and a squelching mire of hoofmarks showed where the cattle were watered; punts drawn up on the mud and nets stretched in the sun suggested fish, at least on Fridays; and, as a hint of better fare, there were ducks on the shining water, bobbing restlessly as the ripples drove in the snoring wind.

They turned attention to the mill. It was hard by the pool, and in winter the water must have been near to lapping it. It was tall and sturdy, and lovingly cared for; on door and sails the orange paint was gleaming; its limewashed walls were a snowy white; and at its top, above the churning shaft that the great sails drove, its short domed roof was sheathed in lead and painted the same bright orange—significant colour. John stared at it grimly, and, without surprise, he noted the tiny window cut in the lead roof and facing to the sea and the gap in the hawes. He pointed it out to Penny and she nodded.

"We need not have doubts of Richard Rimmer," she said. "That's no doubt his house."

It stood beyond the mill, with the granaries in between—a fine new house of thin red brick, with small-paned windows and a panelled door. Its paint was new, its garden trim, its stables sweet and clean; and again John nodded. There was a prosperity to be discerned in Richard Rimmer.

"What now?" he asked, as he found Penny's eyes on him.

"We ride," she said firmly. "We'll need to go north about this moss. There's no track that crosses it, and it's overlate already."

It was. The miles before them were long and tiring, and Langley House was a vague loom in the dusk before the weary horses ended their day at last, and their riders, almost as weary, dismounted before a door that was welcoming and candlelit. Under the black arch of it was Richard Langley, bluff and impatient as he waited for his lagging daughter. He came stumping on the gravel when he heard the horses; but if he had been in anxiety he said nothing of that, and he cut brusquely into John's attempted apologies.

"It's no matter, so that you're safe back and all well." His quick shrewd glance at Penny seemed to reassure him. "Did you run your quarry—on that shore?"

"Why—why, yes, sir."

"Good!" Mr. Langley sounded almost as if he knew why they had been to the shore. "You'll be best now at a table."

He led to the house without more words, and John and Penny had puzzled glances as they handed their horses to a groom. They knew they were late by an hour and more, and they had not expected this warmth, nor this air of knowledge; and it was not till they were rid of their boots and the worst of the dust, had changed their clothes and were down the stair again, that they had the explanation. There was a supper set ready for them, but it was not in the cool stone-windowed dining room; it was set this night in an older room, where the panels were thick and black and the latticed windows were low and small. There were flowers on the smooth oak table and candles set between the flowers, throwing a mellow light on the knives and plates, the pewter dishes and the silver spoons; in the shadows by the cool stone hearth Arabella Langley sat in an elbowchair, her face to the windows that were wide to the summer night; and facing her in another chair, with a folding screen of oak and leather set between him and the window, was the friendly Mr. Barlow.

If Penny was surprised and glad, she was at least not lured into foolishness. She took one swift glance at the open window, and then she stood by the table and almost seemed to address her aunt; nothing in her stance would have hinted to a watcher in the garden that there was a man behind the screen, and John was quick to imitate her. He had much to learn of priests and their ways, he reflected, and Penny had no doubt done all this before; and then, as he stood watchful and alert, he saw that in the blackened oak of the wall behind the screen a long dark crack had opened, as though a swinging panel had begun to turn and could, with one swift push, be wholly turned. He looked quickly away, and he gave no sign; but now he knew why Edward Barlow could be safe in this old house and why he sat in this low dark room, and not in the newer comfort of carved and mullioned stone.

He made no move from his hidden chair, but there was a light in his eyes and a warmth in his voice as he gave them friendly greeting.

"I had need to use this road tonight," he explained, "so I took it upon me to start a little early, that I might hear your tale from the sea."

"But surely——"

Penny was speaking quickly, but with an anxious eye on her aunt and father, and Mr. Barlow laughed softly.

"Be at ease, my Penelope. You have not forfeited their love."

Aunt Arabella had a smile that had a pride in it, and, from beyond the table, her brother spoke gruffly.

"Aye, Ned's being telling us of it, lass—of what you think you've nosed of young Mansell. Parcels of lace, is it? But what's of today, that it kept you so late?"

They were hungry enough to eat as they talked, and John told the tale as best he could from the supper table; he had some sharp questions from Aunt Arabella and some rumbling ones from her brother, and he had frequent help from Penny, who interjected freely as she plied a busy knife. But Mr. Barlow, bright-eyed and attentive, sat it through in silence.

"It has its oddities," was his comment when the tale was done. "What do you say is the pattern of it?"

"I think Penny has said it. Mansell rides for the mere with a servant and a pack-horse. They shoot geese, and then they make for this Rising Sun. They're joined there by others, one of whom is perhaps this Richard Rimmer, and away they go to the shore. There's the tide at ebb, good firm sand, and the lugger standing in. There's a gleam of moon to light them, and the leading light from this mill."

"Nice!" murmured Mr. Barlow. "Nice, indeed!"

"There's a deal in this that's nice. There's a boat pulling through the surf, and hands in plenty to load the lace. And then they're away to the mere, where the dead geese wait by the reeds. They're loaded above the lace, and then it's away again, and safely, for the young moon's down and all's dark. All's ready at the Sun, and there's a half hour there to bait both man and beast. Then away again. And if they should be a trifle late, if the dawn's come before they're at Thornclough, then what of that? Here's a man homing from his sport. He's well known for it—and there are the geese he's shot. Anyone may look at 'em."

"I did," said Penny briefly.

"Ye-es." Mr. Barlow seemed sunk in thought. "You put it together very prettily. But do you say that that's the whole of it?"

"No, I don't." John answered him slowly. "There are too many—Whigs, I think we say—in this for me to be at ease about it. Too many with the tang of rebellion in them——"

"Aye . . ."

It was Mr. Langley's growl from across the table, and John nodded as he went on.

"Just so, sir. There's Roderick Mansell himself. You'll know his ways and the ways of his family."

"We do." It was Penny, speaking grimly, and something in her eye told that her mind was with the blackened stone by the door of Langley House. "We've cause to know those ways."

"As have I," said Mr. Barlow softly, and John could have echoed that. He glanced at the window, small and dark against the night, and for a moment it could have been a window high in a grey stone wall in Newgate.

"I think we all have," he said quietly, and then his tone hardened. "And it's not only Mansell. There are these Rimmers, the one at the Rising Sun and the one who shines a light from his mill. They're old rebels both. And there's Mrs. Waring, of the Green Ribbon Club. And the master of this lugger, out of Holland no doubt. Look where you will, you find a Whig."

"Ye-es," said Mr. Barlow once again. He seemed intent on studying his fingers in the glow of the candles; and, surprisingly, it was Mr. Langley who now thrust himself into the talk. He leaned forward, and there was something in the shrewd puckering of his forehead that set John in mind of Penny; he had seen her look exactly so.

"Seven horsemen, do you say? New stables built at Thornclough, and a lugger coming out of Holland? That's a deal of charges to be at for a parcel of lace."

"It certainly is." John spoke thoughtfully. "You'll mean there'll be some other cause, beyond the lace?"

"Of course there will," said Aunt Arabella suddenly, and she had been sitting so quietly that John was almost startled by her intervention. "And if that family orders it, it will be fouler work than lace. You may be sure of that."

"Aye," he answered her. "I'll not dispute it. But—but if this was devised for some other cause, could it be that Roderick Mansell has put it to his own profit by adding to it some private trade in lace? It would not be past what I've seen of him."

"It would not be past what I've seen of his trollop," said Penny viciously. "What did the love cart cost, John?"

"Sixty guineas, I'd say. And another forty for the greys that draw it. But——"

"But what?"

"It sounds well enough. But what *is* it that's to be landed in secret by Whigs, and at such charges? You'll note that it's no fishing sloop that brings this cargo. It's a two-masted lugger, and of some size. So we must suppose that the cargo is of some size too—or of some weight."

"But it isn't," said Penny. "It can't be."

"Why not?"

"Because it's to come ashore in the jolly boat, and in surf. And then be loaded on a pack-horse. That's why. And there's something else that you've forgot."

"And what?"

"The Levite."

"Who?"

"The Reverend Mr. Roberts—so *she* said."

"Well spoken, my Penelope!" Mr. Barlow was suddenly in smiling approval. "You put all our wits to shame. For we must *not* forget this divine—if divine he be. What became of him, pray? Did Jimmy Jump know anything of that?"

"No. He was not on the banks that night."

"No?" Mr. Barlow seemed to be summing it up. "Yet I think we may perhaps see the loom of things."

"How?" John spoke quietly.

"Need we doubt what the lugger's cargo was on Monday?"

"Mr. Roberts, I suppose."

"Exactly. And that's the true and proper purpose of this lugger." His glance swept round the silent circle. "It's been truly said that lace cannot be all that's landed here. And Penny has well said that the true cargo must be small enough for the jolly boat. And so indeed it is. It's living cargo that freights this lugger."

"Men, you mean?"

"Aye, and secret men. Men who must not take ship from London. Men who must move in shadow."

"Or end at Tyburn." Mr. Langley laughed shortly. "The harbingers of treason. Is that it?"

"I fear it may be." Mr. Barlow was speaking gravely. "But you'll note there's one thing more, and perhaps the key to the whole."

"And what's that?"

"Mrs. Waring's journey to Scotland." Mr. Barlow seemed to wait for an answer; and when none came he spoke again, softly and steadily. "There's been rebellion in Scotland lately, and we must suppose, I think, that something of concern to this Green Ribbon Club has arisen from that. Messengers are needed, one for Holland and one for Scotland—perhaps to milord Argyle. And both must be secret."

"Which means some treason," said Mr. Langley again.

"Perhaps it does. But the club has resources to match the need. There'll be a man post to Tilbury, and thence into the packet for Brill or Flushing—an innocent man who may journey openly. But he has orders for the master of this lugger. Then the messenger for Scotland makes ready, and she's well chosen. Her chariot's fast and well horsed. And who would suspect a lady of such work?"

"I would," said Penny. "I'd suspect her of worse."

"Peace, my Penelope!" Mr. Barlow waved her into silence as he went on. "She needs an escort. But the Holland messenger is ready too, and dressed as a divine. It's very fitting—and who would suppose a divine has messages of treason? So they drive in haste, and Mansell knows nothing of their coming—or he'd not have asked Penny into those parts that day. There'll be orders for Mansell, no doubt—he's to see the one into the lugger and then to escort the other to Scotland. And so, no doubt, it's done."

Mr. Barlow ended, and the room was very still. A candle flickered as the night wind came softly in, and Penny's chair creaked as she stirred. No one spoke, and in the silence Mr. Barlow turned to John.

"You'll perceive," he said, "what follows?"

John stiffened and came more erect in his chair. This seemed to be directed to him alone.

"I think there is the hand of God in this," said Mr. Barlow quietly. "I foretold that a way would be opened, and now it is surely before you. Which is to say there is a duty laid, a task set for you to do."

"Oh?" There was a quality in Mr. Barlow's eyes that was holding John almost speechless. "But——"

"If there is something given here, a way opened, a matter pointed out, it might be at peril of soul that we should put it not to use."

"Aye, no doubt. But—what use?"

"You point it neatly, for that's the core of it. I do not know what use. But if there is one man who may, it would be Nevil Payne. Is there another to see to the heart of this, and to judge what's needed now?"

"No." John was emphatic on that. "Certainly Mr. Payne must be told, and quickly."

"Even so. As you say, and quickly. But not, if you please, by letter."

"Not——" John broke off and stirred unhappily as Mr. Barlow's meaning broke upon him. In cold dismay he turned to Penny, and he read in her eyes that she too had guessed.

"Not by letter," said Mr. Barlow again. "It's a deal too long for that, and too fine. Who will write a letter that shall give a sufficient exactness? And what letter will give answer to all the questions that Nevil Payne will ask? No—it's to be told by word of mouth, and questions answered as they come. Would less suffice—for duty?"

John sat silent, knowing that this was true; and knowing too that it would be for him, and him alone, to bear this tale to London. Again, in the silence, his eyes found Penny's. She had the ghost of a smile for him now, and that heartened him as he turned again to Mr. Barlow.

"Meaning that it's I that must go?"

"I did not say 'must' and I do not say it now. It does not belong to me to say that to you. I offer counsel—no more."

"A nice distinction." John essayed a smile at that. "But your counsel is that one of us should ride forthwith to London?"

"Yes." Mr. Barlow did not evade, and his tone was firm and steady.

"I see." Again John essayed the smile. "And I cannot say that you are wrong. And it seems it's I who must go."

"Who else?" But Mr. Barlow had understood, and his lean face had softened as he glanced at Penny; he was almost smiling when he turned again to John. "You could return to us when duty's done?"

"I—I hope so."

"So do we all," said Mr. Langley quickly; and, in her shadowed corner, his sister nodded swift agreement.

"It's my counsel that you should go," said Mr. Barlow firmly, "and I think it a duty laid upon you. I cannot go myself, for I've an office to fulfil. With his father sick, there are duties for Will Hoghton. And we can scarcely send Penny. So——"

"Precisely."

There seemed to be no avoiding it. Penny's eyes were on him, and his eyebrows gave the question. She nodded.

"You must ride to London, John. And when all's sorted you'll be pleased to ride back." Her smile flickered bravely. "There's yet something to be sorted here."

It wanted an hour of midnight, and there was moonlight on the garden when John went quietly, at Mr. Barlow's side, down the scented path that led to the paddock beyond the hedge. He went in silence, and his thoughts were in a night when Penny had walked this path with him and had sent the white phlox petals crumbling between her fingers; and from that his thoughts went leaping—leaping to the London he must return to, the London of streets and stenches, of clocks and coffeehouses, of Newgate and Whigs and Nevil Payne. It did not allure; and quickly, in the dappling moonlight, his eyes turned to the man who walked at his side, this friendly soft-voiced man whose tone could be so sure, whose precepts so unbending, when he spoke of duties laid and tasks to be fulfilled.

"I have not brought you happiness this night."

Mr. Barlow spoke suddenly, his face coming into the moonlight as he turned, and there was nothing of question in his tone; it was the tone of certainty, and John offered no dispute of it.

"I've no wish to go," he answered quietly. "I see the need and I'll do what's called for. But as for wishes, that's——"

"Our Penelope. Just so."

Mr. Barlow was as soft as ever, but he had given his first word a stress that pointed all his meaning, as though he knew, and would say aloud, that Penny was no longer for him alone to cherish. It set John turning quickly in a surge of gratitude, and by the gate in the hedge Mr. Barlow stopped. A shaft of moonlight was on him, picking his pale face from the blur of his cloak and hat while he seemed to collect his forces; and then he spoke firmly:

"What may befall you in London I do not know, and you may find what the world calls harm. These are very dark and troubled days, and the things of earth are none of them secure. There is rancour and greed and fear, and much else that is from hell. In the seats of power there are men of evil heart, and, daily, men die who seemingly should not. Which does *not* mean"—Mr. Barlow's tone was hardening—"which does not mean that a man should turn his back and seek for himself alone. Happiness is not found that way, and what is found is empty. You may thank God that a path is open before you, even though you like it not. For it is better to be called than not to be called."

In the paddock beyond the gate a slow fall of hooves could be heard, faint and muffled in the long lush grass. Mr. Barlow turned as he heard it; and then, with his hand on the gate, he paused for another word.

"You will not, in the end of things, be the less happy for having done what was set before you. That is the Law. It is to be heeded or not heeded, as men do choose. But it is not to be balked or changed."

He stayed for no more. He went quickly through the gate, and he was drawing his cloak around him as Penny came down the hedge leading a saddled horse. Mr. Barlow's hand came out, and John took it warmly.

"My thanks," he said briefly. "I'll hope to meet again—and soon."

"Amen to that! We'll pray for it, all of us. And when you do return . . ." His quick glance seemed to take in both of them. "I shall hope it may then be proper for me to offer felicitations in happy form."

Again he stayed for no answer. There was a faint clink of spurs as he mounted in the shadow of the hedge, and then Penny spoke quickly.

"You'll have a care, won't you? It's bright tonight—too bright."

"That's not to be mended, Penny, and it's been so before." Mr. Barlow was cool and reassuring. "But these are friendly lanes, and I know where the shadows fall."

He pulled his hat low, and for a moment his face was turned to John.

"God keep you as you journey! Keep and bless you—both!"

Vaguely in the shadows it seemed that his hand had lifted. But already his horse was moving, and the quiet pad of hooves was receding along the hedge as he began his nightly journey into peril of the law. John stood stiffly, and suddenly his hand found Penny's.

Across the paddock there was a blur that moved and seemed to pass through a gap in the hedge. The hoofbeats faded into the night, and in silence John turned to Penny. Her hand was still in his as they moved together through the gate into the garden; and on the scented path he stopped.

"We ought to go in," she said quietly.

"Yes." He took her other hand as well, and slowly he turned her to face the moon. "But it's I that must ride next, Penny—away from you, and for longer."

"I know." Her voice came steadily. "It's in the fate of things, it seems, and we can't mend fate. It's been so before."

Quickly, and for a fleeting moment, her head had turned to her home, to the old and sentient house that stood so gracious in the moonlight, a chequer of black and silver behind the silent trees; and in that instant he knew that her thoughts were with others of her name who had come and gone, and with Arabella, who had said farewells to her men and then had stayed to keep good faith with her name and home.

"Yes," he answered. "It's been so before—and worse. I'll be back in weeks, if——"

"If what?"

She was almost smiling now, and she was looking at the sky rather than at him. His hands drew her closer.

"If God wills and you wish. Will you say that, Penny?"

She turned to him again and stood considering him, her face grave and composed under the moon. Then, slowly, she nodded.

"Of course." For a moment she looked away again. "Come back when you can. You'll be very—welcome."

"That's no answer, Penny. You know it's not."

"Not? But it's——"

"It's no answer from you, Penny." His arms were round her now, and he was pressing her close. "It's a careful answer, and my Penny isn't careful. She couldn't be—the Penny I know—and love."

"John! I——"

"I want your own answer, Penny. From your own true self."

She leaned back as he held her, and her eyes dropped as she looked away.

"We—we ought to go in," she said again.

"I know. But I want the answer—your own."

He heard her quick breathing as she moved in his arms. Slowly her head lifted, and then she was meeting his eyes, her face white as the moonlight found it. He felt her arms come round him, and he saw her lip quiver.

"What is it?" he whispered.

Slowly she nodded.

"Come back to me, John."

The quiver was still in her lips as they came against his; and he forgot the moon and the house and Nevil Payne, and all the world but Penny. Behind them the moon was swinging in the sky, and suddenly the old house took a gleam from the changing light; and its windows began to twinkle, as though it had seen all this before.

23   STUDY OF LUNATIONS   Mr. Payne the writer and Mr. Gadbury the astrologer came by appointment to the Fleece in Chancery Lane to dine with Mr. Leyburne the clockmaker.

It was a tavern discreetly chosen, and John had thought that needful. For when, on his return to the town, he had gone in search of

Mr. Payne, he had found him in the Grecian, chatting amiably with Mr. Gadbury and some others. He had at once invited Mr. Payne to dinner; but it had unfortunately been necessary to give the invitation in the hearing of Mr. Gadbury, who had promptly shown such an eager interest that there had plainly been nothing for it but to invite him too; which was to be regretted. For it was scarcely to be denied that Mr. Gadbury, well intentioned though he might be, was nevertheless a man likely to attract notice in any company; and that was by no means what John desired for his talk with Mr. Payne. So he had drawn swiftly on his knowledge of the taverns near Fleet Street and had been quick to suggest the Fleece in Chancery Lane; and that, he now thought, had been adroitly done. For the Fleece was a tavern set apart for lawyers; it was a house where pending cases were discussed over chops and claret, where briefs were conned over pale canary, where guineas clinked as fees were paid, where attorneys came to attend their clients, and barristers to attend attorneys. The long timbered room, dark and low, was redolent of food and wine and tobacco, and the hurrying servers brushed past men of every sort and humour who sat in the discreet alcoves, their heads together above the wine-stained boards and their voices sunk to a murmur; it was a place of question and consultation, of grave advice and whispered counsel, a place where each was sunk in his own concerns and none gave ear to what his neighbour did; and John, coming early and alone to order the dinner and keep an alcove private, knew that he had chosen well; not even Mr. Gadbury would set an eyebrow lifting here.

Mr. Payne seemed to have that thought also. He came striding down the room, tall and leisurely, and there was a twinkle in his eye as he threaded his way to the alcove.

"You've chosen well," was his greeting, as he slid into his seat. "Not even our Gadbury will call for notice here."

"I hope not. The fact is, I——"

"So did I." Mr. Payne's smile was eloquent. "I know our Gadbury. But I'll remember this house. The 'Fleece' you say it's called?"

"It is."

"It's very apt." Mr. Payne swept a sardonic eye round the company. "*Carnivora legis,* I see. This should suit Gadbury. He likes his dinner."

"Does he indeed?"

"Yes." Mr. Payne had his lazy smile. "Which, to come to the root of it, is why he sees a deal of Mrs. Cellier these days."

"You mean that her hospitality——"

"Is much to Gadbury's taste. Her table's well furnished, as you'll know."

"I do. But how is she, pray?"

"It's what I'm asking you to learn. Myself, I don't frequent her table—these days."

"Oh?"

A server came fussing with the sweet canary that would introduce their dinner, and there was a wary silence as the wine was poured. Then Mr. Payne gave answer.

"Ye-es." He was smiling as he took the scent of the wine. "It's to be deplored, but it's prudent. You'll remember Dangerfield?"

"The captain?"

"So he says. But he's a rogue if ever there was one. Even Gadbury has sense enough to see that. But he's a plausible rogue with a ready tongue, and not ill-favoured. And Mrs. Cellier, whose wits are not of earth, finds him a very pretty fellow."

"Does she? There was a horoscope of this Dangerfield——"

"So I've heard—some scores of times. You should hear Gadbury on it. But you'll see why I keep a proper distance from Mrs. Cellier's. I prefer not to be too well known to this Dangerfield. These are perilous days, and such men make informers. There's one in every sponging house."

"Yes." John nodded. Captain Dangerfield was precisely that. "But what of Gadbury? You say he has sense enough to see it?"

"But not enough to avoid it. It's Mrs. Cellier's dinners, I suppose. And all being said, there's no risk in it for Gadbury. There's nothing to be informed against him."

"He's an astrologer only?"

"Isn't it enough?" Mr. Payne seemed amused. "Gadbury's an oddity, I'll grant, but, as astrologers go, he knows his trade. And astrologers are busy these days."

"Why these days?"

"Because they're troubled days. God knows, they're troubled." Mr. Payne reached for the wine, and his eyes had lost their light. "There may be war at any time, if not with France then with Holland. More likely than either, it will be civil war. Apart from which, you know what a terror walks the town. There are hangings every week at Tyburn, and witnesses ready to take off any man."

"Of the Oates breed?"

"If breed it is. Or are such hirelings bred like maggots—out of slime and corruption? But they'll swear to what they're told, and any one of us may hang next week. Can any man feel safe—or woman either?" The strong voice shook as the brooding words came out. Then Mr. Payne seemed to recover himself, and the light tone was with him again. "Profitable days for Gadbury, you'll see."

"Men seeking solace, is it?"

"And women too. Is it not the way of things? When all's well and the sky's bright, who'll fee an astrologer? But in times like these it's worth a guinea to be told the Sun's nosing up to Jupiter and all's to be heaven next week."

"Is that what Gadbury says?"

"No. But it's what they hope he'll say. And the guinea's paid first."

"I see. And then?"

"Whatever he thinks he sees. There's an honesty in Gadbury. But he has chambers in Westminster and half the Court at his door, which makes him useful for the Court gossip. And sometimes it's more than gossip."

"Is it?" John was looking steadily at him. "If I may say so, you have a way with gossip."

"Have I?" The smile flickered again. "But how?"

"I was thinking of the midwife's gossip—of Mrs. Cellier's. About the lace being sold so cheap."

"Ah, that? I gleaned from your letter that you'd stumbled on something in the North. Is there now some more?"

"For what it's worth, yes. But it's a tangled tale, and———"

"Here's Gadbury."

Mr. Payne's sharp tone had something of warning and something of amusement, and both men turned in their seats with smiles of greeting, which Mr. Gadbury more than returned. He was striding hurriedly into the room, portly and untidy as ever, his wide hat flapping and his brown suit on the point of bursting; his round red face was hot and shining, and, with its twinkling eyes and genial smile, it looked more than ever like a harvest moon. He was beaming with pleasure as he swept the flapping hat from his sandy hair and slid into his seat with a gasp of relief.

"Your pardons, both," he spluttered. "I'm late."

"So we noted," said Mr. Payne drily. "But pardon granted. This wine's amused us."

"The devil it has!" Mr. Gadbury drank thirstily from the glass that John had brimmed for him. "Am I in fault if Saturn hunts the Moon?"

"I shouldn't think so." Mr. Payne toyed with his own glass and spoke solemnly. "I should hardly know whither to address complaint of that. Perhaps to this new place at Greenwich—the Observatory, as they call it. But did you join this hunt?"

"What's that?" Mr. Gadbury was staring blankly at him, and Mr. Payne stayed solemn.

"I don't see how these turmoils in the sky should make you late for dinner. That's all."

"You don't, hey?" Mr. Gadbury blinked, and then suddenly he was grinning happily. "Why then, I've been plagued this forenoon through by a fat and paunchy spice merchant, demanding that I tell him why his ships tarry in the foreign seas, so that he ever waits."

"And why do they?"

"It's what I've been telling the fool, but he's too thick of head to take it in. But the temporal translation of Saturn through the zodiac, requiring some twenty-nine years to accomplish, and the Moon's progression in a natal figure, demanding twenty-nine and one half years, it plainly follows——"

"Of course it does. And the fool did not see it?" Mr. Payne shook a solemn head. "These spice merchants!"

Mr. Gadbury gasped, and for a moment he was redder than before; then he burst out laughing as he reached for the wine and refilled his glass.

"Devil take you!" he grunted. "You may nose your own answers. I'll talk with another. How it is, Mr. Leyburne? You had my letter?"

"I did, and found it good reading. How's Mrs. Cellier, pray?"

"Excellent well, though fevered of one Dangerfield. But of yourself, Mr. Leyburne? Did you find a lady out of Sagittary?"

"Even so." John was meeting his quizzical glance without evasion. "And as you foretold—with heat of head and hair."

"Good!" Either at John's good fortune or his own sagacity, Mr. Gadbury was beaming again. "Tell me more, pray, of your doings in Lancashire——"

"It's what we're here for," said Mr. Payne quietly. "It's why we dine in this scent of snuff and ink. And perhaps . . . But here's our dinner."

"What!" Mr. Gadbury was sniffing eagerly as the servers loaded the table and swept the covers from the gleaming dishes. "What's this? Who's been choosing?"

It had been John's choice, and he had disdained the ordinary and had been at pains to choose well for his guests. There was a fat capon, brown and sizzling from the spit; there was a beefsteak pudding, garnished with larks; there were beans and cabbage to help it on its way; there was the famous apple pudding with the wine sauce that the Fleece was noted for; there were the fruits and comfits and nuts, and the wines to blend with each. It was of the best, for the Fleece knew how things were done, and the hovering servers knew better than to stay in earshot; so the talk could go safely above the pewter and napery of the shining table. John told his tale in unhurried detail, and Mr. Payne listened in silence; but Gadbury was showing signs of excitement even before the capon was done with.

"A mere, is it?" he put in eagerly. "And a secret there? Just so! A rustic place, and water! The Bull and the Scorpion opposing, as I said——"

"True." John let that pass as he went on with his tale; and again Gadbury interrupted.

"I doubt these larks," he said suddenly. He was rooting with a spoon in the steaming depths of the beefsteak pudding. "Who'll say they're not sparrows? But this Richard Rimmer and his mill—Taurus, you understand, Taurus!"

"I beg your pardon, I——"

"Taurus, sir. The Bull!" Mr. Gadbury waved a forkful of beefsteak pudding. "A mill's a rustic thing, a thing of cornfields and earth, and places where cattle are. It comes within the governance of the sign Taurus."

"There's a portion of Taurus just fallen from your fork," said Mr. Payne calmly. "I suggest you resume governance over it."

A grunt of disgust was the answer to that, and John went quietly on with his tale until the servers swooped on the table again and set the apple pudding before them. John pushed it to Gadbury, and the plates with it; he wanted to be free to give heed to Mr. Payne.

"This Jimmy Jump," Mr. Payne was saying. "He seems well disposed, and he's seen what was needed. It's fortunate that he catches shrimps."

Mr. Gadbury flourished an uplifted spoon.

"What sign has governance over shrimps?" he demanded loudly.

"God knows," said Mr. Payne briefly. "I think we may accept it then that Mansell is landing lace as you say. And that's certainly of interest. But——"

"Cancer," said Mr. Gadbury suddenly. He seemed to be following his thoughts aloud. "It must be Cancer. The crab and the shrimp . . ."

He sank into a brooding silence as he ladled the wine sauce, and Mr. Payne was free to bring sober thought to the matter.

"Accepting these landings of lace," he said slowly, "what else did you suppose when you talked of this?"

"We thought that this was not a matter of lace alone. There are too many Whigs in it and too much money spent. The lugger's said to be Dutch, and it's surely under control of the Green Ribbon Club, who may be supposed to have ordered these journeyings by Mrs. Waring and this Roberts. Which puts me in mind, do you know the man?"

"No." Mr. Payne poured wine thoughtfully. "To a point, I think you reason well. Certainly the lace is landed. Certainly that's not the chief purpose. But what the chief purpose is—that's still for guessing."

"We'd guessed it to be ferrying of men—men with treasons and secret letters."

"It could be. Yet I doubt it."

"But Mrs. Waring, to Scotland in such haste—she'll have had letters?"

"Perhaps. But she did not journey in this lugger, and it's the lugger that I speak of."

"But Mr. Roberts?"

"Was in the lugger. But did he carry letters? Again I doubt it."

"Aye, but . . ." The note of obstinacy was in John's voice again. "But when all's said there *is* this lugger. That's not guessing. It *is*. It comes and goes. And here's no guessing. It's fact. And if the cause is not this and not that, then what is it? What is it that brews in Lancashire?"

"Treason." Mr. Gadbury, who had seemed to be asleep over the pudding, was suddenly very much awake; he was sitting up and speaking vigorously. "Treason it is that brews—treason of '41."

" 'Forty-one?"

"Aye—as it was brewing then."

"Oh?" Mr. Payne eyed him steadily. "I'll not deny that mischief brews. We've had warnings enough and to spare. There were men sharpening swords here not a fortnight back——"

"What!" John's voice was sharp.

"Aye, just that. The King was ill at Windsor, and for a moment it seemed that he was like to die. And you could hear the swords grinding then, if you walked these alleys at night. This town's a froth of Whigs, and some at least will fight to keep our James from crown and sceptre. They know what faith he holds."

"It's what I said." Mr. Gadbury was insistent. "It's revolt that brews."

"But urgently? That I doubt." Mr. Payne shook his head. "The King has mended. Revolt's none so urgent now—while the King stays hale. Though there's Monmouth turned out of being captain general, which will sweeten no Whig temper. I wonder now——"

"You wonder too much," said Gadbury briefly. "You think too much and you talk too much. It's time to be doing now."

John jerked upright. A change had come over Gadbury, and not only in his voice. He was sitting forward, tense and determined, and the orange pips went dancing as he pushed his plate away and slapped a well-thumbed book on the table in its place.

"Now listen," he said curtly, and even Mr. Payne listened. There was a dignity in Gadbury now, and with it was authority.

"There were strange conjunctions in July, strange and heavy. For there were Mars and Saturn together in the Scorpion, and, from such a joining of the two infortunes, some mischief must surely flow. And to add to it, both were, in their apparent motions, retrograde."

"What's that?" said John, and Mr. Gadbury swept it aside.

"No matter. But there they were—Saturn, the doom of men, and Mars, the lord of war. Now mark——"

"My dear Gadbury——"

"Mark!" He swept even Mr. Payne aside as he went on. "There's rebellion in the sky. And in the North Parts you've pricked it out."

"Would you tell us how?" said Mr. Payne. "And exactly what he has pricked out in the North Parts?"

"Preparations for the day—for when '41 shall have come again. Don't you see it? There's an army raising, and this Mansell's the quartermaster. He's furnished well with gold—and takes a little for his lady. He's landing stores on this beach of his—swords, maybe, and muskets. He's buying horses and building stables for them. Soon he'll be buying corn and building granaries. And now is the time to stop him."

"Is it?" There was cool disbelief in Mr. Payne. "And how?"

"Get more proof. Swear an information and let him dance at Tyburn. That's how. It's when this signifies, not how. And that's a matter of lunations."

"Of what?"

"Of lunations." Mr. Gadbury was flicking at his book as he spoke. "A lunation is what you'd call a change of Moon. Wherefore the ephemeris. Ha!"

He had apparently found his place, and he was running his finger down a column of close-set figures. John watched intently, his memory flaring of a night at Mrs. Cellier's; and across the table he met amusement in Mr. Payne's swift glance.

"Ha!" Mr. Gadbury sounded decided. "These nights the Moon's lit in the Virgin—a cold and earthy sign, besotted of little things. It will not serve. And next . . ." He flicked his pages quickly. "Next, September the twentieth—that's a week from now, and it will not serve either. The Crab rises and the Fishes culminate. That's no map for hunting treasons."

Mr. Gadbury shook his head and turned another page. Then he looked up to face his bemused listeners.

"Here's our need," he announced solemnly. "Lunation in the Scorpion."

"Indeed?" Mr. Payne spoke with a bland politeness. "A new Moon or a full Moon would it be? And how in the Scorpion?"

Mr. Gadbury set himself to explain.

"There's a new Moon on October the twentieth. At thirty-four minutes gone eight of the morning, and in the ninth degree of Scorpio. Is that plain?"

"New Moon in Scorpio—perfectly. Pray continue. What shall it signify?"

"It shall colour the days that follow. For mark . . . ." Again Mr. Gadbury sought truth in his ephemeris. "It's a little after sunrise, and the ascendant is the twenty-fifth of Scorpio. In which exact degree is Mars—Mars in his own deep sign."

There was excitement in the rich voice, and Mr. Payne looked at him curiously. Gadbury shifted in his chair, and suddenly his eyes were on John.

"That's your time, Mr. Leyburne. The period of that Moon shall lead you to it. Monday, October the twentieth, if you please. And the thirty-fourth minute past eight. There you have it—the day and the hour. Strike no blow till then."

His voice died away, and he turned as though all were settled; he was pouring his wine as the spell broke and John sat back with a sigh. Mr. Payne stirred, and pushed his own glass to be charged.

"That's five weeks hence," he said quietly, "and before then we must do what in us lies. Shaftesbury may not wait till the Moon's in Scorpio."

"There's no profit in fretting. That's the hour, and until then you may burst yourself and come to nothing. There's a reason of inception in all things."

Mr. Payne finished his wine and set his glass down delicately.

"I've had cause to note," he said, "that the gods help best those who help themselves. So, perhaps, do the stars."

"What's that?" Gadbury's wine splashed on the boards as he

whipped round, his mouth open and his red face glowing with excitement. "Help ourselves, is it? But . . ."

His eyes were widening as his sticky fingers flicked the pages of his ephemeris once more. Mr. Payne rose, unnoticed, to his feet.

"I think," he said quietly to John, "that you may not return to your Penelope just yet. There'll be work for you here, these coming days—stars or no stars. At the least there's smuggling to bring home on Mansell, and somehow that's to be contrived."

Mr. Gadbury, sunk in his ephemeris, had forgotten them; he was far away, and he was calling for ink and pens as they slipped quietly from the room.

24   THE CAPTAIN'S PROGRESS   It was some two weeks

later, in the first days of October, that John met Captain Dangerfield.

They had been weeks that did not satisfy. He had been alert to see and hear, and he had gleaned nothing more cogent than that Colonel Mansell, when he was in town, had a lodging in Bride Court, off Fleet Street. But Colonel Mansell was apparently not in town, nor was Mrs. Waring; and from Penny there came a letter which said that neither of them had been seen at Thornclough or anywhere else. Mr. Payne, expert and diligent though he was, had gleaned no more and had confessed to being baffled; and John had retorted sourly that there seemed to be foundation for at least a part of Mr. Gadbury's prediction.

He was in this mood when he met Tom Dangerfield.

It happened at the corner of Water Lane, almost within sound of Mr. Tompion's ticking clocks. John was just out of the shop, after some talk with Mr. Tompion, when he saw the gentleman who was coming down from Temple Bar; he could not well miss seeing him, for this was a gentleman very gay in pale blue velvet and a canary waistcoat, a gentleman who sauntered unsteadily on a long beribboned cane and set his buckled shoes very daintily on cobbles that seemed rougher than he liked. John stared as remembrance came to him; a moment later it came to the captain too, and at once he was bowing unsteadily, his modish hat sweeping the cobbles with its canary plumes.

"God sink and blast me!" said the captain amiably. "It's Mr. Leyburne! Damn, drain and gut me, but it is!"

John's bow had a twitch of amusement. The captain might be a little drunk, but he was certainly doing it well; he had the dress of a fine gentleman, and he was taking the airs of one, too.

"Captain Dangerfield, surely?" John was trying to be hearty. "You've an elegance, sir."

"Oh, aye . . ." The captain lurched erect and then preened himself to be looked at. "But how's it with you, Mr. Ley—Ley——— What's your blasted name?"

"Indifferent well." It would be better not to argue with the captain's present humours, and John was curious to know what had brought the fellow into Fleet Street. "But how's it with you, Captain? You'll be a busy man to have affairs in Fleet Street?"

"Busy enough." The captain leered, and then suddenly grew angry. "I'll not be pumped, sir, d'ye hear? I'll not be pumped."

He seemed to be fumbling for a sword hilt that eluded him, and John eyed him warily; certainly the captain was too drunk to be argued with. But it was easy to confuse the issue.

"A pump?" he said blandly. "To be sure there's a pump, if you've need of one. Good sweet water, too. You'll find it——"

"God gripe your guts!" The mention of water seemed to irritate the captain. "By the holy bellyache . . ."

Beyond doubt the captain was doing it well; this was the very flavour of Whitehall, and John was suddenly aware of a ring of grinning spectators. Then, as quickly as it had come, the captain's anger was gone, and he had linked an arm affectionately into John's.

"God sink and damme! You've a wit, cully, a wit! Water, by the pox! Water!" He was laughing uproariously as he lurched across Water Lane, dragging John with him. "We'll have a bottle on it, by the bowels of Venus we will!"

The words gave John his clue. There was only one excuse this fellow would swallow, and John made it unblushingly.

"Not this present hour," he said. "There's but one thing would part me from you, Captain. But there's a wench who waits——"

"A wench!" The captain's hat went flourishing. "Then what a plague d'ye linger for? Ain't I a gentleman, damme? Would I part a man and his doxy? Get ye gone, and we'll drink another day."

"To be sure! Your servant, Captain!"

"Aye, aye . . ." The captain unlinked his arm and lurched happily down the street. Then of a sudden he turned and was bawling over his shoulder. "Come to my lodging of a night, and I'll find ye a wench or two."

"To be sure, Captain. To be sure!"

"Devil rot me! I'd forgot . . ." The captain blinked as he tried to shake his wits. "In Bride Court yonder. House of Richard Hill. Two pair of stair . . ."

He went unsteadily on his way, and John made a circuit to get back to Mr. Gill's; and it was not until the afternoon was wearing dim that a sudden memory made him thoughtful. If Captain Dangerfield had indeed got a lodging in Bride Court, he must be the near neighbour of Colonel Mansell, who had also a lodging there; and that surely was odd.

It was easily determined. Bride Court, after all, was a small place and of few houses, where everybody would know everybody. John went at dusk, knocked at the first house he came to, and boldly inquired for the lodging of Colonel Mansell. He was answered promptly; the colonel was known to be from town; but his lodging was above-stair in the house opposite, the house of Richard Hill.

They were arguing about schismatics in Child's in the churchyard when John walked in, his cloak pulled tight against the chill of the October night. Mr. Payne detached himself slowly from the circle and called for fresh coffee; and it chanced that he and the newcomer carried their cups to the same corner. John came to the matter quickly; he was terse about it, and Mr. Payne was given the facts shortly. They set him looking grave, and when he spoke his words were plain.

"The rat's what we supposed. He scents more profit with the Whigs, and now he'll play the Judas. He's making up to Mansell."

"Mansell's not in town."

"He soon will be. And then there's a friendly neighbour waiting for him. They'll fall to talk. Very pretty!"

"Very. What's to be done?"

"Ye-es." Mr. Payne seemed to brood. "If Dangerfield knows anything, he's learned it at Mrs. Cellier's. Have you visited there since you were back in town?"

"No."

"Then do. Make it a polite duty, a visit of manners after absence. Being there, follow where your nose leads. You may learn something."

"I'll try. Do I give her warning?"

"Against Dangerfield? Determine that when you have the scent of things. If we're to believe Gadbury, the woman dotes on Dangerfield, and if that's so you'd best be careful."

"I'm quite sure it's so. But I'll attempt her tomorrow. What of this notion of Gadbury's?"

"Which notion? He has so many."

"Of a Whig army raising, and Mansell as quartermaster."

"That?" Mr. Payne took the scent of his coffee. "I'd say the Moon's got out of Scorpio, or wherever it is, and into Gadbury's wits instead. Mansell's of no such weight."

"I—I don't quite——"

Mr. Payne explained himself soberly.

"That the Whigs brew armed revolt is not beyond believing. The temporal power and the schismatic faith hang both upon it, and with it they might be sure of both. If not . . ." Mr. Payne's shoulders lifted eloquently. "The King is with us, of course, and he's no fool, and no coxcomb either—for all his dicing and whoring. And the Whigs have shot their bolt."

"How?"

"Isn't it plain? They meant to have the whole nation in a frenzy with Oates and his dunghill tales. And they haven't done it. They've done it only in the town. The country gentlemen—your Langleys and their like—have kept their heads. They're loyal to the King, even if they do growl and mutter and drink damnation to the Carwell. If trouble comes they'll be loyal to the rim of hell, and Shaftesbury knows it. He's growing desperate, and that's why he might stir trouble now—while he still has the town."

"Which means that Gadbury's right?"

"Not about Mansell. It won't be your red-faced Mansells that

Shaftesbury will turn to if he wants a treason hatched. That's work for a different breed—for Ferguson and his like."

"Who? I've heard that name."

"I put it in a letter-of-news. Ferguson, surnamed the Plotter. A sly-faced rogue who shifts his lodgings thrice a month when the moon's down, who has a dozen names and a hat and cloak for each, a fellow who walks on the shadowed side and looks back as much 'fore. That's Shaftesbury's man, if he wants a treason done."

"It's a pretty picture. I'll remember him. But meantime———"

"Meantime you may look to Dangerfield. Or it may be Tyburn for Gadbury, and perhaps for Mrs. Cellier, too. If Dangerfield takes to informing, he'll follow Oates and swear to plenty. It pays."

"Does it? I'll look to Dangerfield tomorrow."

He went about it warily, sure of Dangerfield's impending treachery and sure that Mrs. Cellier was in more danger than she could easily be persuaded of. She knew too much, and of too many, for her own safety or anybody else's, and Dangerfield had had opportunity, and to spare, for imposing himself on her—a work, as John grimly reflected, to which he would no doubt bring a practised skill; imposing on women was probably Dangerfield's trade.

The moon was full as he went along the Strand, and he noted it with a vague alarm; in two weeks more, it reminded him, there would be that new Moon in Scorpio on which Gadbury seemed to set such weight. He was brooding on that as he turned into Arundel Street and plied the knocker briskly. Even the Moon was the same, and the street was alive with memories—Mansell wounded on the cobbles, and Mr. Barlow limping bravely and speaking of his "little Penelope"; and at once John's thoughts were far away, ranging to the North, where the moon would be as bright on Langley House and the lake by the Park Hall would be black and silver beneath the trees.

A bolt slid, a latch clicked, and John was alert again as the door swung open in a glow of candlelight. The soft-faced Anne, Mrs. Cellier's maid, held the door as he stepped swiftly in, and the candle in her uplifted hand shone on her eager face as she pushed the door to and stood smiling up at him. Some instinct stirred within him, bidding him look carefully at this girl; there would be a cause for this eagerness.

"Mrs. Cellier?" He murmured it politely as he untied his cloak.

"Yes, sir." The soft voice seemed to match her face. "She's above, sir."

"And free?"

"Why yes, sir. I—I think so." She was excited, and John's interest grew keener.

"You think it?" His face slipped suddenly into a smile. This girl was perhaps fifteen, or sixteen at the most, and she would be best dealt with lightly. He let his cloak fall open to show his fine brown coat and his waistcoat of cream brocade with its sash of golden satin; the ringlets fluttered in his periwig as he slipped his fingers under her chin and tilted her face to the light again.

"Oh!" It came as a gasp, but it was not of displeasure.

"You're teasing me, aren't you?"

"No, sir." She tossed her head impishly. "I don't——"

"Oh yes you do. What's your name?" He was tilting her chin again, and her eyes were beginning to sparkle.

"Anne."

It came with another toss of her shapely head, and there was no "sir" this time.

"Anne what?"

"Anne Blake, if it please you."

"It does. So do you. Let me look at you. . . ." He had her chin again, in both his hands this time, and deliberately he turned her face to the light. Then he let go her chin, and as he stepped back he tossed a silver crown in the candlelight and caught it deftly as it twinkled down.

"I'll lay the crown, Anne, that you know just what your mistress is doing, and who she's doing it with. Do you?"

With her eyes on the crown, the girl nodded.

"There's Mr. Gadbury——"

She paused, as though there was more to say; and suddenly he saw that her cheeks had flushed.

"Who else?"

"Captain Dangerfield."

She said it breathlessly, and her tone had changed. She was starry-eyed, and her lip was quivering; and John stood impassive, as understanding rushed upon him. Dangerfield was an even bolder rogue than he had supposed, and his conquest here had not been of the mistress only.

"I see." He spoke gravely. "A very pretty gentleman, the captain."

She nodded eagerly, and he told himself that he must be watchful of this girl; probably she would obey Dangerfield blindly and gladly if he should command her.

"It's very well, Anne." He spoke easily as he tossed the crown to her. "Now be off with you! Ask your mistress if she'll receive me. Run along!"

She got a friendly slap to speed her on her way, and she was laughing over her shoulder as she ran lightly up the stair. Beyond the bend of it he heard her tap lightly, and a man's voice could be heard as a door was opened. Then the parlour door creaked sharply; there was a flutter of feet on the landing, and then Mrs. Cellier was coming down the stair, her blue eyes sparkling under her corn-coloured hair, and excited pleasure in her dainty face.

"Mr. Leyburne!" Her words came rushing as she hurried to greet him. "I've been asking when you'd come—and there's none more welcome. You fare well, I trust? Indeed you look well, very well. It will be the air of the North Parts. And Father Barlow? Pray, how is——"

"He's excellent well, ma'am. And your servant, ma'am! Your servant always!"

He was smiling as he stood there, poised and erect, with his cloak falling sheer and the light glinting on his sword hilt and his buckled shoes; and then he was saluting her in full form, bowing over her outstretched hand and bearing it lightly to his lips. It was perhaps more than the occasion called for, but it was shrewdly judged. Mrs. Cellier's delight was plain in her pretty face.

"Come above," she fluttered. "Come abovestair, pray. And I don't know why you were not above sooner. That foolish Anne of mine . . ."

She was lighting him up the stair as she spoke, and he followed placidly to the parlour, where Captain Dangerfield, bright in his blue-and-canary, was leaning negligently against the hearth, with the sea-coal fire flaring behind him and the silver-mounted candles shedding their light on the sleek black periwig that tumbled across his shoulders. He had picked from the carved stone overhang a tall-stemmed glass, and he was sniffing delicately as he gave an affable nod.

"Servant, sir!" he murmured. "Glad to see ye."

If it was supercilious it was also of the mode; and at least it could be said that the man was sober this night. John made his acknowledgement.

"Yours, sir! To command!"

There was a faint creak as one of the high-backed chairs was pushed back and Mr. Gadbury came politely to his feet, portentous in black velvet and waistcoat of gold brocade which might be supposed to be his Sunday best.

"Ha!" He was wheezing a little, but he was beaming with good humour. "Your servant, Mr. Leyburne! Indeed, we—we are all your servants, ha! ha!"

He was suddenly both pleased and amused, and John stood puzzled; and then Mrs. Cellier slipped quickly past him.

"Gentlemen!" She sounded almost breathless. "You'll know Mr. Leyburne both? He's from the North Parts, and he may tell us what face affairs have there. But Tom, a chair for Mr. Leyburne. . . ."

She was addressing Captain Dangerfield, it seemed, and he set the chair with a flourish while Mrs. Cellier tinkled a silver bell that brought Anne running.

"Wine, girl, wine!" Mrs. Cellier was still fluttering. "The best canary, Anne, and your best foot forward! Run to it. . . ."

There was something overpowering about Mrs. Cellier, and the entire room was in a flutter. John resigned himself to it and allowed himself to be thrust into the brocaded elbowchair, with the hearth to his left and the table to his right. Mrs. Cellier, on her knees with the copper-bound bellows, was blowing the fire to a brighter flame. Anne came running with the wine, and suddenly an outraged Gadbury was fluttering in front of her, muttering angrily as his moist hands closed on the bottle and took it from her; apparently he had some decent notions of how wine should be handled, and he blew his breath noisily as he held it to the candles to see if her haste had clouded it. John watched with amusement; and then, from the corner of his eye, he became aware that Dangerfield, again leaning negligently against the hearth, was quietly taking a sheet of paper from the stone and slipping it into the deep pocket of his coat.

It was not the action that seemed odd, but rather his way of doing it; it was a movement made softly while his eyes were elsewhere, and it was made while John had eyes on Gadbury and Anne; and John, noting that, was alert at once. He had a smile for Anne as she brought him a brimming glass, and then he glanced politely round the room as though to salute them all. Dangerfield was still languid against the hearth; Mrs. Cellier was returning the bellows to the brass hook that was a cherub blowing; Gadbury, with Anne hovering close, was at the table pouring wine; it was all very natural, all in the common course. But at the head of the table was the chair that Gadbury had been using; it was still pushed back as he had left it, and on the table in front of it there were more sheets of paper, with ink and pens convenient. John noted them with amusement; here, no doubt, was the astrologer at his computations.

"Anne! What's this? What do you do?"

Mrs. Cellier's voice cut into his thoughts, and set him turning hastily to see what was amiss; for there had been high anger in her tone. Seemingly she had just turned after hanging up the bellows, and now she was standing rigid, her blue eyes glittering and her lips pressed thin and tight. Dangerfield, no longer languid, was standing stiffly by the hearth; and in front of him, with her shoulder all but touching his, was Anne, turned now to face her mistress. She had apparently been carrying him his wine, and there was the plain appearance that she had somehow got a deal nearer to him than would have been needful for that service. John had perhaps not seen it all; but Mrs. Cellier seemed to have no doubts, and her voice came with a cold crackle.

"Go to your room. I'll school you when my guests are gone. Your manners need some mending."

Anne was white-faced and trembling; her mouth opened as though she would have spoken, and then she seemed to think better of it; and Mrs. Cellier's foot tapped angrily.

"Have you heard me?"

It came viciously, and it seemed to rouse Anne from her daze. Her mouth shut, and somehow she got her feet together and made her curtsey. Then, with her head up and a flush on her cheeks, she passed from the room. The door clicked behind her, and Mrs. Cellier, now white-faced herself, moved close to Dangerfield.

"The little wanton!" she whispered. "It shall not happen again, Tom. I promise you that. You shall not be so treated here."

John sat very still, and his face expressed nothing; to his right he had a glimpse of Gadbury standing stiffly by the table, bottle in one hand and a half-filled glass in the other; by the hearth Mrs. Cellier waited anxiously, her lips still quivering and her eyes intent on Dangerfield; and Dangerfield, his shoulders still against the hearth, was looking pleased. There was a smirk of vanity on his face as he shrugged his shoulders in disclaimer and then bowed over her hand, murmuring some inanity. Her sigh of relief seemed to fill the room, and it left an anxious silence.

It was Gadbury who broke it. He roused himself suddenly, and he was looking very bluff and honest as he sent the wine splashing into the glass.

"It's no matter," he said heartily. "What's to be concerned for? If the girl's a shade forward, what of that? Venus afflicted of Mars, no doubt."

Mrs. Cellier turned quickly, but she had no more to say than a word of thanks as she took the proffered wine. She was smiling as she raised her glass, and the sparkle was back in her eyes as the men raised theirs in salute. But the incident had been revealing. She had been a little too heated over it, a little too stirred within for John to believe that her concern had been for no more than the manners of her maid. Mrs. Cellier was sweet enough on Dangerfield to be vicious to any hint of rivalry, even though it sprang from no more than Anne's youthful ardours. John had another glance at her, and his eyes hardened. Dangerfield had certainly made progress these recent weeks.

But they had all lifted their glasses to him now, and hastily he recalled himself to the present. He accepted it smilingly, and his heels clicked as he lifted to Mrs. Cellier in acknowledgement. She was her feminine and vivacious self as Dangerfield held her chair for her, and she sank into it with a dimpling smile and a charming swish of satin. John, standing with uplifted glass, watched her with pleasure; but as he seated himself he noted a detail that roused his questing thoughts again. Gadbury's sheets of paper had gone from the head of the table.

In itself it was perhaps nothing, perhaps no more than a courteous putting aside of what did not concern the guest; but it linked oddly with Dangerfield's sly pocketing of another paper and it set John's suspicions flaring; something had been astir in this room, and it was something that he was not to know of.

He stayed thereafter for no more than some small talk, and he took his leave within the half hour, well assured that he would learn no more by staying; and, once through the door, he walked briskly, glad to be alone with his seething thoughts. Something had undoubtedly been astir in that firelit room, something that needed to be written down, something that he was not to be told of; and Gadbury, portentous at the head of the table, had the look of being the leader in it. In the darkness of the Strand the image of Gadbury seemed bright before him as he walked—Gadbury, muddleheaded and well-meaning, big and hot at the table as he wrote his sprawling script; and suddenly John had a tremor of quick alarm as he remembered Gadbury at dinner in the Fleece, poring over his book of planets and then spilling the wine in excitement as some thought seemed to come to him.

John found his pace quickening as his thoughts came clear. Whatever had been hatching in that room, Gadbury was surely the leader in it; Mrs. Cellier would be ardently with him, and Dangerfield would be impudently informing himself of it while he waited for Colonel Mansell to return to the house in Bride Court. And Mrs. Cellier was so bemused by Dangerfield that if she were told he had just taken a lodging in that same house she would probably refuse to believe it. John's thoughts became grim. Decidedly Mr. Payne must be told of this on the morrow; and in the meantime it was devoutly to be hoped that Mansell would delay his return some few days longer.

The moon was above the river as he went down Fleet Street, discreetly on the shadowed side; opposite, the houses were stark in the silver light, their doors tight and their shutters up. Only by the turn of Chancery Lane were there signs of life, where a gleam through an open shutter spoke of stirrings in the King's Head tavern. It would be the Green Ribbon Club, and John looked with no friendly eye; and then, as he drew close, he saw what checked his stride and brought him to a staring halt.

A chariot was standing in the roadway there, a chariot slim and elegant, poised on springs of steel. It was sharp-edged and black under the moon, and its horses were of gleaming silver; but in the sunlight he knew they would be grey, and the chariot black and crimson.

25 THE YOUTHFUL ANNE

Mr. Payne must be sought this night, not tomorrow.

That at once seemed certain, and John made briskly for St. Paul's to see who might be in Child's this night. Mr. Payne was not, and John had to try again; and it was a half hour past nine, and getting late for coffeehouses, when he found him in the Grecian. In the half-empty room Mr. Payne took one swift look at John and then swept him into a corner.

"What's this?" he asked bluntly. "You look grave."

"I've cause to."

He told his tale with no prelude more than that, and before it was ended Mr. Payne's looks were matching his own.

"So it's that way, is it?" was his terse comment. "I thought Gadbury was stewing something when we left him in the Fleece that day. This will be his plot, no doubt."

"Plot? But how——"

"It's plain enough, isn't it? Gadbury's staked his credit on something falling out when the Moon's in Scorpio, and now it looks as if he'll give the Moon some help. Does he think he's Ferguson?"

Mr. Payne lapsed into silence, and John sat in a brooding sympathy. Mr. Gadbury might be a very good astrologer, but he would surely be a very bad conspirator; any man must be who conspired with Dangerfield.

"But what sort of plot?" he asked slowly. "And how's it done?"

"As you saw. Three addled heads to mix the tale, and then they write it down. That's what they'd be at tonight." Mr. Payne was becoming sardonic. *"The True and Exact Narration of John Gadbury!* Or would it be *Dangerfield?* More likely it would. He's a Protestant, so he'd be the one to carry it."

"To the King, I should think."

"The King!" John was incredulous. "Dangerfield? To the King?"

"Why not? It could be arranged. Gadbury knows half the Court, and Mrs. Cellier knows the other half. It's easy."

"The hell it is!" John was still staring. "But what *is* this tale that Dangerfield's to carry?"

"At a guess, the one that Gadbury told *us*—about a Whig army, and Mansell as quartermaster."

"Not the lace?"

"They'd hardly plague the King with tales of lace. But the other's a tale of revolt—and Gadbury believes it."

"It's moon-kissed."

"A happy phrase—of Gadbury. But that's the tale he'd use. When all's said, it's the tale he wants. It's a tale to hang Mansell—if the King believed it."

"Oh!" A sudden flicker of excitement died stillborn. "You mean the King would not believe it?"

"He certainly wouldn't. He's had his fill of plots since Oates's time. And anyway he has a doubting mind. Have you seen his eyebrows lift?"

"I have not. But what would he do?"

"Our Royal Charles? He'd look half asleep—which he isn't. Then he'd cock an eyebrow and set to teasing the spaniel. And Dangerfield would be passed to Mr. Secretary—who would no doubt tell him go find some better tale."

Mr. Payne yawned sleepily and called for fresh coffee. He was taking the scent of it when John spoke again.

"We'll agree that Gadbury believes this tale. And Mrs. Cellier?"

"She's fool enough."

"True. And Dangerfield?"

"Will do as he's paid to do. He won't scruple."

"He certainly won't. But do I stand on my head? Do you paint him as a faithful fellow, doing always as he's told to do?"

"Why not? He's paid for it."

"Is he?" John was looking grim. "Then what of Bride Court?"

"Mother of God!" For once it was Mr. Payne who was startled. "I'd forgot that. The same house, you say?"

"The house of Richard Hill. Mansell above one stair. Dangerfield above two."

"Aye . . ." Mr. Payne seemed to have recovered himself. "But it's to be expected, isn't it? Taking pay from each to betray the other? That's Dangerfield."

"I don't doubt it. But how's it done—this time?"

"How?" Mr. Payne's eyes had recovered their light. "He'll have his fee from Gadbury and he'll take this tale to the King. If Charles believes it, there'll be some guineas thrown. If he doesn't—and he won't—Dangerfield will take it to Mansell, and from Mansell to Shaftesbury. And Shaftesbury has some guineas, too."

"So it seems. But why for Dangerfield?"

"Because it's the tale Shaftesbury needs. He could make a second Popish Plot of this, and Mansell a Protestant martyr."

"Martyr?"

"Why not? It's a conspiracy to kill him, isn't it? To get him hanged on false testimony? That's how Shaftesbury would show it. No wonder he'd pay Dangerfield—and Mansell, too, for bringing him."

Mr. Payne slapped down his empty mug, and John stared gloomily at him across the table.

"Isn't there time to call Gadbury off?"

"You can't argue with Gadbury when the stars have been telling him. It makes him worse." Mr. Payne tinkled his cup irritably. "The short of it is that Dangerfield gets paid by the King if he believes it, and by Shaftesbury if he doesn't."

"I see. Then there seems to be only one thing for it—dispose of Dangerfield."

"We can't. That would make *him* the Protestant martyr if Shaftesbury gets a whisper of this. It would be worse, not better."

"Then what's to be done?"

"God knows." Mr. Payne's thoughts so gripped him that he seemed lost to time and space, and John sat in a bleak silence until he roused himself and went to the bar for yet more coffee; and when he returned with the steaming cups Mr. Payne was alert again, and almost at his ease.

"There are perhaps some hopes," he said quietly. "This may not be so pressing as we'd feared. Gadbury is likely to wait till his precious Moon's in Scorpio, and Dangerfield will have to wait on Gadbury. So perhaps there's a further chance."

"Of what?"

"Of warning Gadbury—and Mrs. Cellier. So be pleased to try again, and this time be indiscreet."

"Indis——"

"Yes." Mr. Payne was crisp and sure. "Don't offer a warning direct. That would set them against you. But let it somehow drop that Dangerfield has taken a lodging as Mansell's neighbour. Even Gadbury should see what that means."

"I'll try. Though I've doubts. What more?"

"There's no more that offers. But a little may lead to much—by the grace of God. I'll be in Child's at nights. It's discreet, and you may seek me there." Mr. Payne yawned and looked about him at the empty room and the impatient servers. "We outstay our welcome here, and we'd best be off. And so ends Sunday. . . ."

It had not been a good Sunday, and there was little in Monday that made amends for it. Monday indeed began well; it began as John would have had all days begin; for during the forenoon a letter was brought to him out of the post office, a letter whose scrawling and jagged superscription sent his heart leaping and racing in excitement; this was from Penny.

It was a gossipy letter, as brisk and inconsequential as herself. It was not Penny's way to devote herself to literary composition; she put down words as they came to her, and the result was a letter that talked and rambled as though she were there and speaking; her own ways and moods, her turns of speech, the quick lighting of her eyes and the hot snap of her comments, all came alive and vivid from the sprawling script. She wrote of a chance meeting with Will Hoghton, of a thorn that had lamed her horse, of trouble with Aunt Arabella over some nicety of behaviour in church; her father was showing signs of the gout; there had been a fellow taken poaching on his land. One thing followed another just as it had come to mind, and John read with a delighted interest; it freshened his fragrant memories, and every quirk and turn of it was Penny. His smile was mellowing as he read; and then, on the last sheet, he came to what touched him differently.

Did I tell you Roddy's here? He is, and he's been here this last week, and I think he'll be here another. Anyway, he said yesterday he'd see me at church next Sunday.

John frowned at it, and thoughtfully he turned back to the head of the letter. It was dated the previous Sunday, which meant that the postboys had found good riding these October days. But "next Sunday" must now mean the Sunday just gone—yesterday, when the chariot had been standing by the King's Head tavern; which should mean that Mansell had *not* returned to town with Mrs. Waring. John's forehead puckered over that; and then he returned to the letter.

He wanted me to ride with him this week, and I said I wouldn't. I said he kept a trollop and he could ride with her. I don't know where the trollop is. Nobody's seen her here. But I did see the Levite—the one who was attending on her when she first came that day. And I've seen him twice since, and he was at the church this morning. He must be at Thornclough, and I don't know why.

Nor did John, and it did nothing to smooth his forehead. It was perhaps trivial, but it was a detail that did not fit; and before the evening was done he was concerned with another detail that did not fit. Once again he went in the dusk to Arundel Street, but this time he went in russets, with his cloak drawn tight and his hat pulled low, for the weather had broken sharply and the dusk was grey with the drenching rain. It was a night when men moved quickly to avoid the pattering puddles and the mud that spattered as the coaches crashed and jolted on the cobbles. It was a night for a hackney coach, but John was learning prudence; he went alone and on foot, sure that none would heed him in the dark and rain, and he came to Arundel Street with his cloak sodden and his hat soft and black with water.

The street was cold and wet as he knocked, and he huddled in the doorway to shake his cloak as he waited; then the latch clicked as softly as ever, the door swung as silently, and there was Anne with surprised face and uplifted candle.

John did not hesitate. It was no night for hesitation, and he had stepped briskly in before Anne could speak. She made no demur at it; in silence she pushed the door and slid the bolt, and when she turned to face him he had doffed his hat and was shaking open his cloak.

"Mrs. Cellier?"

He was slipping the cloak from his shoulders as he spoke, and to his surprise Anne shook her head.

"She's from home, sir, this night."

He stopped short, the wet cloak trailing from his arm, and stared at the girl; he had not expected this, and for the moment he was at a nonplus. He was still groping when Anne spoke again.

"She drove out in a coach with the captain at five of the clock. And she told me I might go to bed."

John heard; and suddenly he was alert and questing. There was something behind this. The girl had not waited to be asked; her words had come with a rush, and there had been venom in her tone.

"I see." He nodded calmly. "And whither, do you know?"

"She doesn't tell *me*."

Again it was venomous; and at once he remembered how she had been sent to her bed last night with a promise that she should be schooled when the guests were gone. He eyed her steadily as she stood silently in front of him, and now he noted that her face was white and strained.

"I see," he said again. "You were sent from the room last night, Anne, and we saw no more of you. Did anything follow?"

"Yes."

It came curtly. She was looking him straight in the eye, and there was defiance in her white face.

"She whipped me."

It was defiance and resentment in one, and he stood stiffly while his thoughts raced; there was something out of proportion here; something, perhaps, to be probed when so much might hang on trifles. He handed her his cloak, and he watched in silence while she hung it.

"You may conduct me abovestair," he told her. "I'll write a few words for her."

"Yes, sir."

That came quietly, as though she had recovered herself now, and she held the candle high as she led up the stair and flung open the parlour door for him. She seemed at ease then, and she had herself under command as she lit more candles and found him paper, ink, and pens.

He made his thoughts leave Anne as he took the chair by the table; in writing a word for Mrs. Cellier he meant to write the warning he could not now speak, and it required his best thoughts before his pen went scratching noisily.

I had not supposed that Captain Dangerfield had such happiness this night. I had supposed, indeed, that he was engaged with some companions and a bottle or two at his lodging in Bride Court, and I had even hoped that some disturbances might be occasioned thereby to Colonel Mansell in his lodging below. But it is not so, and another night must serve the need of

John Leyburne

He scanned it quickly and decided that it would do; certainly it meant almost nothing, but it set plainly the one fact that she must know, and it might therefore serve the need.

"How old are you, Anne?" He spoke quietly while he set Mrs. Cellier's name on the folded sheet.

"Sixteen, sir."

"How long have you been with Mrs. Cellier?"

"A year, sir, and two months."

"Then you'll have been whipped before last night?"

"Yes, sir."

"I expect you deserved it?"

She hesitated, and then with a rueful grin she nodded.

"Yes, sir. Those times."

"I see." He flung down his pen and looked up at her. "So it was different last night, was it? Why?"

The girl's face had darkened, and there was mute anger in her eyes. He saw it plainly, and for a moment he was silent as he considered the foolishness that jealousy had led Mrs. Cellier into. On the surface of things it could, indeed, be justified; if the girl's conduct was unseemly it ought to be corrected, and Mrs. Cellier's neighbours would no doubt say that she had done no more than her plain and obvious duty. But she had evidently gone about it in a fashion that had roused a seething resentment, and John was eyeing the girl anxiously as he thought of it. Anne's young affections had already been given to Dangerfield, and it would need but a little flattery now to persuade her to any service he might ask.

"I didn't *do* it."

Anne spoke suddenly, and the tremulous anger in her voice startled him. He looked up sharply.

"What did you not do, Anne?"

"I did not press myself against the captain." She was speaking more steadily now, but the ring in her voice showed how she had been stirred. "I'm called a wanton and a slut and a lecher. And I'm not. I—I——"

She had stopped, and her lip was twisting between her teeth. He turned away and stared at the fire while she fought for control.

"No, Anne," he said quietly. "I do not think you are. But what was it, then, last night?"

She answered him calmly and steadily.

"I carried him his wine. Mr. Gadbury gave it to me to carry, and it's my proper work. He had his back to the hearth there——"

"I remember. And then?"

"He saw me come with the wine. And he pushed himself forward from off the hearth—pushed with his shoulders, I mean. And he seemed to fall forward at me——"

"What's that? You mean he lurched, as it were, and came against you?"

"He came pressing against me." She coloured hotly as she remembered. "And I—I had the wine, so I had to be still. And——"

"And then Mrs. Cellier saw you?"

"Yes, sir."

She ended, and then stood calmly, her big eyes moist and shining. He nodded slowly.

"I'll believe you, Anne."

He found it impossible not to believe her. Dangerfield had no doubt contrived it, and he was not a man to be concerned for anything that Anne might suffer. John felt his mouth hardening.

"But Anne," he said slowly, "you surely explained that to your mistress? Would she not believe you?"

"I wasn't going to tell her. I wouldn't seem to blame *him.*"

"No?" It was a sentiment that John did not share. "But what befell?"

"She had me out of bed—and it hurt. And when I was getting back to bed, she—she called me all those names."

"I understand." He interrupted quickly, thinking that he did not want the details of this; and then he realized that there was still something he must say. He came quietly to his feet.

"You've been hardly done to, Anne. I'm sorry for it. And I believe that it was not your fault and that you've not conducted yourself ill. Now will you get my cloak?"

She made no spoken answer, but he saw the mute gratitude in her face as she went quietly from the room. He heard her go down the stair, and then he stood staring at the fire as he pondered Mrs. Cellier's madness. She was even more of a fool than he had supposed; and that, he thought grimly, was to say a deal. She had betrayed her feelings blatantly, and she had done a mischief that she would not find it easy to mend; and as like as not she would not even have wit enough to perceive that she had done it.

The door opened, and Anne came in with his sodden cloak. He let her help him into it, and there was a gratitude again in the way she fussed about him. She stood happily in front of him when the cloak was set to her liking; and suddenly his eyes were alert as he saw the small locket, a leaf of gold done to the shape of a heart, that was now pendant from her slim young neck. He was sure it had not been there when she had gone for the cloak; and at once he guessed that she was proudly displaying what had before been hidden.

"It's very pretty, Anne."

She flushed happily and tossed her head, and he knew that she wanted to tell him.

"A gift, was it?"

She nodded, and he saw that her breath was coming quickly.

"And from him?"

"Yes." It came breathlessly. "He gave it me three days past, and he said . . ."

Her voice died away. She was smiling into vacancy, and John did not rouse her; he cared nothing for what Dangerfield had said.

She passed him his hat, and his fingers pressed on hers as he took it. Then he was smiling down at her.

"It was well for you, Anne, that she did not see him give it to you."

"She couldn't," came the prompt answer. "She wasn't there. It was at his lodging."

"Anne!"

"Very proper, if you please, sir." She was almost arch about it. "I'd been sent there by my mistress—with a letter."

"Then you're a blameless child." He took the gloves she was

holding out, and he was moving to the door when an odd thought came to him. In the doorway he turned.

"This lodging of his that your mistress sent you to, Anne—where is it?"

"Just off Fleet Street, sir—in Bride Court. The fourth house on the left——"

"I see." His face was impassive, and his eyes were avoiding hers. "I hope Mrs. Cellier gave you good directions."

"Oh yes, sir. She did."

"I see." His grave eyes moved back to hers. "I think, perhaps, I'll not leave this letter for her after all. There's not the need for it."

He hardly noticed that the rain had ceased as he went slowly up Arundel Street. His thoughts were in chaos, and all that he had supposed secure seemed built on sand. Mrs. Cellier *did* know of Dangerfield's new lodging; and could she be so devoid of all perception as not to see the meaning of it? Or had she so succumbed to his persuasions that she would even join at his bidding to betray them all, friends and faith alike?

The faint grey light that suffused the Strand told of a moon bright and high above the clouds, and his thoughts turned darkly to Mr. Gadbury's predictions. The moon was past its full; and night by night it was swinging in the sky, moving on its endless journey through the belt of stars that were the twelve signs of the zodiac. Soon it would slide softly into Scorpio; and what then?

Gadbury might be right, he told himself as he made for Child's in the churchyard where Mr. Payne would be. There might indeed be stirrings when the moon was in the Scorpion; but what sort of stirrings, and to whose hurt? Scorpions, he remembered, had stinging tails and were not always to be accounted friendly.

26 MOON IN SCORPIO

The moon was new on the twentieth of October, and it was a damp grey Monday, cool and windless, with a soft mist of rain wetting the cobbles and lying in glistening beads on the cloaks of those who walked in Fleet Street.

Mr. Gill, of the Clockmakers' Company, was away on affairs, and Mr. Leyburne, watchful in the workshop in his stead, was not in the best of humours. Somehow the belief had hardened in him that Gadbury's prediction would be fulfilled, that this change in the Moon's affairs would bring some changes in the affairs of men; and not, he thought, changes for the better.

Chiming clocks in that little room always set him in mind of Penny, her brown face taut with delight as she fingered a repeating clock and pulled at its silken cord; and he was cherishing that memory as he paced slowly through the workshop to assure himself that all was well before he slipped up the stair for his midmorning ale. For a moment he gave his full attention to the bustle around him, and then his walk checked abruptly; something was amiss.

His face stayed impassive as he turned. There was nothing obviously wrong, but he had been an apprentice and a journeyman, and he knew what the signs were of suppressed excitement in a workshop; the talk was a little more and a little louder than usual; men were watching the door; apprentices were making show of being busied with work that was not theirs; and one apprentice was missing altogether.

John took it all in with an experienced eye; then he strolled to the bench that the missing lad shared with another.

"Where," he demanded, "is Harry?"

"Out for a minute, sir." The lad at the bench looked up from the weights he was threading on the cord of gut that would hang them in a clock. "We're just out of resin, sir."

"Resin, is it?" John nodded, and moved across the workshop again; it was an old tale, and he came to a halt by the senior journeyman.

"Where's young Harry?" he asked again. "And don't *you* tell me it's resin."

"Resin?" The man laughed openly. "They all think they're the first——"

"So did we. But where's Harry?"

"Down the street, and agog for news. There's some stir down Bride Court way. Matter of smuggling. The excisemen are there. . . ."

John's face stayed impassive, and he had no show of interest as he

turned away. But two minutes later, when young Harry slipped innocently through the door with a lump of resin prominent in his grubby
fist, he was sharply called into Mr. Gill's small room and questioned
more about what he had seen than why he had been to see it. And
then Mr. Gill returned to his shop.

It was John's turn to make polite excuses, and then he was away
himself, careless of the drizzling rain, and not staying even to pull a
cloak about his shoulders. Young Harry had been specific that there
were excisemen in Bride Court at the fourth house on the left; and
that something was stirring could hardly be doubted.

The press was thick at the opening of the court. There was a clutter
of apprentices, a journeyman or two, and the usual rabble of by-
standers sprung from nowhere; and they were all intent on some stir
within the court, where a hackney coach was standing. John had to
use his shoulders to get through the crowd, and once he was in the
court he saw what he had expected to see; the coach was by the fourth
house on the left, the house of Richard Hill, and by the open door of
that house three burly fellows were lounging.

There was a stir and sigh in the crowd as a man appeared from the
house and spoke urgently to one of the three who lounged by the door;
the fellow nodded and then went elbowing through the crowd, bawling
noisily for passage; he disappeared into Fleet Street, and a couple of
minutes later there was a clop of hooves and a rattle of wheels as a
second hackney coach came edging into the court; it drew up by the
other, and then affairs moved swiftly. Roderick Mansell, his red face
flushed and hot, came from the house with excisemen to left and right
of him; Captain Dangerfield followed, similarly escorted, and then
came a man in sky blue, whose silver lace and air of consequence
hinted that he had authority in this; he carried a roll of papers, and
the fellows by the door jumped to attention as he appeared. Mansell
entered the one coach and Dangerfield the other, and John waited for
no more; he wriggled through the crowd and hurried into Fleet Street
to call a coach for his own hire.

What followed was easy. The two coaches came rumbling from the
court and went jolting up Fleet Street, past Fetter Lane, past Chancery
Lane and the King's Head tavern, and on almost to the City boundary;
here, within a score of paces of Temple Bar, they drew up before the

house of Mr. Caldwell, the goldsmith; and the third coach, which had moved discreetly behind them, drew into the side as though its single passenger were bound for the Rainbow. Colonel Mansell stepped from the one coach and Captain Dangerfield from the other; the chief of the excisemen stepped out with him, still clutching his papers, and all of them entered hurriedly into the house of Mr. Caldwell. John saw it all as he made leisurely search for the shilling that should pay his coachman, and then, for the better look of things, he went strolling into the Rainbow. Mr. Caldwell, the goldsmith, was also a justice of the peace, and it might therefore be supposed that the excisemen had found some smuggled lace and had at once carried Colonel Mansell before the nearest justice. But why had Dangerfield been taken too? That was something to be discovered.

John came thoughtfully from the Rainbow and made his way briskly down Fleet Street to Mr. Gill's. Mr. Caldwell was a very prosperous goldsmith, and his house and shop swarmed with apprentices; one apprentice would always talk to another, and all of them had long ears and a trick of knowing their master's affairs. The matter should not be difficult, and John went at it as soon as he was back in the workshop.

Young Harry, whose ears were said to be the longest at Mr. Gill's, was called aside and given crisp orders; his eyes widened as he took them in, and they widened further as he took the shilling that followed; then, with his sharp young face agog with excitement, he was out of the workshop at a run and scurrying up Fleet Street. Mr. Leyburne, of the Clockmakers' Company, walked calmly round the workshop and went to dinner.

It was half-past one by the chiming clocks when he returned to the workshop and called young Harry into Mr. Gill's now empty room, and at once it was plain that Mr. Caldwell's apprentices had been willing enough to talk. Young Harry had it pat. An information had been laid before the Excise that Colonel Mansell had some uncustomed lace at his chambers in Bride Court. It was a Captain Dangerfield who had laid that information.

John queried it sharply, but the lad stuck to it. Mr. Caldwell's apprentices must have listened with avidity, and Harry seemed sure of his facts. It was Captain Dangerfield who had laid the information, and the captain had accompanied the excisemen to search the colonel's lodging. Unfortunately no lace had been found, but there had been something else.

Young Harry was twitching with excitement as he went on. The search had ended in the colonel's bedchamber; it had come to an end, and the chief exciseman had been rendering apologies, when Captain Dangerfield had suddenly made his discovery. He had given a great shout of "Treason!"

"Of what?"

John's voice cut in sharply. This was by no means what he had expected, but Harry stuck firmly to it. That was what the captain had shouted, and as soon as he had shouted it he had plunged his hand behind the head of the colonel's bed and had brought out a roll of papers; and these papers had contained a plot.

"The devil they did!" John was beginning to wonder whether he had heard aright. "What sort of a plot?"

But for once Harry was at a loss. This was something he did not know, and he wasted no time on it. He hurried on to what he did know; the excisemen, he said, had refused to become involved in this; instead they had carried both men before the nearest justice, and Mr. Caldwell had perforce given them a hearing; and the end of that had been that he had disbelieved in the plot. He had committed Captain Dangerfield to Newgate on a charge of forgery; and he had honourably discharged Colonel Mansell, who was now back in his lodging in Bride Court.

"The devil!" said Mr. Leyburne once again.

It was a sentiment echoed that evening by Mr. Payne. John was in search of him as soon as dusk was come, and in Child's Mr. Payne took one swift glance at John's face and then swept him into a discreet alcove.

"Gadbury!" was his terse comment as John came to an end.

"You mean that Gadbury——"

"Of course he did. The pattern's plain. Perhaps we should have guessed the truth when you had it that Mrs. Cellier knew of his lodging. It was all part of their plot. Gadbury wrote those papers—no doubt of Mansell as a quartermaster—and it was for Dangerfield to take them to Mansell's room and there discover them. The excisemen, of course, were to be witnesses to it. A nice touch that, and it had a pretty tinge of truth in it. I suppose any informer likes a tinge of truth if he may have it."

"And then he bungled it." John spoke grimly. "And what's to be expected now?"

"Something worse. He'll tell what tale will get him out of Newgate."

"He could, I suppose, even tell the truth?"

"He could, but he won't. It's not in his nature. He'll hatch some slyness and then preen himself on it."

"Let's hope he'll hang himself on it."

"Amen! But he's more likely to hang Gadbury on it. And where, by the way, *is* Gadbury?"

"God knows."

"You sound sour. But I'm in earnest. Dangerfield has a forgery charged against him, and his way out of that is to reveal a plot."

"What plot?"

"Any plot. So we may expect some pretty tale, spiced to suit Shaftesbury."

"If he can get at Shaftesbury—from Newgate."

"He knows Newgate, doesn't he, and every turnkey in it?" Mr. Payne seemed to brush that aside. "Our only hope is that, at the root of it, Dangerfield's a fool. There was a fine sprouting imagination in Oates, but Dangerfield hasn't got it. If he takes to fiction it will be something workaday. From Oates we'd have had a tale worth hearing. But not from Dangerfield. It's not in his talents. It will be something near at home, something about folk he knows. And that's why we must see Gadbury."

"To warn him?"

"He needs it, doesn't he? And that must be your work. For me, I'll see what's to be learned. I'll get me to the Grecian now. It's the place for such whispers." Mr. Payne came briskly to his feet and adjusted his cloak. "Gadbury is for you, if you can find him. So is Mrs. Cellier."

They parted at the corner of Arundel Street, and John turned down towards Mrs. Cellier's. He was as likely, he thought, to find Gadbury there as elsewhere, but in that he was wrong; Gadbury was not there, and neither was Mrs. Cellier. John's quiet and wary knock brought Anne to the door, and, when he had stepped within, it needed only one glance to assure him that all was not well with Anne. He looked keenly as she lowered the candle.

"You've been crying, Anne."

He spoke gravely, but she had no answer that was in words; the girl's head was down and she was biting at the crumpled handkerchief that was screwed tight between her fingers; he had to wait while she recovered herself, and then she spoke breathlessly.

"Is he safe?" The words came with a rush. "Will they get him out?"

"Captain Dangerfield, you mean?" He was speaking almost lightly, and Anne nodded eagerly at the name. "I can't say *when* they'll have him out, Anne, but no doubt they will. The captain, I think, is in no great danger."

"Oh!" Her voice was fluttering. "That's—that's the truth?"

"It is."

The words came grimly as he reflected that it was most damnably the truth; it was John Gadbury and some others who were in danger, not Tom Dangerfield. It was a fleeting thought, but it woke his mind to realities, and at once he was considering Anne again.

"Where is your mistress?" he asked her.

"She's from home, sir. She went out an hour since—with Mr. Gadbury. It—it's about bail for him, sir."

"For the captain?"

"Yes, sir. They—they went to the Grecian, sir."

"Did they, indeed?" He was considering her thoughtfully, but he had some kindly feeling for this distraught girl, and he was smiling as he pulled his cloak tight.

"Be of good cheer, Anne. All men have friends. And you have some too."

He leaned forward and touched her cheek lightly, and a moment later she let him into the dark street. He walked quickly, relieved to be away, and relieved also that it would be Mr. Payne who would have to deal with Gadbury in the Grecian. It might be a difficult task; and more than that would be difficult, he reflected, before this Moon should have come to its full in the stinging Scorpion.

27 WARRANT FOR SEARCH   Mr. Payne was taking his coffee when John walked into Child's the next evening; and at once he made it plain that he had himself met Gadbury and Mrs. Cellier in the Grecian.

"The Moon in a Scorpion?" was his comment. "Myself, I'd say it was in Gadbury's head."

"It's so, is it?"

"It's just so. I told him in the plainest words what his danger is, and he'll have none of it." Mr. Payne's cup tinkled as he set it down forcefully. "There's Mars in the Bull just now, it seems, and the Scorpion's opposed. So alarms are to be expected. And that's all there's to it."

"What is?"

"What I've said. Or rather it's what Gadbury said. He pulled out his almanack to prove it."

"But this Bull——"

"I wish it had hay on its horn. It might gut Dangerfield for us then. I want more coffee."

Mr. Payne gestured to a server, and John sat silent while the coffee was brought.

"What of Mrs. Cellier?" he asked then.

"She's mad. Sick for love." Mr. Payne spoke pungently. "It's poor Tom Dangerfield. Tom, Tom, Tom—poor faithful Tom! That's the burden of it."

"I see." John's voice came steadily. "I mind Gadbury's saying she'd Mercury combust somewhere and her wits were addled."

"Addled! They're gone in stinking corruption. From lovesick women, good God deliver us!"

"Amen to that! But what does Gadbury say to all this? He must say something."

"He says all will be well in the *next* New Moon. That's in the Archer, it seems."

"Is he mad also? A Scorpion, and a Bull, and now an Archer! *Why* an Archer?"

"It's the day house of Jupiter."

"What is?"

"The Archer is."

"What!"

"So Gadbury says. Have you a horse?"

"Certainly I've a horse. But——"

"The Archer's got one too. He's a mounted Archer. That's what put me in mind of it."

"Of what?"

"Horses. Planets in the Archer give love of horses. Thus Gadbury."

Mr. Payne tasted his coffee delicately, and for a moment John's thoughts were far away. For a moment the sun and wind of a northern shore were his; and there was Penny, vivid in the summer light on the dappled grey she sat so lovingly; Penny trotting by the creaming tide with the careless ease that was her own. She flared for an instant before him, bright and alluring, and then she was gone; and again he was in Child's in the churchyard, in the murk of an October night, and Mr. Payne was setting down his cup.

"We may have need of horses."

Mr. Payne was speaking gravely, and John hastily disposed himself to listen; this did not sound trivial.

"I said I'd visit Whitehall this day, and I did not have to seek for gossip. The place was buzzing with it. And the short of it is that Dangerfield's to come before the Council."

"Oh? Meaning what?"

"Need you ask? The Privy Council's above such dregs as forgers. If he's appearing before them he's appearing as an informer, and as nothing else. He's to reveal a plot."

"I see." John spoke quietly. "And when does he do it?"

"Monday. That's when the Council next sits, and God knows what he'll say. The more in a plot the better, and there'd be room in it for you and me. Which is why I speak of horses. We may have to ride for it, and at short warning. You'd best have all prepared."

It was hardly to be disputed, and there seemed nothing to be done except to look to horse and harness; nor could more be known till Monday or later, and John went home with the unhappy thought that the days till Monday would be long and anxious.

They were. They dragged most tediously, and they were enlivened only by the coming from the post office of another letter directed in the bold and inky script he knew was Penny's. He took it eagerly, and the rustle of grass and the clop of hooves seemed to come to him as he broke the seal; and one piece of news she had for him, when he had plucked it from her ramble of words:

Will Hoghton's a good friend. His father has the gout still, but each time he can set foot to the ground Will has ridden to the shore to learn if the Widow Jump has news, and yesterday I rode with him, though it was blowing out of the northwest and I could see the rain coming. I rode to the Park Hall because I thought I might see Uncle Ned. I can talk to him. Sometimes he's the only one I can talk to—except you. But he wasn't there. Will says Sir H. Mansell and the other justices are a deal hotter against the papists now than they used to be, so all the papists have troubles and that makes Uncle Ned busy. But Will was making ready to ride to the shore, so I said I'd ride with him, even though the rain had started. It was getting gusty too, but it was better than turning to home again and being clapped behind doors. Aunt Arabella always wants to do that when there's a puddle of water and I might get my feet wet.

It was past noon when we got to the shore, and Aunt Arabella would have had the vapours to see me. It was a full gale now, blowing like the wrath of God, and you couldn't see for the rain. It was through my cloak and down my neck and into my boots, and my hair was like the sea wrack, and Will said I looked like a mermaid gone rusty. But the widow had a fire of sea wood, all crackling and spluttering, and that dried us. Jimmy was there too. He baited the horses and the widow baited us, and it wasn't shrimps, either. Will and I ate most of a ham between us. Of course we asked Jimmy if he'd seen anything of late, and he said he had. There's been that lugger in again, the week before when the moon was at swell. He could not see much because it was raining and there was a murk on the moon, but he did make out that there were four men that came on horses, and when they made off again there were only three and a led horse. So what of that? Will thinks it was the Levite gone again, and so do I.

It was a good day, for all the wet of it, though it wasn't good for me when I got home. It was near dusk at the Park Hall, and then Will rode all the way back here with me, but we were too late, and my father and Aunt Arabella were near frantick, because I had not said I was riding far that day. I'll tell you more when you come. But when are you coming?

John wished he knew. He would have given much to know. In his present humours there seemed nothing fitter to be wished for than the long lonely ride to the North. Penny had come alive to him in that rambling tale; and from those artless phrases there had come too the memory of Will Hoghton, friendly and solid; of the Widow Jump, birdlike and bright of eye; of the salt wind by her door, and the marram grass that shivered in the hawes; of the screaming gulls, and the white surf on the cool wet sand. He read it again, and yet again; he looked out through the workshop window to the damp murk of London in a wet October; and he knew that there was nothing to be done but wait for Monday and the meeting of the Council. He could not desert Mr. Payne, nor the others, at this juncture, and the less so since Mr. Payne had pointed out the danger; journey to the North Parts now would have a look of flight, and there was no course in honour but to wait for Monday.

Monday came. It took an age to come, but it came; and it came as wet and sickly as the other days had been. The workshop was dim and grey as a drizzle of rain blurred the windows, and through the day there were candles burning, that the journeymen might see their work; the dusk came early that night, and John was away in the first wet greyness of it to seek Mr. Payne at Child's; and he was into his second coffee before Mr. Payne's tall, loose-limbed figure appeared through the press of divines who crowded round the fire.

"What is it?" John spoke abruptly. "Let me have the worst of it."

"I don't know the worst of it." Mr. Payne seemed more concerned to taste his coffee. "It was not what I'd expected."

"No? But what *was* it?"

"One of those quirks of Fate. The Council met at noon, and they'd more to consider than a slug like Dangerfield, so they left him to the last. But in midafternoon they had some affair of coining, and a fellow from the Mint came running with some papers that might be called for. And he's no sooner in the anteroom than he calls out against Dangerfield, naming him as a rogue that's wanted, and for clipping coin."

"Oh ho!"

"You may say it. And there was a rare commotion. The Mint man shouts at Dangerfield. Dangerfield shouts back that he's son of a

whore. The guards thump their halberds and shout at both, and half
a score of gentlemen call on God to damn 'em. And at once there's
Dangerfield and the Mint man haled before their lordships to be
questioned. And soon it's plain the Mint man has the truth of it. Apart
from coining, Dangerfield's been pilloried twice, and he's broken gaol
to miss a third stand. In short he's a known and noted rogue, and now
he's so committed. But now it's coining that's against him—and that's
high treason. It's pains of death if they press that against him."

"As they will—surely?"

"They might." Mr. Payne gazed dreamily at his coffee. "Or they
might not. It depends, no doubt, upon his memory. But I think the
affair looks better than it did. He's a rogue now, and he'll have to show
some evidence, if they're to heed him. And has he got any?"

"No."

"Then he'll perhaps try to make some. A few days will show. If all's
well by Sunday we may breathe again. If not, it's horses—if Fortune
smiles."

"Yes." John steadied his breath. "What more?"

"Nothing. Except that tomorrow I'll get me to Westminster and call
on Gadbury—to be sure he's still at large."

"At large?"

"Precisely. For that's our touchstone. And do you the same for Mrs.
Cellier. If they're both at large, all's well. If not . . ."

The tightening of his lips said the rest, and John nodded.

"If not, it's horses?"

"Maybe. So we could meet here at—nine, shall we say?"

"If you wish."

"I do." Mr. Payne was grim. "We must know that *we* are still at
large."

"Good God!"

"Amen! And the same each night this week, if you please."

They parted on that, and John was not without matter for thought
as he hovered alertly in the workshop the next day. What path his
thoughts were running appeared at noon, when the shop was empty
and all were at dinner. He slipped in alone and made for the bench
where the oilstones lay for the sharpening of tools; and for a half hour
he was busy with his sword, working at both edges from the point six

inches up; he brought a craftsman's precision to the work, and when it was done he tested the cut of it on a falling strand of wool.

He went out in the late dusk, thankful for the mist of rain that still kept the cobbles shining, and he went warily down Arundel Street, alert for a coach, or perhaps a chariot, that might be standing before the door. But all was quiet, and the street was dark and empty as he plied the knocker softly. Then the door swung silently, and Anne was smiling at him, her face a little flushed in the light of her upheld candle; that was what he had expected; what he had not expected was that Anne spoke first.

"She's from home, sir. It's all dark here. She went out an hour since."

"Oh?" He was in some surprise. "Do you know whither?"

"Yes, sir. To Man's coffeehouse, she said. She went with Mr. Gadbury."

"Man's?" His surprise was open now, for Man's in Whitehall was the coffeehouse of the courtiers, the most fashionable house in town; it was not a likely choice for Gadbury and Mrs. Cellier.

"Yes, sir. And they said that if you were to call I was to say they were at Man's to meet Mr. Payne."

"To meet——" John broke off as the feeling closed on him that something was amiss. Mr. Payne would certainly not choose Man's.

He thanked the girl and took an abrupt departure. The sooner he was at Man's, he thought, the sooner he would know what was amiss, and in the Strand he looked eagerly for a hackney coach. But no coach appeared; he had to go on foot, and it was a full twenty minutes before he turned into the long dark alley that led to Man's. He hurried down it under the gaze of the rabble of lackeys and linkboys who waited there for their masters, and then he climbed quickly up the stair to the fragrance of coffee that flowed from the upper room. It was a fragrance of coffee only, with no fume of tobacco to pollute it; there was an elegance at Man's, and tobacco was not in favour. There were faces that turned and eyebrows that lifted as John came through the door in russets that were discreetly bare of everything that glittered, but he paid no heed to that; he was scanning the candlelit room in search of the two he sought, and it was quickly apparent that they were not there. He made sure of it, moving idly round the room to peer into every corner, and then he took his coffee to a chair by the wall, where he could sit while he watched the door; he called for more coffee and then he stretched his legs and lounged at ease. His thoughts went drifting; and soon they were with Penny, and he was asking himself what she did this night, how she had spent the day; and then he was pondering the lugger that came so discreetly in, and had perhaps as passenger the Levite, Mr. Roberts. . . .

He came from his thoughts abruptly, and wondered whether he had been asleep. Certainly he had lost all count of time, and he was startled when he glanced at the long clock that ticked behind the door; it was a quarter-past eight, and he must have been here for an hour and more. The coffee in his cup was cold, and he sat erect in something like alarm and considered what was to be done. Certainly he must keep his appointment with Mr. Payne at nine o'clock, since that was to be the proof that all was still well; but to get to Child's he must pass along the Strand, and there would be time to turn into Arundel Street on the way; and that, no doubt, would be as well, for Mr. Payne would surely wish to know where Mrs. Cellier was.

It was scarcely half-past eight when he plied her knocker once more, and the door swung open with a promptness that surprised him; seemingly Anne was in surprise also, as though she had not expected to see him a second time this night; but he paid no heed to that, and his voice was crisp as he asked for Mrs. Cellier.

"Why, yes, sir." Anne answered him quietly. "She came back an hour since, and she's above."

"If you please, then . . ."

Mrs. Cellier was surprised too, and she took no pains to hide it. But she was also pleased, and she did not hide that either; she gave him a rushing welcome, threw more sea-coals on the fire, sent Anne running for the wine, and showed herself in no way disposed to raise an eyebrow at his coming alone and in the hours of dark.

"Where is he?" she demanded quickly.

"But who, ma'am?"

"Mr. Payne, of course. He sent for me——"

"Sent?"

"To be sure, sir, to be sure." There was indignation in her voice, and it had heightened her colour as she stood beneath the candles.

"Mr. Gadbury came to me at dusk. We—we've been trying to make a bail for poor Tom——"

"Aye, ma'am." He was not interested in poor Tom. "And then?"

"Why then, sir, there was a gentleman came, a Mr. Warburton. A very pretty gentleman——"

"No doubt, ma'am. But what said he?"

"Why, he stayed but a moment—only to say he was friend to Mr. Payne and that Mr. Payne had most urgent cause to see me at Man's."

"Whither you then went? I see."

"Certainly I went. What else should I do? And Mr. Gadbury——"

"Went with you. I know. You must have left before I got there."

He told her swiftly of his own movements, and then he turned thoughtfully to the fire as she filled his glass.

"Then where," she asked plaintively, "is Mr. Payne? We stayed an hour for him. But where is he?"

"I wish I knew."

His face was hard as he sipped his wine. Something was undoubtedly amiss; it would not be like Mr. Payne to break an appointment made so urgently; and then the thought came rushing that there was something spurious here. Who was this Mr. Warburton? And was it the way of Mr. Payne to send so odd a message by an unknown man? And why to so unlikely a house as Man's?

A knocking, harsh and exigent, came at the outer door, and John whipped round as it broke his thought. Mrs. Cellier moved to the door, and then checked as Anne's young feet went pattering below the stair.

"Now we'll know," she fluttered. "This must be he. He'll have come to tell us."

"I doubt it."

He spoke grimly as he went quickly across the room. Abruptly he flung open the parlour door that he might hear better. Below him the bolt slid and the latch clicked; and then a voice, hard and peremptory, spoke curtly.

"Anne Blake?"

"Yes. But——"

"Servant to Elizabeth Cellier?"

"Why, yes."

"Stand back. We're to search this house. Here's a justice of the peace. And a warrant signed."

28

THE WHIG JUSTICE   What followed was so swift and sure that John was left without illusions; this had been pre-concerted.

Feet crunched on the stair, slow and menacing, and Mrs. Cellier shrank back against the hearth as the parlour door was kicked fully open and men came in; the burly red-faced fellow who came first had the air of a tipstaff, and the four who followed were his underlings. But none of these signified; command lay here with the man who came last, the tall thin-lipped man in the prim black velvet; and one glance at him told John who this was and what kind of trap had closed; this was Sir William Waller.

Recognition was mutual and immediate. John needed no second glance to know the justice who had committed him to Newgate on an April night; and the justice, for his part, stared at John in plain surprise.

"Where's Gadbury?" he snapped.

"Not here."

John snapped it back. It was perhaps injudicious, but it was born of a hot anger as he realized what was coming. Sir William, besides being a justice, was a man of note among the Whigs, and not a man to stir in the murk of an October night if there were not something more than chance to lure him.

"You're pert, it seems." Sir William's cold eyes were on John as he spoke. "We'll mend that in season. Your name's Leyburne, I think? And you've been in Newgate?"

"By a justice's blunder, I have."

A faint flush crept into the justice's cheeks, and then he nodded.

"A justice's, you think? We'll give you cause to think differently."

He turned away as if John no longer existed, and his hard eyes were on Mrs. Cellier as he drew a paper from the deep pocket of his coat.

"Elizabeth Cellier?"

"You well know, sir, that I——"

His white hand waved imperiously to cut her short.

"I know perhaps more than you suppose. Is this your house?"

"It is."

"Here's warrant for search. Read it."

He thrust it under her nose, and then affairs moved swiftly. John was pushed into a corner under guard, Mrs. Cellier to another, and at once the tipstaff was busy upturning furniture, opening presses, flinging their contents to the floor; he went at it noisily, and he was heedless of what he smashed; he turned the trim parlour into a chaos of splintered wood and broken china, a crazy litter of chair legs, books, and draperies, with the spilt wine dribbling on silken cushions and an inkpot flung on top to ruin all; yet always he seemed more intent to damage than to probe, and the haste of it did not sort with any serious search.

"Enough! Try within."

The justice spoke curtly, and a moment later the same ruin was being wrought in the elegance of Mrs. Cellier's bedchamber; again she and John were witnesses under guard, and again there was hardly more than pretence of search.

"Enough. The kitchen."

Sir William snapped again, and again the search was transferred. The tipstaff went clumping down the stair, and others after him, and behind the stair they found a door into the big stone-flagged kitchen. It was a cheerful room, gay and neat, lit by a pair of candles and warm from the red fire that shimmered in the hearth; a table, scrubbed and white, had the centre, and under the window was a long slab of slate that made a working bench; in the opposite wall was a door that might have led to a larder, and, left and right of the door, tubs were standing, with staves of shining oak and hoops of twinkling brass. There was a stir as Anne rose from a low chair and stood before the fire; she spoke no word, but she was tense and pale; her breath was fluttering, and there was a quiver at her lip. Her eyes, too, were oddly bright; and John, looking with all his senses quickened, remembered that this was a girl who doted on Tom Dangerfield and had some cause for resentments against her mistress. He had a swift and sickening guess of what was coming; and in that moment his eyes met Anne's, and he knew.

The tipstaff went at it again, flinging plates and dishes from the racks and sending them in tinkling ruin to the floor. Then he turned to the gleaming tubs by the wall, and the brass-hinged lid of the first went clattering against the wall as he flung it up; he dived his arm into the tub, and flour went spattering over the floor; he dived into the second tub, and a fistful of oatmeal went whirling across the room. Then the fellow gave a yell of triumph; he spat exultantly as he plunged his arm into the tub again; and from it he pulled a roll of papers, neatly tied with tape.

"Ha!"

It came from the doorway, where the justice was standing under the lintel, his face impassive and his lips pressed thin and tight. The tipstaff shook the papers and blew vigorously to clear them of the clinging meal. Then he moved clumsily across the room and passed the roll to his master. Anne, silent by the fire, had her glittering eyes on Mrs. Cellier.

John turned without illusions and saw Sir William deftly untie the tape and smooth the score of sheets it had contained; he flicked them between his fingers and took hasty glances at what was written; then he turned coldly to Mrs. Cellier.

"These will do your business, ma'am. False and libellous statements, I see." He flicked at the sheets again. "Lying notes of a so-called plot. Alleged to be of a Presbyterian army. Colonel Roderick Mansell supposedly as quartermaster. Very significant, ma'am, very significant."

"I don't know what you're about, sir." Mrs. Cellier had a creditable air of truculence. "I know nothing of these papers. Nor am I at fault if Presbyterians plot treason. I'm not of that crew, sir."

"You may pray to God you were. You're a damned whoring, grovelling, idol-kissing papist, and you'll shortly wish that you were not." Sir William's eyes were bulging with a cold fury as he spoke. "There's a fellow Dangerfield now in Newgate. He's been here a deal of late, I'm told."

"Sir!" She was white-faced and trembling as she stood between the guards. "Are you supposing——"

"I'm supposing nothing. Here's evidence, not supposing." His fury was scorching as his knuckles rapped against the papers in his other hand. "This Dangerfield pretends to find notes of a lying plot in the lodging of Colonel Mansell—notes that he placed himself, as he now admits."

"Admits?" Her voice was suddenly shrill. "Do you say——"

"I say admits." His wrath cut her short as he flicked the sheets again. "And here's the full setting-out of what those notes were drawn from. Conspiracy to perjure—to the hurt of Colonel Mansell. That will be the shape of this."

"Mansell, is it?"

John spoke suddenly and unbidden, and Sir William turned on him with a face of cold menace that would have left another quaking. But John was beyond that; the irritations of weeks had crystallized into an icy anger that left him careless of this pale-faced Whig.

"Ye-es, Mansell," he drawled. "And it's not as though he were in need of further blackening."

"What's that?" Sir William's voice had risen to a shout. "You'll hold your tongue, you——"

"I shall not. I shall hold it neither here nor before the Council."

"Council?"

The word crackled, and for a moment there was a throbbing silence in the room. And John's eyes narrowed as he sensed the note that had been in the word; it had been high anger, to be sure, but under the anger, deep and far away, there had surely been a quiver of alarm. It was enough, and in that fleeting instant John had made his guess and formed his resolution.

"A very pretty fellow, Mansell," he observed drily. "There's something of Holland about him. Of Holland and the North Parts. And there's something of it about his friends, too. . . ."

His eyes were pin points now, but their gaze was steady on the fine Dutch lace that foamed at Sir William's neck, white against the soft black velvet. Sir William, he had remembered, was also of the Green Ribbon Club, and certainly its members shared some secrets; that they shared another was by no means impossible.

"Enough!" Sir William had apparently recovered, and his voice came harshly. "This is not a season for insolence. You're to be examined on oath and in form. Take them along."

His crew did it with a practised skill. Two of them had Mrs. Cellier by the wrists and elbows and were hustling her down the stair. The other pair seized on John, and for a moment they held him fast while the tipstaff lurched towards him and plucked his sword from its sheath; the fellow grinned as he saw the glint of it, and as John was pulled to the stair he was viciously pricked in the back with his own steel. It sent him white with fury, but the two rogues had him fast and there was nothing to be done—except remember.

There was a cold mist of rain sweeping up Arundel Street, and the lanterns of the waiting coaches cut it in glinting cones. There were three coaches, and John was hustled into the second, the two tight-gripping fellows with him; dimly he was aware of Mrs. Cellier entering the first, and then there was the crack of a whip and the rumble of wheels as the horses toiled up the slope to the Strand. They turned westward into it, and in matter of minutes they had halted at Sir William Waller's house near Charing Cross; and then John had to wait. He was taken to a cold dim room which looked as if it were commonly so used; and here, between two surly guards, he had to wait, fuming and fidgeting, asking himself how it was faring with Mrs. Cellier and what Mr. Payne had supposed when nine o'clock had gone. But fuming and fidgeting were of no avail, and a full two hours had gone before he was at last summoned once more to the presence of the justice; and when he was taken blinking into the light his first glance showed him what confirmed his belief that Sir William had been rendered wary; cool and elegant in an elbowchair sat the fashionable Mrs. Waring.

He stiffened and stood very still, his thoughts clearing as his eyes sorted themselves to the lights. His hint about lace had indeed alarmed Sir William, and the lady had been summoned perhaps because it touched her nearly, perhaps to judge whether what John might say was dangerous or not; no other supposition fitted, and it plainly meant that Sir William knew more than he ought to know. That was a heartening thought, and John, with his temper chilled and hardened by his wait, was in a humour to make the most of it.

"You'll first be sworn."

The justice spoke frostily, and John made no demur; this could not be refused, and he was at this moment too cool to blunder himself into the wrong. A dry and wizened fellow, sitting in clerkly black at the head of the table, dropped his quill and reached for a Bible; and John's eyes went wandering as he repeated the oath. It was a good setting for a justice; the waxed oak table was bright with candles, and behind the table, his face just out of their light and his back to the long curtains that screened the windows, Sir William sat, dignified and austere in a leather-backed chair. Paper and pens and a silver inkstand were before him; and to the side of them, its steel vivid against the gleaming oak, John's sword lay under the candles; that quickened his memory, and his eyes had hardened as he glanced to where Mrs. Waring, in crimson velvet and a soft black cloak, sat watchful by the warm and glowing hearth.

The wizened clerk tiptoed to his place and dipped his pen with a flourish. Sir William leaned forward and produced a dry cough; then he leaned further forward and seemed engrossed in the papers before him; again he coughed, and suddenly John understood. This dry cough was meant to impress him, and the sooner it was disturbed the better; Sir William was no doubt accustomed to submissive men, and it might school him to deal now with another sort.

The cough came again, and Sir William leaned back at his ease and pursed his thin lips. He spoke formally and coldly.

"These papers, Mr. Leyburne, which you lately saw seized in the house of Mrs. Cellier—since they're evidence of perjury, or of intent or conspiracy to perjure, and since they are from the house of Mrs. Cellier, and since you were taken at some ease with Mrs. Cellier, and since——"

"There's a deal of 'since' in this. It will have a meaning, no doubt."

Sir William gasped. He was plainly not used to this sort of insolence.

"Meaning?" His voice was perceptibly rougher. "More meaning than you'll care for. And the short of it is that you'd best make some explanations."

"Of what, if you please?"

"Of what I've said. Of these papers."

"Of their content, is it? Or of how they got there? I know both."

"Do you now? You're perhaps overbold in that. And it's the over-bold cock whose neck is wrung." Sir William's smile was acid. "Then since you know so much, let's hear it, pray. How came these papers to be where they were?"

"Oh, that?" John sounded almost airy. "This rogue Dangerfield in Newgate—he's no doubt been suborned."

"Suborned?" Sir William sounded indignant.

"Why not? There are rogues in plenty who'd attempt it. Or perhaps he was fearful of his neck. So he told a tale, a lying tale——"

"Lying, is it? I've known other men do that."

"So have I. Shall we let it pass?"

Sir William was erect in his chair, his face taut and his nostrils dilating; but he checked on the brink of speech, and then nodded grimly, as if to say that he would pass what he would not forget; and John's voice became sardonic.

"So Dangerfield tells a tale, and it gets to the right ears—long ones. After that it's soon concerted, and there'd be some clerkly rogue to write what's spelt to him. Then there's a fellow whose true name I'll not sweat to learn. But he calls himself Warburton. A very pretty rogue, this Warburton. . . ."

He paused, and in the silence he heard Sir William's hard breathing; there was a tautness in his face as John continued.

"He waits for dark, and then he comes tapping at the door, this scum called Warburton. And he has a tale for Mrs. Cellier, a tale to take her from her home and lead her a mile away. And she's no sooner safe away from home than he's tapping at the door again, this Warburton. It's her maid he'll speak with now, a girl lately punished by her mistress. No doubt he has a sly tongue, this Warburton—a sly tongue, and perhaps a pretty face. He has a roll of papers in his pocket too, and a tale of what Tom Dangerfield expects. And the girl's young——"

"Good God!" Sir William had found his tongue at last. "What frenzy's this? Are you drunk, do you say?"

"I've been sitting in your damned anteroom too long to have a hope of it. Shall I continue?"

"You shall not." Sir William flung back in his chair and sat glaring. "I'll hear no more till you've found your manners."

"Then you'd best question your tipstaff instead."

"My tip—— Are you mad?"

Sir William seemed near choking, and John nodded affably.

"He could at least say who told him where to look."

"God give me calm!" Sir William was clutching his elbowchair with a grip that blanched his knuckles. "You're in midsummer madness. You may come from it and eat your words, or I'll commit you this instant."

"Will you? And for what, I wonder? But it's not midsummer, and when it was I was not here. I was in the North Parts. I learned a deal in the North Parts."

He saw the twitch of Mrs. Waring's eyes, and then he stepped back and spoke crisply.

"We might perhaps now end this play. Do you listen, Sir William? First, you know full well I'd no more to do with those papers than the man in the Moon. Second, you've no cause to move against me but to serve your Roderick Mansell. Third, you——"

"You shall not bring Colonel Mansell into this."

"Shall I not?" For a moment his eyes turned openly to Mrs. Waring. "Then why bring in his—er——"

"The pox!" She spoke for the first time. "What's that you call me?"

"I don't remember calling you anything, ma'am—so far. Nor do I wish to. You haven't my interest." He turned again to the open-mouthed justice. "So you'd best decide, sir. You may commit me if you choose, and on what charge you choose. But you may note that I'm not in fear of you, and that not *all* the Privy Council are of your Whiggamore club. There'll be some who'd lend an ear to me."

He paused as if he would have an answer, but no answer came; Sir William sat twitching in a speechless fury, and it was John who broke the silence.

"Then I'll take my leave." He bowed ceremoniously to Mrs. Waring. "My felicitations, if you please, to your spiritual adviser."

"My——" She gasped and sat staring.

"Mr. Roberts, I think he styled himself. A most devout man. And you, sir . . ." He turned at leisure to Sir William. "Commend me, pray, to poor Dangerfield—and Oates and Bedloe, and the rest."

He bowed again, and he was making for the door when he remembered his sword that lay on the shining table. He went back and took it from the oak; and it was naked in his hand as he went quietly from the room.

There were three men dozing by the fire in the candlelit hall, and they scrambled hastily to their feet as they saw his set face and the bare steel in his hand; two were those who had sat with him in the coach, but the third was the tipstaff who had pricked him with the sword.

John halted; and the blood of the Leyburnes was red and hot as he eyed the tipstaff.

"When scum of your sort lays hand upon a gentleman there's need for schooling."

His arm swung back and he used the sword as a switch. The fellow got the flat of it across his face, and he went reeling with a cry of pain that set the others shrinking; and John nodded grimly. He glanced at the tall clock at the foot of the stair and saw that it wanted five minutes to midnight. Then without another word he stepped into the outer darkness.

The rain had cleared; there were clear stars above him, and the roofs of the houses were sharp against a spangled sky. The wind was from the river, and there was an edge in it that set him pulling his cloak tight as he halted, dazed and bewildered by relief after tension. He was weary beyond belief, and all his wish was to relax and sleep; and that, as he knew, was precisely what he must not do. His thoughts were clearing as the night wind cooled his head, and he knew that there was a duty on him now; Mrs. Cellier had disappeared, and it was hardly to be doubted that she had been committed; and what else would be supposed of himself, since he had not been in Child's at the promised hour? There was something to be told here; and for Mrs. Cellier there might be something that could be done.

His head went back as he braced his shoulders and felt that his sword was free; then, warily and watchfully, he walked through the shadows to Lincoln's Inn Fields and the lodging of Mr. Payne.

29 THE GREAT POPE-BURNING   The King was about to turn papist; the Parliament was to be dissolved, and on a signal given by the Jesuits there was to be a great killing of Protestants.

Who started the tale nobody seemed to know. But it swept like a flame through the taverns and the coffeehouses, the shops and markets, the streets and alleys; and it was a tale that wrought a change in the town as Protestant fears went flaring. Apprentices saw to their clubs; journeymen kept little lead-tipped flails convenient in their pockets; merchants locked up their plate and secreted their cash; citizens locked up their daughters and put an extra bolt on the door; a divine preached the Word while his churchwardens stood by his pulpit with their swords drawn. It was a tale that set men in mind of Mr. Oates, and there were not many who asked whence it came or what truth it had.

That Oates had had a hand in it was a thought that occurred to John, and he said as much to Mr. Payne when they met in Child's one night. Mr. Payne nodded briefly.

"It's now or never for Shaftesbury. The country's sick of him and his howling Whigs. Is there more from Waller?"

"Waller?" It was almost a week since John's encounter with Sir William, and he had begun to hope that it could be forgotten. "No, nothing. They must suppose I know more than I truly do."

"Perhaps. But that doesn't extend to Mrs. Cellier. She's still in the Gatehouse, and there's no disposition to take bail for her. There'll be something signified by·that. We may expect some further move, I think."

It was an expectation soon fulfilled. On the Sunday night Mr. Payne came grimly into Child's and announced without prelude that Gadbury was in Newgate. John sat in dismay, and Mr. Payne gave the rest of it tersely.

"They took him this morning as he came from Mass. They carried him before Waller—Waller again, you see—and now he's in Newgate. And I don't suppose they'll allow a bail for him either."

"No?" The thought of the genial boisterous Gadbury cooped in Newgate was not pleasant, and John knew only too well what Newgate could be like. "When's it for trial, do you think?"

"That's another oddity. Where's Mansell?"

"I don't know. I've not seen him."

"Nor have I. Yet the whole of this depends on Mansell."

"How?"

"Because it's Mansell they say was to be conspired against. It was in

Mansell's lodging that Dangerfield found papers. It's Mansell who's named as quartermaster in this plot the stars told Gadbury of. It all turns on Mansell. If it comes to trial, any jury would expect to see Mansell. If there's no Mansell, there'll be no conviction. In fact there'll be no trial. And again I ask, where is Mansell?"

"What . . ." John stared in surprise. "What's hinted there?"

"I don't know. I wish I did. But just when he should be here he's gone. I've a feeling that something's brewing, and I doubt if you should continue to meet me here each night. I might be dangerous company for you."

"How?"

"Isn't it plain—in these days?" Mr. Payne's smile was bitter. "You, after all, are a Protestant, and——"

"I wish to keep touch."

"That's stoutly said. But not, I think, always here. We'll make some changes. . . ."

They did. They made them with a frequency that was as bewildering as it was meant to be. They met at Rider's by the Chapel of the Rolls in Chancery Lane; at the Union in Cornhill, where their talk was spoiled by hawkers from the bookshops nearby; at the Sultan's Head in Aldersgate, where men in sober clothes spoke of the Good Old Cause and recalled in nasal tones the days of the Lord Protector; at Garraway's by the Exchange, where the surgeons met and the talk was of clysters and bloodlettings and cuttings for the stone; at John's in Birchin Lane, where the sea captains came and talk could be heard of the Indies and the Spice Islands and the green Sargasso, where the sea cows grazed; and once they were at Procter's by the Charing Cross, which was the house that Dangerfield had used—and it was while they were in Procter's that a fellow came rushing to shout that he had just met Tom Dangerfield, free and at large, and with a pardon for all offences in his pocket. They exchanged glances and went out of Procter's without another word, for neither of them had any wish to meet Tom Dangerfield; and pardon could only mean that he was to be used as a witness against his betters.

But it was, as Mr. Payne pointed out, a thing they might have foreseen, and soon John had almost forgotten it as the town began to buzz with talk of a great procession the Whigs were to make on Monday week. There would be musicians to lead it and torches to light it; men of quality would ride behind the torches; and at the centre of the procession, where the torches would be brightest and the press thickest, there would be the Bishop of Rome, carried in a full and proper effigy to be fitly burned when the procession was done. The Green Ribbon Club would have charge of all, and there would be ale and claret so that all good Protestants might drink damnation to the papists; and the Earl of Shaftesbury would be on the balcony of the King's Head tavern as the procession passed that way, and would exchange salutes with any trueborn Englishman whose heart was in the Good Old Cause.

"And what," John asked acidly, "is the Good Old Cause?"

"Whiggery and damned rebellion," said Mr. Payne promptly. "It's a phrase the Saints first used in the Usurper's day, and now they're putting it out again."

"Are they? But what's it for? This marching with torches, I mean."

"To show what friends the Whigs can muster. And no doubt to stir some hatreds."

"Against whom?"

"It's the burning of a pope, isn't it? Beyond which you'll have noted the date."

"Not specially."

"November the seventeenth. And that was the accession day of Queen Elizabeth."

"Was it? But why remind us?"

"Because, besides being a Protestant, she was a Tudor. And I suppose that to celebrate that day is to say you love a Tudor better than a Stuart. Shaftesbury's in a mood to try anything. Have you noted that there are Scots in the town?"

"No?"

"They move softly, but they're here—emissaries no doubt of Argyle."

"Now why Argyle?" John was beginning to feel lost in this maze.

"Because he's another Whig. And if it could be concerted that he and Shaftesbury strike together——"

"Is it likely?"

"No. Argyle's cautious. And though he has men in plenty they're not well furnished. But it could be concerted. And there's a tale come to me yesterday that Ferguson's in town. I'd supposed him in Holland."

"What of him?"

"He spews plots. I've said so before. And if *he's* the envoy in this . . ."

Mr. Payne became gloomy, and John parted from him without much regret; his own spirits, he thought, were being lowered in this air of plots and forebodings, and his heart was in the North Parts with Penny and her dappled grey.

He had a letter from Penny at the end of the week, and it did nothing to raise his spirits; it was in her usual chattering style, but the core of it was disturbing.

Roddy's back here now. I don't know where he's been nor why, but he's back, and he doesn't seem to have much to do except ride after me. He says he's finished with the trollop and he'll never see her again and she wasn't a trollop anyway—or at least she wasn't his. He said it three times over and very fiercely, pressing his hat against his heart and swearing it by all sorts of names I'd never heard of. And why, do you suppose? Because he wants to marry me. He said that very fiercely too, and about six times over. I told him I thought she was his trollop, and if she wasn't this week she would be again next week. Roddy wasn't pleased. He flapped his hat on his heart again and said he'd always loved me, and I told him he'd better love the trollop instead.

But it's no jest really, at least not for me. I told you I was in trouble for riding with Will to the shore that day. They cooped me here for a week, not letting me ride even beyond our gates, but now it's worse. It's a lot worse. Because with Roddy riding each day to fall in with me whenever I stirred abroad, and always with talk of being wed, I grew wearied and was fool enough to tell my father. And between that and his gout I've not heard such words from him before. He threw his crutch across the room, and he was shouting to heaven to blast, sink, rot, curse, and damn him, when Aunt Arabella came in, and when she'd discovered what it was for I think she was madder than he. They took counsel what to do, and the short of it is that I'm cooped more straitly than before, and as far as I can see forever and ever. I'm not even to go so far as the gates. I may not stir beyond the rim of the lawns, where I may be seen from the house. Think of me, riding round and round a blasted lawn!

But that's no great matter really. The other's a deal worse. Which is that I was also fool enough to let Will know the shape things had, and Will was so stark mad that he said if it went on he'd pick a quarrel with Roddy and let it go to swords. So on that account alone I must never dare to stir out. Will dead in such an affair is more than I can bear thought of, but suppose it was Roddy killed? You know what follows if a papist kills a Protestant. They don't call it an affair then. They call it murder and they hang the papist, and I think I'd have to hang myself then. So here I'm cooped, and here I stay. But when are you coming? They'll let me ride with you, if with no other. And I don't want to ride with any other. You know I don't.

It was not a letter to soothe a lovesick man, and John was in something near a fever when he had brooded on it through the day; of necessity, because he had to speak of it to somebody, he spoke of it to Mr. Payne.

"I ask when I may depart for the North Parts."

"You need not ask. You're a free man. There's none can detain you."

"There are decencies. I'm committed in this with you and Gadbury—as you well know."

"Not every man would say it." Mr. Payne's eyes were very bright and keen. "But perhaps every Leyburne would."

"I—I hope so. But of departing?"

"If you ask my wishes, they are that you stay some few days more —but only few. This is Saturday. The club have their Pope-Burning, as they now style it, on Monday. That may lead to—anything. It's in some sort of a trial of strength, and among much more it may determine how far they can press it against Gadbury and Mrs. Cellier. By Tuesday night we may perhaps guess the answer, and if you'd stay till then you could bear word to Father Barlow, who's much concerned for Mrs. Cellier. I ask no more."

"So be it!" John nodded decidedly. "I ride on Wednesday."

"By all means. And if this weather holds you'll have a wet ride. You'll be lucky if you're not bogged."

It was, indeed, as wet and sickly an autumn as John could remember, and he would have given much for one frosty morning with the roofs white and a crackle on the ground. But it stayed mild beyond the season; there was never a hint of frost, and day by day there was the rain, one day as a misty drizzle and another as a pattering stream. The store the Whigs set upon their Pope-Burning was plain from the way the work was pressed against the weather. They put orange streamers across the streets from one Whig window to another, and every streamer had the Tudor Rose; where no friendly window was opposite, they put out flags or they let the streamers fall in damp festoons against the fronts of houses; and before the houses they put old barrels with an inch of pitch in the bottom and a stuffing of oil-soaked rags to fire the pitch. There were short poles, pitched, and wrapped with the oily rags, to stand in the barrels and flare like candles when the great procession should pass; there were rag-stuffed images of papists, of the Pope, of the King of France, of the Earl of Castlemaine, and of many another, all greased and oiled and set ready by the barrels; and when the lord mayor remembered '66 and sent word that these things were not to be done, these risks not taken, the people laughed at him; it would be hard enough, they said, to get a torch to burn this year, let alone the town. They went on with their preparations, and at the King's Head tavern the come-and-go grew faster as the club gave oversight to every detail; day and night there were horses tethered and coaches waiting in Chancery Lane, and often a black-and-crimson chariot could be seen in the waiting press. It had a look of chaos; but abovestair in the tavern there were men who knew what they were about, and, as the week end passed, the town took an air of frenzy. There were divines enough who were ardent Whigs, and on the Sunday the town was told what was expected of it; in a hundred pulpits Bibles were banged and sounding boards set booming, as the Good Old Cause was preached; and when evening was come the churches were packed again as Protestants crowded under the candles to hear what their duty was against the plots of Rome. There were divines indeed, and not a few, who told a different tale, who preached of the King and his prerogative, of the duty of men to obey the Lord's Anointed; but these were not the divines that made the noise that night. And when the preachings were done, when the churches were emptied and the candles blown, there were noises of other sorts to keep the town astir, and not all of them were noises proper to a Sunday; from many a house there was a thump of drums and a twitter of flutes as musicians made ready to earn their fees; from others there was a chanting of psalms, as men who had marched with the Saints vowed to the Lord of Hosts that at need they would march again; and from streets and houses many came the rasp and ring of steel as the grindstones whirled and the swords and knives grew keen against whatever need should come.

Then it was Monday, and the weather had cleared at last; it had not cleared wholly and there was no speck of blue in the sullen sky; but at least the rain had stopped, and when dusk was come there was no more than a thin mist to blend with the smoke from the flaming barrels and put a halo round each flaring torch. Mr. Payne took some risks that night, and John shared them with him. They pressed together into the arch of the Inner Temple opposite the King's Head tavern in the very heart of Whiggery, and they had to be there at dusk. They were lucky, indeed, to get into the arch at all, and it was not achieved without some use of elbows; and when they were in they had a full two hours to wait, while the crowd grew thicker and pressed so tight that there was soon not space to stamp a foot against the chill of the November night. Patrols of armed Whigs moved busily in the street, pressing back the crowd and keeping the centre clear, and in the centre the musicians played, and tumblers and mountebanks were let loose to keep the crowd in good humour. Little by little the street grew bright as torches were lit, as candles came in windows and fire was put to the oil rags in the barrels; they were damp and slow to start, but one by one they made their heat and went blazing in crimson flame and waves of whirling smoke; then, on the tavern's balcony, a score of torches went flaring in a crackle of resin and a stream of soaring sparks. It lent a touch of madness to the scene; the crowd quivered, and the street was a crimson frenzy as the whirling smoke sent the shadows leaping over the steel of swords and the white of upturned faces; for a moment there was a hush, broken only by the hiss and crackle of flame; then on the balcony, short and slender, his eyes aglow and his black-and-crimson matching the smoke and flame, the Earl of Shaftesbury was standing below the torches.

He had timed it perfectly, and when the madness of cheering had died it was echoed by the roar of distant cheers; faces turned, women leaned from windows, and men climbed to whatever they could grasp as the swelling cheers came nearer; they were by St. Paul's; they were on Ludgate Hill; they were at the bottom of it; they were in Fleet Street, past Lombard Lane, past Fetter Lane; and then above the cheers there was the bang of drums and the blare of trumpets. A hundred torches came streaming by, and then there were the marching men, swinging lustily; and then the horses as the gentlemen rode by, swords out and eyes uplifted to salute milord in his torchlit eyrie. They passed, and for a moment there was nothing. The street seemed oddly dark, and in the surprise of it the tension mounted. Then came torches again, but a half dozen only, and dim and flickering; and behind these torches, drawn on some low trolley and vague and ghastly in the light, was the white and waxen effigy of the murdered Edmund Godfrey; the thing lolled horribly, its neck awry and a sword thrust through its loins; and behind it, propping it up and twitching its limbs, was a man dressed as a Jesuit, a crucifix in one uplifted hand and a dripping dagger in the other. There was a gasp and roar from the crowd, and then a low hiss of seething anger; but then, before they could give it vent, there were torches again, torches primed with sulphur so that there was a tinge of hell-fire in their light; and after the torches, rumbling and clattering behind its coal-black horses, came the cart. It was, in truth, a very ordinary cart; it was a dung cart, and it still had a reek that betrayed its proper use; but it was painted blood red now, and in it, high in a gilded chair and swaying drunkenly to every lurch of the cart, was the obscene and potbellied image of a pope in vestments. It had been done with a bitter care, a great wax image with an arm that swayed and jerked as though in benediction; it had a triple crown and a bloodstained sceptre, and in its lecherous leering face there was a thick-lipped mouth that seemed to chatter as the head lurched and jolted.

The crowd was in a frenzy, swaying and roaring as the hideous thing went by, and for some it was the climax. Yet not for all; for now there were drums again, and after the drums a led horse came— a horse led alone and without a rider—its harness of the plainest and its saddlecloth of russet; and then came a troop of horse, grizzled and elderly men, riding four abreast and with a rare precision; and from the crowd there came a roar almost of delirium as they saw the ridged steel caps, the prim white collars over the steel of breastplates, the long basket-hilted swords uplifted in salute. For these were the furnishings of '45 and these were the veterans of '45, the men of Marston Moor and Naseby, of Preston and Dunbar, grandfathers now, but riding as they had ridden long ago; and suddenly the roar of welcome died as men knew who the rider should have been of the saddled horse that led this troop; it died into a gasp, and then it broke again as a wild exultant chant, the great deep-chested chant that men remembered: *"Ironsides! Ironsides! Ironsides!"*

The riders passed, and the crash and rattle of the drums grew faint along the Strand. There was a stir and sway from the crowd as tension eased, and John found himself pressed against his neighbour and then released again. He shook himself, and found that he had been sweating. Then, on a whim, he looked up and saw Lord Shaftesbury leaning over the rail of his balcony, his tiny figure tense and his flaxen periwig lurid in the torchlight; he had whipped out his sword as the troop went by, and in the style of the theatre he had saluted that horse without a rider; now he was leaning over the rail, watching curiously as the troop rode on, and behind him some men who had been in the shadows had moved forward also. It brought them under the glare of the torches; and suddenly John was staring at sight of one of them; he had seen that sharp, thin face before, that face with the Roman nose, the blotchy skin, and the periwig pulled low; and for a moment memory had him in a dusty road by Thornclough, with a chariot halted and Penny at words with Mrs. Waring.

He turned and spoke quickly to Mr. Payne.

"That man up yonder, behind milord——"

"Where? What?"

"He's Roberts. The Levite, as Penny——"

"God in heaven!" Mr. Payne reared suddenly erect. "Roberts! It's Ferguson!"

"What——"

"Come away. . . ." Mr. Payne's fingers were tight on his arm. "That's Ferguson. Gadbury's right, and there *is* a plot. You ride at dawn."

30

"'41 IS COME AGAIN" The post road to the North lay sodden under the rain; the ruts were filled with water and the track was a squelching mire. It was far from the dusty road that John had known in June; it lay under the November rain, stark and empty, and there was nothing but the quiet wind, the patter of the rain, and the *plug* and *plop* of hooves in the mud. But this was the silence that healed; and for all the toll and weariness of it, it allowed a man to think.

He had eight long days of it before he came to Langley House, and in the North there was a kicking wind and spattering gouts of water that came tearing from the trees. He rode the last morning in a full gale, pressing the speed at the last as he went down the lane by the dry-stone wall; and then he was holding St. Christopher in iron as he plied the knocker; and even St. Christopher seemed to smile in welcome. After that it was breathless; the white-haired steward in gentle greeting; Aunt Arabella, poised and cool, but plainly glad to see him; and then Penny, wet and muddy from the stables, but careless of that as she went boisterously at him with a flood of questions.

It was the same Penny; there was never a doubt of that, and his breath was coming quickly as he saw her eager face and vivid hair; he was almost laughing as he tried to stem her rush of questions, and in the end it was Aunt Arabella who had to intervene to protect him.

"Penny! Penny!" She was almost laughing herself. "Have some pity, do! He's a guest new come, and he's still in his boots."

"In his boots, is he?" Penny's eyebrows were suddenly twitching. "I can't see any boots. I can't see anything but mud."

But the short hint had been enough for her, and already her cool good sense was showing. Her chatter rippled on, but even while she talked she was pushing him into a chair that he might be rid of his boots; and it was no sooner done than she had him in charge again and was leading him up the stair. In his bedchamber there was dry wood stacked in the hearth, with a tinderbox set ready, and Penny waited for no servants. She dropped on her knees by the hearth, and the flint went tinkling on the steel as she struck them fiercely together; the spark flew into the tinder, and at once she was crouching over it, blowing vigorously to fan the dull red glow that was spreading in the box.

John left her to it while he looked round him with a questing interest. He had sent no warning of his coming, but surely this was a room prepared? He looked round again and was sure of it; and the preparation had been more than tentative. There were signs of care in this; the shutters were off the windows; the bed had had its curtains opened and its sheets and pillows set; there were candles new and ready in the gleaming pewter; the tall clothespress by the wall was dry and open, and its shelves had been strewn with lavender; and, as a final touch, on the table by the bed was Mr. Barlow's clock, Penny's own repeater, with its silken cord trailing and its tick coming sweetly from behind its gilt and ebony. He saw her initials on it in the gold he had cut himself, and his breath caught in his throat as a rushing thought came surging; all else in the room might be courtesy, but this was Penny's own.

His gaze came back to her as she crouched before the hearth. Already the tinder had lighted the slender wooden match, and with that she had fired the shavings that were scattered below the high-piled wood. The blue smoke rose in waves, and then came back as the sea wind hit the chimney; again the shavings flared, and Penny reached for the bellows; she had an expert touch, and the flame was hissing against the sticks as John came close behind her.

He stood in silence for a moment, watching her shoulders move to the rhythm of the bellows; she seemed intent on that, and she gave no sign of having heard him come behind her.

"Did you have word of my coming here?"

"No."

Her answer came shortly, and its tone expressed nothing. The sigh of the bellows and the hiss of the flame filled the silence as the dry sticks took the fire.

"How should I? Your letters never said it."

She spoke quietly, her back still to him and her eyes on the gathering fire; and again her tone told him nothing.

"No." He spoke almost shyly. "But I couldn't say it. I never knew. It was all—all mad in the town. But I thought——"

"Thought what?"

She was still intent on the fire, but her tone had changed; there had been a quickness in it, and that roused him.

"I thought this seemed a room set ready."

"It is." Her answer came tersely. "You didn't tell me, so I had to guess. And I guessed wrong."

"Wrong?"

"What else? I kept guessing wrong. I've had the room ready this month and more."

She turned to him at last, dropping the bellows and coming quickly to her feet.

"I thought you'd be away three weeks, perhaps four. And you've been away ten. And I've never known how it would be or what would come next. Your letters never told me much."

"There wasn't much to tell—that made sense. And when I did leave there wasn't time for letters. It was short warning."

"John! What do you mean? Are you——"

"No! No!" He had her hands in his as he heard the quick alarm in her voice. "No, Penny. I did *not* mean that."

"You're sure?" She was still hard and strained. "John, you're not——"

"No." He answered her firmly. "No, Penny. I'm not in flight. And all's well—for us."

"Oh!"

She was still eyeing him anxiously, but she seemed to find assurance now. She made no resistance as he drew her to him.

"It's all well, my Penny. And I'm back at last. And that's heaven."

Deliberately and without haste he pressed his lips on hers; and suddenly she was clinging to him as though she could not be sure he was real.

"Yes." His voice came as a whisper, while the sticks went crackling in the hearth and the wind sent the blue smoke puffing. "I'm come to you again, my dear. And it's not for parting—now."

Footsteps, brisk and light, came in the passage beyond the door, and he whipped round to face it. Penny stooped hastily for the bellows as Aunt Arabella came marching in.

"Is all as you'd wish it?" she asked him brusquely. "Are you cared for now?"

"Wholly as I'd wish it, ma'am." He was avoiding Penny's eye. "I'm most finely cared for."

"So you should be." She ran an expert eye round the room. "I don't know why you're blowing that fire, Penny. There's not the need for it now. Can't you see that?"

"Yes, dear Aunt."

Penny got demurely to her feet and hung the bellows on the hook. John plunged hastily into another topic.

"I owe some apology, ma'am, that I come to you thus. I'm sorry I could send no warning."

"So were we." She was looking him directly in the eye. "The truth is, we've been in some anxiety for you."

"I'm sorry for that, ma'am. But why, pray? There was not the need."

"Was there not?" Her eyes were steadily on his. "Edward Barlow thought there was."

"Oh?" He was quickly alert. "But may I know what he said?"

"He didn't say anything." Penny thrust herself suddenly into the talk. "He just kept on talking of God ordering all things with an infinite wisdom. And that's his way of saying he wishes God would order 'em differently."

"Penny!" Aunt Arabella sounded scandalized. "You may stop such talk and get from the room. Mr. Leyburne will wish to change his dress, and not to hear such nonsense. Now be off with you!"

Aunt Arabella made a stately progress to the door, sweeping her niece in front of her. But under the lintel of it she turned, as if on afterthought, and then she spoke deliberately.

"What Ned Barlow *did* say was that he had frequent letters from Mr. Payne, who said there was great turmoil in the town and that no man could be accounted safe." She paused, bright-eyed and erect, as he stood before her. "But Mr. Payne said also that through all of it you were most constantly at his side, bearing yourself most truly."

There was a swish of taffeta, the click of a latch, and she was gone;

and he was alone in the friendly room, with the scent of lavender, the crackle of the fire, and the tick of Mr. Barlow's clock.

He dined with them at leisure in the warm oak-panelled room whose mullioned windows gave on the wind-swept garden; and Richard Langley, hobbling on a stick, with his right foot swathed in bandages, made no secret of being glad to see him.

"You're well come," he said heartily. "These are no sweet times to live in. I'd supposed once, when the King was home again, that we'd done with the troubles for my lifetime. But now . . ." He shook himself, and seemed to decide that this was no fit talk for the dinner table. "But as I've said, you're well come. It's time Penny had company. She's found it hard of late, and little ease of movement."

"I've not had any movement," said Penny briefly.

"Aye, lass. That we know. But there's a need in things at times."

"So I'm told—frequently." She turned, and looked steadily at her aunt. "Am I now to be released?"

"Somewhat. You've been told you may at all times ride in proper company."

They were firm words, but they were softly said; and her eyes, watchfully on Penny, had a softness in them too. John noted it thankfully, and with it he noted something more. Aunt Arabella was quieter now than he remembered her, and when he looked attentively he saw that her face was white and strained. There had been some ferment working here.

What that ferment was he began to understand when evening came. There was little said at dinner, and he was, indeed, in no fit state to say it. He was so tired from eight days of winter roads that before they left the table Penny had told him bluntly that she had known a foundered horse look better; he had a face of chalk, she said, with blood in his eyes and cobwebs round them, and he would be a deal better for a sleep. She was highhanded about it, and he had neither will nor wish to resist her; so she had her way, and he spent the afternoon in a sleep that was oblivion, deep and unbroken.

He came to his tale in the evening. He told it after supper, when they were back in the parlour, with the wine and the candles and the shimmering glow of the fire; and it needed less explaining than he had supposed it would. Mr. Payne's letters-of-news, as well as his letters to Mr. Barlow, had done their work well, and the Langleys had a shrewd and decent grasp of affairs in London. They knew, indeed, nothing of Dangerfield, and nothing of Gadbury except his repute as an astrologer; and of Mrs. Cellier they knew only that she had befriended Mr. Barlow. But at least they knew the shape and trend of affairs in town, and they could see the meanings of things; and to John's surprise they were more ready than he had himself been to credit Gadbury's tale of an army preparing, and of Mansell as its quartermaster.

"It sorts with that family," said Aunt Arabella tersely, and at once her brother was nodding his assent.

"It was so in '41," he told them quietly. "In that year also, men were looking forward and Mansell was making ready. And when it came he had a troop prepared, and pikes set ready."

"And blew our door," said Penny viciously.

"Aye, he did. And that, from all I've heard, was the whole of his soldiering. His true work was the furnishing of men for the Parliament. For which, if you please, he's first a justice and then knighted."

"Just so. Like father, like son!" Aunt Arabella nodded sagaciously. "Myself, I'll believe Mr. Gadbury. He's a most excellent astrologer, I'm told. But Mr. Payne disbelieves it, do you say?"

"He did. But he doesn't now. There's more. . . ."

John went on to tell of the great Pope-Burning. He told of it in full, giving the details, the order of procession, the glint and colour of it. But when he had told of the horse that was led alone, and of the white-collared steel-capped troop that had followed it, he came to a sudden end and looked round him with a quick alarm. All was not quite as it had been. There was a tension in this firelit room; and in the quiet of it Mr. Langley spoke bitterly.

"Even so—as we saw them once."

He lapsed into silence, staring into the fire while his sister sat rigid; and Penny, as if to ease it, tiptoed to the table and poured wine for them all; and as her father took his glass he spoke across the hearth to his sister.

"We are back, I think, in the days of our youth, and '41 is come again. In that year too we saw the shape of it, and were looking to horse and sword."

The silence took the room again as he sat staring. In the shadows Penny stood rigid, frozen in her walk and with a glass still poured and brimming in her hand. Aunt Arabella sat stiffly, intent on her brother's face; and he, meeting her eye, spoke again.

"You—and Penny—you could care for our house again?"

"Richard!" She had jerked back, and her voice was urgent. "Have some thought for things. And with your gout——"

"The gout's none so crippling. I find some ease in a bandage. That's all."

John pressed back in his chair and found his breath coming quickly. For the meaning of this was not in doubt; tone and face had said what words left vague, and it was very plain and simple. If all were as it seemed to be, if '41 were come again, if the times were such that a man must again take horse and sword to the King, then Richard Langley knew where duty lay; if it should come again to the push of it, then, gout or no gout, there should be a man ride out from Langley House.

There would, indeed, be two; for, without a word said, John knew that he too was committed to this. It was not only a matter of loyalty to friends, of what Penny would think if he shirked; beyond all that it was a duty, a thing he owed to his name; there would be a Leyburne riding out from Cunswick.

Beyond the hearth, Aunt Arabella stirred. She relaxed and had the ghost of a smile for her brother.

"I think, Richard, you go a little swiftly. Things are not yet driven quite so far."

"No indeed." John leaned forward and spoke firmly. He had just remembered that he had not yet ended his tale. "It may not ever come so far—which is why I'm here. I was saying that Mr. Payne no longer disbelieves, or wholly disbelieves, this tale of a plot and an army raising. That's because upon that balcony he saw one Ferguson. . . ."

He went on to explain it, and he had no arduous task. Ferguson the Plotter was a name made familiar by Mr. Payne's letters-of-news, and that he might now be employed between the English Whigs and the Scottish was not hard to comprehend; but when John came to the identity of this Ferguson with the Reverend Mr. Roberts there was a startled gasp as Penny came jumping to her feet.

"What's that?" she cried excitedly. "The Levite? The Levite's Ferguson?"

"He is. But the fellow's no mere envoy, and that's what signifies. He's of weight beyond that, and if there's a plot here he's likely to be the manager of it. And he's been so oddly interested in that shore beyond the mere that——"

A knocking, soft and urgent, fell on the shutters beyond the tight-closed windows, a knocking that was repeated and had a rhythm in it. Penny took one glance at her aunt and then ran to the door, with John after her in quick alarm. He followed her across the dimly lighted hall, where a single candle flickered, and then she plunged quickly into the gloom of an unlit passage. Far down it, as he groped his way after her, he heard the slide of a bolt, and then a creak and a long howl as the night wind came roaring in; it came up the passage, buffeting him as he made his way against it, and when at last he came to the door there was a man with his shoulder to it, forcing it against the wind. It clicked to, and as Penny slid the bolt the man stood upright, vague and shadowy in the gloom.

"Ah, Mr. Leyburne!" Mr. Barlow's voice was as soft as ever. "I had hoped for talk with you."

31 WIND FROM THE SEA   They took him without ado to the parlour, where Arabella Langley was quick with anxious questions; and for all his soothing answers Mr. Barlow could not hide it that his life of late had been in more than the usual hazard. Sir Henry Mansell, stirring himself as a Whig and a justice, had lately spared no pains to take him; and that he had *not* been taken, he smilingly observed, must be attributed, under God, to the watchfulness of Will Hoghton and the loyalties of many humble folk. But all was still well, and his coming tonight was not an alarm of flight; he had merely hoped for a word with Mr. Leyburne.

"And here he is," growled Mr. Langley. "Though how the devil you knew——"

"Whispers pass," said Mr. Barlow blandly. "I was in sleep this day and woke at dusk. And they told me that he had arrived at noon."

"True, sir." John spoke cheerfully. "It was exactly so. Your whispers serve you well."

"I've need of them. And not all of them are comforting." For a moment the dark eyes were anxiously on Penny, and then he turned to her father. "Has Sir Henry been pressing something? Forgive me that I should ask."

"Now damn your whispers!" Mr. Langley was staring at him. "What's this you've heard?"

"What you evidently suppose." Mr. Barlow was very calm and steady. "There's a tale that the Mansells were here yesterday, the pair of them—Sir Henry and young Roderick. And I could think of a purpose in that."

There was a hush in the room. Mr. Langley was sitting awkwardly in his chair, his bandaged foot impeding him as he tried to come upright. By the hearth, his sister sat very still, and, beyond it, Penny was standing mute. Mr. Barlow sat placidly; he glanced round the circle and then sipped his wine; and it was Aunt Arabella who spoke first.

"Richard," she said quietly, "I do not think this need be a secret from Ned. Or from Mr. Leyburne."

"No." His answer came slowly, and if there was a grumble in his tone it was at least quiet. He paused as if to collect his thoughts, and then he made brief answer.

"If you must have it," he said, "Mansell came here yesterday with what he called an offer of marriage—for Penny, on behalf of his son."

It was short and terse, and he looked into the fire when he had said it. John's chair creaked suddenly as his feet pushed at the carpet; he had not known of this; and Penny, in the shadows, stood very still and tense. Mr. Barlow nodded.

"It's what I'd guessed," he said quietly. "And you answered?"

"What you might also have guessed. That Penny's not for marriage yet, and that when she does wed it won't be into the family of a damned thieving rebel."

"Ah!" John's sigh of relief escaped him before he knew it. The notion of Penny's being betrothed to Roderick Mansell was something to make him choke, and he twitched in quick relief at the answer. But then Mr. Barlow spoke again, and his tone was grave.

"I see," he said slowly. "An admirable sentiment, no doubt. And truly I'd be sorry . . ."

His brooding eyes strayed to Penny, as his thoughts had surely done.

"You'd be more than sorry." The growl was coming back to Mr. Langley's voice. "So what's at odds then?"

"The wisdom of it," Mr. Barlow spoke steadily. "To refuse was needful. But to refuse so? Was it judicious?"

"Damn your soft words!" The growl was thunder now. "It's plain words that are needed for such as Mansell, and he's had them plain enough to remember. He'll not come here again."

"Not in friendship, certainly."

"Then how else? Are we supposing——" Mr. Langley stopped, and for a moment he was staring; and when he spoke again his voice was quiet. "So you suppose it also, do you?"

"Suppose what, if you please?"

"What we're all supposing. That '41 is come again."

"That? Surely not?"

"Surely yes." Mr. Langley laughed shortly. "And when I put Mansell through the door I bade him look to the stone of it. That's Mansell's way. It was, and it is."

"Aye indeed. But——"

"There are no 'buts' to this. He's had his answer, and that's an end."

"I hope so."

Mr. Barlow's voice expressed nothing, and his quiet comment said the more for that. It set John looking sharply, while his quick thoughts sought the meaning. That Sir Henry would have a keen resentment was not to be doubted, and it would not be the less for the thin-lipped primness of the man; and if hope of an heiress had gone, there would be no cause left for the restraint that had kept a truce and cold civility between these families. Something might be expected if opportunity should serve; and for a moment the scene in Fleet Street came alive again—the shouts and cheers, the flaring torches, the marching men, the troop of horse, and the call of *"Ironsides!"* throbbing in the dark. The memory flared as the torches had done; and then it quickly faded as Arabella Langley spoke.

"Ned!" She was leaning forward, speaking anxiously. "You don't think there's matter here to hurt *you?*"

"Hardly so much." He was quick on that. "To be truthful about it, Sir Henry is doing all he can at that already. Indeed——"

"Yes?" It came as an urgent whisper, and he paused. Then he had half a smile as he went on.

"That's one cause why I'm here tonight. It's been decided that I'm to move quarters. It's none so safe, now, at the Park Hall."

"Oh?" It was Mr. Langley who spoke in surprise. "But what's this, Ned?"

"It's young Will's notion. He thinks Sir Henry is grown so urgent that he may use his powers as a justice and search the Park Hall. And if I should then be in sleep there—you see?"

Certainly John saw. He saw very clearly, and he had the memory of the search of Mrs. Cellier's; he nodded quick approval.

"If that's the risk," he said quietly, "you'll be best away."

"So Will says. And I've my hosts to consider. If I'm not there to be taken they can't be charged with harbouring. So I'm to move into Wigan—perhaps tomorrow night, perhaps the night after. Which is why I sought you this night—you and Mr. Leyburne."

He turned to John with the half-smile on his face again, and he had the air of one glad to be rid of these tedious preliminaries. Yet before he came to what was plainly at the front of his thoughts he had another word to say; and he was almost casual about it.

"Let me discharge my conscience," he said easily. "I've a word for you from Will Hoghton, and I'd all but forgot it. But he bade me say he learns from Jimmy Jump that there's a lugger now lying off by North Meols, and waiting, it seems, until this storm shall abate. He——"

"What! It waits, and we——"

"Easy, John! Easy——"

It was Penny who had intervened. She had slipped round the circle as John came excitedly to his feet, and now her hand was quickly on his arm.

"Easy!" she said again, and with the calm of one who understood. "There'll be no haste. Uncle Ned had the words for it."

"What words, if you please?"

"Until this storm shall abate. Don't you hear the wind?"

He had forgotten that. But he flung his head back, listening; and at once, as he heard the howl and moan of it and felt the shake and quiver of the house, he was at ease; there would be no landings on that open shore while this continued.

"It does not abate yet," said Penny quietly. "So you may give ear to Uncle Ned."

"Say rather, give tongue," said Mr. Barlow pleasantly. "You'll have guessed what I've come to hear. How is it with Mrs. Cellier?"

It was midnight when Mr. Barlow at length took horse and was lost in the noisy dark. John held his stirrup as he mounted, and Penny was at his side, her cloak pulled tight against the roaring wind. They saw him go, and then they ran together to the door as a splutter of rain and a flurry of whirling leaves came suddenly on the wind; and with the door still open Penny turned and stood staring out at the night.

"The just word," she said slowly. "It abates nothing. And it won't, for another day—at the least."

"No?" He was suddenly close against her in the dark. "There are other things that abate nothing. And won't—ever."

She spun towards him, alert at his tone; he slipped his arms round her as she turned, and he had kissed her before she could speak. For a moment she was limp and pliant in his arms, a moment long enough to make all plain; and then suddenly she was thrusting back, and he sensed the grin that the darkness hid.

"You'll blame the wind, I suppose, if Aunt Arabella sees my hair?"

"I shall not." He knew the mood that had her now. "I shall blame you—all that you are."

"Oh? And you suppose she'll believe it?"

"Yes—if she has a memory."

A light flickered at the turn of the passage, and quavering shadows came dancing on the walls. He stretched out his arm and pulled the door shut; then he turned, and quickly and lightly he kissed her again as the candle came to the corner. A stick thumped on the boards, and Richard Langley came hobbling into view.

"What's to do?" he called. "Is Ned away? Your aunt's in alarm."

"So am I."

It was Penny, and there was a suspicious shake in her voice; evidently her father had noted it, and he was eyeing her warily as he spoke again.

"In alarm, are you? And at what?"

"It's John. He's been kissing me in the dark."

"And what the devil else should he do in the dark? Go tell your aunt."

"Tell her what?"

"What you please. Be off with you. She's feared for Ned—— You and your lingering here!"

"I was kept."

"Were you? And now you're being hastened. Run——"

He swung his stick at her as she stepped past him, and it smacked across her as she went. Her surprised yelp mingled with her gurgle of laughter, and at the turn of the passage she paused to look back at them.

"Didn't dear Aunt ever linger in the dark?"

Her grin was impudent as she spoke; and then she was gone, light-footed and eager. Mr. Langley turned, and the shadows went cavorting as he raised his candle.

"God sends sons and the devil daughters," he growled. "An imp from the pit, that one! But Ned *is* safe away?"

His tone had sobered suddenly, and John made haste to conform to it.

"Aye, sir. Safe away. As for Penny and—and what——"

"As for Penny, she's like a horse." Her father interrupted gruffly, but there was no displeasure in his tone. "A horse kept to the stable. Too much corn and no exercise. Take her out, if you please. Take her out and bring her home tired. That's what she needs."

"I will." John was prompt and fervent on it. "Tomorrow, if she'll come."

She would. She had had more than enough of being kept within the gates, and she and John were away together the next morning and as soon as breakfast was done. They rode under ragged cloud, and the wind set their cloaks twitching and made them bend their heads as they turned into it; for they were riding westwards towards the Park Hall in the teeth of the wind. It was not the most pleasant of rides, and there were spatters of rain to add to the buffeting of the wind, but it was a ride they were sure they must take. There was Will Hoghton to be seen again, and his short message of the stormbound lugger must assuredly be looked into. So they went steadily to the west, and before they were at journey's end a slit of blue winked through a cloud, shut again, opened, and then seemed to stay.

There was a grimness on the Park Hall. The gravelled drive was dead with leaves, wet and slippery; the lake was menacing, with shivering ripples on the cold black water; the trees were bleak and bare; and the grass beneath the boughs, where a gracious shade had been in the summer days, was a litter of leaves and fallen twigs. But if winter had gripped the house it had not gripped Will Hoghton; he was out in the wind to greet them, and his welcome was as warm and his handshake as cordial as the ale he had ready for them.

"I've been spicing it," he explained as he swept them into the parlour. "It's better so these days—and hot. I guessed you'd be coming——"

"A safe guess." John drank gladly at the rich hot ale. "I'm glad to see you. It's been a long time. But I'm told that all's not well with you—and yours."

"No." There was a note almost of resignation. "It's a portent of the times, it seems."

"Ye-es. And the times are not good. You're told of the set of things?"

"Tolerably. Or should I say intolerably?" Will's shoulders shrugged. "But to put it simply, we have Mr. Payne's letter-of-news each week, and he does not cloud matters."

"He clouds them less in speech. Which is why I'm here. It imports to learn what Mansell does. You know why?"

"Again—tolerably. Which is to say Father Barlow told me of it when he was back last night."

"He's safe, Will?" Penny spoke sharply, almost anxiously, and Will's nod was reassuring.

"Perfectly. He was in by dawn."

"You awake and watching, I suppose?" She was beginning to sound indignant. "It's no proper life, Will, for either of you."

"Be at ease, Penny." The answer came placidly. "Perhaps it isn't. But it ends tomorrow."

"How?" She sounded almost alarmed.

"He moves quarters. There's nothing safe here, with Sir Henry the nearest justice. So he's for Wigan. He'll be lost in the press there."

"Oh! But he's to be cared for?"

"Of course." Again Will's smile was placid. "One of your folk, John. His new host is a clockmaker, Hilton by name, and known as a religious man."

It was apparently Will's way of saying that Mr. Hilton was a papist, and John accepted it easily.

"It's fortunate," was his comment. "They can talk of clocks together."

"That's why he's going. It's how they became acquainted."

"Is it?" Penny sounded impatient. "But why doesn't he go today?"

"Because he must go by night, and then he must get past the watch. And tomorrow is Hilton's night in the watch. That's why."

"Oh!" Penny grunted. "I hope it's not too late."

"So do I. And indeed the time's running short." Will's voice had become graver. "I think we may expect something, and soon."

"This lugger, do you mean?"

"In part. But there's another trifle. John—when was it you got here? Yesterday noon, was it not?"

"You're well informed—as usual. It was."

Will nodded.

"I think we all but met. I rode to the Boar's Head for the letter-of-news, and I must have left just before you got there. Did you halt there?"

"No. I was in some haste."

"No doubt." Will had a quick glance at Penny. "But if you had called there you might have heard of me. I'd been asking if they'd seen you—having a notion it was time you came. Of course they hadn't seen you."

"No—if I hadn't got there."

"No." Will repeated it firmly. "They'd not seen you. They'd seen only one traveller of late who had interest for me. She was there the day before."

"*She?*"

Penny's word snapped as she came erect in her chair, and Will was smiling as he nodded.

"Exactly so, Penny. A most elegant lady. Travelling alone in a chariot of black and crimson. A smart pair of greys."

"The trollop, was it? And the Levite?"

"No. Travelling alone. And she took the road for Thornclough."

"Blast her!"

"Precisely." Will nodded his agreement. "But you'll note that she travelled alone—none so proper, perhaps, for any lady. We may argue some urgency from that."

"Yes?" John was erect too. "What are you suspecting, Will?"

"I don't know. But she surely heralds something, and it may break our peace."

"It may." John spoke grimly. "The last time I saw that lady was at Sir William Waller's—and she was no herald of peace then. There's a portent in her, Will, and we'd best bestir ourselves. Now what's this of a lugger? When do we ride?"

"Tomorrow."

"Not before?"

"Easy, John! There's no hurry. This wind is not done yet, as Penny will tell you."

"She has told me."

"Then believe her. But tomorrow . . ." He went strolling to the window, and he was staring out as he spoke. "Certainly tomorrow, and not later."

Penny went running to his side, and John after her; and one glance sufficed. The blue rift had broadened in the clouds, and a shaft of pale sunlight was playing on the rippling lake.

"It will blow out in the night," said Will decisively. "We'll ride tomorrow. And there'll be a swelling moon."

32 THE GEESE FLY LOW   Parbold Hill was bleak under the grey cloud, and the wind from the sea was sweeping up it with a force that set hats twitching and the horses' manes rippling. It

was not, indeed, the wind of yesterday, but there was enough of it as it swept up the hill to set John clutching at his cloak and drawing it tight about him; at his side, Will Hoghton sat easily on his horse and gazed steadily down at the cold black sheet that was the Martin Mere.

"Have you seen it so—before?"

"No." John's answer was brief as he stared at the distant water. "I saw it in summer, and it was silver then."

It was not silver now, and John knew that it would not be silver again till it was touched by the summer light. Under this winter sky it was black, a black forlorn and cold, and the scattered islets were fewer, the trees shorter, and the fringe of marshland nearer; the mere was wider than it had been, and its waters higher. John voiced his thoughts at once.

"It's bigger," he said. "The rains, would it be?"

"That—and the wind." Will was clutching his hat as he spoke. "A good nor'wester sets the seas driving over."

Will gathered up his cloak and then led cautiously down towards the river that curled, thin and black, at the foot of the hill. John followed in silence, his eyes on the loose stones and his thoughts on a day of summer light when he had followed Penny down this hill and had let his horse stumble because he was too intent on her. He was not so tempted now, for Penny was not with them. To her mutinous disgust she had been left at home, and John had for once been in declared agreement with her aunt and father. He had spoken his mind firmly on it, well knowing that he must; what was in hand this day might not be work for Penny.

His eyes turned thoughtfully to Will Hoghton, jogging slowly down the track in front of him, sturdy and thickset, with a sword sheath pushing at his cloak and a pair of holsters made fast to his saddle for the pistols which, as a papist, he ought not to have had. Plainly Will knew the dangers, but he was as calm and placid as ever, and at the bottom of the hill he fell back to let John lead at the narrow bridge that spanned the swollen river. Under the grey sky the black water was swirling and rippling as the horses clattered over, and suddenly, in the clear winter light, the walls of Ormskirk seemed plain and close.

"We'll call on Tom Greenhalgh," said Will cheerfully. "He spices a pretty ale at the Rose there."

"I can do with it. You think we'll find trouble this night?"

"It could be." Will seemed quite unperturbed. "But I think we can look to ourselves. It's Father Barlow I'm concerned for."

"Oh? How?"

"Because he moves quarters tonight. I told you. Evan Hilton is of the watch tonight, and he's to be at the Standishgate at midnight. It looks well enough, but one never knows. There could be a chance encounter, and I'll be glad when the night's safe done."

"Ye-es. What of ourselves, if it's not an improper thought?"

"For the night, trust in God." Will spoke soberly and with a calm certainty; and then suddenly a smile was in his face. "But at this present moment we'll trust in Tom Greenhalgh."

It was a trust well given. Tom Greenhalgh was alert this November day, and he was out to greet them as they trotted over the grey cobbles of the market place and dismounted before the glowing red that was the Rose of Lancaster. It was creaking in the wind as he led them beneath it to his door and to the quiet room that looked on the wintry garden; but there was a sizzling fire of logs in the fine stone hearth, and as he bowed them before it he took the long iron poker and thrust it deep into the red and shimmering ash beneath the logs.

"Sea-coal makes a good fire," he said genially, "and it's cheaper here than logs. But it will not mull ale as the wood ash does. Your pardons, gentlemen . . ."

He slipped quietly from the room, and almost before they had loosened their cloaks he was back with the pewter mugs of ale. He set them on the hearth, sifted in spices, and stirred; twice he tasted delicately with a spoon before he was satisfied with the blend; then he took the glowing poker from the fire, held it by his cheek to test the heat of it, and with a nod of satisfaction he plunged the glowing tip of it deep into one of the pewter mugs. The ale came hissing in a seething froth, and its deep amber turned to the yellow of the close-packed bubbles as a wave of warm steam rose billowing from the hearth. The scent of spices drifted across the room as he withdrew the poker and thrust it back beneath the logs.

"Which is how we do it in this county—or used to." A little unsteadily he got to his feet and proffered the mug to John. "There's a wisdom that lies in time, and men forget what their fathers knew. Pray taste it, sir, and tell me."

It was hot and mellow, and almost creamy to the taste; and the spices had blended to a harmony that John had never known in ale before. He said so, and Tom Greenhalgh was plainly pleased.

"That's the wood ash," he explained. "It's carried with the poker and it salts the whole."

He was spicing the second ale as he spoke, and Will Hoghton, sitting with his hands outstretched to the fire, looked across at John.

"It's also the ale," he said. "You'd not get it so at the Sun yonder. It's sea-coal there, and ale of the second sort—not the October. Isn't that so, Tom?"

"Aye, sir. It is. And rightly."

"Why rightly?"

"What he sells, sir, is fit enough for them that drink it."

Again the steam rose as he plunged the poker into the second ale, and fragrant wisps went curling from the hearth, up past the fine stone shelf, where candles now were where summer flowers had been, up past the deep gilt frame of the portrait that hung in splendour; and from the canvas the Earl of Derby looked down with a smile that seemed to approve that sentiment.

"I see." Will spoke quietly as he took the frothing ale. "The same folk still, is it? And in the nighttime?"

"Aye, sir—the same. And last Saturday."

"When the wind was high?"

"Just so, sir. They went—and soon returned."

"Thwarted by wind, no doubt. And called at the Sun for their cup?"

"I'll suppose so, sir. Certainly they called."

"Good! Then all seems plain. Ourselves, we'll be on the shore this night, and——"

"Aye, sir. God grant it so—and bring you safe. But more of the ale, sirs?"

"I'll not say no. But thereafter we must ride."

They rode within minutes, and the rested horses took it briskly. Soon they were out on the open plain, vast and desolate; and there, to the north, was the Martin Mere, chill and dark in the wintry light, an ocean of water, rippling and wind-swept. The fringing reeds showed darkly, and the lap and gurgle of the water came clearly above the soft thudding of the hooves. To the left, the marsh stretched level, and beyond it, stark and clear against the sky, was the mill of Richard Rimmer, the black bars of its sails swinging in the wind; the hamlet by the mill was clear in view, a low huddle of white by the dark of the Otter Pool, and John waved at it.

"A fine Whig mill," he said briefly. "It will show a red light, we'll hope, tonight."

Will nodded. "Aye, through the gap in the hawes. On a leading line."

They went on steadily, and the beat of the hooves grew slower as the track grew wetter; the mere was before them and behind them, and it filled their world, imposing its silence and hushing all words. They rode quietly, each in his own thoughts, until before them the far rim of the mere was seen, and beyond it the yellow line that was the sand of the tumbled hawes. The wind was snoring now, and there was a clean tang of salt in it; and suddenly John was jerked from his thoughts by a shrill harsh scream. He flung back his head, and there above him were the white-winged gulls, wheeling and soaring in their fretful tumult; and below him was the thin sod with the yellow streaks of sand, streaks that were broadening and running into one.

They left the sod behind and plunged into the trackless hawes, and then out to the hard-ribbed sand of the open shore; and at once, and without a word spoken, they had halted by the flotsam of the tidemark, and Will was pointing to the horizon. Hull down in the west, its spars black against the sky, was a two-masted lugger, hove to under a jib and a close-reefed driver.

"There she is!" said Will. "Riding it out. But the wind's dying, and she'll be in this night."

"Under a swelling moon?"

"A little more than that. It's none so far from full. And . . ." He glanced shrewdly round him. "What time would it be?"

"Now? Past noon—a half hour past."

Will nodded, and his eyes strayed across the wet sand to the white line of the surf that foamed and seethed beyond.

"The tide's making, you see. It's about half flood. High water perhaps at three, and low water at nine—under the moon. It's very convenient."

"Very." John clung to his hat as he stared into the wind. "Now where's Jimmy Jump?"

They rode briskly along the sand, watchful for the track that opened through the hawes by the Birkdale hamlet. It was soon found, and then they were at the thatched and limewashed cottage with the path of sea-washed shells; it was as trim as ever, its door gleaming, its windows bright, and its single chimney smoking; the two-wheeled cart was still standing by the garden with its shafts cocked up; and by it, wintry in sea boots and a tarpaulin jacket, was the squat and sturdy shape of Jimmy Jump, busy with brush and bucket as he scrubbed its salt-caked timbers. He looked round as he heard the thud of horses in the sand, and at once he had come towards them, a welcoming grin on his face and his wet brush dripping water.

"Eh, it's Mr. Leyburne!" was his greeting as the grin widened on his sunburned face. "And I'm right glad of it."

"And I, Jimmy. I'm back from London, do you see, and——"

"Aye, I see. And Mr. Hoghton too. I'd half thought to see you, sir, with the wind dropping."

"Just so." It was plain in Will's tone that he had seen the point. "The lugger's in the offing, I see."

"Aye, he's there. It'll be tonight's ebb that——"

"Jimmy!"

It was shrill and sudden, and it set the men turning quickly; and there by her open door was the Widow Jump, fierce and small as she stood in bright-eyed welcome. John swept his hat punctiliously, and her eyes grew even brighter; but she made no comment that was direct.

"Jimmy!" she barked again. "Put your brush down, you great oaf, and be at baiting horses. What do you think you——"

"Aye, aye." His voice cut in heartily. "I'll do that, and you be at baiting the gentlemen."

She needed no telling. She was already waving them in, and before their eyes were used to the gloom of it there was a cloth spread on the scrubbed table, and a glow and flicker from a fire she had newly raked. She was a whirl of defiant apology; there was nothing in these parts, she said, but pigs and fish, and with this gale there wasn't any fish and they would have to make the best of that. The crackle and scent of frying ham came from the hearth to make her meaning clearer, and Will Hoghton grinned and said he had heard that these parts had some hens as well.

"Eggs!" The widow snorted with seeming contempt. "Who counts eggs? But you can have some if you want some."

They ate with zest; and Jimmy, coming in from seeing to the horses, settled himself on a stool by the fire and was plainly willing to talk. His mother stayed silent and let him; she was attentive to her guests' needs, and her darting birdlike glances missed nothing; but her sturdy good sense kept her from intruding on a talk that quickly became technical. Jimmy was the expert here; the night tide, he said, would begin to make before nine, and a little after eight would be the hour when nearest approach might be had to the deep-water channel; it would therefore be the lugger's hour. But the delay made by the storm had set the moon nearer to its full, and by nine it would be high to the south, shining along the shore instead of hanging low across the sea, as it had done when the lugger had come before.

"And that's our chance, d'ye see," said Jimmy. "It'll be a clear night, by the looks of things, and we can work to the north and have 'em up-moon. That's how you see at night."

Clearly he took it for granted that he was coming too, and they were glad enough that he should; and then Will looked inquiringly across the table.

"I think you are captain in this enterprise, John. So what comes next? Is it Ormskirk, to await their coming?"

"No." John spoke decisively. "It's the Martin Mere."

"The mere? Why?"

"Because we don't know for certain what's done on the mere. We think Mansell goes there at dusk for geese to cover these ridings-out. But we don't know for certain. So I think we'll be by the mere at dusk."

"Then perhaps we'd best be moving. North about the mere, I think. Do you know the brow?"

"The Mere Brow? Yes, Penny once showed it me."

"It has more trees than the rest of the mere, and the reeds are taller.

And you need some cover if you're to come at the geese. That's where Mansell should be."

They rode in the wane of the afternoon, leaving the widow preparing for their return and Jimmy watchful of the lugger and the shore. They rode warily, keeping to the line of the hawes and making a careful circuit round North Meols, and the light was fading when at last they left the coast, splashed through the sodden channel where the mere touched the sea, and went quietly up the gentle slope of the brow. The wind had died, and under the thin high cloud the sky was chill and grey; only in the west was there a touch of gold, where behind the clouds the sun was falling; and from the gold came a soft cool breeze that hardly stirred the mere. On the brow the wind-bent trees were still, and on the thin wet turf the horses padded softly; and little by little, as they went, the mere cast its spell. Endlessly it stretched to the south, black and quiet, fringed with secretive reeds, and on its islands the trees hung stark and gaunt above the water. Nothing stirred; all was silence, the forgotten silence of the mere. The horses went softly on; and the riders had eyes on the mere, and not a word to say. They were at the top of the brow and were sitting stiffly on their horses, staring at the water, when Will broke the silence.

"We'd best leave our horses," was all he said. "Down the slope there, where they'll not be seen."

John nodded, and in silence they walked the horses down the further slope, away from the mere, and set them to a grazing tether. Slowly they walked back, and then Will looked about him thoughtfully.

"We must not stay here," he said. "If Mansell comes from the east, as he should, he'll have us in the sky and against the afterglow. We'll be better in the reeds."

They went quietly down until the willows were left behind and the turf had given place to the cold black soil, where the thin grass straggled and the mare's-tails were straight and green. Then the soil grew softer and began to stick; rivulets of water were in it, and became pools; the pools grew larger, and tall reeds were growing from the water; and suddenly, before their feet, there was nothing else. Reeds and water filled the world, and the mere had imposed itself. Nothing moved; nothing broke the stillness but the lap of water in the reeds.

"It's almost time." Will's voice was almost a whisper. "You see the light?"

John looked up, almost startled at a human voice, and at once he saw what was meant. The grey and gold had left the clouds, and a strange and lemon-coloured light had filled the sky, a light from the west, cold, serene, and clear; under it the mere was black, and the lap and gurgle of it tinkled in the silence.

"Look!"

Will had John by the arm, swinging him round as he spoke. Far out over the mere a goose was in flight, fast and low above the water; it was a speeding shape against the lemon sky, its neck outstretched and its great wings beating firmly, and as it passed out of sight behind the island trees another shot up in its wake, and another, and another. They came into view again beyond the island, circling the mere fast and low, a thin black skein in a lighted sky; and behind them a second flight was up, and then a third had come from nowhere.

"Where's Mansell?" said Will suddenly. "It's his hour."

"Is it?" John's thoughts and eyes were not with Mansell. He was staring at a sky that seemed filled with sound, and for this brief moment the silence of the mere had gone. All about him, near and far, the geese were taking flight, speeding in their skeins and circling above the water; they were in the distance, black dots against the lemon sky, and they were so near and low above him that he heard the whirr of wings and the hiss of air through pinions; and then, of a sudden, they were calling, shrill and loud, as if orders for the night were being given by the leaders and answered by the skeins.

A skein broke away, following with fine precision as its leader made for the sea; a second followed, flying fast and straight for the distant banks. Then a third broke clear, streaming out of the circle and soaring to clear the brow; it was scarcely a hundred yards away, and suddenly, as it went, there was a red flash of flame from the reeds below, and the thunder of a fowling piece came rolling across the mere. The leader dipped and went fluttering, and as John spun round with Will's hand tightening on his arm the fowling piece flamed out again.

"Good cover," said Will grimly. "He's nearer than I'd thought. And he's no 'prentice hand."

The mere was in tumult. The shooting was rapid now, and the flame and thunder of it cut through the whirr of wings and the splash and thud of the falling birds; a horse whinnied, and somewhere in the reeds a dog was barking. Caution was needless, and Will swept the reeds aside that he might better hear the shots.

"Every ten seconds," he said calmly. "There'll be men loading for him. Come——"

He led quickly through the reeds in the deepening dusk, and John followed closely; and as Will moved into the loom of a stark and straggling willow the shooting stopped abruptly. Feet crunched in the distant reeds; the dog scurried noisily; and that was all. Slowly the mere imposed itself again. Undisturbed, the skeins flew out to the lonely banks; undisturbed, the last few stragglers rose from the mere, and their shrill *arck! arck!* came echoing as they formed their skein; then they were gone, dark specks against the last pale glimmer of the lemon light, and the mere was itself again. There was nothing in the silence but the sigh of the night wind and the lap and ripple of the water. John spoke in a hushed whisper.

"Where are they? We must see more closely."

"Loading the pack-horse, I expect. Keep off the reeds. They're noisy."

They moved cautiously from tree to tree, edging away from the water to the slope of the brow, and suddenly Will stopped against the trunk of a willow and was peering cautiously.

"What the devil?" he whispered. "Here's more than we'd supposed."

The mere was below them, smooth and quiet, and the last light of the sky was mirrored in the water; against its glimmer were men and horses, vague black shadows in the dark, and the number of them set John staring.

"How—how many?" he asked blankly.

"Men, perhaps four. Horses, a score at the least."

"Yes." In the dark, John stood staring as he tried to count the shadows. "Many beasts and few men—that should be pack-horses."

"But what are they all for?"

"That's to be learned—tonight." John spoke grimly. "Though there's one thing learned now."

"What?"

"Why Thornclough must have fine new stables. What next?"

"Departure—if we're not to be seen. Look . . ."

Inland, to the east, the thinning cloud could be seen, picked out by a pallid glow that had touched its ragged fringe; the men and horses by the mere took sharper line as the water began to gleam, and Will pressed back into the shadows.

"Moonrise," he said softly. "And the sky's clearing. Come away. . . ."

33 THE SWELLING MOON

The fine dry sand went sliding under the hooves as Jimmy Jump led them from his mother's house and down the trodden track, through the hawes, to the lonely silence of the shore. The sky had cleared, as Will had said it would, and to the south the crescent moon hung above the hawes, red and clear; the night wind was coming from the sea, soft and cool, and the rested horses went briskly in the nip of it. Jimmy led confidently to the distant banks; he took a sinuous course, warily skirting the pools and the softer sand, and coming at last to a great arched bank, hard and ribbed and wet; and there before them, where the bank fell away, was the heave and gleam of water and the white foam of the incoming tide.

They drew rein by the seethe and splash of it, and for a moment there was silence as they looked around. Far down the hawes the moon was climbing, and the light of it lay along the black-ribbed sand like a bar of gold; the nearer hawes were lost in a surging gloom, and not a light showed, nor any hint of waking men. Seaward the sky was clear, but there was no gleam of light, nor any loom or shadow to give hint of a lugger stealing in, dark and silent under shortened sail; there was nothing but the surf, the fanning wind, and the bright cold stars.

"He's there."

It was Jimmy's voice, sardonic and reassuring. He had turned his face to the sea, and with his head thrown back he was sniffing at the wind as though he would smell this creeping Dutchman.

"Aye, he's there," he repeated confidently. "He'll have greased his blocks and stood hands at every sheet. And a hand in the chains with——"

Jimmy stopped abruptly. Out over the sea, perhaps a mile beyond the surf, an eye of gleaming red had sprung into being, heaving and rocking against the stars.

"That's him," said Jimmy briskly. "Now where's the shore party?"

He swung round, the others with him, to scan the dark loom of the hawes, but they looked in vain. The moon was higher now, and the trail of it was turning silver, but nothing stirred; no light showed in the hawes; no beat of hooves woke the silent shore.

"What of this leading light?" said John suddenly. "It shines from the mill, does it not? Through the hawes?"

"Aye, it does an' all." Jimmy spoke confidently. "And it would shine before he'd show his. We're off the line of it, that's all."

He put his cob to a trot, southward by the cream of the surf. A furlong sufficed, and then with one accord they drew rein as the light opened up, clear and bright and seeming to hang in the very heart of the hawes.

"Excellent," said Will softly. "How far does it run?"

"Quiet! And listen——"

John slapped his saddle to enforce his words. At once there was silence, heads thrown back and ears alert; and in the silence they heard it clearly—the confused low rumble of a host of hooves thudding on the hard sand. Then he spoke urgently.

"Down-moon!" he snapped. "Or they'll be upon us."

He swung his horse without waiting for an answer, and at once the others followed, trotting quietly to the north and away from the silver moon; and they were a full furlong down the trail of it when they halted and turned their horses again. In silence they waited, sitting tensely and staring up the silver trail of sand. Under his cloak John's hand was on his sword hilt, and at his side he saw Will reach softly forward to the holsters that hung from his saddle. Jimmy saw it too, and chuckled.

"They'll not see us down-moon," he said reassuringly. "Try it."

John did. He spared a quick glance over his shoulder and was convinced; down the moon-trail all was gloom, and nothing and no-body would be seen at a furlong's length.

"There!"

He spun round again as he heard Will's soft word; and hard and black in the silver light was the shape of a horseman, moving across the shining sand. Another followed, and another. One by one, six riders crossed the silver trail, full into the light and then out of it, so that only the loom of them remained as they halted by the breaking surf; and after them came the pack-horses, a dozen of them in a patient string, and two more riders to tend them as they went.

"Eight," said Will quietly. "Those you spoke of, and Richard Rimmer added, no doubt. But a dozen pack-horses? There's more to this than lace. What now? Can you see?"

It was Jimmy who showed them what to do. Without speaking, he walked his horse into the sea, and the others followed him, through the breakers and the sizzling undertow and into the heave and swell of the tide. Here they halted, with the crests of the swells splashing at their boots and the horses' bellies; and from here they looked again up-moon.

The moon-trail had moved with them, and now it was a track of heaving surf, curling and breaking on the sand; and up it, clustered by the edge of the tide, with the first white water streaming and sizzling by their feet, were the men and horses. John and Will watched tensely, and with no thought of more; but Jimmy's eyes had turned to the sea.

"There she is," he said calmly, and the others turned to him on the instant; and there, vague and shadowy in the uncertain distance, was a black shape on the heaving water, a shape that had two tall and raking masts and some shadows that must be sails. And John had hardly made sure of it when Will's hand was on his arm to direct him to something more; there was another shape now in the lighted band below the moon—a boat under oars that was pulling for the shore. It grounded, and at once there were men in the surf, grasping the gunwales and heaving it in.

What followed was not to be clearly seen. There was a press of men about the boat, heaving and lifting, and the clutter of them hid all else. Three times the boat put off to the dark loom of the lugger, and three times it came again to the surf and the shining sand; one by one the panniered pack-horses were led to the water's edge to take their loads; and then it was surely Mansell's burly figure that stood alone by the water in last talk with the tall stooping man who had seemed to command the boat and who seemed now to take something from his pocket. John's eyes narrowed as he saw it; he had remembered Mr. Payne's guess that letters would be landed here.

Whatever it was, Mansell seemed to take it; and then, as the boat pushed off, he stood for a moment by the water's edge with his arm raised, as if in farewell. Then he turned, walked briskly to his horse, and swung into his saddle; and at once the whole cavalcade was moving. It went slowly, the loaded pack-horses doing little more than walk, and it made directly across the banks to the low line of the hawes. Warily lost in the dimness down the moon, the three watchers kept pace.

They plunged into the dark tangle of the hawes, and, by some devious route that surely only Richard Rimmer knew, they came out to the endless plain beyond. The watchers followed, and there to their right was the Otter Pool, sleek and shining in the moonlight; to their left the marsh stretched into the night, black and shadowy, and the steady plod of the pack-horses could be heard on the track that girded it. North about they went, steadily round the marsh, until to their left was the mere, down the moon-trail and therefore dim and vague. And suddenly the pack-horses and their guard had left the track and were making towards it.

"You see?" said Will sharply. "It's the mere they go to."

"Of course—for the geese. But we'll be up-moon if we follow them there. We must work round."

It was easier said than done, and a quarter hour had passed before they had made their circuit and could see under the moon the shapes of men and horses grouped by the shining water. Then, at Will's insistence, they dismounted and went on foot in a light-toed silence. It brought them in safety to a tangled clump of willows, where the boughs were silver and the shadows pitch; and as they slipped into that shielding dark there was a splash and gurgle of water, soft and gentle, from the mere.

It came again, and then a silence; then reeds rustled noisily, and the tense watchers pressed against the willow boughs as they strained their eyes to see. Before them, clear in the moonlight, the horses waited by the rippling mere at a place where a tongue of water ran through the reeds to the marshy rim; and, as they watched, the reeds that fringed this channel swayed and parted and a dark shape slid into the tongue of water. It turned and came towards the shore; and John's hand was on Jimmy's shoulder.

"What is it?" he whispered.

"A punt," said Jimmy promptly. "And men in it."

It came slowly in, and it had four men paddling gently. It grounded, and something was lifted in; then it moved away again, and the tall reeds rustled as it thrust between them; and again, as the rustling stopped, there was a soft and gurgling splash.

"Very pretty!" said Will beneath his breath. "Buried treasure—and the mere keeps its secret."

Three times more the punt moved in and out; three times more the gentle splash told of a secret given to the mere; and then, as the punt made its last return, it was pushed into the thick reeds by the shore, and there left. There was bustle as men mounted and pack-horses were linked together; and then the rumble of hooves came again, muffled by the sedgy soil as the cavalcade moved off.

"Do we follow?" said Will.

"We do not." John's answer was prompt and decisive. "It's our work tonight to learn what these men do—and what they've hidden in the mere."

It was the practical Jimmy who showed them how to do it. They waited until all sound of hooves had died into the night, and then Jimmy was groping in the outer reeds.

"There'll be a mooring somewhere," he said.

It was soon found—a stake, deep in the mud and with a rope made fast to it. Jimmy hauled, and the reeds swayed and rustled as the punt came slowly into sight. It was Jimmy who took command as they paddled cautiously down the narrow lane of water that ran from the shore; and it was Jimmy who found the gap in the reeds at the side of the lane. He swung the punt expertly, and the reeds parted as it drove between them.

There was not far to go. In a score of yards there was another clearing in the reeds, a round pool of open water, black and rippling;

and as the punt slid into it Jimmy dropped his paddle and was in the bows, peering keenly. Then suddenly his long arm was reaching to the water to grasp at a billet of wood that floated there.

"This'll be it," he said. "Or one of 'em."

A wave of his other hand completed his meaning, for it showed that the wooden billet did not float alone; from rim to rim the pool was dotted with its fellows, floating low and still.

"Very pretty!" said Will again. "And now the mere does *not* keep its secret."

Jimmy heaved the wood inboard, and with it came a thin rope, wet and dripping; he heaved on that, and soon a stouter rope appeared, made fast to the thin one. Jimmy grasped the knot and ran his fingers over it expertly.

"Nicely married," was his comment, and it sounded as though he approved.

He heaved again, and this time there was weight—too much for him in the lurching punt, and Will lent his own thick arms to the work as well, till the dark water broke in a flurry of white and Jimmy was leaning out to grasp at what had come.

Between them they tumbled it to the bottom of the punt, and John risked a flash of flint and tinder that they might see the better. It was a wooden case, long and slender, stoutly built and tarred, and it had a flat lid, securely nailed. Jimmy produced a ferocious knife, found the joint and prized; he got his fingers under, and, with a slow creak of pulling nails, the lid reared up. Jimmy's hands were in the case at once, and he needed no light to tell him what he was handling.

"Muskets," he said briefly, and he pulled one out to be seen.

There were six of them in the case, each wrapped in grease and rag, and John gave himself to quick computing.

"Six to a case," he said. "Two cases to a horse, and twelve horses. That's twelve dozen in a night. And how many nights?"

"That's a guess." Will spoke sombrely as he thrust the thing back into its case. "Ten, perhaps—or twelve."

"Even ten makes fifteen hundred odd."

"Unless some of it was powder and shot."

"Very like. Small wonder that Ferguson saw fit to look at this himself. Here's the heart of rebellion—hidden in this mere, and to be had at short call."

"It won't be—soon." Will's voice was grim. "*You* may see to that."

"I will. Now how's the time, do you suppose?"

"Past eleven—by the moon."

"Then we'd best be riding. I'll have Penny growing concerned."

"I *am* concerned—for Father Barlow. He should have been safe till he rode for Wigan. But I'll be glad of news. It's Justice Mansell in our house with a warrant that I fear. It's in his powers."

There was anxiety in Will's steady tone, and John found spur enough in that. In minutes the muskets had been safely sunk again, the punt stowed among the reeds, and farewells said to Jimmy. Then they were at horse again, riding round the rim of the mere to Scarisbrick and beyond. But they did not enter Ormskirk, glad though they would have been of Tom Greenhalgh's ale; they were not minded to meet Mansell and his men leaving the Rising Sun, and Will took no chances; he led on remote and rustic tracks, keeping to the north of the town, and sinking soon into a brooding silence that matched John's mood, as concern for a hiding priest became his also; he had a warm feeling for Edward Barlow, and he knew what was done at Tyburn could be done as savagely at Lancaster.

The early-risen moon was dropping now, and its light had turned to gold and then to a dusky red before they came at last to the post road. They halted there for a parting word, sitting their horses on the dusty ribbon of it and peering at each other's faces in the last glimmer of the moonlight.

"My thanks," said John slowly. "For all you've done. Most grateful thanks."

"They're neither due nor asked. There's a duty in things these days. What comes next?"

"Find justices who are not Whigs. Take them to the mere."

"Richard Langley will find them for you." Suddenly in the gloom Will laughed. "You heard how he turned the Mansells from his door —when they'd have bid for Penny?"

"Blast them! I did."

"You still sound sour. But we'd best be parting. You know your way from here?"

"Yes. Across this road, and then——"

Southward a pistol shot cracked in the night, and Will's horse reared suddenly at the sound of it. To the south there was a flurry of hooves on the rutted road, and then another shot, and another; the hooves were nearer now, and louder, and the racing horse was almost at the bend of the road when John edged back into the shadows of the fringing trees.

"What the devil!" he muttered as Will joined him.

It was not without cause. Whoever had this horse was riding like a madman, and bright sparks flew between stones and hooves as he took the bend. Behind him were hooves again, a flurry of them, and from the curve of the road a pistol flamed again, the red spurt of it stabbing the shadowed dark. John jerked back as the shot went whistling, and he was still taut when the first lone rider went tearing by, madly through the dark tree-shadows and out into the gleam of the moon beyond. Something in the loom of him stirred a memory, and as John groped for it he heard Will's startled word.

"God! It's Ned!"

The pursuit came roaring, a wild clatter of men and horses; and suddenly Will was in the open road, his horse across it and his gloved hands plucking at his holsters. There was a yell of fury as a man swerved to clear him, and then John was in the road at his side, utterly blocking what was left of it and bringing the riders to a frenzied panting halt. There were five of them, and there could be no mistaking the burly thickset loom of Roderick Mansell.

In the dark, John's hand was suddenly on Will's, pressing it down and forcing the half-drawn pistol back into its holster. A coldness had come to him under this spur of danger, and he was remembering that Will was a papist, forbidden pistols and open to the law—as given by Sir Henry Mansell. This must be his own work now, not Will's; and it was with Mansell that his own score lay. He was remembering that when Mansell spoke furiously.

"Stand clear!" he shouted. "From the road—in the King's name!"

"The King's?" John's voice came slow and cool, and still his restraining hand was on Will. "The King's, is it? Or Shaftesbury's?"

"What the devil! Stand clear!"

Again Mansell tried to move his horse through. But Will was

stolidly across the road, and John was blocking what remained of it; and in the far distance the roar of hooves had died to a soft drone as John spoke again.

"Is it the Brisk Boys loose? Or the Mohawks? Or a crew of thieving lackeys?"

"Lackeys!" Mansell was almost choking. "Now blast and——" He broke off as if a thought had come to him. "Leyburne, is it? And who's this?"

"William Hoghton, sir—at your service."

Will's voice was very steady as he made his answer; and suddenly, and without any mirth, Mansell laughed.

"It would be! And makes a priest's escape. For which you'll answer, both of you. You'll ride with me to Thornclough, and——"

"Are you a justice these days?"

John's voice cut sharply in, and Mansell wheeled furiously on him. "Am I a——"

"A justice, I said. And if not, you'll use the King's name less noisily, and with fewer pistol shots. Further—Colonel Mansell, is it not?"

"You know damned well——"

"Further then . . ." Again John cut him short. "If you've a wish to continue living, you'll mend your manners—mend them by a deal —when you speak to me."

"What—*what* was that?" Mansell's voice was suddenly hushed and threatening.

"You know well enough what it was—and is. I've measured your sword before, and found it a poor, rough thing. And I'll eat no insolence from *you*. Now, is that plain?"

The hush quivered beneath the silent trees as Mansell sat rigid. John was as still as he, and Will was like a statue. The hush lengthened, and a horse moved and pawed at a stone beneath it; and then Mansell found his voice.

"Plainer than you'll care for—tomorrow. You'll hear from me."

Without another word he pulled his cloak tight and wheeled his horse; and he had something of dignity as he trotted away, his silent servants with him.

34

THE BROKEN NIGHT There was a sigh of easing breath as Will turned slowly.

"Rash of you, John. You've provoked something."

"I've provoked a rat, that's all. And there'll be no more heard of him. What I said was true."

"About what?"

"About his swordplay. Also, we have him now as a smuggler."

"He doesn't know that yet. Or——" Will's voice hardened suddenly. "Or does he?"

"Does he? Now how do you mean by that?"

"No." Will seemed to be trying to speak lightly. "I suppose he doesn't, yet. He was too heated to think. But he must have seen which lane we came from."

"And what of it?"

"Only that we could have come from nowhere but the mere. And if he *does* begin to think when he's cooled——"

"I see." John spoke steadily as he saw what was possible. "He'll guess where we were and what we've seen? Then perhaps we'd better seek those justices before he's done his thinking. But Will—what of tonight? That *was* your Father Barlow, surely?"

"It was." The anxiety was back in Will's voice. "I suppose he was riding for Wigan when he met them. If Mansell and his crew left the Sun about that time——"

"I see. They'd have come upon him at the post road?"

"They must have done—a mile south of here. We kept to the north, remember."

"I do. But what now? This is your matter, and I'll serve you in it."

"I don't know. Is he hurt, do you think? Those pistol balls came close."

"If he's hurt he's not badly hurt. He was riding too well for that. But where would he make for? The Park Hall?"

"He might. It's home to him. But it's the house they'd search first, and he'd think of that too."

"Then where else?"

"He . . ." Will hesitated. "He might be at Langley House. They'd not say him nay there, any of them."

"If he could rouse them without tumult."

"There's you to come in yet. Which means Penny astir, at the least."

"Bless her! Then perhaps we'd best part?"

"I'm sure of it. And John?"

"Yes?"

"Whoever has news of him tells the other."

"Be sure of that." John wheeled his horse. "God keep you, Will!"

"Keep all of us, you mean—in these days. But fare you well!"

The moon was down and the sky was a cold bright twinkle of stars when John came at last to the dark loom that was Langley House; and as his horse clopped wearily on the gravel there was the soft slide of a bolt, and then the arch of the door took sudden shape in a glow of candlelight.

"John?"

It was Penny, alert and welcoming in the lighted doorway as he swung stiffly from his saddle; and as he walked unsteadily to the house, his feet numb in his boots, she came impulsively to meet him, and she pressed herself against him with an eagerness that hinted at anxieties relieved.

"Is it well?" she whispered as she flung her head back.

"Very well."

He stayed for a moment smiling down at her, and then he kissed her again before he would release her.

"It's very well," he repeated. "We've learned it all."

A groom came sleepily from the side of the house to take his horse, and then Penny was close at his side as he went slowly through the door; but as she pushed it to behind them she spoke excitedly.

"It's well here too," she told him. "We've a guest new come."

"Mr. Barlow, do you mean?"

He spoke sharply as memory came rushing to revive his fears, memory of racing hooves and pistol shots that flamed in the night; and Penny's face changed quickly at his tone.

"Why, no . . ." She was plainly alarmed. "But what——"

She broke off as the parlour door swung open; and under the lintel of it, tall and big, the lazy smile on his face and his hand outstretched in greeting, was the friendly Mr. Payne.

"I leave you in no peace," he said cheerfully. "Always I disturb you."

"Indeed no." John pulled the gloves hastily from his chilled fingers. "You set me in surprise. That's all."

"It's perhaps enough—or will be." A well remembered note was coming into the crisp voice. "But between one thing and another in the town I thought I'd best learn things for myself. So I made bold to arrive unbidden."

"I see." John spoke slowly. "But what——"

"What's that of Uncle Ned?"

Penny cut in urgently, as though this came first and the affairs of the town could wait; and her voice must have carried clearly, for there were quick footfalls within the parlour as Aunt Arabella came hastily to the door.

"Is this something of Ned?" she asked urgently.

There was nothing for it but to tell them the tale, and it left them in an anxious silence. Mr. Payne stood brooding by the parlour fire; Mr. Langley tried to be bluff and hearty, and then gave it up as he saw his sister's face; and it was John who had to fill the silence by telling the earlier tale, the tale of the moon on the silver sand, the boat in the creaming surf, and the horsemen by the silent mere. It came from him slowly, for he told it from the table while Penny plied him with beef and bread and hot spiced ale; but it was a cheering tale, and a happy thought of success was with him as he ended.

"So all's now well," he told them buoyantly. "We've seen what's done and we've seen who does it. And we can guess what it's done for. And all that's needed now is to seek good justices."

There was a fine confidence in his voice, and then he waited happily for their comments. There was a slow nod of assent from Aunt Arabella, a rumble of approval from her brother, and a quick pat on the head from Penny. But from Mr. Payne there was nothing. He was still standing by the hearth, with his big shoulders propped against it and his lean face set and grave; he had flung one arm along the stone of the mantelshelf, and his fingers were drumming on it as his fine eyes clouded in the tight web of his thought. John watched with something of apprehension, and he knew that all could not be well; he had seen Mr. Payne look like this before. And suddenly Penny's hand was softly on his arm, as though she had sensed that he had a need of comfort.

The drumming finger stopped. Mr. Payne seemed to rouse himself, and his arm dropped from the shelf as he turned.

"I'll agree," he said slowly, "that we know now what is done and why. But for proving it, for bringing it home on these Mansells—for that you need witnesses. Or at least, the justices will. And of witnesses we have only one."

"One?" John echoed it in surprise. "I've said that there were three of us who——"

"Three men—yes." Mr. Payne seemed to sweep that aside. "But only one Protestant. It won't be enough."

He seemed to go into his thoughts again, and John sat silent, with elation gone. It was a thing not to be disputed; no justice would give weight to a papist's oath.

Mr. Payne stirred himself again.

"A small packet, did you say? And passed to Mansell by this man from the boat?"

"Yes—or so it looked. A tall and stooping fellow. The moon was very bright, and——"

"Just so." Mr. Payne nodded. "It would be the letters, without a doubt. And that, we may suppose, accounts for Mrs. Waring."

"Mrs. Waring?"

"Did you not say she had come? She's been the messenger to Argyle before, and that's surely to be her work again. She arrived when the lugger was due, did she not?"

"She did. And then there was the storm——"

"Exactly. And now she'll be making ready. I'll guess that her chariot's called for dawn, and then she'll be for Scotland again—no doubt with Mansell as her escort. And those letters are the key to all."

There was a stress on his last words that gave them meaning, and it was Richard Langley who voiced the question.

"How?" he asked quickly. "How are these letters——"

"They'll turn the lock." Mr. Payne turned to his host as he explained it. "These muskets in the mere won't hang the Mansells—nor even set them into flight. There's but one good witness, and they'll outswear him. At the worst they'll be suspect and they'll lose their muskets. And without the letters, that's all. And in the town they'll hang Gadbury and Mrs. Cellier—a virtuous Colonel Mansell giving evidence against them. They might even hang this Will Hoghton here —swearing the muskets as his work."

"What's that?" Penny was on her feet in consternation. "Hang our Will, do you say?"

"I certainly do. There have been worse things done than that, these latter days." Mr. Payne, the papist, spoke bitterly. "Which is why the letters are the key. Without doubt they're of treason, and that's what's needed. Once they're taken, the letters will prove the muskets and the muskets will prove the letters. And it's Holland for the Mansells—or Tyburn."

"And Gadbury?"

"Will go free. With Mansell gone there'll be nothing against him, as I've said before. So it's matter now of these letters. This Mrs. Waring, now . . ." Mr. Payne had his eyes on John. "She'll start at dawn, no doubt. But where *is* this Thornclough? And what road will she take?"

"Good God!" John sat up, startled by the tone of it. "You don't think of turning highway cull, do you?"

"Why not?" The answer came grimly. "In these times I'm like to be hanged for something in the end. So as well for that as for less."

"Hell!" John was staring at him while the others sat aghast. "Do have *some* thought for your safety."

"I try to. And it would also be well to give some thought to yours."

"What!"

"Even so." Mr. Payne was as grim as before. "Forgive me if I speak plainly—but you're a danger to the Mansells, are you not? Perhaps their only danger."

"Perhaps I am. But do they know——"

"Probably they do. They're not fools. You say he could have guessed from the road you were on that you'd been at the mere?"

"Why, yes—but——"

"And there's still a charge of assault lying against you, which could still be pressed. Did you, by any chance, make any admission tonight of having wounded him before?"

"I—I think I did."

"Unfortunate!" Mr. Payne spoke almost drily. "His servants could no doubt be witnesses to that. So I think we may expect them——"

He broke off sharply, as though some new thought had come to him, and again his eyes were clouding as he sank himself in it. By the hearth, Mr. Langley gestured for the wine, and Penny went on tiptoe to pour for them all.

"There is perhaps a hope here." Mr. Payne broke the strained silence, and his tone was brisker now. "However they may hope to silence you, you are still a danger till they've done it. And from what I know of Mansell I doubt if he'll start for Scotland—or Mrs. Waring either—till they know their backs are safe. So perhaps we have a little time."

"Oh, indeed?"

"Yes." If John's question had a sardonic ring, Mr. Payne did not seem to have noticed it. "When all's said, they're some three days late from the storm, so one day more may not signify. Where the devil's Barlow?"

"Is that your first thought of him?"

Aunt Arabella had spoken suddenly, and in chill reproof, and Mr. Payne turned to her at once.

"I beg your pardon, ma'am. Truly I do." His voice was soft and gentle as he saw her strained and anxious face. "I've had a deal else to think of, as you well know. But indeed we must find him, and quickly. And not for his own sake only. In all these parts he knows the secret lanes—aye, and the secret men—as I do not. And his counsel's needed here. Where would he be, do you think?"

"Be?" John hastily collected his wits as he saw that the question was for him. "The Park Hall, I should suppose. It's his home, and Will thought he'd make for there or here. And he isn't here, so——"

"What about Wigan?" said Penny sharply. "He was to go there, wasn't he?"

"He'd not try that road again, with the Mansells on it. There's nothing sure, and he may have other hides. But my own guess is the Park Hall."

"Probably." Mr. Payne straightened himself and spoke with crisp decision. "And it's certainly the only one we can try. Could you lend me a horse, sir?"

"Eh—what's that?" Mr. Langley seemed surprised. "A horse, is it, and at this hour? Why, what—what *is* the hour?"

"Close on four," said Penny.

"Time to be a-going," said Mr. Payne firmly. "Myself, I'm rested, but my horse will not be. So——"

"To be sure." Mr. Langley still sounded surprised. "You're free enough of a horse, if you think it needful."

"I do. Now where *is* the Park Hall, pray? How do I find my way?"

"You won't," said Penny tersely. "Unless you first go to the Boar's Head—past Thornclough."

"Certainly not that way. But what other?"

"It's what I'm saying. There's none other that you'll find. It's dark now, and there'll be mist in the lanes."

"Then I'll need a guide."

Mr. Payne sounded determined, and his quick glance at John was a plain hint. But John was not allowed to answer it. Penny spoke first, and she sounded as determined as Mr. Payne.

"No you don't, John. You've been riding since dawn—I won't guess how many miles. It's time you were in bed."

"Now, Penny——"

"It's time you were in bed. And anyway, you don't know our lanes yet. You'd be lost yourself, and Mr. Payne with you."

That was true, and he knew it was. It put him to silence; and, bright-eyed and confident, Penny turned to Mr. Payne.

"I'll myself be your guide, sir," she told him cheerfully. "And I shall not lose you."

There was a chorus of protest and denial, and Penny swept it aside. It was a service needed, she said, and there was none but herself to do it. She was imperious about it, and John was chary of opposing her; Aunt Arabella was plainly thinking of her Ned, and Richard Langley was as plainly proud of this spirit in his daughter. So Penny had her way, and she went at a run for her riding clothes while John led Mr. Payne to the stables; it was not a moment to set the grooms chattering, and they saw to the horses themselves.

The first hint of dawn was in a paling sky, and a thin mist was hanging by the trees, when they led the horses to the cold dark of the gravel; and at the first clop of hooves the door swung open in a glow of light and Penny came quickly out. John held her stirrup as she mounted her beloved grey, and in the dark he saw her lean down to him.

"Don't stay here thinking about me," she whispered. "Get into bed. It's time you did."

"I will. But have a care for yourself."

"It looks as if I'm to have a care for others—and all of 'em papists." He heard her quick laugh in the dark. "And I'm going to enjoy it. It'll be a grand morning when the sun's once up."

There was the scrape of a boot and a soft clink of spurs as Mr. Payne swung into his saddle, and Penny stayed for no more. Her gloved hand pressed quickly on his shoulder, and then she was away, Mr. Payne close at her side. John stood stiffly as the darkness took them and the hoofbeats died into the mist; then he yawned wearily as he turned to go in. For a moment he stood, looking up at the waning stars, and suddenly he thought of Gadbury—Gadbury cooped in Newgate, and perhaps at this moment peering through a small high window at these stars he said he served. There had been no lack of truth in Gadbury's prediction of stirrings when the Moon was in the Scorpion. But that other moon, the moon whose silver trail had lighted the sand and the mere this night—was that the Moon in the Archer, which Gadbury had said would make all well?

He went quietly through the door, and had thought enough to slide the bolt behind him. In the parlour the candles had been blown, and Mr. Langley, out of his chair at last, was hobbling awkwardly on a stick; the carrying-candles were ready on the table, and Aunt Arabella handed one to John as soon as he appeared; evidently all was ready for belated bedtime.

"They're safe away." He answered the unspoken question as he took the candle. "Penny seems happy enough."

"So she should be!" Her father almost grunted. "What's the weather like?"

"A fine clear morning, sir—or will be. Fine and cold."

"Aye." The hobbling man spoke wistfully. "A good horse, and a good man with her. A November morning, a hoar on the grass, and a good sun lifting. What more does the girl want? What more does anybody want?"

"News of Ned Barlow," said his sister quietly. "That's what's wanted now, and it's what she's riding for."

"Aye . . ." He was suddenly embarrassed, as though he should not have forgotten this. "But she may as well——"

A knocking came softly on the shutters, a knocking whose odd rhythm John had heard before. The talk died like a blown candle; and, as the three of them turned to the windows, the knocking came again and seemed to falter, as if the hand that made it had faltered too; and John waited for no more. He went running to the hall, where a single candle burned, and then down the dark and unlit passage that Penny had used on a night of wind and rain. He found the door and groped in the dark for the bolt; and as he swung the door fiercely open he heard Arabella's hurrying feet on the creaking boards behind him. It was Edward Barlow, as he had known it must be; he was a cloaked and muffled shape against the first pink glow of dawn, and he was clinging to the doorpost as though to support himself, and sagging at the knees as though his strength were all but gone; and even as John got an arm round him he lurched and slipped, and all his weight came forward as his will gave way at last.

It was Arabella Langley, taut and white, who was captain of them all in the hour that followed. She found the ragged hole in his cloak where the pistol ball had entered, and with a gasp of relief she found the other hole where it had torn its way out; and after that she thought of everything. She had him out of the parlour, where servants would soon intrude, and away to the forgotten room in the older parts, where a panel turned in the blackened oak to give hide at need to a hunted man; she had the leather jerkin off him, and she cut away the blood-soaked shirt from the jagged wound where the ball had torn his arm-pit; she sponged and washed and probed, until she was sure that the worst of his hurt was loss of blood from a wound he could not stanch unaided; she had her brother bringing him hot sweet wine, and she had even wit enough to tell John to go outside and do something with his horse.

She set him a pretty problem there. He went into a wan grey world where the mist was white and the eastern sky was streaked with flames of red, and after some search he found the sorrel mare quietly at graze in the curving drive; and one look at her showed that neck and saddle were stained alike with blood. It was not a sight to leave for the public eye, and he had to work quickly. A riot of matted bramble below a hedge served well enough as a hide for saddle and harness; and then, because it was overlate for stables, where grooms would soon be waking, he led the mare down the well-remembered path that was so sweet and scented in the summer days; she followed patiently behind him into the paddock where Penny had led her under an August moon, and there he did what he could at her neck with a swab of cold wet grass. It was poor work, but the best he could do, and then he turned her loose to find what graze she could in the frosty field. Again it was the best he could do, and of concealment there was none if anybody chose to look; he could only hope that, in such a place as this, one horse more or less would take nobody's eye.

There were red shafts of sun thinning the mist and lighting the white hoar of the grass when he passed again through the low gate to the garden; and the path was alive with memories that set him to walk unseeing as he thought of Penny, riding through this crackling morning with Mr. Payne as friendly escort. Penny, he thought, had had the best of this; she would have had less pleasing work if she had stayed at home and let another ride into the dawn.

He came slowly from the garden, and he straightened himself wearily as he remembered that there was a wounded man within the house, and more to be done yet for the care of him. He was brooding on that when a quick clop of horses broke upon him, and his first and only thought was that here was Penny at last, trotting through the sunlight to home and him. He spun round eagerly; and up the bend of the drive came a cavalcade of horsemen, a full dozen and more, following in ordered rank behind a leader who was surely Sir Henry Mansell. He stared in cold dismay, and the icy thought gripped him that Mr. Barlow lay helpless within and that here was what he had seen before at Mrs. Cellier's—a party come to search, with a justice of the peace, and a warrant signed.

35

RED SKY AT MORNING It went with a sickening precision.

Sir Henry Mansell, his cheeks pinched and blue in the cold and his thick black cloak pulled tightly round him, took one piercing glance at John, and then his gloved hand waved imperiously. Three men broke instantly from the troop and came at a noisy gallop across the gravel, their drawn swords flashing in the sun, and John had no chance of escape; unarmed and on foot, he could do no more than stand between them as they crowded round him in a threatening silence. Again Sir Henry's gloved hand waved, to send two more parties galloping left and right about the house, as if to cut off all escape; and with a clatter of hooves and a jingle of spurs the rest dismounted and went running to the great door.

Sir Henry came last, and he was in no hurry to dismount. He sat erect and watchful on his horse while men knocked on the tight-shut door, and others ran left and right in search of another. There was a moment before they found it, and John, standing stiff and silent between his guards, had a chance to think. The promptness with which he had been seized had been ominous, and the thought was hardening in him that he himself was the quarry they hunted here. This Whig justice was not concerned with justice; he and his son had made the true guess that the secret of the mere was out, and they were concerned to make it safe.

The thought took seconds only, and then from the side of the house an exultant shout told that the small unbolted door had been found by which he had let himself out in search of the sorrel mare; and at once there were men storming through it, while the justice sat impassive, as prim and rigid as before. Between his guards John stood as stiffly, while memory came of Sir William Waller; and with it there came the memory of Mrs. Waring, warm in her black-and-crimson as she sat by Sir William's hearth. But where was she now, on this cold white morning? Was her chariot already bouncing and clattering to the North

along these rimed and frozen roads? And where was Roderick
Mansell?

The bolt of the door clanged noisily; it was pulled fiercely open, and
Sir Henry's men came pouring out as though inviting him to enter. He
nodded, and without haste he swung from his saddle and walked
slowly to the door; he stood for a moment in the arch of it, staring at
the blackened stone as though a memory had him; then, in the same
thin-lipped silence, he went within; and John was left with his thoughts
and his silent guards.

They had dismounted now, and they were standing round him with
their swords still drawn as his thoughts turned anxiously to what was
going forward within the house. And suddenly he realized that he did
not even know where Edward Barlow was, nor whether there had
been time enough to get him past a panel that turned in a forgotten
room; but certainly he was in the house, and white and weak from a
wound that——

He swung round sharply as another sound broke in. Down the bend
of the drive a horse's hooves could be heard, quiet and unhurried, and
in another moment, as the rider came in sight, John was standing a
shade more stiffly than before; this was Roderick Mansell, and there
could be no mistaking the burly form of him as he trotted easily over
the whitened gravel and swung from his horse in the glittering sunlight. He stood for a moment by the door, his bridle still in his hand
while he regarded John with a cold and hostile stare.

"You're back from your rovings, are you?" he said curtly.

"As are you, it seems." There was a hint of menace in John's steady
tone. "And you rove a deal, I'm told. Did you have good shooting?"

"At Barlow, is it?" The rough voice seemed rougher now. "You
know damned well——"

"I know nothing of a Barlow. Were you not shooting at geese—on
the Martin Mere?"

"Was I?" The ice-blue eyes had narrowed. "You've a deal too much
to say. You're a fool, and a long-nosed fool, and this time there'll be
an end of you. There are witnesses in plenty now, and you're for
Newgate again, and then Tyburn."

"Then perhaps we'll meet there, Colonel." It came swift and smooth as the scorpion's sting. "Or would it perhaps be Lancaster for you? I don't know all their ways in this county—but I'm learning."

"You're learning, are you?" It came truculently, and it had an ugly ring in it. "You may perhaps have learned too much."

"Just so, Colonel. I thought you'd think that."

The noisy truculence faded from Colonel Mansell, and something colder and harder took its place. His blue eyes were almost pin points as he stood in a staring silence, and something of the high colour seemed to fade from his cheeks. Then, without any haste, he moved slowly to the door; and as he went he spoke over his shoulder to the guards.

"Bring him along."

He disappeared under the arch, and John had a moment for thought before they took him in. He need hardly doubt, after that exchange, that the Mansells were here to make themselves safe from a danger they knew he could bring upon them. But what of Mrs. Waring? Had she started already for the North with the seeds of danger left to sprout and grow behind her? Or was she impatiently at Thornclough, waiting for the reassuring word and the escort who would ride beside her? His thought was hardening on that as his guards closed round him. Even if she were making light of the danger here, she could hardly take that moorland road to the North without some fitting escort.

They marched him into the house, and a fellow standing by the stair told them where next to go; and it was not to the fine stone parlour. Instead he was marched the length of the house, away from the clean new stone and into the older wing of oaken beams and panels black with age; and it was not hard to guess why. There was a priest to be taken here, a priest's hide to be found, and where should it be but in this old and rambling wing? And quickly the sickening image came of the friendly Mr. Barlow lying torn and wounded in some vile hole behind these panels, lying with the dust and the rats while the noise of search came nearer and hope of help grew less. It was no pretty picture, and John's thoughts were turning savage as the tramp of boots rang before him and behind him on the creaking boards. The thick shape of Roderick Mansell was flickering before him now, Mansell riding insolently in the sunlight to a door his kin had forced and blackened in the days gone by, Mansell swaggering at his ease by lawns and gravel that belonged to Penny and her dappled grey. The image flared; and then his hot fury went as a cold clear thought came leaping. Why had Roderick Mansell come alone and late? There could surely be none but Mrs. Waring who could have kept him back this day; which must surely mean that she had *not* begun her journey, that she was perhaps none so far away, and that Mansell had lingered for some word with her before thrusting himself into the work that was doing here.

The thought ended as he was marched into the room where the secret panel was, the room which in the hours of dark had seen a fainting man brought in to have a wet wound dressed and a blood-soaked shirt cut off. There was sunlight in the window now, and a glittering mist was in the shaft of it, where the pounding boots had raised a sea of dust. A half dozen men were ranged against the wall, one with his back to the very panel where the secret was, and Roderick Mansell, red and truculent, was stiffly in front of them. In the room's centre Sir Henry Mansell, his warrant crackling in his hand, was giving heed to a man who stood before him. Arabella Langley might have been carved from ice as she sat by the cold hearth in a chair she had swung to show the back of it; and in the sunlit window Richard Langley was showing the same contempt as he stared through the window at the whitened grass and the rime on the frosted trees. He seemed to hear nothing as Sir Henry spoke.

"You've heard what's told me," he was saying. "There's a mare found in your paddock with some daubs of blood—a sorrel, as Barlow is said to ride. And here's your floor still wet. There's been some swabbing done, and a wound dressed here no doubt. Do you still deny it?"

He had no answer. Richard Langley moved no muscle; Arabella stayed a frozen rock; and an angry flush was coming to Sir Henry's face as he turned threateningly to John.

"You'll be a privy to the whole of this. It's a work that would fit you. You're a crawling, grovelling papist who makes pretence to be an honest man, and you're ripe for Tyburn Tree. There's a warrant against you, as you've cause to know, and you'll do well to buy your neck. Where was Barlow put?"

The question cracked viciously, as though it would bruise by the sheer force of it, and for a moment John was numbed. Then he recovered as his own cold anger hardened, and the scorpion's sting was in his tone again as he flung his answer back.

"I know nothing of a Barlow. I'm concerned with rebels, not with priests."

"You'll be concerned with what I say. Here's——"

"I'm concerned with what you *are*. And if we're to speak of warrants there's another coming. Do you stay for it, I wonder? Or are you for Holland while there's still some time allowed you?"

There was a soft hiss of breath, and Sir Henry was a poised snake in the sunlight. From the hearth Arabella took a fleeting glance, bright-eyed and commending; and from behind the table Roderick Mansell laughed with a fine bravado.

"Here's a drunken cur!" he hooted. "Is it some tale your priests have told you? And who cares? It'll be all one at Tyburn. They've a fine way there with tongues."

But Sir Henry did not join his laughter. He was standing very still and upright, while the dust went sparkling round him and the sun found flecks of silver in his aging beard; and when he spoke his tone had changed.

"You are very prone to error, Mr. Leyburne," he said softly. "There is *not* a warrant coming. Your mad tale is not yet taken to my fellow justices. And if it *is* taken, and if they do look to it, they'll find it's not at all as you've supposed."

"No?"

"No." The word was firm and sure. "They'll learn that some muskets and the like were lately put upon this coast and carried to the mere by certain papists hereabouts, one William Hoghton being chief among them."

"Very pretty! You're a justice, did you say?"

"I am."

"I'd not have guessed it. You've the impudence of a carted crimp."

"Have I?" Sir Henry's voice rang cold and hard. "You'll find there are witnesses to what I've said."

"One Titus Oates being chief among 'em, I'll suppose. Tell your tale to another. You grow tedious."

"A jury of Assize may think differently. They'll hang you on the one charge and Hoghton on the other. And Barlow shall hang between you. Now do you buy your neck, and theirs, or don't you?"

"A bargain, is it? It would be—from you."

"Do you or don't you?"

"I don't."

"You insist on hanging Barlow, too?"

"You haven't got Barlow. He isn't here."

"Do you take me for a fool?" Sir Henry snapped his fingers as though in exasperation. "You've heard my last word. Now what's your answer? And let me have it plain."

"Go to the devil. Is that plain?"

Sir Henry's head reared up, and again the poise of the snake was his. But then he controlled himself, and, thin-lipped and white, he turned to the waiting men with orders crisp and hard. He knew exactly what his powers as a justice were, and he used them to the full. His men obeyed with a speed that suggested they were not new to this work of search, and he drove them to it with a precision that blended cold venom with exact observance of the law. It had the noise, the litter, and the wanton wrecking that Sir William Waller's search had had. It was thorough to brutality. Locks snapped and wood splintered as crowbars were used in earnest; curtains ripped as they were torn from walls, and the white plaster went flying into dust as the crowbars jabbed into walls and ceilings; the black oak ripped into streaks of white as the bars drove through the panels, and twice the very bricks were prized from walls where a hollow echo was fancied; hearths were probed and banged, and even the stones of them were lifted; ladders were thrust up chimneys, and hard-faced men went climbing; and half the treads were levered from the stair lest a cavity should lurk beneath.

The sun was above the trees and the white rime was off the branches before the end came. A panel split beneath a jabbing crowbar, and the split ran straight and true instead of following the grain. It was enough. The bars drove in remorselessly; then the brick-backed panel came swinging on its silent hinge as the bolt was torn away, and it was Roderick Mansell, his sword flashing in the sun, who made ready to leap into the dark hole that had opened. But so much was not needed. From behind the oak there was a stir and the scrape of a dragging foot, and Edward Barlow came slowly to the opening, his head and shoulders bent as he moved painfully in the dark low space. He was blinking as he met the light, and his bloodless face was taut with pain; but his first glance across the room was for Arabella Langley.

"I'm most sorry," he told her gently, "that so much should have come upon you because of me."

"Ned!"

It was a grating whisper, and her face was a twisted agony as she hid it in her hands. In the window Richard had turned to the room again, his face set and white. And in the silence the priest spoke softly to the purring Whig.

"And what, sir, would you have of me? I am Edward Barlow."

"And a Massing priest, treasonably within the realm?"

"I serve God—and the mission."

"For which you'll hang. And you——" Sir Henry turned viciously on Richard Langley. "You and your sister both, you're for Assize also. Comforting a Romish priest."

"I doubt it." Richard spoke shortly. "You're a thieving, smuggling rebel. You've lived and swelled and fattened on it, and all you seek is money. Now what's your price?"

"You offer insults, I think." But there was smooth satisfaction in Sir Henry's tone. "It's to be probed further. But not in this dust and cold. There'll be warmth elsewhere."

They went under close guard to the fine stone parlour where a fire crackled in the hearth and the mullioned windows gave on the wintry garden; and what Sir Henry's purpose was in moving them became apparent as he softly shut the door. For now they were alone; the guards had been left beyond the tight-shut door, and Sir Henry could speak his mind.

He came slowly from the door, and his hard eyes swept round the room; from the priest, weak in a chair with his face as white as the bandage on his shoulder, to Richard, standing stiffly at his sister's side; to Roderick Mansell, preening himself by the hearth, and at last to John, alert and alone by the window. Then he seemed to pick his words with care.

"There are certain charges I've been lately put to, and they'll need to be defrayed. They're considerable, as you'll find." His eyes flickered to Richard for an instant, and then they were on John again. "But what signifies more, Mr. Leyburne—do you heed me now?"

There was a plain threat in that, and the way he stopped gave sudden point to it. But John was not to be shaken; he had already guessed what was coming, and he spoke his own word first.

"What signifies is your own preservation, no doubt, from a proven charge of treason. And you'll bid high for my silence? Is that it?"

"It is not." Sir Henry was quick on it, almost too quick. "I've told you there are witnesses against you. Your tale's a foolishness, no more. But it might, perhaps, be in some sort an inconvenience."

"It certainly might."

"Be so good as to listen. Whatever tale you may tell of me, and even supposing you find some fool to heed it, it will not save this Barlow here. He'll hang—for a moment. And he'll then be drawn alive."

He flung the last words brutally, lifting his voice to a gloating roar of triumph; and across the room Arabella Langley twitched in anguish as she looked down on the white strained face of the man who was all but son to her. Her eyes glazed as though they could already see that last horror on the stark, high gallows; and in that agony of thought her mute glance turned to John.

Sir Henry saw it, and on the instant he pounced.

"It's a high price for obstinacy, Mr. Leyburne—when others pay it. There are some who think so, if you do not."

John stood silent, staring savagely at him, but he knew he was defeated now. He could not look again at those glazed and shuddering eyes, and there seemed no other way.

"What is it that you ask of me?" he said slowly.

"Merely a statement, duly signed and certified, of what you have lately seen—and not seen."

"No more?" John's thoughts were rushing as he sought to temporize. "Certified by the justices, I suppose. The usual three?"

"Don't be a fool. It will be certified by those I choose to name. And they will not be——"

A clop of hooves and a quiet jingle of harness broke into his words, and John spun in the window to see the riders who were coming easily across the gravel. There were three of them, Penny on her grey, Mr. Payne at her one side, and Will Hoghton at her other.

"What the devil!" Sir Henry was in the window too. "But who might this be?"

"That?" Roderick Mansell took a hasty look. "God's life, it's Payne! I know the rogue in the town, sir—as busy a papist as breeds."

"Is he so?" The justice sounded pleased. "Then there'll be matter against him. And I've said there's enough to hang young Hoghton. Let them come in—by all means."

He spoke crisp orders to the men beyond the door, and he was rubbing his hands in satisfaction as he came back to a room that was very quiet and still. The threat in his words had been plain, and now he had another and a worse. It came in the same purring tone as John was staring, aghast, from the window at the rush of armed men who poured from the door as the riders dismounted.

"A hot and busy papist, do you say?" Sir Henry was rubbing his hands again. "Young Hoghton harbours priests, and Miss Penelope rides between them."

"What's that?" John had spun on his heel again.

"I don't know what it is—yet." The stress was ominous. "But it's tainted company, and——"

The latch rattled as the door was flung open, and Will Hoghton held it while Penny came marching in, with Mr. Payne towering beside her. They came briskly until they caught sight of Mr. Barlow, white and bandaged in his chair; and then Mr. Payne checked sharply in his stride, while Penny went running openmouthed to the man whose soft smile was all for her as she dropped on her knees by his chair.

"Uncle Ned! What is it? Are you hurt—much?"

"No, my Penny." His smile was even softer. "And I've been well tended."

Penny's quick glance was at her aunt, as though she well knew who had tended him; and one sight of that taut and twisted face set her jumping to her feet to round savagely on Sir Henry Mansell.

"What's this?" she shouted. "What have you——"

"Easy, Penny!" Will Hoghton was at her side, and his hand was on her shoulder. "It's not that way."

She stared at him suspiciously, but she let him have his way, and she was silent as Mr. Payne spoke quietly.

"What is your hurt?" he asked. "And where have you been? There's none of us could find you."

"I'm sorry. I came here late. I had been a little faint, you see. It—it was a pistol ball."

"From this gutterblood?"

Mr. Payne's jerk of the head showed who was meant, and Roderick Mansell came storming in a red-faced fury.

"What!" It was a high-pitched shout. "Will you say that word again?"

"Gutterblood," said Mr. Payne calmly. The lazy smile was with him again, but the twist of it was bitter. "It's how you serve Shaftesbury, is it not?"

"God's life, you——"

"You should read the Third Commandment. And perhaps the Ninth also. Do you find me offensive?"

"Find . . ."

Colonel Mansell stood speechless in a choking fury, and Mr. Payne had lost his smile.

"Your swordplay's rough, I'm told. But if you've a mind to display your talents you may come outside to the gravel—now. And I'll spare you a journey into Holland."

The colonel stood staring, while the red flush paled from his cheeks and his eyes noted the long limbs, the big shoulders, the hint of easy strength in the man who stood before him. His mouth dropped open, as if the words would not come; and while he stood defeated his father spoke to restore a situation which Mr. Payne had looked like seizing.

"You'll please to recall that I'm a justice. And I'll have no brawling here—or elsewhere."

"Not even pistol balls?"

"Nor insolence either. Your name's Payne, I'm told?"

"It is."

"And a nosing papist. And you another——" He glanced acidly at Will. "I'd not supposed that Miss Penelope used such company, and it's perhaps fortunate——"

"It *is*."

"What's that?"

Mr. Payne's interjection had been oddly dry, and Sir Henry seemed disconcerted. In the window John stirred suddenly as he caught the tone of it; and then he saw that Penny, with her temper now recovered, was standing against the wall and looking uncommonly pleased with herself.

"I said it was fortunate," said Mr. Payne calmly. "Shall we now make an end?"

"End?" Sir Henry's voice had a rasp. "Are you———"

"End, I said. You're taken in a treason, you and your brawling son."

"Oh?" Sir Henry stepped back, and his stare was minatory before he spoke with a sly cold menace. "It's sworn before me by divers witnesses that muskets and other stores of war were lately put on shore by you and this William———"

"Hoghton and I, was it? Surely Mr. Leyburne, too?"

"Quite surely, I'd say."

"You certainly would. Did we also write letters to Argyle?"

Sir Henry twitched. Visibly and certainly he twitched; and across the room the colonel was almost on his toes before he could check his sudden swing towards his father.

"Now what's this?" Sir Henry had recovered, and his face was impassive again. "Do you hint some further lie?"

"I hint nothing." Mr. Payne spoke curtly, and then he turned to John. "But I *did* suggest that Mrs. Waring would———"

"Mrs.———"

"Your trollop, Roddy."

Penny's contemptuous tone cut coldly into what else the colonel would have said, and his gasp of fury left a silence which Mr. Payne promptly filled.

"I suggested, you remember, that she would not start for Scotland until they were sure of matters here. Though I hardly supposed she'd linger so lovingly and close."

"God's life!" It came as a rending shout. "Have you———"

"Yes."

The one short word swept the colonel into speechless silence, and at the tone of it Sir Henry's cold eyes seemed to widen. Richard

Langley started forward, and John found his breath coming quickly.

"Tell me," he said urgently. "What is it?"

"What you've guessed." Mr. Payne spoke calmly. "We came upon that chariot as we rode back here——tucked under the trees, and not a furlong from the gates. Plainly she was waiting——"

"S'blood!" The colonel's voice was back in a screaming fury. "You damned whoreson papist! You've put your poxy hands on——" He turned shrill and wild-eyed to his father. "Robbery on the road! And they can hang for it, all three!"

"And no doubt will." Sir Henry was making a fine show of calm. "Continue, sir. You seem to be confessing something."

"Confessing?" The colonel was shouting again. "He's told us he's a highway thief—a damned gaol-rotted gibbet-sprouting bridle cull!"

"A fine word for *you*, Penny," said Will Hoghton, calmly.

"*You?*"

Mansell's voice was cracking as he whipped round, and Mr. Payne was bland as he gave the explanation.

"I've said it was fortunate that we had Miss Penelope with us. The lady, you understand, had hid the letters upon her person, and as a matter of propriety——"

"Don't ask where she had 'em," said Penny darkly.

"I see." Sir Henry cleared his throat. "So it's a confessed robbery, and you know what will follow. But first we'll recover what you've taken."

"Don't be a fool," said Mr. Payne, as the justice made for the door. "By all means call your rabble if you think we're so simple as to bring such trophies here. Do you choose it so?"

The question had a ring that brought Sir Henry to a startled halt; and when he turned, with one hand still on the door, he found that Mr. Payne was dominating the room. His voice came resonantly.

"We took—or Miss Penelope took—three papers from Mrs. Waring, all directed to milord Argyle. The first, from Ferguson in Amsterdam, bade him call men for instant rising and march them into England—arms to be furnished here by the trusty Sir Henry Mansell. The next—signed Henry Mansell, his most obedient—says amen to that, and assures him the arms are ready. And the third is a hand list of those arms, writ and signed by Roderick Mansell—also his most obedient."

The strong voice ended, and Mr. Payne gave his back to the justice as he went strolling to the window. He peered through it as though he were expecting someone.

"Do you stay for it?" he asked. "Or do you go?"

In the quivering silence father looked helplessly at son; and it was the soft-voiced Mr. Barlow who found them the excuse they needed.

"I trust," he said gently, "that this Mrs. Waring did not come to any hurt."

"My God!"

Roderick Mansell wheeled as though he had urgent duty, and at once he had flung the door open and was bawling for his horse.

"A further assault, is it? Then that's to be looked to."

The justice had kept his poise, and it was still his when he hurried out after his son. There was a shouting and turmoil, a flurry of hooves and harness, and then the whole troop of them were away, their sword hilts flashing and the gravel spurting as they rode madly at the bend of the drive and were lost behind the leafless trees.

"They're well gone," said Mr. Payne bitterly. "And it's better so. They'll not breathe at ease this side of Holland."

He turned quickly, and his whole face had changed as he moved to Mr. Barlow's side.

"But how is it?" he asked anxiously. "Say that it's no great hurt?"
"Ned?"

Arabella Langley was close at his other side, and there was a light in her eyes again.

"Why, no . . ." Mr. Barlow spread his arms, and his one hand took Mr. Payne's and the other was in hers. "There is great mercy shown to me, and great love from many."

His eyes were shining as they drew closer to him, and Richard Langley moved hastily into the window; then he spoke sharply.

"Penny!" He sounded his own gruff self again. "Be pleased to see to your horses. They're trampling the borders."

Penny took one look through the glass and went running to the door. John was after her on the instant, and Will Hoghton was at his side as he followed her through the blackened arch into the cold crisp air of the morning. Will seized hastily on his own horse and Mr. Payne's, but Penny's grey had gone roaming further. It was down by the bend of the drive, finding what graze it could; and as Penny went briskly after it John went as briskly after her.

She was round the bend when he came up with her, and she did not have to call her horse. He came of himself, nuzzling against her as though he thought it more than time she gave him some attention; and she was close against him, her face upturned to the sun, when John came close behind her.

"I grow jealous," he said softly.

"You?" She spun round lightly, and at once he had her hands in his. "Then you shouldn't be. He's my very true friend, and I love him."

"Penny! I'm more jealous than before."

"Oh?" She pushed away the horse, who was nuzzling at her ear, and she twisted so that the sun was on her face again. "And why?"

"You well know why. Because you've said you love him, and you haven't said it to me."

"Haven't I?" He saw her lip quiver. "Haven't I, John?"

"No." His arms were round her, and she let herself come to him. "Then say it to me now."

"Could I?" She was smiling up at him as he pressed her closer. "Perhaps I could."

He felt his heart go pounding as she pressed back in his arms and seemed to wait. For a moment she was still, as he held her in the ecstasy that is not of time. Then, as he drew her slowly to him, the grey horse grew impatient, and thrust his nose between them.